Contents

PENGUIN ⟨ᴘ⟩ CLASSICS

PARZIVAL

WOLFRAM VON ESCHENBACH was the greatest of the medieval German narrative poets. Very little is known about his life, but it is generally accepted that he belonged to a Bavarian family of the lower nobility, that he may have served a Franconian lord and that for the better part of his creative period he enjoyed the patronage of the great medieval German maecenas Hermann, Landgrave of Thuringia. He probably died between 1220 and 1230.

Although Wolfram left some brilliant lyric poems, chiefly dawn songs of his youth, it is in his narrative poems – *Parzival*, the unfinished *Willehalm* and so-called *Titurel* fragments – that his claim to be a poet of world stature lies. *Parzival*, on which Richard Wagner based his music-drama *Parsifal*, is a romance of self-perfection in knighthood, in which both the chivalric and the spiritual receive their due; *Titurel* narrates in an elegiac measure the story of Signe and Schionatulander prior to their appearances in *Parzival*; *Willehalm* is a crusading poem with epic qualities which tells the story of the famous William of Toulouse.

•

ARTHUR THOMAS HATTO was Head of the Department of German, Queen Mary College, University of London, from 1938 until his retirement in 1977, and was Professor of German Language and Literature at the same university from 1953 to 1977. He is now Professor Emeritus in German at the University of London. He was assistant for English at the University of Berne (1932–5), and during the Second World War worked in the Foreign Office (1939–45). Since 1960 he has been a Governor of the School of Oriental and African Studies, University of London, where in 1970 he gave the Foundation Lecture, with the title 'Shamanism and Epic Poetry in Northern Asia'.

His other publications include *The Memorial Feast for Kökötöykhan* – a Kirghiz epic, edited, translated and with a commentary. His translations for Penguin Classics are Gottfried's *Tristan* and the fragments of Thomas's *Tristran* (together in one volume) and the *Nibelungenlied*, and with this, his third volume for the series he has made available to the English-reading public a substantial portion of the finest narrative poetry of the medieval German Golden Age.

Professor Hatto is now living in retirement in the enjoyment of a Leverhulme Emeritus Fellowship in support of his studies of epic poetry in Central Asia and Siberia. He is married and has one daughter.

PARZIVAL

Wolfram von Eschenbach

TRANSLATED BY
A. T. HATTO

PENGUIN BOOKS

Penguin Books Ltd, Harmondsworth, Middlesex, England
Viking Penguin Inc., 40 West 23rd Street, New York, New York 10010, U.S.A.
Penguin Books Australia Ltd, Ringwood, Victoria, Australia
Penguin Books Canada Limited, 2801 John Street, Markham, Ontario, Canada L3R 1B4
Penguin Books (N.Z.) Ltd, 182–190 Wairau Road, Auckland 10, New Zealand

—

This translation first published 1980
Reprinted 1982, 1984, 1986

—

—

Printed and bound in Great Britain by
Cox & Wyman Ltd, Reading
Set in Linotype Granjon

Foreword

Parzival is the retelling and ending by one genius, Wolfram von Eschenbach (*fl. c.* 1195–1225), of the unfinished romance of another, the *Perceval* of Chrétien de Troyes, a poem otherwise known from its prologue as *Li contes del graal* or 'The story of the Grail'. Chrétien's poem is the earliest extant narrative of the Grail, though he tells us that his patron Philip, Count of Flanders, had lent him its 'book', presumably in one or other respect a source, but a work of absolutely unknown content.

Wolfram, whose great stature as a poet is known independently from his earlier love-poetry and his later epic *Willehalm* and elegiac *Titurel*, rose magnificently to the challenge of retelling and completing Chrétien's mystery story, achieving it in a very different and indeed inimitable style.

If, glimpsing the title 'Parzival', the reader picks up this book in the hope of finding the Story of the Grail, he will not find it. He will find instead the Story of *a* Grail, together with everything else he is entitled to expect of a story told by one of the world's great narrative poets and humorists. There never was a Story of *the* Grail, and never could be. On the other hand there were stories of as many different Grails as there were writers or syndicates exploiting the potent name.

Chrétien himself first speaks of *a* 'graal', and it is clear from the best (though not all) manuscripts of *Perceval* that he intended a vessel, some sort of dish like the one named 'gradalis' in Medieval Latin, from which the Old French 'gra(d)al' took its rise. After introducing *a* graal into his narrative, Chrétien logically refers to it as *the* graal when he has occasion to mention it again. In the present state of our knowledge the notion cannot be disproved that Chrétien, the originator of Arthurian romance in the higher courtly mode, also launched the subsidiary genre of Grail Romances in his *Perceval* of *post* 1181 A.D.;

which is not the same as saying that there were no narratives or cults centred on esoteric vessels or other objects before *Perceval*, for if one chooses to take the matter loosely one can go far beyond Byzantium in space and, if licentiously, as far back in time as the Pharaohs.

How open a question the physical nature of 'the Grail' still was in *c.* 1200, when Wolfram embarked on his *Parzival*, is shown by the fact that his Grail – he calls it 'Grâl' – was a Stone, and that although it had the loftiest spiritual connections it also had some very earthy aspects, since it served up meats hot or cold, wild or tame, and a whole variety of alcoholic beverages to individual taste, so that, as has been wittily observed, it also functioned as 'un buffet ambulant'. Since the French scribes of some of the surviving manuscripts of the *Perceval* show themselves unaware that Chrétien's Graal was a vessel, the German Wolfram, with a knowledge of French that left something to be desired, could readily be forgiven for being unaware of it. On the other hand, Wolfram was sufficiently strong-minded to set aside any prior knowledge he might have had that Chrétien's Graal was a vessel and choose a Stone as apter to his purpose. At the other extreme, Robert de Boron in his *Joseph d'Arimathie*, composed some time between *Perceval* and 1199, not only has the Graal as a vessel – the Chalice of the Last Supper – but also fills it with Blood from the Cross, anticipating if not already clinching the pious pun 'San greal (Holy Grail): Sang real (True Blood)'.

All that the Grails of medieval romance have in common is the function of indicating a goal worth striving for or preserving, and in content at least a modicum of sanctity.

These preliminary remarks on 'the Grail' are intended to free the reader's thoughts from any distorting impressions or expectations he may have gained from Malory, or from nineteenth-century poetry or music drama, so that he can take as they come the many and varied scenes from medieval courtly life as Wolfram paints them – scenes which despite their Arthurian setting are of course based upon the style of life which Wolfram knew at the German courts of the very brilliant Hohenstauffen period.

Thanks to the food-producing powers of the Gral, peasants are dispensed with by the Gral Community, and even outside in the world at large they are rarely mentioned, while because of the Gral's direct link with Heaven both for the annual regeneration of its powers and the decisive news-flashes it receives, priests are required only for the odd baptism and marriage, which is again reflected in what is narrated of the world outside. In this way, Wolfram freed his noble listeners from all memory of bad conscience towards the peasantry and of humiliation at the hands of the clergy, whether from the pulpit or in the confessional, in order to focus their attention entirely on the problems of knights and ladies whilst entertaining them, that is, on loyalty in love real or ritualized, on loyalty within family or feudal bonds, on fighting and bloodshed, and on a proper relationship with God.

At one point in his poem Wolfram humorously wonders how it is possible for so impecunious a knight as himself to describe such wealth and luxury as he unfolds. We in our turn wonder, with no humour but on the contrary with much bitterness, how it was possible for a knight of such humble station and education to enshrine in his poetry an understanding of the Christian message deeper and truer than that of all the popes and most of the saints of his day, touching not only Christendom but also Heathendom, after a century of Crusades. Comprehend this miracle we cannot, but gratefully accept it we can – and are indeed compelled so to do, as under Wolfram's virile and gentle guidance we read how God loved knights and ladies as well as He loved peasants and clergy, and perhaps all the more indulgently because in many ways they were morally more exposed.

Wolfram von Eschenbach was a ministerialis or technically 'unfree' knight bound to the service of a lord, though *qua* knight he was free to defend his honour anywhere and evidently also able to change his patron, finding his main benefactor in this respect not in the neighbourhood of his native Eschenbach but in Thuringia with its famous maecenas, the Landgrave Hermann. Although Eschenbach is in Franconia, Wolfram alludes to himself as a Bavarian, and it is permissible to see Eschenbach as the mid-point of a series of concentric circles linking localities at ever-increasing distances – with a proportionate increase in vagueness and fantastic charm – from the tourneying-ground of Klein-Amberg, only a few miles east of Eschenbach, to furthermost Asia where the sky comes down. Such knights ministerial as Wolfram were the main bearers of the great efflorescence of secular poetry in Germany in the first half of the Hohenstauffen period, when poetry became emancipated from clerical domination. Bright boys of the subservient nobility were picked out and sent to monastery schools to learn the Three R's so that their lords could administer at least their territories for themselves while their consciences remained in clerical hands.

Like Wolfram's statement that he was following a Grail romance not by Chrétien but by the otherwise unknown 'Kyot the Provençal',* his claim not to know his A B C must be discounted as one of his many tactical jokes. In his Apology, inserted between the second and third chapters, Wolfram takes his stand not as a poet but as a knight, and in such bold and definite terms that he would have been howled down by the roughnecks of Thuringia had he not been a crack-jouster. In this proud stance he roundly disclaims that his story can be a book. This is clearly mockery of his senior, the poet Hartmann von Aue, who introduced and excused his masterpieces *Der arme Heinrich* and *Iwein* as the fruits of a scholar's leisure. With his *Erec* and *Iwein*, Hartmann was the unassailable Arthurian narrator – until Wolfram von Eschenbach flung down his gauntlet (p. 83), a challenge which the great Gottfried von Strassburg rebutted with much parody and persiflage in the Literary Excursus of his *Tristan* (Penguin Classics, p. 105). All that we can safely glean from these exchanges to the present purpose is that Wolfram neither was nor claimed

* See p. 427.

to be learned (notably in Latin), as both Hartmann and Gott-fried clearly were. Some who take Wolfram's assertion of analphabetism seriously point to strange transmogrifications in his riot of exotic names, and infer oral transmission. Yet this born bard-improvisator, only half-submerged by his con-ventional 'literary' persona, absorbed information about the world *vastly* from any available source, and at least one scholar who cites the transmogrifications goes on to speak of Wolfram's unbounded delight in manipulating language somewhat in the manner of J. R. R. Tolkien, though of course with less real freedom. The view of the present writer is that Wolfram had a practical grasp of letters and numbers adequate to supervising, say, his lord's falconers, his general stores, gold plate, cavalry horses, uniforms, munitions of war and other logistical affairs for the field of battle, under the Marshal – all matters with which he betrays an uncommon technical familiarity.

Some scattered topical references, as well as polemical ex-changes embedded in the text, enable us to date Wolfram's *Parzival* between the years approaching 1200 and those follow-ing 1210, the richest years in the history of medieval German poetry; for they also saw the appearance of the *Nibelungenlied, Iwein, Tristan,* and the superlative political poetry of Walther von der Vogelweide, not to mention his love-lyrics and those of several other fine poets.

There is evidence that after finishing *Parzival,* which he assembled according to a loose-leaf system – some pages sent flying round Germany never caught up with the main sheaf – Wolfram returned to it to patch and touch it up. One minor strand of narrative in *Parzival,* derived from a single short scene of Chrétien's, that of the tragic young lovers Sigune and Schionatulander, so obsessed him and his audience that after the four scenes given them in *Parzival* he told the prior history of the pair in elegiac strophes of his own devising in the miscalled *Titurel.* Whether before, during or after the making of *Titurel,* Wolfram retold almost to the end the Old French *La bataille d'Aliscans* in his epic *Willehalm,* soon to be pub-lished in English from other hands in this same series. *Wille-halm* was based upon a *chanson de geste* and deals with the double clash of two great armies, the Frankish and the Saracenic, who seek a crucial decision amid vast carnage undreamt of in the sporting *Parzival*. In *Willehalm*, Wolfram again rose superbly to the challenge, which of its nature took him to greater heights.

Writing in a dense, sententious and at times consciously gnomic style, Wolfram makes heavy demands on his audiences. As a faithful translator I have in the main passed his demands on to my readers. Many passages of the original have virtually no syntactical structure – *Parzival* is definitely no book – and so the bare act of translation has inevitably tidied them up. Thus the reader must imagine Wolfram to be in one sense rougher and less tidy than he appears in these pages. In another sense he is tidier than I could possibly render him, in that his compelling thought derives much structure from his sappy and vigorous use of medieval German courtly couplets. Most characteristic of his style is a succession of verse-sprung statements in which he leaves it to his audience to supply the logical nexus, as we often do in living speech. In my translation I have left to the reader as much of this work required of him by Wolfram as I safely could, chiefly by means of innumerable dashes and colons. If my pages tend to look a little odd, then so does my original. I offer no apology, since otherwise I should have had to apologize to Wolfram for watering him down more than was absolutely necessary. For to translate this extraordinary poet, more than any other I know, is to risk watering him down unbearably. The consolation is that when one has dared to do so the flavour may still be recognizable.

For the further guidance of the reader I have furnished an Introduction to a Second Reading after my translation. Here I can truthfully say – and it is a tribute to Wolfram's supercharged utterance – that my Introduction to a Second Reading could have been many times its length without diffuseness or repetition. When that insight dawned on me I stopped it.

I am indebted to so many scholars at home and abroad over the half century during which I have been at grips with *Parzival* that, contrary to usage, I make no specific Acknowledgements here bar one. To have done otherwise would have been invidious, since many would inevitably have been overlooked. I have thanked them all privately in any case and I now thank them again in my heart. For very recent and expert advice, however, in a field that is virtually all his own, I thank my old friend and colleague F. P. Pickering, Professor Emeritus of the University of Reading, who made it possible for me to identify the area within which my enlightened publishers should seek and find the illustration on the outer cover. Finally, I wish to express my gratitude to my friend and colleague Dr Marion Gibbs for her vigilant and perspicacious reading of the proofs when as a teacher she was already fully engaged.

A. T. HATTO

Chapter 1

IF vacillation dwell with the heart the soul will rue it. Shame and honour clash where the courage of a steadfast man is motley like the magpie. But such a man may yet make merry, for Heaven and Hell have equal part in him. Infidelity's friend is black all over and takes on a murky hue, while the man of loyal temper holds to the white.

This winged comparison is too swift for unripe wits. They lack the power to grasp it. For it will wrench past them like a startled hare! So it is with a dull mirror or a blind man's dream. These reveal faces in dim outline: but the dark image does not abide, it gives but a moment's joy. Who tweaks my palm where never a hair did grow? He would have learnt close grips indeed! Were I to cry 'Oh!' in fear of that it would mark me as a fool. Shall I find loyalty where it must vanish, like fire in a well or dew in the sun?

On the other hand I have yet to meet a man so wise that he would not gladly know what guidance this story requires, what edification it brings. The tale never loses heart, but flees and pursues, turns tail and wheels to the attack and doles out blame and praise. The man who follows all these vicissitudes and neither sits too long nor goes astray and otherwise knows where he stands has been well served by mother wit.

Feigned friendship leads to the fire, it destroys a man's nobility like hail. Its loyalty is so short in the tail that if it meet in the wood with gadflies it will not quit a bite in three.

These manifold distinctions do not all relate to men. I shall set these marks as a challenge to women. Let any who would learn from me beware to whom she takes her honour and good name, beware whom she makes free of her love and precious person, lest she regret the loss of both chastity and affection. With God as my witness I bid good women observe restraint. The lock guarding all good ways is modesty – I need not wish

them any better fortune. The false will gain a name for falsity.
– How lasting is thin ice in August's torrid sun? Their credit
will pass as soon away. The beauty of many has been praised
far and wide; but if their hearts be counterfeit I rate them as
I should* a bead set in gold. But I do not reckon it a tawdry
thing when the noble ruby with all its virtues is fashioned
into base brass, for this I would liken to the spirit of true
womanhood. When a woman acts to the best of her nature
you will not find me surveying her complexion or probing
what shields her heart: if she be well proofed *within* her
breast her good name is safe from harm.

Now if I were to judge of men and women as I know them
a long story it would be. Hear, then, what manner of tale this
is, telling of things both pleasant and sad, with joy and trouble
for company. Grant there were three of me, each with skill
to match mine: there would still be need of unbridled inspira-
tion to tell you what, single-handed, I have a mind to tell!]†

I will renew a tale that tells of great fidelity, of inborn
womanhood and manly virtue so straight as never was bent
in any test of hardness. Steel that he was, his courage never
failed him, his conquering hand seized many a glorious prize
when he came to battle. Dauntless man, though laggard in
discretion! – Thus I salute the hero. – Sweet balm to woman's
eyes, yet woman's heart's disease! Shunner of all wrongdoing!
As yet he is unborn to this story whom I have chosen for the
part, the man of whom this tale is told and all the marvels
in it.

There is a custom still observed today wherever our western
neighbours' laws prevail. It holds even on German soil in one
odd corner – you don't need me to tell you that! Whoever it
was that held those territories yonder ruled – nor was it shame

* In medieval German, *ich solde* was pronounced *i solde* in faster
speech. Wolfram thus embeds the name of Isolde in his anti-*Tristan*
polemic.
† The passage in brackets is a later self-interpolation *contra* Gottfried
von Strassburg, to whose *Tristan* it alludes, in answer to Gottfried's
polemic in the Literary Excursus of that poem. See Penguin Classics,
p. 105.

to him – that the eldest brother (strange though true) should have his father's whole inheritance. That death should sever the rights of which their father's life assured them was the cadets' misfortune. Before, they held in common. Now, the eldest holds alone. Was that not a wise man who laid it down that age should have possessions? – 'Youth has its fill of good things, eld of sighs and sorrows'! – 'There never was a fate so pitiful as age *cum* poverty!' I will not palter with the truth: that kings, counts, dukes should suffer dispossession of their acres, all but the oldest son – what an outlandish ordinance!

Thus it was that heroic Gahmuret, the daring yet restrained, lost lands and strongholds where his sire with pomp and royal sway had borne crown and sceptre till he met his death in knightly combat. He was bitterly lamented, having kept honour and faith entire till the end. His elder son then summoned the princes of the realm. They came in brilliant style, for they were entitled beyond question to receive great fiefs from him. Now when they had come to court and their claims had been heard and their fiefs confirmed, hear how they proceeded. Prompted by loyalty the whole assembly, rich and poor, humbly and earnestly petitioned the King to show his love for Gahmuret as a brother, and dignify himself by leaving him an Honour from his lands so that all might see whence the knight derived his freedom and his title, and not utterly dispossess him.

The King received this gladly. 'You know how to ask in reason,' he said. 'I will grant you this and more. Do you not call my brother "Gahmuret of Anjou"? Anjou is my country. Let both be named from it!' And his majesty continued 'My brother may look to me for staunch support in more than I can name at such short notice. He shall be a member of my Household. Truly, I shall prove to you that we two had one mother. He has little, I enough. This I shall share with him so liberally that my heavenly bliss shall not be at stake in the eyes of Him that giveth and taketh. – With justice to dispense He may do either!'

When they saw that their lord was loyal it was a happy day for those mighty princes. Each made his separate bow of thanks. Nor was Gahmuret slow to voice the assent which his heart had spoken.

'My lord and brother,' he said good-naturedly, 'had I the wish to be an inmate of your noble House or that of any other man it would have been idle comfort I had secured. But loyal and discerning that you are, consider my reputation and advise me with an eye to present circumstances: it is here you can lend a helping hand. I own nothing but my equipment. Had I achieved more with it, such as had brought me wide renown, I should be remembered somewhere in the world. I have sixteen squires,' he went on, 'of whom six are cased in steel. Give me in addition four pages of gentle birth and breeding. These shall share fully in all my prizes. I am off to see the world – not the first time I have ranged abroad. If fortune watches over me perhaps I shall win the recognition of a good lady and then, if I am worthy and am allowed to serve her, reason tells me I shall not do better than conduct the affair in all sincerity. May God lead me along the paths of good fortune! When our father Gandin ruled your kingdom we used to ride in company, suffering many a doleful pang for love. You were a knight and thief in one, you knew how to woo and conceal! How I wish that I too had the trick of stealing love, had your skill, and found true favour in my partner!'

The King sighed, 'Alas!' he cried, 'that I ever set eyes on you, for my heart that was whole you have cut in two with your jesting and still do, if we must part. My father left us both great wealth. I will mark you out an equal share, for I love you from my heart. Dazzling gems, red gold, men, weapons, mounts, clothes – accept as much from me as will let you travel as you please and maintain your name for generosity. Yours are the pick of manly virtues. Though you had been born of Gylstram, or had you hailed from Hromgla, I should always have given you that place in my affections which you now hold. You are my brother, never doubt it!'

'It is your courtesy that makes you praise me so, my lord. Then help me in that measure. If you and my mother wish to give away your worldly goods my fortunes will rise not fall.

18

But my heart is set on the heights! I do not know why it quickens so – *here* – as though it would burst. Oh where is my ambition taking me? I shall attempt it if I can. The day is approaching when I must leave.'

The King gave him all and more than he had asked: five chargers, picked and tried, strong, swift and spirited, the best in all his lands, numerous vessels of gold and many ingots. The King was pleased to fill him four sumpter-panniers with these things, and then, at his command, a pile of precious stones was added. When the panniers were full, the squires who were in charge of them were clothed in fine tunics and given good mounts. Then, when Gahmuret went into his mother's presence and she clasped him in her arms so tight, grief would be checked no longer.

'Fil li roy Gandin,' said this womanly woman, 'will you no longer stay with me? Oh, was it not I that bore you? And you are Gandin's child no less. Is God blind where He should help or is He deaf that He does not lend an ear to me? Am I to bear fresh sorrows? I have buried my heart's own vigour, my eyes' sweet pleasure! If God means to rob me further, Judge though He be, then the talk I hear of His succouring us is all lies, seeing that He thus abandons me!'

'God console you for my father, ma'am,' replied the young Angevin, 'there is good cause for you and me to lament him, but none for any man to bring sad news of me. I am for the wars in foreign parts to mend my fortunes. That, ma'am, is the turn my life has taken.'

'Dear son,' said the Queen, 'since you are set on serving a great lady and winning her love, do not disdain these things of mine to help you on your way. Tell your chamberlains to receive from me four heavy sumpter-panniers containing broad silks entire that never knew the scissors, and many lengths of samite. Sweet son, if you would make me happy, name the day of your return.'

'Madam, I do not even know what lands shall see me, only – whichever path I take on leaving you – you will have dealt by me nobly and as befits the honour of a knight. The King, too, has dismissed me in a way that calls for my dutiful thanks. I am sure you will cherish him the more, whatever comes of me.'

The story tells us that this dauntless hero had, from the love and friendship of a lady, received costly gifts to the value of a thousand marks. (Whenever Jew asks pawn today, he would not turn up his nose, but take them at that price.) A certain lady-love of his had sent them to him. There was profit in his service: women's love and a kind reception. But cure of his love-pangs it brought him none!

The warrior took his leave, never to set eyes on mother, brother or brother's lands again. This was great loss to many. He warmly thanked all who had shown him marks of favour before he left. He thought it more than his due: of his courtesy he never let it appear that they had done it because bound. In disposition he was as straight as straight could be. Those who proclaim their own worth court incredulity: so let a man's neighbours and those who witness his exploits abroad vouch for it – then his tale would be believed!

Gahmuret cultivated self-control and moderation in all things. He was not given to boasting, endured great honour calmly and was free of loose desires. Yet the noble man knew of no crowned head, whether king, emperor or empress, in whose household he would care to serve except his whose hand was highest over the nations of the earth. Such was his inmost wish.

He had heard there was a man in Baghdad so powerful that two thirds of the earth or more were subject to him, and whose name was so revered that, in the heathen tongue, he was called 'The Baruc'. So irresistible was the power he wielded that many kings were subject to him for all their crowns.

The Barucate stands today. See how they dispense the Christian rite in Rome, as enjoined on us by Holy Baptism: in the other place you see the infidel order. They get their papal law from Baghdad, and, so far as it is free of crooks and crannies, deem it straight! The Baruc gives them bulls of indulgence for their sins.

There were once two brothers of Babylon, Pompeius and

Ipomidon, from whom the Baruc seized Niniveh, which had always belonged to their forbears. They were giving a very good account of themselves when the young Angevin appeared on the scene. Gahmuret found favour with the Baruc, and, noble man, accepted his pay for service there and then.

You will not mind if he has to have a different coat-of-arms from the one his father Gandin bequeathed him? As one who aspired to preferment, his lordship displayed Anchors on his trappers, cut from dazzling ermine. The rest – his shield and vestments – had to follow suit. His harness was greener than an emerald, of the colour of the silken fabric known as Achmardi,* finer than brocade, of which he ordered a tabard and a surcoat. Anchors ermine were sewn on these, with cord-of-gold for cable.

His Anchors had essayed neither main nor headland, they had not bitten anywhere. A noble exile, never finding billet or rest, he had to bear this burdensome device, these Anchor-signs, from land to land.

Through how many lands did he ride, or sail around in ships? If I must swear to these, my word of honour as a knight, upon my oath, is telling you just as my source tells me – I have no other witness. It says that his manly vigour won the first place in heathendom, in Persia and Morocco. In other places, too, Damascus and Aleppo, and wherever knights gave battle, in Arabia and under the walls of Araby, his prowess achieved it that none would challenge him in single fight. Such was the fame he won there. The ambition in his heart reached out for glory. All others' deeds crumbled and fell away in his path almost to nothingness. This was the lesson all had to learn who met him in joust. He strove with undeflected courage – such was the verdict in Baghdad.

From there he made his way to the Kingdom of Zazamanc. Here people were all lamenting the death of Isenhart who had

---

* It is a fact that especially *green* fabrics of silk were exported from North Syria to Western and Central Europe. *Achmardi* has not been recognized in Arabic, but since Wolfram actually mentions 'emerald,' it would be rash totally to reject the Arabic *az-zumurrudī* 'emeraldine' as the oral source through trade.

lost his life in the service of a lady. It was sweet and constant Belacane who had brought him to this pass. She had never allowed him to enjoy her love, so now he lay dead for love of her. His kinsmen were avenging him in open war and ambush, and were beleaguering the lady with their armies. When Gahmuret came to her country she was making a stout defence. Vridebrant of Scotland and the men of his fleet had burned the land before retiring.

Now hear what befel our knight. Tossed thither by stormy seas and but narrowly escaping death he came sailing into the harbour up to the Queen's palace, where he was observed by many eyes. He looked out on to the plain. Many tents were pitched all round the town, except towards the sea. Two great armies lay there. He sent to inquire whose town it was, for neither he nor any of his mariners knew of it. They told his envoys that it was Patelamunt and sent their message with friendly tokens, imploring him by their gods to aid them – they were in great need, fighting for survival.

When the young Angevin heard of their wretched sufferings he offered his services for hire, as many knights still do, else they must give him some other reason why he should endure their enemies' spite. Sick and sound alike answered him then with one voice that their gold and jewels were his, he should be master of it all and want for nothing if he stayed with them. Yet he had no need of hire: for as to gold of Arabia he had brought numerous lumps of it with him! And the people of Zazamanc were all as dark as night – he had had enough of their company! Nevertheless he gave orders for quarters to be taken, and they were only too pleased to give him the best. The ladies were still reclining at their windows, looking on and taking careful note of his squires and of the details of his turn-out.

I do not know how many sable furs the generous warrior bore on his shield of ermine. The Queen's Marshal made it out to be a great Anchor, and very glad he was to see it there. His eyes told him he had seen this knight before, or else his double. That must have been at the time of the Baruc's siege of Alexandria, where Gahmuret's prowess had been quite unequalled.

Thus great-hearted Gahmuret rode into town in style. He ordered ten sumpters to be loaded. These marched through the streets followed by twenty squires on horseback. His baggage-train could be seen ahead: unmounted pages, cooks and scullions, they had gone on in advance. After the squires rode twelve noble pages, some of whom were Saracens, well-bred and with engaging manners. After these, horses with trappers of cendale were led, eight in a bunch. The ninth carried Gahmuret's saddle. The shield I mentioned was borne beside it by a merry page. Next rode trumpeters, such as are still in demand today. A drummer beat his tabor and tossed it high into the air. His lordship would have thought it a poor show had there been no flautists, no good fiddlers three! These all passed on with measured step. The great man brought up the rear himself with his master-mariner, an esteemed and experienced man.

All the inhabitants were Moors, every man and woman of them. The knight saw a profusion of battered shields pierced through and through by spears, many of them hanging on doors and walls. There was weeping there, and wailing. Numbers of men had been laid on beds in the windows for the fresh air, so badly wounded that even when they had had the doctor they could not recover. They had been in among the enemy, and such has always been the lot of those who would not flee. Countless horses were being led back past him gashed by spear and sword. He saw many dusky ladies on either side of him whose colour resembled the raven's.

His host received him amiably. This had a pleasant outcome for him later. What a very gallant man he was! In charge of one of the great Gates, he had delivered many a hack and thrust. With him Gahmuret found a number of knights, their arms in slings and heads in bandages. But their wounds were not such as to keep them from fighting, they had not lost their vigour.

The Burgrave begged his guest in the friendliest way to dispose of him and his without ceremony. He led Gahmuret to his wife, who then kissed him, which was little to his liking. They then went for refreshments. This done, the Marshal left him and went before the Queen to claim a rich reward for the news he was bringing.

'Madam,' he said, 'our cares have given way to joy! The man we are entertaining here is a knight of such high quality that we must forever thank the gods for their grace in bringing him to us.'

'Now tell me, I command you, who is this knight?'

'He is a proud warrior, a high-born Angevin, who has taken the pay of the Baruc himself. You should see how little he spares himself, when he is unleashed! How beautifully he swerves away and veers to the attack! He shows his enemies what mischief means! I saw him fighting gloriously when the Babylonians were out to relieve Alexandria and drive the Baruc off by force. What hosts were felled there in that rout! It was there that the charming fellow exerted himself so mightily that there was nothing they could do but run away. He is given the reputation of having distinguished himself beyond all others in many lands.'

'Now watch for a suitable occasion and see that he comes and talks to me here. We have an armistice today, you know, so that the gallant man can ride up here to me – or must I go to him? His skin is a different colour from ours. I only hope this is no sore point with him? I wish I had known of it before. I would show him all honour if my councillors wished it. If it is his pleasure to approach me, how shall I receive him? Is he near enough to me in birth for my kiss not to be thrown away?'

'He is known to be a scion of royal stock, let my life be pledge for it, ma'am. I will tell your princes to robe themselves and wait on you until he and I ride up. Instruct your ladies. For I shall go down at once and bring you the noble stranger so well-endowed with charming qualities.'

No sooner said than done. The Marshal went briskly about his mistress's bidding. Rich robes – I heard they were *very* costly – were quickly brought for Gahmuret, and these he donned. To meet his wishes they were embellished with heavy Anchors of Arabian gold. Then he, who well knew how to requite a love-gift, mounted a horse which a jouster from

Babylon had once ridden against him – he had thrust him off it, to the latter's chagrin! You ask 'Did his host bear him company?' He and all his knights! And indeed they were happy to do so. They rode on together and dismounted before the Palace, where many knights were assembled in splendid robes. Linking hands, his pages preceded him, two and two. Their lord found a bevy of ladies there in exquisite gowns. As they lit on the Angevin the Queen's eyes did great hurt to her. He looked so very winsome that, irresistibly, he un-locked her heart which until that time her femininity had kept locked fast. She advanced a pace or two towards her guest and bade him kiss her, and then led him to the wall that faced the enemy, and there, under its broad windows, they sat down on a quilt of samite spread on a soft divan. If anything is 'brighter than the day' the Queen does not resemble it. She had a woman's heart and was all that a knight could want in other ways, but not 'like the dewy rose' – she was of a swarthy aspect. Her crown was a bright ruby through which her head was visible. The lady of the land told her guest what pleasure his coming gave her.

'My lord, I have heard much of your prowess as a knight. I beg you of your courtesy to forgive me if I complain to you of sorrows that touch my heart.'

'You shall not call on my aid in vain, ma'am. Whatever it is that has vexed or vexes you, if this right hand can ward it off, let it be duly appointed to your service. I am but one man, but if any has wronged you, or wrongs you still, I interpose my shield. But that will scarcely cow the enemy.'

At this a prince politely interposed, 'If we had a leader our enemies would not escape so lightly, now that Vridebrant has sailed away. Back at home he is freeing his own country, now that the kinsmen of King Hernant (whom he slew for Her-linde's sake) are harrying him; for they will not refrain of their own accord. But he has left some stout fighters behind: Duke Hiuteger, who has wrought great havoc on us, and all his company. They fight with skill and vigour. Gaschier of Normandy, too, that grand old campaigner, has many mercen-aries here and Kaylet of Hoskurast knights in greater number, a host of warlike strangers. It was Vridebrant, King of Scots, with four allies, who brought them to this country, together with many warriors fighting for their hire. Down by the sea to the west lie Isenhart's men, their eyes streaming with tears. Never, since their lord was slain in joust, have they been seen anywhere but they were overwhelmed with grief. It rains in their hearts to overflowing.'

'Tell me, if it is your pleasure, why they hem you in so fiercely with their armies,' the stranger asked his hostess, like the gallant man he was. 'You have so many brave fighting men. It saddens me to see them borne down by the malice of enemies bent on ruining them.'

'I will tell you, sir, since you wish it. A noble knight once served me. Fine qualities burgeoned on him like blossoms on a spray. This knight was brave and discerning. Loyalty bore fruit in him nourished from deep roots. His breeding excelled all breeding. He was more modest than a woman. He was brave and daring. No hand more liberal ever grew on knight in any land before. (What will happen when we are gone I do not know, let others say.) He was untutored in the ways of perfidy. In hue he was a blackamoor like me. His father was King Tankanis. He too had high renown. My suitor's name was Isenhart. As a woman I betrayed myself to let him serve me for love without his bringing it to a happy consummation, so that I must forever rue it. People imagine I sent him to his death, but treachery is not in my nature, though his vassals accuse me of it. I loved him more than they and do not lack witnesses to vouch for it, since the gods, both his and mine, know the truth of it. Many were the love-pangs I suffered for him, yet my woman's shyness made me delay his reward – and the end to my remorse! My virgin state spurred him to win fame in many feats of arms. At last I put him to the test to see if he would prove a lover. Proof was soon forthcoming. He gave away his war-gear for my sake. That Pavilion standing there like a palace was his, Scots brought it to this battlefield. Rid of his equipment he did not spare himself. Life seemed to have lost its charm for him, for he sought many an encounter bare of his armour. At this time a prince of my court named Prothizilas,

26

a fearless man, rode out to try his fortunes, but disaster over-took him. It was no sham death that he took from his joust in the Forest of Azagouc with a brave man who also met his end there – Isenhart my suitor! They each received a spear through shield and body. Wretched woman, I mourn it still, nor shall I ever cease to regret their deaths. The affection I bear them blossoms forth in grief. I was never yet wife to any man.'

It seemed to Gahmuret that although she was an infidel, a more affectionate spirit of womanliness had never stolen over a woman's heart. Her modest ways were a pure baptism, as was the rain that fell on her – the flood descending from her eyes down to her sabled breast. Her pleasures in life were devotion to sorrow and grief's true doctrine.

'The King of Scots invaded me from overseas with all his army,' she went on. 'He was Isenhart's cousin on his mother's side. It was not in their power to do me greater hurt than I had already sustained in Isenhart, I must say.' The lady fell to sighing. Through her tears she cast many a shy glance at Gahmuret, as between strangers, and her eyes told her heart he was well made. She was a judge of fair complexions, too, since before this she had seen many a fair-skinned heathen. With this there was born between them a steadfast longing – she gazed at him, and he at her.

At length she ordered them to pour the farewell drink, though had she dared she would have left it. She was vexed that her command was not ignored, for it has never failed to dismiss gallants who would have dallied with the ladies. Yet her life had become his, and he had inspired her with the feeling that his life too was hers.

He rose to his feet. 'I am inconveniencing you, ma'am,' he said. 'I have been forgetting myself, sitting here so long. It troubles your humble servant deeply to see you so distressed. I am yours to command, my lady. My vengeance shall be wherever you desire.'

'I well believe it, sir,' said she.

His host the Burgrave is not neglectful of his entertainment. He asks him if he would care to ride out and take the air. –

'And see the battlefield, and the defences at the Gates?'
Gahmuret, worthy knight, replied that he would indeed like
to view the scene of combat.

A merry company of knights rode down with him, both
young and old. They conducted him round the sixteen Gates
and explained at length how not one had been barred – 'Day
or night since revenge was sought for Isenhart. The fighting
between us has hung in the balance, yet all that time not one
was closed. Loyal Isenhart's men have given battle before
eight Gates and have inflicted great losses on us. These noble
princes and vassals of the King of Azagouc fight fiercely.'

A gay pennant was flying above the brave troop before
each Gate, showing a knight pierced through with a lance-
thrust in the manner of Isenhart's death. From this his army
had chosen its device.

'To assuage their grief our answer is this: our pennants
show a woman with two fingers of one hand raised in oath,
proclaiming she had never suffered so much as since that day
when Isenhart was slain – his loss was torment to her heart.
And so the Lady Queen Belacane's image was raised aloft in
black upon a ground of white samite, as soon as we recognized
their emblem, which could only add to the loyal woman's grief.
Ours are planted high above the Gates. Before the other eight
we are still hemmed in by proud Vridebrant's army, Christian
folk from over the sea. Each Gate is in the care of a prince who
sallies forth to battle with his banner. We have captured one of
Gaschier's counts, and he is offering us a large ransom. He
is a son of Kaylet's sister, so that any damage Kaylet does must
be paid for by this other. We rarely have such luck! Between
the moat and their encampment there is a stretch of country
some thirty courses broad, sand, not turf. Many jousts take
place there.'

Gahmuret's host had more to tell him. 'There is a knight
who never fails to seek a joust before the walls. If the lady
who sent him here were to fail to reward him for such love-
service what profit would his thirst for battle bring him then?
This man is the proud Hiuteger. I must tell you further that
this reckless knight has halted before the Palace Gate, equipped

and ready each morning since we were first besieged here. Add to that, we have come back from jousting with the gallant man with his love-tokens thrust through our shields, precious stones valued as of high price when retrieved by the heralds! He has unseated many knights of ours. He likes to show himself, and our ladies too commend him. A man who is praised by the ladies soon acquires a reputation: fame and all his heart's desire are there at his command.'

The weary sun had now gathered in his bright glances to himself again, and it was time to make an end of their outing. The stranger rode in with his host and found his supper waiting.

I must tell you about the viands. They were brought to the board with due form and the company were served as befitted knights. The puissant Queen came to his table in great state. (Here was heron, there was fish.) Accompanied by her young ladies she had come expressly to see for herself that Gahmuret was well cared for. She knelt – despite his protests – and with her own hand carved him a good helping. She was happy in her guest! She presented his cup and saw to all his needs. He for his part took careful note of all she said and did. His minstrels sat at the lower end of his table, his chaplain on the other side.

He looked at the lady bashfully and said with many blushes: 'I am not accustomed to such honour as you show me, Ma'am. If I may offer you my opinion, only such hospitality was needed as I deserve. Nor would I have had you ride down here. If I may ask a favour, Ma'am, let me strike a happy mean. You do me too much honour.'

She insisted on going over to where his pages were seated and told them to fall to, thinking thus to honour her guest. The gratitude these young gentlemen felt for the Queen was boundless. Nor did she omit to go up to the master of the house and his lady the Burgravine. Raising her cup she said: 'Let me commend our guest to you, since it is you who have the honour. I beg you, bear this well in mind.' She took leave of them but sought her guest again. His heart was burdened with the love she inspired; and she too had been brought to the same pass by him, as her heart and eyes averred – they had to make common cause with her.

'My lord, command me,' she said with shy restraint. 'Whatever you ask I will provide, since you deserve it. Now let me take my leave. If you find everything comfortable here we shall all be very happy.' Four candles led the way in candlesticks of gold, and she was riding to a place where there were plenty!

They did not go on with their supper. The knight was sad, yet happy. He was glad at the great honour that was shown him. But he was molested from another quarter, by imperious Love, humbler of soaring spirits.

The lady of the house withdrew and hurried to her chamber. Gahmuret's bed was made with care, and host said to guest 'Sleep sound, and rest yourself tonight, for you will need it.' Then the host dismissed his retainers.

The beds of the stranger's pages lay all round him with their heads turned towards him, for such was his custom. Great candles stood there burning brightly. The hero lost his patience with the night for dragging on so. With thoughts of the dusky Moorish Queen he fell from swoon to swoon, he whipped from side to side like an osier, setting all his joints a-cracking. He was on fire for love and battle. Now pray his wish be granted! His heart pounded till it echoed, it was near to bursting with battle-lust, so that it arched the warrior's breast as the sinew does the crossbow – so keen was his desire!

He lay without sleep till he saw the grey of dawn. It had not begun to glow before he told a chaplain to make ready for Mass, which the latter then sang for God and his master. Straightway they brought Gahmuret's armour, and off he rode to where jousting was to be had.

He then promptly mounted a war-horse trained to the headlong charge and the swift gallop and that was quick to respond whichever way he wheeled it. You could see his Anchor towering above his helmet as he was led towards the Gate, where men and women alike declared they had never seen so enchanting a warrior – why, their gods must look like him! They carried stout spears along with him. How was he caparisoned? His charger was clad in iron to ward off hack and thrust. Above this lay a second, lighter covering of green samite, which added little to the weight. His tabard and his surcoat were also green, of Achmardi woven in the town of Araby – I lie to none. The thong of his shield – all its gear – was of bright new corded silk adorned with gemstones, its boss was of reddish gold refined in fire. He served for Love's wages: thoughts of a fierce battle left him unmoved.

The Queen was reclining in a window with a number of her ladies. Now see where his enemy Hiuteger stands, having halted at the spot where honour had come to him before! When he saw this knight gallop up 'When and how did this Frenchman arrive in the country,' he mused, 'if I took him for a Moor I'd be a fool at best.' Their mounts that were already leaping forward they spurred from the gallop to full tilt. They showed their knightly mettle, their thrusts were well and truly meant, they were not make-believe. Splinters from brave Hiuteger's lance flew skywards, but his opponent swept him over the cruppers on to the grass, little though Hiuteger was used to it. Gahmuret rode him down and trampled him, but he refused to own himself beaten and made many efforts to recover himself, yet the other's lance was pinning him down by the arm and he was demanding his surrender. Hiuteger had found his master.

'Who has defeated me?' he asked the gallant man.

The victor made swift answer. 'I am Gahmuret of Anjou!'

'I give you my parole,' replied the other.

Gahmuret accepted it and sent him in. This won him much praise from the ladies looking on.

But Gaschier of Normandy was riding up at speed, a proud and fearless warrior and a jouster of great power. Handsome Gahmuret was ready to receive him in a second clash. His lance-head was broad, the shaft stout: the strangers were immediately engaged. The scales were soon tipped: down went Gaschier, horse and all, under the shock of the joust, and he was forced to surrender willy-nilly.

'Your hand on it, which gave so good an account of itself!'

said doughty Gahmuret. 'Now ride to the army of the Scots and ask them to refrain from attacking us, if they would be so kind. Then follow me into the town.'

His order – or request – was duly carried out. The Scots were forced to call off the fight.

Kaylet was next to ride up. Gahmuret turned aside, since Kaylet was his cousin on his mother's side. What cause had he to harm him? The Spaniard pursued him with loud cries. Kaylet's helmet bore an Ostrich-crest. He was arrayed in flowing silk, as I am bound to tell, and the meadow rang with the little bells he wore as he passed through it. Ah, flower of manly beauty! He outshone all but two, of a later generation: Lot's son Beacurs and Parzival, who were yet to come. These were still unborn: but in later days they were singled out for beauty.

Gaschier seized Kaylet's bridle. 'Your wildness will be tamed, believe me, if you oppose the Angevin, riding there with my surrender. Take my advice, which is also a request, my lord. I have promised Gahmuret that I will turn you all from battle, he has my hand on it. For love of me, press on no more, or he will show you his mettle when it comes to blows.'

'If he is my cousin, Gahmuret fil li roi Gandin,' replied King Kaylet, 'I have no quarrel with him! Let go my bridle!'

'I will not let go before I see your head bared! – My own is rocking!' Kaylet unlaced his helmet and doffed it.

Gahmuret had more fighting to do. As yet the morning was but half spent and the townsfolk who had seen this joust were glad it was so. They all hurried along to the outermost defences, for he seemed to them like a net: whatever came beneath was trapped! He mounted a fresh horse (so I was told) which flew along barely touching the ground, was equally apt in the left or right wheel, courageous in battle and, for all its pace, was easily checked. Thus mounted, what did he achieve? Deeds such as move me to commend his valour! He rode within sight of the Moors as they lay with their host, westwards down by the sea.

There was a prince named Razalic, the mightiest man of Azagouc. Day after day he never failed to set out for the town in search of jousting. In this his race did not belie him, he was a scion of royal stock. Yet the warrior of Anjou ended his prowess with a swift check-mate, with the result that a dusky lady who had sent Razalic there was deeply grieved that any should defeat him. Without prompting, a squire had handed his master a spear with a bamboo shaft, and with it Gahmuret had thrust the Moor over his cruppers clean on to the sand. But Gahmuret did not let him lie for long before taking him prisoner.

With this the war was high and dry, and Gahmuret had covered himself in glory.

Gahmuret then caught sight of eight pennants floating in the direction of the town. He quickly told his gallant captive to turn them back. He then ordered him to follow him in. Razalic complied, for so necessity decreed.

Nor had Gaschier failed to appear. It was this that first told the Burgrave that his guest had taken the field. If like an ostrich he did not swallow iron and flint-stones it was because there were none to hand. He was so angry that he roared and bellowed like a lion! Tearing his hair, he said 'What a fool I am despite my years! The gods have sent me a brave and noble guest, but if he is overwhelmed in the fighting I shall lose my honour beyond recall. What are my shield and sword for? – If anyone tells me I shall take it as an insult!'

With that he left his men and spurred towards the Gate. A squire approached him bearing a shield painted on both sides in the likeness of a man who had been transpierced by a lance. It had been made in Isenhart's country. He also carried a helmet and a sword which Razalic had brought to the wars to prove his mettle. But the swarthy heathen had been parted from it despite his far-flung reputation! If in later days he died unbaptized may He Who works all wonders have mercy upon him!

The Burgrave had never seen a sight that gladdened him so much. He recognized the emblem and galloped through the Gateway. There at his station was his young guest, turning to cross lances with an adversary. His host took him by the arm and led him in again. Thus Gahmuret unhorsed no others that day.

'Tell me, sir,' said Lahfilirost schachtelacunt 'was it you who defeated Razalic? If so, our land is safe from war for ever, since he is lord of all the Moors, of all those loyal men of Isenhart who have inflicted such loss on us. Our troubles are at an end. It was at the beck of an angry god that they came to invade us with their armies. But now their power of waging war is broken.'

Lahfilirost led Gahmuret in, much to his annoyance. The Queen came riding out to meet him. She took his bridle and unlaced his ventail. Gahmuret's host had to surrender him. But Gahmuret's squires kept close to his heels. The subtle Queen led her guest through the town for all to see – the champion! When she judged the time had come she dismounted.

'Bless me, what trusty squires you are! Do you think you are going to lose him? He will be made comfortable without your aid. Here is his horse, now take it away. *I* am his companion here!'

Up in the Palace he saw many ladies. The Queen disarmed him with her own dark hands. There was a magnificent bed with a sable coverlet, where a new though private honour awaited him. They were now alone: the young ladies-in-waiting had left the room and closed the doors behind them. The Queen yielded to sweet and noble love with Gahmuret, her heart's own darling, little though their skins matched in colour.

The townsfolk brought rich offerings for their gods. Do you remember what gallant Razalic was told to do when he left the war? He kept his promise faithfully. But his grief for his master Isenhart broke out afresh.

From the shouting, the Burgrave guessed that Gahmuret had come, for the Princes of the Queen's land of Zazamanc were streaming to the Palace to thank and congratulate him on his glorious achievement. He had thrust down a couple of dozen knights in straight joust and brought in the mounts of most as prizes. Three captives of princely rank, attended by many knights, were riding to the Palace to present themselves at Court.

The lord of all these lands, having slept and taken refreshment, was attired in magnificent robes. She who had been called maiden but who was now a woman, led him out by the hand. 'I and my lands are subject to this knight,' she said, 'if enemies will concede it.'

Gahmuret made a request which met with ready assent. 'Approach, lord Razalic, and kiss my wife! You, too, my lord Gaschier!' He also asked proud Hiuteger the Scot, still smarting from his lance-wound, to kiss her on the lips. He invited them all to be seated, but himself remained standing. 'I should also like to see my cousin, if I could do so without offence to his captor,' were his politic words. 'I am bound to free him as a kinsman.' The Queen laughed. She ordered the knight to be fetched, and soon the charming young count was elbowing his way through the throng. He had been wounded in battle, but had also distinguished himself there. He had been brought to the wars by Gaschier the Norman. His father was French, his mother was Kaylet's sister. He had been bred up at court and had come in the service of a lady. His name was Killirjacac. He excelled all other men in beauty.

As soon as Gahmuret saw him – their very faces proclaimed their relationship, since they resembled each other closely – he asked the Queen to kiss and embrace him. 'Now come over here to me, too,' said Gahmuret and he kissed him on his own account. They were delighted to see one another.

'Ah, my charming young man,' continued Gahmuret, 'why do you expose your tender person here? Was it at the command of a lady?'

'The ladies command me very little, sir. My uncle Gaschier brought me here, he knows best why himself. I maintain a thousand knights here, ready at his service. I marched to the place of assembly at Rouen in Normandy, bringing him young fighting-men. I left Champagne for his sake. Now misfortune is turning her treacherous arts against him – unless through a generous deed you add lustre to your name. If it be your wish, let him profit from my friendship: soften his ordeal!'

'Follow your own advice. Go with my lord Gaschier and fetch me Kaylet.'

They went to do the warrior's bidding and returned with Kaylet as they had been asked. He too was affectionately received by Gahmuret, and the puissant Queen embraced him warmly. She kissed the handsome knight, nor did she demean herself, since he was her consort's cousin and a king in his own right.

'I swear, lord Kaylet,' said Gahmuret with a laugh, 'if I were to take Toledo, say, and all your lands of Spain just to please the king of Gascony who is always attacking you so fiercely, I should be thought disloyal, you being my cousin. Yet *you* have the pick of the old guard with you here! Who forced you to join this expedition?'

'My uncle Schiltunc commanded me to serve him,' answered the proud young warrior. 'Vridebrant is his son-in-law, it was of his prompting that I joined Vridebrant. Because of his wife, Vridebrant has six thousand warlike knights from me alone. I brought others, too, to serve his cause, but some of them have since gone away. Formidable contingents were here for love of the Scots: two kings from Greenland, redoubtable fighting-men, in great strength, with a veritable torrent of knights and many ships. I was much taken by their troops. Morholt, too, who fights with brains as well as brawn, was here. All these have gone away. I shall dispose of my men as My Lady instructs me. She shall see how ready I am to serve her. No need to thank me for my service, either. After all, we are related! Her dashing knights are now all yours. If, like mine, they were Christians, and their skins were of the same colour, the king has not been crowned who would not find them a handful! But, I wonder, whatever brought you here? Tell me how it all happened.'

'Yesterday I came, today I am lord of the realm. The Queen took me prisoner with her own hand, and I, yielding to discretion, defended myself with love!'

'It seems to me that you owe your double victory over the opposing armies to the charming way you fight.'

'You mean because I ran away from you? You challenged me at the top of your voice – what did you hope to force from me? Only now is the time for parley.'

'Your Anchor there meant nothing to me: my mother's brother-in-law Gandin never took it to the field.'

'But I knew your Ostrich, and the Serpent's Head on your shield. Your Ostrich perched high, it was not nesting! I could see from your behaviour that my capturing those two men had annoyed you. They gave a very good account of themselves.'

'I fancy I should have fared no better. I must say that if the most loathsome devil had triumphed over the brave as you have done, the ladies would have eaten him for sugar-candy!'

'You overpraise me.'

'No, I cannot flatter – ask me to help you some other way.'

They summoned Razalic. 'My cousin Gahmuret took you prisoner with his own hands,' said Kaylet courteously.

'That is so, my lord. In him I have recognized a warrior to whom my land of Azagouc will never deny allegiance, seeing that lord Isenhart can never wear a crown there. He was slain in the service of the lady who is now your cousin's wife, he gave his life to win her love. Yet I have forgiven her with my kiss. I have lost a lord and kinsman. If your cousin will follow chivalric custom and make amends for Isenhart, I will fold my hands to him in homage. He will have wealth and honour, then, and all that Tankanis bequeathed to Isenhart, whose body lies embalmed out there with the army. No day has passed when I have not gazed on his wounds, since this spear tore through his heart.' The gallant knight drew it from his bosom by a silken cord, then slipped it back next the bare skin. 'The day is far from done. If my lord Killirjacac will bear my message to the army as I ask him, the Princes will ride back in company with him.' – and he sent a ring to them.

Soon they were passing through the town on their way to the Palace, all those that were of princely rank, their faces black as Hell. Then by the taking and giving of pennants Gahmuret enfeoffed the Princes of Azagouc. Not one but was happy with his fief: yet the better part remained in the hands of Gahmuret, their lord.

These had been the first. But then the lords of Zazamanc approached him. At their mistress's bidding they received their lands and revenues from him with great ceremony, each

37

according to his due. Poverty had fled their lord! Prothizilas, who was of princely line, had left a duchy, and this Gahmuret gave in fee to one who had never failed in battle and had won great honour there – Lahfilirost schachtelacunt! He received it with pennant there and then. The noble Princes of Azagouc took Hiuteger the Scot and Norman Gaschier and.went before their sovereign. At their request he set these prisoners free, for which they thanked him.

'Make our lord a present of the Pavilion, as a reward for his rare exploit,' they urged Hiuteger. 'Isenhart was snatched away from us as the result of his giving Vridebrant the proudest possession of our land: there was nothing on earth to compare with that Helmet of hard, thick adamant, that trusty friend in battle! The victim of unrequited love, he staked his whole happiness, and now pays the price in person on this bier!'

Hiuteger promised with his hand on it that when he returned to his country he would try to recover the Helmet from his over-lord and return it in good order. This he did without being pressed.

The assembled Princes all crowded in to take leave of the King, and then left the Palace. Although his lands had been sadly ravaged, Gahmuret continued to shower such bounties on them, you would have thought the trees bore gold! He doled out lavish gifts. Vassals and kinsmen relieved the hero of his property, for such was the Queen's pleasure.

Prior to these happy nuptials there had been many and great dissensions. Peace was made as follows. This is no fabri-cation of mine – I was *told* that Isenhart was buried with royal honours by his friends, who of their own accord laid out fully a year's revenue from his lands on it. But Gahmuret decreed that Isenhart's men should retain his great possessions and administer them separately.

Next morning the besiegers quitted the field before the fortress. Those who had been there now parted company, bear-ing many litters as they went.

The plain was bare of their encampments but for that grand Pavilion! The King commanded it to be taken aboard. He spread the tale among the people that he was going to take it to Azagouc, but in this he was deceiving them.

And so the proud warrior sojourned there, till finding no deeds of arms to perform he began to pine and fret, so that his happiness turned to sorrow. Yet the dusky lady was dearer to him than life. Never was there a woman of comelier form. Her heart, too, was ever mindful of the truly modest woman's ways that were in constant attendance on it.

He asked his Sevillano to make ready for sea by a fixed hour. The man had been his pilot over many miles before: indeed, he had brought him there.

'Conceal it from the blackamoors,' said that wily mariner (who was himself not of Moorish hue). 'My cogs are so fast that they will never come up with us. We must put out with all speed.' Gahmuret gave orders to ship his gold.

And now I must tell you of a parting. That very night the noble man set sail, in secret. At the time when he gave his wife the slip she was twelve weeks gone with child. How swift the wind that drives them away!

In her purse the lady found a letter in her husband's hand, in French, a tongue she knew. Its legend was as follows:

Herein one love salutes another, and sends its love. Like a thief I have sailed away. I *had* to steal away to spare our tears. Madam, I cannot conceal it that did you but live within my rite I would long for you to all eternity. Even now my passion gives me endless torment! If our child has the aspect of a man, I swear he will be brave. He is of the House of Anjou. Love will be his Mistress. In battle he will be a hail-storm and a hard neighbour to his enemies. I would have my son know that his grandsire was named Gandin and met his death in battle. Gandin's father suffered the same fate – Addanz was his name. He was of British race. His shield never stayed whole for long. He and Utepandragun were the children of two brothers, whose names are written here: the one Lazaliez, Brickus the other. Their father's name was Mazadan. A fairy, Terdelaschoye, lured him to the land of Feimurgan: her heart was moored to him. My race descends from this pair, nor will it ever cease to shed its lustre. Each has worn his crown in turn, each had his meed of honour. Madam, you can still win me, if you will be baptized.

She did not wish it otherwise. 'How soon that can be done! I will be christened with all speed if only he will come back. To whom else has the courtly warrior left the fruits of his love? Out on you, sweet dalliance, if I am to be assailed by bitter memories now and ever after! I would gladly be baptized to the glory of God,' the lady continued, 'and live according to his liking!' Grief had at her with hack and thrust. Her happiness 'found the withered branch', as turtle-doves still do. They keep such faith that when they lose their mates they never fail to seek the withered bough.

When her time came, the lady was delivered of a son. His skin was pied. It had pleased God to make a marvel of him, for he was both black and white. The Queen fell to kissing his white spots, time and time again. The name she gave her little boy was Feirefiz* the Angevin. When he grew up he cleared whole forests – so many lances did he shatter, punching holes in shields. His hair and all his skin were particoloured like a magpie.

More than a year had passed since Gahmuret was acclaimed in Zazamanc on gaining the victory, and still he tossed on the sea at the mercy of the scudding winds. But now he descried a silken sail, gleaming red, and then a ship. It was bringing messengers from Vridebrant to lady Belacane, asking her to pardon him for having invested her, though he had lost a kinsman because of her. They had also brought the Adamant, a sword, a hauberk and a pair of greaves.

Here is a marvel for your ears: their courses met! My source swears to it. They made it all over to him, and Gahmuret for his part promised he would convey the message with his own lips, when he returned to her. I was told that the sea carried him into a haven, from where he went to Seville. There the gallant man paid off his pilot for all his toil, with a rich reward of gold. They parted company, much to that mariner's sorrow.

* Quasi *vair fils*, meaning 'Pied Son'.

Chapter 2

GAHMURET knew the king in that land of Spain, for it was his cousin Kaylet. He set out for Toledo to find him, but Kaylet had left in search of tournaments where there was to be no sparing of shields! Then Gahmuret too, as my source assures me, told his men to equip him with gay lances, each with its pennant of green cendale displaying three Anchors of ermine so proud that all acclaimed their splendour. They were long and broad, and from where they were tied a span below the lance-head reached almost down to the hand. A hundred of these had been made for the gallant man and were now being carried in his train by his cousin's people, who contrived to show him their love and esteem nobly and in a way that pleased their lord.

Gahmuret ranged after Kaylet for I do not know how long until in the land of Waleis he saw the encampments of foreign knights, a crowd of pavilions pitched on the meadow before Kanvoleis. – By your leave this is true, I am not romancing. He told his men to rein in and sent his discreet young squire-in-chief ahead with orders to find a camping ground within the town, and his squire went about it with all speed. Others followed leading sumpters. Not a house did he see that was not covered with shields as by a second roof, its sides draped with hangings and all palisaded with lances.

The Queen of Waleis had bidden a tournament at Kanvoleis in terms that still scare a coward when he sees such a proclamation afoot – he is no man to take part in it! She was a maiden not yet come to woman's estate and offered two lands and her person to whoever most distinguished himself, news that caused many to be thrust over their cruppers down on to the young grass. Those who took a toss of this sort were judged to have lost their throw! Yet fearless warriors took part in it and proved their mettle as knights. Many a horse was spurred to the headlong gallop, many swords were set a-ringing.

A pontoon bridge led over a sheet of water to a meadow, but access was barred by a gate. Unabashed, the young squire opened it – and there above stood the Palace! The Queen was sitting at the windows with a bevy of noble ladies, and they began to take note of what the squires were about below, for these had made their plans and were raising a pavilion of state. A king had given it up for a love that brought him no return, moved by passion as he was for Belacane. A rare, luxurious pavilion needing thirty pack-horses to carry it, it was erected after much labour. Add to that, the meadow was broad enough for the guys to be fully braced. Noble Gahmuret was breakfasting outside the town while this was being done. But when it was ready he busied his thoughts as to how he could cut a courtly figure riding up. No great time was spent on that. Each of his squires tied five of his lances together in a bundle and carried a sixth in his hands with pennant flying – in such style did the proud man ride!

The news reached the Queen's entourage that a complete stranger from a distant land was about to arrive.

'His attendants, both French and infidel, are elegant. But judging by their speech some may well be Angevins. They bear themselves proudly, and their clothes are very fine – well cut, there is no denying it. I was with his squires and found them above criticism. They say that if anyone needs anything and petitions their master, he will part him from his cares. I asked who he was, and they told me straight that he was the King of Zazamanc.' Such was the news a page had brought her.

'Look! What a pavilion! Your crown and lands would not fetch half the price!'

'I will not have you rate it so highly, though I admit it belongs to a lord who cannot know what poverty means. But', went on the Queen, 'why doesn't he come in himself?' and she sent a page to inquire.

Meanwhile the warrior was marching through the town in high state, waking those who slept. The gleam of many shields met his eyes. Ahead of him clarions rang out shrilly, shattering the air, a pair of timbrels were tossed and thumped, rousing the echoes. This din was heard all over the town, but it was mingled with the music of flutes, since the men were playing a march.

Now we must not lose sight of their master's entry, flanked by fiddlers on horseback.

The noble knight was wearing a pair of light summer high-boots over his bare legs, one of which he had cocked up in front of him over his horse's back. His full lips shone like rubies, red as fire. From each and every angle he was radiantly handsome. His hair was fair and curly where it fell away from the expensive hat that covered his head. His mantle was of green samite. At the front, trimmings of sable stood out black against a tunic of dazzling white. There was a great press of people trying to catch a glimpse of him, and many questions were asked as to who this beardless young knight parading such magnificence could be. The news went round in a moment, his retinue made no secret of it.

These and the others began to make for the bridge. The radiance shed by the Queen brought his leg down smartly into position, he strained like a falcon that has sighted its quarry. The warrior felt he liked his quarters. As to his hostess the Queen of Waleis, she was quite content.

It reached the ears of the King of Spain that the famous Pavilion which Gahmuret had acquired at Patelamunt at the request of the gallant Razalic had now been reared on the Leoplane, and it was a knight who told him. Abandoning himself to his delight, Kaylet gambolled like a deer.

'I saw your cousin arriving in all his old pride,' went on the knight. 'There are a hundred banners planted on the green-sward before his high Pavilion, and a shield, all green. On each pennant of cendale the brave man is displaying three Anchors ermine.'

'If he is here with his crest and armour, believe me, you will see how he spoils another's charge, how with his onrush he throws all into confusion! For a long time now King Hardiz has been giving me his fierce attention and pressing me hard, but when they cross lances here Gahmuret will lay him low! My fortunes are not yet on the way out!'

43

Kaylet at once sent messengers to where Gaschier the Norman and handsome Killirjacac were encamped with a large retinue. It was at Kaylet's request that they had come. Now they accompanied him to the Pavilion, where they welcomed the King of Zazamanc most affectionately. In their opinion they had had to wait too long before seeing him again, and they loyally said as much. Gahmuret asked them what knights were there.

'There are knights from distant lands whom Love has goaded here,' his cousin answered, 'a host of fearless warriors. King Utepandragun has many Britons here. Yet one thing sticks in his flesh like a thorn: he has lost his wife, mother of Arthur. The lady went off with a priest well versed in magic, and Arthur chased off after them. We are now in the third year since he lost his son and wife. But his son-in-law, Lot of Norway, is here, an adept in chivalrous combat and a noble, sagacious knight who is as slow to do a treacherous deed as he is swift to pursue honour. His son Gawan is here, not yet of a strength to do deeds of arms. The boy was with me here. If he could break a lance, he says, if he could be sure he were strong enough, he would like to be doing a knight's work! How soon the urge begins with him! The King of Patrigalt has brought a whole forest of lances with him: but his exploits do not count, for the men of Portugal are here! We call them "the Daredevils", they are bent on holing shields. There are the Provençals, too, with their brightly coloured blazons. The Waleis are here: they owe it to their weight of numbers here at home that they can press their attacks at will clean through the others' onset. There are many knights unknown to me by name who have come in service of ladies. As to those I *have* named, we are all encamped in grand style inside the town at the Queen's invitation. Now let me name for you those who have camped in the field outside and make light of our ability to make a fight of it. The noble King of Ascalun and the proud King of Arragon; Cidegast of Logroys and Brandelidelin, King of Punturteis. Bold Lähelin is there, too, and Morholt of Ireland, who has been forcing some acceptable ransoms from us. Out there on the plain lie the proud Alemans. The Duke of Brabant has ridden to this country for love of King Hardiz of Gascony. – The King had given him his sister Alize, so his services here were rewarded in advance. All these oppose me fiercely. But now I shall rely on you. Remember your kith and kin and help me by the love you bear me.'

'If my service brings you any honour here,' said the King of Zazamanc, 'you must not feel indebted to me. Let us make common cause. Does not your Ostrich stand up as ever, scorning his Nest? Then you must carry your Serpent's Head against Hardiz's Demi-Griffin! I will cast my Anchor into the surge of his attack with intent to land – but he will have to pick his way ashore over his horse's tail down on to the sand! If he and I were pitted against each other, either I would down him or he me, I guarantee you on oath.'

It was with feelings of unmixed pleasure that Kaylet rode back to his quarters. Then, suddenly, there were shouts of two proud warriors being heralded, Schiolarz of Poitou and Gurnemanz de Graharz, who were jousting on the meadow. This promptly led to the Vesper Tournament,* for six rode up on this side, some three on the other, and these were joined by perhaps as many as a whole troop. These began the work of knights in earnest, there was no stopping it.

It was still round about noon, and the King of Zazamanc was lying in his Pavilion, when it came to his ears that the charging squadrons were growing broad and long out on the plain, as is the way with the chivalric order, whereupon he too made his way out with many a gay pennant. He held aloof from the swift galloping, since he wished to study at leisure how both sides were acquitting themselves. His carpet was spread on the meadow, where charge was embroiled with charge and mounts neighed dolefully under lance-thrusts. Round him were squires and a clanging of swords. How they strove for glory whose swords rang out so! There was a loud splintering of lances – no need to ask where! His tent-hangings were serried charges, woven by knights' hands!

This noble sport was near enough for the ladies in the

*A preliminary tournament fought on the eve of a tournament proper.

Palace to watch the warriors' toil. But the Queen was sad at heart that the King of Zazamanc was not in the hurly-burly with the others. 'Ah, where is the man of whom I have heard such marvels?'

[Now the King of France had died, Gahmuret's passion for whose wife had often reduced him to dire straits, and his noble Queen, impelled by her great longing, had sent to Kanvoleis to inquire whether Gahmuret had returned from the heathen to his native land.]*

Great things were done by many a brave knight of slender means who did not aspire to the lofty prize proclaimed by Queen Herzeloyde in her Conditions, to wit, her lands and royal person. They were out for other pawn.

Now Gahmuret too was caparisoned in that same armour by which his wife was to have been reconciled with Vridebrant of Scotland, who had sent it as a gift to make amends for the crushing load of battle he had laid on her. There was nothing on earth that could compare with it. Gahmuret gazed at the Adamant that was his peerless helmet. On it they laced an Anchor inlaid with precious stones, all of great size. It was indeed a heavy burden. The stranger was now caparisoned.

With what was his shield embellished, you ask? A priceless boss of gold of Araby had been riveted on to it, a dead-weight for the man who had to bear it. It shone with a reddish lustre so that you could see your own face in it. Beneath it was a sable Anchor. I myself would not mind having what he ordered to be put on him, for it was many pounds in worth.† His tabard was of ample width – I doubt if any has taken its equal to battle since – and its hem reached down to the carpet. If I am any judge, it shone like a live fire burning in the night. There was no spot of faded colour. Its dazzling light did not elude one's gaze – a weak eye could have cut itself upon it! It was figured with gold torn from a rock in the Caucasus Mountain by the claws of griffins, who guarded it then as they still do today. People go there from Araby and gain possession of it by guile

* This passage occurs in all manuscripts after the place marked by †
below, where it does not belong. It must therefore be a misplaced after-
thought, essential as it is as this strand of the tale unwinds.

– there is none so rare in any other place – and take it back to Araby, where green Achmardis and rich brocades are woven. That tabard was not at all like other vestments.

He quickly slung his shield round his neck. Here stood a fine charger clad in iron almost down to its hooves, and here were pages shouting his battle-cry! Seeing it ready he leapt into the saddle.

The warrior expended many lances at full tilt. He cut clean through the others' charge and out at the far side. The Ostrich followed hard after the Anchor. Gahmuret thrust Poytwin de Prienlascors over his cruppers and many other distinguished men whose surrender he obtained. All those knights who bore the cross – of poverty – reaped the benefit of the hero's labours, since he gave them his captured horses. He was a source of heavy gain to them.

Four identical banners were borne against him, displaying a Griffin's Tail, beneath each of which rode a brave troop. Their lord was versed in battle-tactics. Though it was a Griffin's latter half to which these men belonged, it struck like hail in battle. That expert knight the King of Gascony bore the Griffin's forward half on his shield. His turn-out was such as ladies admire. Glimpsing the Ostrich on a helmet he spurred ahead of the others – but the Anchor reached him first! The noble King of Zazamanc thrust him over his crupper and made him prisoner. There was a great mêlée there. Deep furrows were trampled flat as a threshing-floor, and swords did a deal of combing. A whole forest of lances were shattered and many knights were downed. I am told they picked their way back to the rear where the cowards were lurking.

The fighting was now so near that the ladies were able to see clearly who were distinguishing themselves. From the spear of Riwalin, who sought a lady's favour, splinters showered down like a fresh fall of snow. He was King of Lohneis and whenever he charged there was a sound of splitting and cracking. Morholt robbed the Inners of a knight by hoisting him bodily from the saddle on to his own before him, a rough trick indeed! The knight's name was Killirjacac, from whom King Lac had just received such pay as a falling man earns from the ground. Killirjacac had been doing very well there: but the strong man had had an itch to defeat him without sword and so had taken the noble knight in that fashion.

Kaylet thrust the Duke of Brabant over his crupper – the Prince's name was Lambekin. What did his followers do? They gave him cover with their swords, those warriors thirsted for battle. Then the King of Àrragon pushed old Utepandragun over his horse's tail down on to the meadow – the King of Britain! – where he lay in a bed of flowers! How courteous of me, when all is said and done, to couch the noble Briton so rarely under the walls of Kanvoleis in a spot untrodden by vulgar feet and, to tell the truth, unlikely ever so to be in time to come. He did not need to keep his seat on the horse he had bestridden! Yet he was not forgotten for long: those who were fighting above him gave cover with their swords. There was no lack of furious charging.

Then up came the King of Punturteis. He was laid low before Kanvoleis on to his horse's tracks, and there he lay while it sped on. This was proud Gahmuret's work. – 'Charge, my lord, charge, charge!' They found his cousin Kaylet locked in the charge made by the men of Punturteis and about to be taken prisoner.

At this point the going grew very rough. After King Brandelidelin had been snatched from his fellows they had taken this other king. Various noblemen were running or walking in armour. They had had their hides tanned for them with kicks and cudgels, their skins were black with bruises – contusions were the prizes these fine warriors got! I do not say it to adorn my tale, but rest was a thing despised here. Those worthies had been spurred thither by Love, with many a bright shield and crested helmet now coated with dust. The field was of short green grass sprinkled here and there with flowers. Falling upon this were such knights as had been destined for the honour. *My* heart can indulge such ambitions, provided I keep my seat on my steed!

Now the King of Zazamanc rode out from the mêlée for a rested mount. They unlaced the Adamant, but only to give him a breather, not with any thought of bravado. They also peeled off his coif. His mouth was red and proud.

The chaplain of a lady I have mentioned before arrived there attended by three little pages. They were escorted by sturdy young squires leading sumpters. These envoys had been sent by the Queen Ampflise. Her shrewd chaplain was swift to recognize the knight.

'Bien sei venuz, beas sir,' he said, addressing him in French, 'on my Lady's part and mine! That is, on the part of the Queen of France, who is pricked by the lance of passion you inspire in her.' He handed him a letter in which the gentleman found greetings and a tiny ring meant as a safe-conduct and token of identity, since the lady had once had it as a gift from the Angevin. At the sight of her hand he bowed. Would you care to hear what it said?

I who have been disconsolate ever since I knew I loved you, send you love and greetings. The passion you inspire in me is a lock and bar on my heart and on its happiness. I am dying of love for you. If your love is to elude me, then surely Love will do me mischief. Return, and from my hands receive a crown, sceptre and kingdom that have been bequeathed to me. The love you arouse has won it for you. As requital accept these costly gifts in four panniers. I also wish you to be my knight at Kanvoleis, chief city of the land of Waleis. If this comes to the eyes of the Queen there, what do I care? It could not harm me much, for I am lovelier and mightier than she and know how to lend Love's exchanges more charm. If you have a mind to cherish a noble passion, then in return for love requited take my crown!

This was all he found in the letter. A squire drew Gahmuret's coif on to his head again. He had not a care on his mind. They laced on the hard, thick Adamant, he was now impatient to exert himself. Yet he gave orders for the envoys to be conducted into the Pavilion to rest.

Wherever there was a press, Gahmuret made a clearance. Some had bad luck, others good. But whoever missed his chance of doing great things could still make up for lost time: there was ample opportunity to hand. They only needed to ride a joust here or join the charging squadrons over there. They dropped such refinements as 'friendly thrusts' as they are called. Staunch friendships were wrenched apart by the violence of their fury. In such cases crooked deeds are rarely straightened out again: there was no umpire to lay down the law as to what knights might or might not do. If a man won anything he kept it. Nor did he care if the other resented it. Those performing the high office of the shield there with scant fear for the cost had come from many lands.

Gahmuret complied at once with Ampflise's request that he should be her knight as conveyed to him in her letter. Just watch him, now that he is unleashed! Is it Love and courage that urge him on so? Great affection and strong attachment renew his powers.

But now Gahmuret saw King Lot turn his shield to where the fight was thickest. Lot was borne round well-nigh face about, but Gahmuret prevented it. His charge broke the sides of the enemy's wedge, and he unhorsed the King of Arragon with his bamboo spear. That king's name was Schaffilor. The spear with which he had brought the proud knight down bore no pennant, since he had brought it with him from the heathen lands. Schaffilor's friends defended him stoutly, but Gahmuret took him prisoner none the less.

The Inners soon forced the Outers to make for the open country at great speed. Their Vespers were bringing a good yield of fighting! You would have thought it a thoroughgoing tournament, for many shattered lances lay around.

Lähelin now grew furious.

'Are we going to be put to shame in this fashion? It is the doing of the man who wears the Anchor. One of us two will lay the other where he will not lie softly before this day is out! They have come very near to beating us!'

The momentum of their charge assured this pair of ample room. It was now something more than mere sport. They set about it with such a will that they threatened to clear the forest, for they had but a common need: '*Lance*, sir, *lance*, lance!' But in the end Lähelin was forced to suffer a cruel humiliation. The King of Zazamanc thrust him over his crupper to the full length of his bamboo-mounted lance and collected his surrender. But however easily knights went down before him, I would find it pleasanter to gather ripe pears.

There were many who, finding themselves on his line of attack, cried 'Look out, here comes the Anchor!' But an Angevin prince came galloping his way with upturned shield, expressing grief which utterly possessed him. Gahmuret knew its blazon. Why did he turn away? By your leave I will tell you. His affectionate brother, proud Galoes, fil li roy Gandin, bestowed it some time before Love had caused his death in single combat.

Gahmuret unlaced his helmet. He cut no more paths through grass or dust with his attacks, as befitted his deep sorrow. He wrangled with himself for not having pestered cousin Kaylet to tell him what his brother meant by not joining in this tournament. Alas, he did not know how his brother had died at Muntori. Gahmuret already had trouble enough on his mind, tormented as he was by his love for a noble queen. (She too suffered great distress on his account subsequently and died of loyal grief.)

Although Gahmuret was now in mourning he had nevertheless in the space of half a day broken so many lances that had a tournament ensued a whole forest would have been cleared. No less than a hundred painted ones had been issued for him, yet the proud man had squandered the lot. His bright pennants were now the property of the heralds and poursuivants, as was their privilege. He rode towards his Pavilion and was followed by the Queen of Waleis's page, who bagged his precious tabard, pierced and hacked as it was. The boy then took it to show the ladies. It was still resplendent with gold, gleaming like a fiery furnace, and spoke of wealth and magnificence.

'It was a noble lady sent you to this country, Tabard, together with this knight,' said the Queen gaily. 'Now propriety demands that the others who have come to try their fortunes here should not be slighted. Let all take note of my good will, for all are my kin through Adam's rib. Yet when all is said and done, I believe that Gahmuret's deeds have won most praise.'

The others continued their noble sport with such fury that they were banging away lustily till nightfall. The Inners had fought the Outers back to their pavilions, and but for the King of Ascalun and Morholt of Ireland would have galloped in through their guy-ropes.

Some had won their throw, others lost. Many had come to grief, others to honour and glory. But now it is time to part them – nobody here can see a thing! Mine-Host-that-holds-the-Stakes won't give them any light! Who would want to gamble in the dark? That is asking too much of weary men.

The darkness was quite forgotten where Gahmuret sat in what might have been broad daylight, though it was not. There were in fact huge lights made of countless bunches of tiny candles. Many fine quilts had been laid over olive leaves, many broad carpets spread with care before them.

The Queen rode up to his guy-ropes with a bevy of noble ladies. She wished to have a look at the noble King of Zazamanc. A crowd of weary knights pressed after her. The table-cloths were removed before she entered the Pavilion. Her host leapt to his feet, followed by four captive kings who for their part were attended by many princes, and received her with due ceremony. Having looked him up and down she liked him.

'Here where I have found you, you are host,' said the Lady of Waleis happily. 'Yet I am Mistress of this land. If it is your pleasure that I welcome you with a kiss I assent to it.'

'I shall have your kiss,' he answered, 'provided that these lords are kissed as well. If kings or princes are to be passed over I dare not ask it of you.'

'So be it. I have met none of them before.'

She kissed all whose rank entitled them to it as Gahmuret had requested. He then begged the Queen to be seated. My lord Brandelidelin took his seat beside the lady. Green rushes wet with dew had been scattered over the carpet – on which sat a man who delighted the Queen of Waleis, though desire for his love gave her much ado. As he went to take his seat, he passed so close that she caught at him and pulled him down beside her on the other side. She was a maiden, not a woman, who made him sit so near. Now would you like to hear her name? – The Queen Herzeloyde! Her paternal aunt was Rischoyde, whom Kaylet, Gahmuret's cousin on his mother's side, had married. Lady Herzeloyde shed such a radiance that had the candles expired she would have given sufficient light on her own. Gahmuret would have been more than ready to return her love had not bereavement cast down the broad-based pinnacle of his joy.

They exchanged salutations as etiquette required. After a while cup-bearers appeared with some decorative work from Azagouc whose magnificence none could mistake, fine large goblets of precious crystal with no gold! Those who carried them were pages of gentle birth. They were tribute from Isenhart's country which he had offered so often to Lady Belacane, in hope of easing his suffering. They presented their liquor in crystal of both cornelian and emerald, though some were of ruby too.

Two knights rode up to the Pavilion on parole. They had been taken by the Outers and were now returning. One of them was Kaylet.

'What is the matter?' Kaylet asked, seeing Gahmuret sitting there with downcast face. 'You are acclaimed by all as having won my lady Herzeloyde together with her lands. Men of all countries here assert it, the Britons, Irish, French, Brabanters, and those who speak the local Waleis: they all accept your victory and concede that none can compete with you in a game of this sort. I have authentic proof before my eyes here: your strength and courage cannot be said to have been asleep when you got these gentlemen into difficulties, men who have never before had to offer their parole – my lord Brandelidelin, bold Lähelin, Hardiz and Schaffilor! (Alas for Razalic the Moor whom you also taught surrender at Patelamunt!) From all this your fame in battle seeks the heights and far horizons!'

'My lady will think you insane to puff me in this fashion,' said Gahmuret. 'You won't succeed in marketing me, for someone or other will see my flaws. You have been over-lavish with your praises. But tell me, how did you get back?'

'The worthy folk of Punturteis have set me and this Champagnard free to go where we please. If you will free my lord Brandelidelin, Morholt will not detain my nephew, whom he snatched from us. Otherwise my nephew and I will be held to ransom. I beg you to do us the favour. The Vespers were such hard going that there will be no tournament here at Kanvoleis this time. This I know for certain: the hard core of the Outers are sitting here. So tell me how they could ever stand up to us? Like it or not, you have greatly distinguished yourself.'

The Queen addressed a request to Gahmuret that was dear to her heart. 'You must give me satisfaction in the claims I have on you, and your servant asks it as a favour. But if you grant me these wishes only at cost to your renown, then let me go my way.'

At this the chaplain of the modest, discreet Queen Ampflise leapt to his feet.

'I object!' he said. 'By rights he is my lady's who sent me to woo him here. She is consuming herself in longing for him and so has a title to love him. It is she who should possess him, since she more than all other women loves him. Here are her three princely envoys, pages above reproach. The first is Lanzidant. He is from Greenland and of high degree. He came to France and has learned the language. The second is Liadarz fil li cunt Schiolarz.' Now who was the third? Listen to a strange story. His mother was Beaflurs, his father Pansamurs. They were of fairy race. He, their child, is Liahturteltart.

All three made haste to stand before him.

'Sire,' they said, 'if you have discernment you can play hazard without stakes, for the Queen of France has dealt you a chance that is *bound* to win you noble love. Unclouded happiness is yours for the taking!'

While this embassy was being heard, Kaylet who had preceded it was sitting under the edge of the Queen's mantle.*
'Tell me,' she asked him confidentially, 'have you received any other injuries? I saw the marks of blows on you.' Then the lovely woman felt his bruises with her soft white hands that bore the signs of God's own handiwork. She found that his cheeks, chin and nose were badly bruised and battered. His wife was the Queen's aunt and so Herzeloyde had done him the

* A privilege of close relationship.

honour of taking him by the hand and making him sit beside her.

Turning to Gahmuret she addressed him courteously. 'The noble Queen of France is urging her love on you. Now honour all women in me and let me bring my case to court. Remain in these parts till I receive judgment, else you will leave me in disgrace.'

The noble man gave his word, and she took her leave and went. There was no need for a stool: Kaylet, worthy knight, lifted her straight on to her palfrey and then rejoined his friends.

'Your sister Alize once offered me love,' said Kaylet to Hardiz, 'and I accepted it. She has now been provided for in another quarter and with greater distinction than if it had been with me. I beg you of your courtesy, put aside your anger. She is now Prince Lambekin's. Though she wears no crown she has attained illustrious rank. Hainault and Brabant pay homage to her, with many a good knight. Turn your thoughts in friendship towards me once again, restore me to your good graces and rest assured of my desire to serve you.'

The King of Gascony answered him like the spirited man he was.

'Your words were always honeyed; but if a man you had greatly wronged were to call you to account he would think it prudent to overlook it, were he, like me, your cousin's prisoner!'

'*He* is incapable of wronging anyone! Gahmuret is bound to set you free. That will be the first thing I ask. And then, when you are at liberty, the time will come when I shall have earned acceptance as your friend. Surely you have had enough time to swallow your injured pride? But however you treat me, your sister would not kill me.'

They all laughed at his words. But their mirth soon turned to sadness. Their host's old love was pricking him so that he was longing to be back. – Grief is a sharp goad. They all realized that he was struggling with his sorrow and that his spirits were not up to it.

'How inconsiderate of you,' said his cousin, chidingly.

'No, I cannot help my sad thoughts, I am full of longing for the Queen. I left a lady at Patelamunt the memory of whom – pure sweet woman! – wounds me to the heart. Her noble modesty fills me with sad longing for her love. She gave me a land and a people. Lady Belacane robs me of a man's whole happiness! But it is very manly too to be ashamed of one's fickleness. Yet that lady tied me up for safekeeping, with the result that I found no fighting. I fancied jousting would free me from the dumps, and have done some here. Now many an ignorant fellow may think that it was her black skin I ran away from, but in my eyes she was as bright as the sun! The thought of her womanly excellence afflicts me, for if noblesse were a shield she would be its centre-piece. That is one thing I have to lament, but there is another. I have seen my brother's escutcheon carried in reverse.'

Alas for those words! The tale took a sad turn then. The noble Spaniard's eyes filled with tears.

'Ah, foolish Queen! It was for your love that he gave his life, Galoes, whom all women should lament with loyal affection, if they wish their ways to be commended when they are spoken of! O Queen of Averre, however little it may trouble you, I have lost a kinsman, thanks to you! He died a knight's death in a fatal joust wearing your favours. His Princes and companions here bear heartfelt witness to their grief. Sorrow has bidden them turn their shields' broad ends to earth in the style of a funeral cortège. Such are the knightly deeds they do here. They are bowed in grief, now that my cousin Galoes will strive no more to win his lady's love.'

The news of his brother's death came as a second blow.

'With what sorrow to me have my Anchor's flukes struck land!' were his sad words. He then divested himself of his blazons, his doleful mien proclaiming deep distress. 'Galoes of Anjou,' he continued with true affection, 'one needs to look no further. The man who excels you in manly accomplishments was never yet born! True magnanimity blossomed from your heart and there bore fruit! How remembrance of your goodness affects me! – How does my poor unhappy mother Schoette take it?' he asked Kaylet.

56

'As must move God to pity. With having lost Gandin and then Galoes, your brother, and missing you at her side, death broke her heart too.'

'Now summon up all your courage,' said King Hardiz, 'for if you are a man you must not voice your grief beyond measure.'

But alas, Gahmuret's anguish was too great. A torrent gushed from his eyes. He saw to the comfort of his knights and then retired to his quarters, a little tent of samite. The whole night through he suffered pangs of grief.

When the new day dawned the Inner and the Outer parties all agreed – all who bore arms, young and old, the timid and the brave – that they would not go jousting. Even when the mid-morning sun was shining down they were so raw from fighting and their mounts so jaded with spurring that the reckless brotherhood were still overcome by great weariness.

The Queen now rode out in person to the knights in the field and fetched them back with her into the town. Once within the Gates she invited the foremost to ride to the Leoplane. They all complied with her request and came to where the mourning King of Zazamanc was having Mass sung for him. After the benediction, Lady Herzeloyde stepped forward and laid solemn claim to him, voicing her plea with general assent.

'I have a wife, Ma'am,' he replied, 'whom I love more dearly than life itself. But even if I had none I would still know a way of eluding you, if my rights are to be respected.'

'You must give up the Mooress in favour of my love,' said she. 'In the Sacrament of Baptism there is greater virtue. Now divorce yourself from heathenry and love me as our rites enjoin, for I am desperately in love with you. Or is the Queen of France to baulk my claim? Her envoys spoke honeyed words, they made the most of their message and played their game to the board's edge.'

'Yes, she is my true Mistress. I brought her gifts and my manners back with me to Anjou. My lady's help is with me still today, for it was she, a woman free of the failings of her sex, who brought me up. At the time we were both children, yet happy in each other's company. Queen Ampflise is a glory

57

to her sex. Charming woman, she equipped me with the best her lands could muster. Poorer then than now, I was glad to have it – but still count me among the poor! You ought to have pity on me, Ma'am. My noble brother is dead. I beg you of your courtesy not to press me. Let Love repair to happy haunts: grief is all I have for company.'

'Do not let me pine away any longer. Come, tell me how you mean to defend yourself.'

'I shall answer you straight to the point! Proclamation was made that there would be a tournament here: yet none took place. There are many witnesses to bear me out.'

'The tournament was crippled by the vespers, the wild were made so tame here that the tournament lapsed.'

'I exerted myself in defence of your town with others who did well. You ought to exempt me from this suit – many knights did better here than I. Your rights and claims on me are lame and amount to no more than the courtesy you extend to all, if I may have it.'

The knight and the maiden, so my tale informs me, appointed an arbiter to hear the lady's plea. It was then approaching noon. Judgment was pronounced forthwith:

That any knight, the which, being come into these parts for deeds of arms, has laced his helmet on and gained the palm, that same shall the Queen have and hold.

To which the court assented.

'Sire,' she said, 'you are now mine. You will find that I shall try to merit your favour and make you so happy that you will rise above your grief.'

Nevertheless he was tormented by grief. But April suns were past and were followed by short tender shoots of greenest grass – the meadows were one unbroken stretch of green – which inspires faint hearts with courage and makes them top o' the world. In response to the sweet May breezes, trees were out in blossom everywhere. Gahmuret was fated by his fairy blood to love or sue for love – and here was a friend disposed to grant it! He turned his eyes on the Lady Herzeloyde and with a winning smile spoke these courteous words: 'Madam, if I am to find life tolerable with you do not chaperone me. For if my sorrows ever leave me I should like to go out jousting. If you will not let me go to tournaments I have not forgotten my old trick, how once before I gave my wife the slip. Her too I won by deeds of arms. When she tied me up to keep me from fighting I left her land and people.'

'Make your own terms, my lord,' she said. 'I shall leave you to do much as you please.'

'I wish to break a good many lances yet. You must allow me, Ma'am, to attend one tournament a month.'

She promised it, as I was told, and he received those lands and the maiden too.

The three young lords of Ampflise's had been standing there with her chaplain while judgment and assent were being given. The chaplain had heard and seen it all. 'It came to my lady's ears,' he told Gahmuret softly, 'that you distinguished yourself above all others at Patelamunt and were master of two crowns. But she too has a kingdom and a mind to bestow her person and possessions on you.'

'It was she who made a knight of me, and I must steadfastly abide by the statutes of that order as the high calling of the shield obliges me. Had I not taken shield from her this never could have happened, since, like it or not, I am bound by a knightly verdict. Go back, give her my humble respects and tell her that in any event I will be her Knight. Though I were offered all the crowns in the world it is for her that I endure the deepest longing.'

He offered them great treasure, but they declined his gifts. The envoys returned to their country without disgrace to their mistress. They did not ask leave to go, as may easily happen in anger today. Those boys, her princely pages, were almost blind from weeping.

Those who had carried their shields point uppermost were told by a friend of theirs out in the field that 'Lady Herzeloyde has asserted her claim to the Angevin.'

'But who was here from Anjou? I am sorry to say our lord is elsewhere, seeking renown among the Saracens. And that is what hurts us most at present.'

'The man who came out best here and unhorsed so many knights and hacked and thrust so mightily and wore the magnificent Anchor on his gem-studded helmet – he is the man you mean! King Kaylet told me *that* Angevin is Gahmuret! He has had a great success here.'

They raced for their horses. When they arrived where their lord was sitting their robes were wet with tears. They embraced him, and he them. Joy and grief were there together.

Gahmuret kissed these loyal vassals. 'Do not lament my brother to excess,' he told them. 'I will stand you in his stead. Turn up the shield as it was meant to be. Hold to the paths of happiness. I must wear my father's blazon, since my Anchor has struck his land. The Anchor marks a soldier of fortune: let any who pleases adopt it for his charge. I have come to wealth and power and must now bear myself as one who means to live. If I am to be lord of a people my grief would pain them too. Lady Herzeloyde, help me persuade these kings and princes gathered here kindly to defer their departures till you have granted me what love requires of love.'

He and she urged their pleas together, and the nobles readily assented. They all withdrew to their quarters.

'Now entrust yourself to my keeping,' said the Queen to her lover. She then led him along secret passages. (Wherever their host had disappeared to, the guests were well looked after.) His and her retinues were merged. Save for two noble pages, he went unaccompanied. The Queen and her young ladies led him to where he found happiness, and all his sorrows vanished. Grief was discomfited, and zest in life renewed, as it must always be at the side of one's beloved. My lady Queen Herzeloyde gave up her maidenhead. Nor did they spare their lips but began to consume them with kisses, and ward off grief from joy.

This over, Gahmuret did a courteous thing. He freed the prisoners he had taken. As for Hardiz and Kaylet, why, he reconciled them! Then followed such festivities that if any has equalled them since I should say he was a very mighty man. Gahmuret saw to it that his treasure was not spared. They doled out Arab gold to poor knights one and all. To the Kings,

60

Gahmuret himself gave precious stones, nor did he forget the Princes gathered there. The vagrant minstrel folk were very glad, for they too shared in the rich bounty. Now let the guests ride off, whoever they are: the Angevin has given them leave to go.

They hammered the sable Panther on to his shield as his father had borne it before him. Over his hauberk he wore a small white silken shift of the Queen's (the one who was now his wife) as it came from her naked body. – They saw no less than eighteen pierced by lances and hacked through by swords, before he left the lady. She used to slip them on again over her bare skin when her darling returned from jousting after riddling countless shields. The love of these two expressed a deep attachment.

Gahmuret had honour enough as it was when his manly courage took him overseas into the thick of battle. How his expedition grieves me! He received a reliable message that his lord the Baruc had been overrun by Babylonians, the first of whom the story calls Ipomidon, the second Pompeius. The latter was a proud and noble man – not the Pompey who fled away from Rome in ancient times in fear of Julius Caesar. His uncle on his mother's side was King Nebuchadnezzar, who read in lying books that he was himself a god! – People now would laugh it to scorn. They did not spare their persons or property. They were brothers, and of high descent, indeed from Ninus, who reigned before Baghdad was founded and who also founded Niniveh. The Baruc had declared these two cities tributary to him, and they smarted under the shame and loss. As a result, a great deal was won and forfeited on either side. Warriors were seen at grips there. Thus Gahmuret embarked for overseas and found the Baruc under arms. However much his journey grieves me personally, Gahmuret was received with great joy.

Of what happened there, of how their fortunes stood with win or loss, Lady Herzeloyde knew not a thing. Lovely in person, she was dazzling as sunshine and possessed of wealth as well as youth and superabundant happiness. She had all and more than one can wish for. She practised the arts of well-doing and so won the liking of her people. The Lady Queen Herzeloyde's whole way of life brought her a rich return of praise, and her modest ways were much commended. She was Queen over three lands: she was mistress of Waleis and Anjou and wore the crown of Norgals in its capital city of Kingrivals. Her husband was so dear to her that if any other woman in the world had won so fine a friend, what would she have cared? She could have suffered it without bitterness.

When he had been away for half a year she was counting on his returning: this was the hope that sustained her. The blade of her contentment then snapped at the very hilt. Alas and lack-a-day that virtue should fruit in such sorrow and devotion give rise to such grief! But such is the way of the world: joy today and grief tomorrow.

One noonday the lady lay in troubled sleep, when a dreadful vision came to her. It seemed to her as though a shooting-star swept her to the upper air where a host of fiery thunderbolts assailed her, flying at her all together so that her long tresses hissed and crackled with sparks. The thunder pealed with loud claps and showered down tears of fire. As she came to herself again a griffin snatched at her right hand – whereat all was changed for her! For now she marvelled at how she was mothering a serpent which then rent her womb and how a dragon sucked at her breasts and flew swiftly away and vanished from her sight! It had torn her heart from her body! Such terrors had she to behold! Never since has such anguish befallen a woman in her sleep. Till then she had been all that a knight could desire. Ah, the pity of it! This is all to change. Henceforth she will wear grief's pallor. Her losses grow apace. Sorrows to come are on their way to her.

The lady fell to kicking and writhing, moaning and wailing in her sleep, things unknown in her before. Some young ladies were sitting there: they leapt to the bedside and woke her.

At this point Tampanis, her husband's prudent squire-in-chief, rode in accompanied by numerous little pages. Then happiness was no more. With weeping and wailing they told of their lord's death. This so afflicted her that she fell in a swoon.

'How was my lord overcome, so well armed that he was?' asked the knights.

Hard pressed by his grief, the squire nevertheless answered those warriors.

'Long life did not attend my lord. Plagued by the great heat, he removed his coif. Cursed heathenish cunning robbed us of our good warrior! A knight had got blood of billy-goat into a flask and then smashed it on the Adamant, which grew softer than a puff-ball. May He whom painters still depict as the Lamb, with the Cross between His hooves, compassionate what was done that day! When they rode in their companies to engage, you should have seen how they fought there! The Baruc's horse defended themselves with mighty valour. Many a shield was pierced there as they raced to the encounter on Baghdad's plains. The charging squadrons wound their way into each other and pennants were intermingled. Many a proud knight fell there.

'Compared with the deeds my lord performed the glory of the others shrank to nothing. But then Ipomidon rode up. He paid him back in lethal coin for once having thrust him down at Alexandria with many thousand knights looking on. My true-hearted lord turned to face this king: but the other's thrust taught him what it was to die! The point of the lance cut clean through his helmet, such a hole was bored through his head that the splinter of the shaft remained there. Yet the stalwart kept his seat and rode out of battle a dying man on to a broad mead. Soon his chaplain was kneeling at his side, while in brief words he made his confession and sent this shift and the lance that severed him from us. He died without reproach. He commended his squires and pages to the Queen.

'They conveyed him to Baghdad. The Baruc gave no thought to the cost – the tomb in which the spotless hero lies was embellished with gold and precious stones – a fortune went to its making. His young body was embalmed. Many suffered torments of grief. The stone above his grave is a costly ruby through which his body shines! Our wishes were respected in that a Cross was set above his grave in the manner of the Crucifixion from when Christ redeemed us by His death, to

63

comfort him and guard his soul. The Baruc defrayed the expense. It cost him a rare emerald. We did all this without assistance from the infidel, since the Cross whose blessing the death of Christ conferred upon us, is not in the keeping of their rite. The heathen worship Gahmuret in all seriousness as they do their own estimable god, yet not to the glory of the Cross or because of Christian teaching that will loose our bonds at the Judgment, but because his manly loyalty, his confession and repentance give him a bright radiance in Heaven. In him, deceit and treachery were at a low ebb.

'Upon the Adamant, his helmet, they engraved an epitaph and fixed it to the Cross above his grave. The Inscription reads:

'Through this Helm a lance-thrust struck a noble Hero, Gahmuret by name, a mighty King who ruled three lands, each one of which conferred a Crown with its train of mighty Princes. He was born of Anjou and lost his life before Baghdad in the Baruc's cause. His fame shot up so high that none will ever reach its mark wherever men shall judge of knights hereafter. There is no mother's child to whom this Hero swore surrender, that is, within the Chivalric Order! He gave help and manly counsel to his friends and never failed them. For women he suffered bitter love-pangs. Baptized, he followed the Christian rite. It is no lie but truth to say that his death distressed the Saracens. The Hero strove for fair renown in all his conscious days and so died a renownèd Knight. He won the victory over all that is perfidious. Now ask God's Mercy on the man that lies here.'

Such was the squire's account. Many men of Waleis wept for all to see. They had good cause for their sorrow.

The Lady was carrying a child that was already quickening in her womb, but they let her lie unaided. The child had been alive for eighteen weeks,* and its mother the Queen Herzeloyde was wrestling with Death. It was witless of those others not to help the woman, for she carried in her womb one destined to be the flower of chivalry if Death will but pass him by. But then a wise old man who had come to condole with her bent

* Life was reckoned from the first quickening in the second half of pregnancy.

64

over her as she fought Death. He forced her teeth apart, and they splashed water into her mouth. She returned to her senses at once.

'Ah me, what has become of my darling?' she cried, wailing in lamentation for him. 'The noble fame of Gahmuret was what filled my heart with joy, but his reckless ardour took him from me. I was younger than he by far, yet I am his mother and his bride, bearing as I do himself and his life's seed here, which we in our love did give and receive. If God is steadfast in his purpose, may he allow this seed to come to fruit, for I have suffered too great a loss in my consort. How cruelly Death has dealt by me! Gahmuret never shared a woman's love but he rejoiced in her joys and was saddened by her sorrows. It was manly devotion moved him in this, for he was devoid of all villainy.'

Now hear another thing the Lady did. She clasped her belly and the child within in her hands and arms, and said: 'I pray God to send me the noble fruit of Gahmuret! This is the prayer I cherish in my heart – God keep me from foolish desperation! If I were to kill myself while carrying his love-seed it would be the second death of Gahmuret, who was as true to me as a man can be.'

The Lady did not care who saw it – she tore her shift from her bosom and busied herself with her soft white breasts. With a woman's instinct she pressed them to her red lips. 'It is yours to hold a babe's nourishment,' said this woman grown wise, 'and you have sent it on ahead ever since I felt the quickening.' It was just what she wanted to see, this food above the heart, the milk within her breasts! Queen though she was, she pressed it out. 'Milk, how loyal of you to have come! Were I not baptized already you would have marked my christening! Often, now, I shall sprinkle myself with you, as with my tears, both alone and in the presence of others, for I shall mourn for Gahmuret.'

The Lady asked them to bring the bloody shift in which Gahmuret had lost his life at the head of the Baruc's company and met a warrior's death with the élan of a man of courage. She also asked after the lance that had done him to death.

Ipomidon of Niniveh, that proud and noble Babylonian, had paid him back in such warlike coin that her shift was hacked to rags and tatters. She made as if to put it on as in former days when her husband was back from tournaments: but they took it from her hands.

The foremost men in the land lodged the lance with its blood in the minster as people lodge the dead. Then all showed their grief in Gahmuret's land.

A fortnight later the Lady was delivered of a babe, a son so big in the bone that she scarce survived.

With this the story has made its cast, and its beginning is marked. For only now is he born to whom the tale is dedicated Of his sire's joys and last extremity, of his life and death, you have heard some part. Now learn from where the hero of this story comes to you and how he was kept from harm. They concealed from him knowledge of chivalry until he could think for himself!

When the Queen had regained her senses and taken her babe to her arms she and the other ladies studied the little piddler between his legs. And what a fuss they had to make of him, seeing him shaped like a man! In course of time he grew to be a smith – with swords! – and he struck many sparks from helmets, since his heart was of manly mettle.

The Queen loved to kiss him, over and over again. 'Bon fiz, cher fiz, bea fiz,' she said with tender insistence. She quickly took the dun-red points – by which I mean the tiny beaks of her breasts – and thrust them into his little mouth. She had carried him in her womb and was now herself his nurse. This lady who shunned the failings of her sex reared her child at the breast. It was as though her prayers had restored Gahmuret to her arms again. Yet she did not give way to frivolity: humility stood by her.

'The Queen of Heaven gave her breasts to Jesus,' she said pensively, 'who in the fullness of time received a bitter death on the Cross in human shape for love of us and thereby proved His devotion. Whoever makes light of His anger, his soul will fare ill at the Judgment, however pure of heart he is or may have been. This I know for sure.'

The lady of the land besprinkled herself with the dew of her sorrowing heart, her eyes rained down upon her body. All a woman's affection was hers. She lent her lips to both sighs and laughter. She rejoiced in the birth of her son, yet her gay spirit was drowned at sorrow's ford.

Wolfram's Apology

I F any speaks better concerning women than I, he may do so
without my resenting it. It would please me to learn of their
great pleasure. From one alone would I withhold my loyal
service – having found her unfaithful, my anger towards her
does not change.

I am Wolfram of Eschenbach and something of a minne-
singer. Like a tongs I clench on my anger for a woman who has
so mishandled me that I cannot choose but be her enemy. For
this I suffer the hostility of others. Oh, why do they behave
so? Yet although I deplore their enmity, it is womanly feeling
that prompts them, since I said something I ought never to
have said,* and wronged myself as well, which will scarce ever
happen again. On the other hand, they should not gallop
ahead of themselves and charge at my palisade – they will meet
stiff opposition there! I have not lost my ability to judge
shrewdly of their ways and behaviour. Yet I will champion any
woman of modest character, touching her good name – any
pain she suffered I should take very much to heart.

When a poet cries 'Check-mate!' to all ladies to advance his
own particular one,† his praise limps of the spavin. Whichever
lady cares to inspect my patent – and not only see but hear it –
I shall not mislead her. My hereditary Office is the Shield! I
should think any lady weak of understanding who loved me
for mere songs unbacked by manly deeds. If I desire a good
woman's love and fail to win love's reward from her with
shield and lance, let her favour me accordingly. A man who
aims at love through chivalric exploits gambles for high stakes.

Unless the ladies thought it flattery, I should go on offering

* Wolfram must have attacked his Lady in a love-song which has not
survived, see pp. 175 and 438.
† Reinmar, the favoured poet at the court of Vienna, had done so and
had also attracted the shafts of Walther von der Vogelweide for his sally.

you things as yet unheard of in this story, I would continue this tale of adventure for you. But let whoever wishes me to do so, not take it as a book. I haven't a letter to my name!* No few poets make their start from them: but this story goes its way without the guidance of books. Rather than that it be taken for a book, I should prefer to sit naked in my tub without a towel – provided I had my scrubber!

* See p. 10.

Chapter 3

IT saddens me that so many bear the name of woman. They all have the same clear voices. Many are quick to deceit, some are free of it. Thus there are two sides to the question. In my heart I am embarrassed that all are named alike. Womanliness, as long as you remain true to yourself, you and fidelity shall remain inseparable!

Many hold that poverty is good for nothing. Yet if one suffers it for fidelity's sake one's soul shall escape Hellfire.

There was a woman suffered poverty for fidelity's sake so that her gift was renewed in Heaven with infinite bounty. I do not suppose there are many alive today who in their youth would give up earthly riches for heavenly glory. Not one is known to me. Men and women are all the same as I see them: they would shirk it, one and all.

Rich in possessions, Lady Herzeloyde estranged herself from her three kingdoms. She bore a load of care. Falsity was so absent from her heart that eye and ear could find no trace of it. To her the sun seemed but a mist. She fled the world's delights. In her eyes day and night were all one. Her heart was obsessed with grief.

Set on grief, the Lady withdrew from her possessions to a forest in the wilds of Soltane – not to the meadows to be among flowers. She had no mind for garlands, were they red or of colours less gay, so entire was the sorrow in her heart. To this retreat she took the son of noble Gahmuret for refuge. Her followers had to clear the ground and make it arable.

How she cosseted her son! Before he arrived at years of discretion she summoned her people, man and woman, and forbade them all on pain of death ever to breathe the name of 'knight' – 'For if my darling were to learn of knighthood I should be very heavy-hearted. Now have your wits about you

70

and keep him in the dark concerning knighthood and all that has to do with it!'

Things took their hazardous course. Buried away in this fashion the boy was reared in the wilds of Soltane, cheated of a royal style of life in all things, except that he would cut bow and arrows with his own hands and shoot at the flocks of birds there. But when he had shot a bird that had been singing full throat but a moment before, he would burst into tears and, clutching at his hair, wreak vengeance on his own head.

He was proud and handsome. He washed himself in the meadow on the river-bank each morning. He had no care in the world save the singing of the birds overhead. Its sweetness pierced him to the heart and brought a tightness to his breast. All in tears he ran to the Queen.

'Who has been vexing you?' she asked. 'You went out to the meadow didn't you?'

But he was unable to tell her anything, as may easily happen with children today.

She pursued this in her thoughts for a long while. One day she saw him gaping up at the trees to see where the happy clamour of the birds was coming from. She realized then that it was their piping that brought the tightness to his breast. In this her son was the victim of amorous desire to which his race was heir. Lady Herzeloyde now turned her hatred on the birds. But why ...? She did not know. She wished to put an end to their singing. She ordered her ploughmen and drovers to hurry out and wring the necks of all the birds they could lay hands on! But the birds were better mounted! Some few escaped their deaths, a number survived to make merry with song.

'Why are they angry with the little birds?' the boy asked the Queen. He begged an immediate truce for them. His mother kissed him on his lips. 'Oh why do I forget and thwart the will of Him Who is God on high?' she asked. 'Are the birds to leave their happiness for me?'

But the boy was quick to ask 'Oh mother, what is God?'

'My son, I shall tell you, just as it is. He Who took on a

shape in the likeness of Man is brighter than the sun. My child, take this wise saying to heart: pray to Him when in need. His steadfast love never yet failed the world. Then there is one called Lord of Hell. He is black, perfidy cleaves to him. Turn your thoughts away from him and treacherous despair.'

His mother told him about Light and Darkness and how different they are. This done, the nimble boy dashed off and far away.

He learned how to swing his javelin, and with it he shot many deer of which mother and household had the benefit. In snow or after thaw, his shooting did deadly work on the game. Now listen to this strange thing! When he had brought down a beast so heavy that it would have burdened a mule he carried it home unquartered as it was!

One day he was hunting down a long slope. He had just broken off a twig for a decoy-call when he heard the echo of hoof-beats on the path nearby. He began to balance his javelin. 'What was that I heard?' said he. 'If only the Devil would come in all his terrible fierceness I would stand up to him for sure. My mother tells me dreadful tales about him. I suppose she has lost her courage.' Thus he stood there ready for the fray.

But look! Here come three knights at the gallop as fine as you could wish and armed from heel to crown! The boy thought each a god for sure. Nor did he remain standing any longer, but fell to his knees on the path. 'Help, God!' he cried at the top of his voice. 'Thou hast the power to help!'

The foremost lost his temper at the sight of this boy lying in mid-path. 'This stupid Waleis is slowing us down.' (The Waleis, I must tell you, share the same distinction as we Bavarians, but are even denser than Bavarian folk, though stout men with their weapons. Whoever is born in either land will blossom into a prodigy of tact and courtesy!)

At this moment a knight rode up, giving his horse free rein. He was beautifully turned out. He was riding armed in hot pursuit of others who were well away. For a pair of knights had carried off a lady from his country. This warrior considered it a great disgrace and was angry at the wrong that was being done to the poor young lady riding some way ahead. The other three here were his vassals. He was mounted on a fine castilian. His shield was badly battered. His name was Karnah-karnanz leh cuns Ulterlec. 'Who is blocking our way?' he asked and immediately came upon the boy.

To the boy he seemed like some god, never had he seen a thing so bright. The knight's tabard lightly brushed the dew, his well-adjusted stirrups rang with the music of tiny golden bells to the fore on either leg. His right arm too jingled with bells wherever he thrust or swung it. This was to give music to his sword-play, for he was hot in pursuit of fame! Such was the style the great prince rode in, magnificently caparisoned.

'Have you seen two knights, my boy?' Karnahkarnanz asked him, the very coronal of manly beauty. 'They are backsliders from chivalry, ravishers devoid of honour who have carried off a girl by force.' But whatever he was saying, the boy thought he was God, of whom Herzeloyde had spoken when explaining the Light. 'Now help me, most helpful God!' was his earnest cry. Fil li roy Gahmuret fell to his knees in urgent prayer.

'I am not God,' replied the prince, 'though I gladly do His will. If you had eyes in your head you would see four knights before you.'

'You said "knights"! – What are they? If you lack godlike power, then tell me, who gives knighthood?'

'King Arthur does so. Were you to come under his roof, young sir, you need never blush for the knight he would make of you. I should think you are of noble stock.'

The knights looked him up and down, and indeed he bore the marks of God's own handiwork. I have it from my source, which told me the truth of the matter, that from Adam's day till then none turned out better for looks than he, so that women praised him far and wide.

The boy said another thing that made them laugh. 'Oh Sir God, what can you be? There are so many little rings tied on you, up here and down there!' And the lad's hand was tugging at all the iron he could find on the prince. 'My mother's young ladies carry their rings on ribbons,' he said, examining the knight's armour, 'but theirs do not lie so tight together. – And what is it for, this thing that makes you look so trim?' his whim

73

prompted him to ask the prince. 'I can't pick any of it off.'

The prince showed him his sword. 'Now, look. If a man attacks me I fight him off with blows, and to defend myself from his I have to put this on. Against arrows and lance-thrusts too I must arm myself like this.'

'If the deer wore their hides like that,' the boy replied, 'my javelin would never wound a single one. Lots fall dead at my feet!'

The knights were angry that their prince stood talking with this fool of a boy. 'May God protect you!' said the prince. 'How I wish I had your looks! If only you had some sense in you, God would have left you nothing to wish for. May the power of God keep harm far from you!'

The prince and his men rode off and galloped to a field in the forest. There the courtly man found Lady Herzeloyde's plough-hands, and no worse calamity ever befell her people. He saw them busy furrowing. First they sowed, then they harrowed, jerking their goads over sturdy oxen.

The prince gave them good morning and asked if they had seen a young lady in distress? They could not do otherwise than answer his question. 'Two knights and a young lady rode past this morning, the lady in fear and anguish. Those who led her were spurring hard.' This was Meljahkanz. Karnahkarnanz was to overtake him and by force of arms win back the lady, who until that moment had been very dejected. She was Imane de Beafontane.

The ploughmen were in despair. 'How did we come to do this?' they asked themselves as the knights dashed past. 'If our young master has seen the war-scarred helmets these knights are wearing we have betrayed our trust. We shall have hard words from the Queen for this, and serve us right, for he ran along with us this morning while she was still asleep.'

True enough, the lad lost interest in shooting deer, great or small. He went to find his mother and told her a tale that sent her reeling. His words had given her such a shock that she lay at his feet in a swoon.

When the Queen regained her senses, although her spirits had failed her before, she now asked 'My son, who told you of the Order of Chivalry? How did you come to hear of it?'

'Mother, I saw four knights brighter even than God – *they* told me about knighthood. Arthur's kingly power must guide me to knightly honour and the Office of the Shield!'

This gave rise to new grief. The Lady was at her wit's end to find a means of wooing him from his purpose. The noble, simple lad kept pestering her for a horse. 'I will not deny him,' she told herself, though she regretted it in her heart. 'But it will have to be the wretchedest nag. People are much given to mockery,' she continued in her thoughts. 'My child shall wear fool's clothing over his white skin. Then, if he is roughly handled, he will surely come back to me.'

Ah, the pity of it! The Lady took some sackcloth and cut him a doublet and breeches all of a piece down to the middle of his gleaming white legs – regular fool's clothes. To crown it there was a cowl. From a fresh raw calf-hide a pair of buskins were cut to the shape of his legs. This was not done without much weeping and wailing.

After thinking matters over she asked him to stay that night. 'You must not go before I have taught you some sense. When riding across country avoid murky fords. Where they are clear and shallow trot in briskly. Make it your custom to greet all and sundry. If a wise grey-haired man offers to teach you good manners as he would well know how, do as he says with a will, do not fly into a passion. Let me give you this advice, my son. Wherever you can win a lady's ring and greeting, take it – it will rid you of the dumps. Waste no time, but kiss and embrace her. It will bring you good fortune and raise your spirits, granted she be chaste and good. You must learn another thing, my son. Arrogant bold Lähelin has wrested two lands, Waleis and Norgals, from your Princes. By rights they should subserve you. Turkentals, one of your Princes, was killed by him, and he killed your people or took them prisoner.'

'I will avenge this, mother, if God pleases. My javelin shall wound him yet!'

When the sun shone out next morning the boy was quickly resolved – he was impatient to be off in search of Arthur! Queen Herzeloyde kissed him and ran out after him. There

75

then happened a most pitiful thing. When she could no longer see her son – he rode off, and who does not regret it? – the loyal Lady fell to the ground, where sorrow gave her such a cut that Death did not hold off.

Her steadfast death preserved the Lady from Hell's torments. O happy woman for having been a mother! Thus did a root of virtue, stem of humility, go the way that brings reward. Alas, that we no longer have her kindred with us to the eleventh remove! For lack of them all too many are debased today. But true-hearted women must now ask a blessing on the boy who here sets out and leaves her.

Now the handsome lad was riding towards the Forest of Brizljan when he came to a stream which a cock would have crossed with ease. Though its waters were darkened only by the flowers and grass on its banks, the boy left the ford and knowing no better followed the stream all day. He spent the night as best he could till the bright sun shone out on him. Then all alone he made for a ford that was fine and clear.

On the farther bank the meadow was graced by a pavilion on which a fortune in three-colour samite had been lavished. It was lofty and spacious and its seams were trimmed with fine galloons. It had a leather cover hanging there for drawing across when it looked like rain. Duke Orilus de Lalander! – he it was whose wife the boy found lying there beneath it, the exalted Duchess, a lovely sight and all a knight could wish in a mistress! Her name was Jeschute.

The lady had fallen asleep. She wore Love's blazon – a mouth of translucent red, torment to the hearts of amorous knights. She slept with parted lips that wore the flames of Love's hot fire. Thus lay the loveliest challenge to adventure imaginable! Her gleaming close-set teeth lay in neat rows of snow-white ivory. (I fancy none will accustom me to kissing so well praised a mouth! Such things never come my way.) Her sable coverlet barely reached her hips, for on her lord's departure the heat had caused her to push it down. Her figure was neat and trim: no art was lacking there, since God Himself had fashioned her sweet body. Nor was that all. The adorable woman was slender of arm and white of hand. Here on one of them the boy spied a ring, which drew him to the couch. And there he began to struggle with the Duchess. The handsome lad was thinking of his mother and how she had told him to capture women's rings – and so he had leapt from the carpet straight upon the couch! Sweet modest woman, she sat up with a start to find the boy in her arms. How could she go on sleeping?

'Who does me this dishonour?' the high-bred lady asked in shame and anger. 'Young gentleman, you make too free. Address yourself elsewhere, if you please.'

The lady wailed loudly. He paid no attention to what she said but forced her mouth to his. Wasting no time, he crushed her breast to his, duchess or no duchess, and also took a ring. On her shift he saw a brooch and roughly tore it off. The lady was armed as women are: but to her his strength was an army's. Nevertheless there was quite a tussle of it.

But now the boy complained of hunger. 'Don't eat me,' said the dazzling lady. 'If you had any sense you would choose some other food. There's some bread over there, and wine, and a brace of partridges served by a maid who scarcely meant them for you.'

Little did he care where his hostess sat – he ate a good bellyful and drank some heavy draughts to follow. The lady thought his stay in the pavilion tedious. She took him for a page who had lost his reason. For sheer embarrassment she was breaking out into a sweat. 'Young man,' the Duchess managed to say, 'I must ask you to leave my ring behind, and my brooch, too. Take yourself off, for if my husband comes you will have to endure such anger as you would gladly have been spared.'

'Why should I fear your husband's rage?' the boy replied. 'But if it wounds your honour I will gladly go away.' He then went up to the couch, and another kiss was taken, much to the Duchess's annoyance. The lad then rode off without asking leave, though he did say 'God be with you! – That's what my mother told me.'

The lad was delighted with his spoils. When he had ridden on for some time, for close on a mile, there came a man about whom I wish to tell you. From the traces in the dew he could see that his lady had suffered an intrusion. Some of the guys had been kicked out, and here a boy had trampled the grass. The noble, illustrious prince discovered his wife inside, most wretched.

'Alas, madam,' said proud Orilus, 'is it for this that I have addressed my service to you? My glorious exploits all end here in disgrace! You have another lover!'

With tearful eyes the lady offered her denial, protesting she was innocent. He did not believe a word of it. 'A mad fool rode this way,' she ventured timidly. 'Of all the people I have ever seen I never saw any so handsome. He took my ring and brooch against my will.'

'Ah, you liked his looks! You made a pair with him!'

'God forbid!' she cried. 'His buskins and his javelin were too near to be overlooked. You ought to be ashamed to say such a thing! To love in such a quarter would lower a princess.'

'Madam, I have done you no wrong,' rejoined the prince, 'unless one thing rankles with you: that for my sake you renounced the title of "Queen" to assume that of "Duchess". But in that exchange it is I who am the loser. When all is said, my mettle is so keen that your brother Erec fil li roy Lac* has cause to hate you for it. The critics judge my reputation above cavil, except that he unhorsed me before Prurin. Yet, since then, I won glory from him at Karnant, for I thrust him over his crupper with a straight joust to win his surrender – my lance took your favour clean through his shield! Little did I then dream that you would take another lover, my lady Jeschute!

'I beg you credit this, madam – proud Galoes fil li roy Gandin was slain by a thrust of mine. Nor were you far away when Plihopliheri rode out to break a lance with me and pressed me hard: but my lance swung him over his crupper so that his saddle ceased to irk him! I have won glory on many occasions and brought down many knights. Yet I have failed to reap the fruits, as this deep disgrace informs me. They hate me,

* See p. 412.

one and all, those men of the Table Round, eight of whom I unhorsed at Kanedic in view of a bevy of young ladies when I was competing for the Sparrowhawk. I won the Prize for you, for myself the victory. Watching with you was Arthur, who has my sweet sister Cunneware with him in his palace. Until she sets eyes on the most illustrious man in the world her mouth will never wear a laugh.

'If only that man would come my way! There would be some fighting here like this morning's, when I fought a prince who challenged me and did him some mischief! – My lance-thrust stretched him out dead!

'I will not speak of anger and how, often, men have struck their wives for less. If in duty or by favour I owe you anything you will have to shift without it. I shall warm to your white arms no more, where I have lain enamoured many a happy day, now past. I will make your red lips fade and teach their colour to your eyes. I will rob your happiness of splendour and school your heart in sighs.'

The princess looked up at her husband and said with pitiful mouth, 'Show by how you treat me that you respect the honour of knighthood. You are true and discerning: you also have me enough in your power to inflict much suffering on me. So listen first to my defence, I beg you in the name of all my sex. Time enough to punish me afterwards. Granted I were killed by someone else, so that your honour were not lowered, how-ever soon death came to me I would think that moment sweet, now that I am the object of your hatred!'

'You are growing too proud for my liking, madam,' replied the prince. 'I will put a check on this so far as you are con-cerned. – There will be no more eating and drinking together, our sharing one bed is over and done with. You shall have no clothes other than those I found you sitting in. For bridle you shall have a rope of bast. Your palfrey shall go hungry. Your pretty saddle will get the worst of it!' And he quickly ripped and tore the samite away and then smashed the saddle she used to ride in. Modest, true-hearted woman, she had to suffer his spite. Finally he retied the saddle with strings of bast. His rage was all too sudden for her.

'Let us ride, madam,' he said straightaway. 'If I should light on the man who enjoyed your favours here – how I would relish it! – I would try my fortune against him, though he breathed fire like a raging dragon!' All thought of laughter gone, and in tears, the wretched lady set out dolefully. Whatever she endured she did not mind it, only that her husband suffered so. His unhappiness so distressed her that she would have found death more kind. Her faithful love deserves your pity, since from now on she is to suffer great tribulation. Though I were hated by the whole sex, the wrong done to Lady Jeschute could not fail to anger me.

Thus they rode off following the trail.

The boy ahead was in a great hurry too. But the resolute lad did not know they were pursuing him. Indeed, the good youth was passing the time of day with all he saw as he approached them, adding 'That's what my mother told me'.

Now our simple lad was riding down a slope when he heard a woman's voice. Below a spur of rock a lady was lamenting from heartfelt grief. Her whole happiness had snapped in two. The boy rode swiftly towards her. Now listen to what the lady was at. Mistress Sigune was sitting there tearing out her long brown tresses by the roots in despair! The boy's eyes began to range: they lit on Prince Schionatulander, dead, in the maiden's lap. Her thoughts were of unalleviated sorrow.

'Downcast or cheerful, my mother told me to greet them all. God keep you,' said the boy. 'It's a sad thing I see in your lap there. Who gave you that wounded knight?' And he went on unabashed, 'Who shot him? Was it with a javelin? It looks to me as if he's dead, ma'am. If you will tell me about the man who killed him I will gladly fight him, provided I can ride him down.' And the stout lad clutched at his quiver full of keen javelins. He still had the two gages he had torn from Jeschute when a deed of youthful folly was done. Had he learnt his father's noble ways, which remained with him all his life, the tilting would have been more on the mark, back there where the Duchess had sat all alone! Now, thanks to him, she was to suffer great misery. For a year and more her husband did not approach her. The woman was much wronged.

Now hear about Sigune. She could express her grief most dolefully.

'You have much to commend you,' she told the boy. 'All honour to your sweet youth and charming looks! The day will come, I know, when you will be blessed with good fortune. No javelin came his way: this knight lost his life in a joust.* You are of loyal stock to feel such pity for him.' Before she would let him ride she asked him his name, declaring his looks bore the marks of God's own handiwork.

' "Bon fiz, cher fiz, bea fiz" – that's what they used to call me, those who knew me at home.' At these words she at once knew his name. Now hear him named by his true name so that you may know who is lord of this story as he stands there talking with the girl.

'Upon my word, you are Parzival!' said she of the red lips. 'Your name means "Pierce-through-the heart".† Great love ploughed just such a furrow through your mother's heart. When he died, your father left sorrow for her portion. It is not to boast that I tell you, but your mother is my mother's sister, and I will tell you plainly who you are. Your father was an Angevin. On your mother's side you are a Waleis and born of Kanvoleis. I know for a fact that you are King of Norgals too and by rights should wear a crown in the capital city of King-rivals. This Prince, who kept his faith unscarred, was slain on your account whilst guarding your lands, as always. My sweet young charming man, two brothers have done you great wrong: Lähelin robbed you of two kingdoms; Orilus has slain this knight in battle with the lance and your paternal uncle as well. Me too he has left in misery. This Prince from your country served me irreproachably while your mother was fostering me. Dear, kind cousin, let me tell you how it came about. It was a Setter's Leash that brought him this sharp death which he got in the service of us both, bringing me to the extremity of grief, so much do I love him. Where were my

* It was *infra dig.* both to use missiles on one's enemies and to be killed by missiles.
† A play on the French form of the name read as 'Perce à val'.

poor wits, that I denied him enjoyment of love? From this prime source of grief my happiness is slashed to shreds and now I love him dead!'*

'Cousin,' he said, 'your sufferings grieve me, and my disgrace is great. If ever I have power to avenge it I will settle the account.' He was all impatient to go and fight, but she gave him the wrong direction, fearing he would be killed and she take greater harm.

He took a broad, paved road that led to the men of Britain. Whoever came riding or walking by, whether knight or merchant, he promptly gave all a greeting, declaring his mother had said he should. Nor had she erred in giving him this counsel.

With the approach of evening, great weariness came over him. Soon the simple fellow saw a fair-sized house. Within lived a churlish host of a kind that still sprouts from boorish stock today. He was a fisherman, a man without a saving grace. With hunger for guide the boy rode in and told the master how famished he was.

'I'd not give you half a loaf in thirty years,' said the man. 'If anyone thinks he'll catch me being generous, all for nothing, he's wasting his time! I don't fend for any but myself, after that my children. You won't get in here if you wait for the rest of the day. But if you had a penny or something you could pawn, I'd take you in at once.' The boy offered him Lady Jeschute's brooch there and then. When the boor saw it his mouth broke into a grin. 'If you will stay with us, dear child,' he said, 'all of us here will treat you with respect.'

'If you feed me well tonight, and tomorrow show me the right way to Arthur whom I love, this gold will be yours.'

'I will,' said the boor. 'Never did I see so well made a boy. I'll take you up to the King's Round Table to see what comes of it all.'

The boy stayed the night there. Next morning saw him miles away – he was scarce able to wait for daylight. His host made

* The earlier events of this story are told in Wolfram's elegiac poem 'Titurel', so miscalled, since its subject is the child-love of Sigune and Schionatulander.

ready and ran ahead, while the boy followed on horseback: both were in a hurry.

Sir Hartmann of Aue, I am sending a stranger to the Palace to visit your lord and lady, King Arthur and Queen Ginover.* Kindly shield him from mockery. He is no fiddle or rote. In the name of all that is seemly let people find something else to strum on! – otherwise your Lady Enite† and her mother Karsnafite will be dragged through the mill and their reputations lowered! If I am to twist my mouth to jibes, with jibes I will defend my friend!

The fisherman and the noble boy were approaching a great city: they were near enough to see that it was Nantes. 'God be with you, child,' said the one. 'Look, that's where you ride in.' 'Do guide me further,' replied the backward youth. 'I'll take good care I don't! The retainers are all so fine, it wouldn't do at all for a peasant to approach them!'

The boy rode on alone to a fair-sized meadow bright with flowers. No Kurvenal‡ had reared him, he knew nothing of fine manners, as is often the case with a stay-at-home. His bridle was of bast and his little palfrey very feeble – its stumblings often brought it to its knees. No new leather had been nailed to its saddle anywhere. As to samite or ermine, not a bit could you see on him. He had no need of cords for a mantle: instead of suckeny and surcoat he had taken his javelin. His father, whose style was highly spoken of, was better dressed on the carpet at Kanvoleis.

Riding towards this lad who had never known the sweat of fear there came a knight whom he greeted as usual with a 'God keep you! That's what my mother told me.'

'God reward both you and her, young sir,' said the knight. A son of Arthur's paternal aunt, the warrior had been reared by Utepandragun and was moreover laying claim to Britain as

* Hartmann was the first great poet to introduce Arthurian romances into German literature, in his *Erec* and *Iwein*. He was therefore the doyen of medieval German poets 'at Arthur's Court'. Aspiring to outshine or at least equal his senior, Wolfram issues this guarded challenge.

† The heroine of Hartmann's *Erec*.

‡ Tutor to Tristan in the romance of that name.

his heritage. His name was Ither of Gaheviez and he was otherwise called 'The Red Knight', for his gear was so red that it infected the eye with its redness! His charger was a swift sorrel, its crinière red all over, its trappers were of red samite, his shield redder than fire. His surcoat, well and amply cut to his figure, was all red. Lance-head and shaft were both of them red. The warrior's sword was all red as he had wished it, but well hardened at its edges. And the finely chased goblet which this King of Cucumerlant had standing in his hand, having seized it from the Table Round, was entirely of red gold. His skin was white, his hair red. Frankly he addressed the boy.

'A blessing on your good looks! It was a fine woman brought you to the world. Bless the mother that bore you! I never saw so handsome a form. You are the very glance of Love, her victory and defeat. For the joy of many a woman will triumph in you, then grief for you lie heavy on her. Dear friend, if you are going in, please tell Arthur and his men that none shall see me run away. I shall gladly wait here for any who cares to arm for a joust. Let none of them think it a romantic adventure: I rode to the Table Round and claimed my lands. My clumsy hand snatched up this cup, and so the wine was spilt into my lady Ginover's lap. This I did to assert my title. Now had I, instead, upended a burning wisp of straw, I would have smeared myself with soot: but this I did not do!' said the gallant warrior. 'Nor did I do so for the sake of plunder: my Crown exempts me from the need. Now, friend, tell the Queen that I splashed her without intent, in the presence of nobles who forgot their weapons. Kings or princes, why do they let their host go thirsty, why do they not fetch his golden cup for him? If they do not, their bounding fame will lag behind!'

'I will do as you ask,' the boy replied, and leaving him, rode into Nantes.

Here little children followed him into the courtyard before the Palace, where there was a great stir. He was at once the centre of a jostling crowd. Iwanet, a frank young page, leapt forward and offered him company. 'God keep you!' said the boy. 'My mother told me to say so before I left her house. I see a lot of Arthurs here – which is to make me a knight?' Iwanet laughed. 'You can't see the right one here,' he said, 'but you soon will.' And he led him into the Palace where the noble Household had foregathered. Above the din he managed to say 'God keep you all, especially the King and his Lady! I had strict orders from my mother to give them a special greeting. Those, too, whose fame entitles them to a seat at the Table Round. But one thing escapes my knowledge: I do not know who is master here within. A knight I saw shining red all over gave a message for him that he will wait for him outside there. I think he wants to fight. He is sorry too that he spilt the wine over the Queen. Oh, if only *I* had received his trappings from the King! I would be very happy then, it looks so fit for a knight!'

The fearless lad was charged and jostled from side to side. They examined his appearance, which told its own story – handsomer progeny was never sir'd or madam'd. God was in a pleasant mood when he made Parzival, whom no terrors could abash.

And so the boy in whom God had contrived perfection was brought into Arthur's presence. To dislike him was not possible. On leaving the Palace where she had been splashed with wine the Queen, too, had a look at him.

'God reward you for your greeting, young sir,' said Arthur as he gazed at the raw young man. 'I would gladly deserve it with life and wealth, I assure you!'

'Would to God it were so! It seems a year to me, all this time I go unknighted. I cannot say it makes me very happy. Now don't put me off any longer but do what it takes to make a knight of me!'

'I shall gladly do so as long as honour is with me,' replied his host. 'You are so very charming that the gift I shall make you master of will be a magnificent one. Believe me, I should hate to be denied. Wait until tomorrow. I shall equip you well.'

The noble youth stood there trampling like a bustard. 'I do not ask for anything here,' he said. 'A knight came riding towards me. If I can't have his armour I shan't care who talks of the King's gifts. My mother will give me something just as well, she's a queen, you know.'

'The man this armour sits on is so formidable,' Arthur told the boy, 'that I dare not give it you. Even now, and through no fault of mine, I am denied his favour and lead a wretched life of it. He is Ither of Gaheviez and has shattered all my happiness.'

'You would be a mean king to stick at such a gift. Give it him,' said Keie, 'and unleash him on Ither out there in the field. If anyone is to bring us back the goblet, here stands the whip, there the top. Let the boy flog him round – they'll commend it to the ladies! He must face odds in many a tussle yet. I am concerned for the life of neither. To win a boar's head one must sacrifice the hounds.'

'I should be sorry to deny him, but I fear he may be killed, this boy I should be helping to knighthood,' was Arthur's loyal response. But the lad accepted the gift – with dire results as it proved.

And now he raced away from the King, while young and old pressed after him. Iwanet took him by the hand and led him past a low gallery. He surveyed it from end to end. It was indeed so low that he witnessed a thing up there which saddened him.

It was the Queen's pleasure to be sitting there in person with knights and ladies at the windows, and they all began to observe him. The proud and radiant Lady Cunneware was sitting there too. She never laughed nor ever would till she saw the man who held the palm or was destined to win it. Else she would rather die. She had refrained from laughing altogether till the boy went riding past. But now her lovely lips parted in a laugh that caused her back to smart! For Keie the Seneschal seized my lady Cunneware de Lalant by her curly hair, he wound her long tresses round his hand and clenched her without a door-hinge.* Her back was taking no oath, yet a staff was so applied to it that its weight sank through clothes and skin till its swishing died away.

'You have dismissed your good name with contumely,' he

* The reference is to the medieval hinge, one arm of which could embrace the whole width of a door, clamping together with its prongs all the planks of which the door was made.

said, quite beside himself, 'but I am the net that retrieves it. I shall hammer it back into you so that you feel it in your bones. So many worthy men have ridden to Arthur's forecourt and into his Palace and failed to make you laugh, and now you laugh for one who has no notion of knightly deportment!'

Anger leads to great excess. His right to strike this maiden, whose friends were so very sorry for her, would not have been upheld before the Emperor. Even had she been a knight, these blows would have been unseemly, for she was a princess born. Had her brothers Orilus and Lähelin been looking on, fewer blows would have been struck there.

Mute Antanor, whom from his silence people thought a fool, had refrained from speech for the same reason as she from laughter. He was going to say no word till the maiden laughed who had just been thrashed. And now that she had laughed he opened his mouth and said to Keie 'God knows, Sir Seneschal, it was because of the boy that Cunneware de Lalant was beaten. He will fritter your jollity away for that one day, however lonely and friendless he may be.'

'Since the first words you utter are to threaten me, I swear you will have little joy of it!' Antanor's hide was tanned for him, and clouting fists had much to whisper in the ears of this knowing fool – Keie was swift to act. Young Parzival had to stand by and watch while Antanor and the lady suffered. Their distress angered him to the very core. He kept on clutching at his javelin, but there was such a throng before the Queen that he could not hurl it.

Then Iwanet took leave of fil li roy Gahmuret, who set out alone for the meadow to join Ither. He brought Ither news that none of those within were eager to break a lance. 'The King made me a gift. I told him, as you asked me, that you spilt the wine accidently and were annoyed at having been so clumsy. Not one has relish for a fight. Give me what you are riding on and all your gear as well. It was given me up at the Palace. I'm to be made a knight in it. If you begrudge it I'll take back my greeting. So if you are wise you will give it me.'

'If Arthur gave you my armour,' replied the King of Cucumerlant, 'and granted you succeed in winning it from me, then he also gave you my life! So this is the way he favours his friends! Was there something in the past that earned you his good will? – Your services are prompt to find their reward.'

'I dare to deserve what is due to me, and there is no denying that he gave it me! Hand it over and stop your wrangling! I will be a page no longer, I must follow the Calling of the Shield.' He snatched at the other's bridle: 'You are Lähelin, aren't you, of whom my mother complained to me?'

The knight reversed his lance and thrust at the boy with such might that he and his little nag came tumbling down on the flowers. The warrior was quick-tempered. He beat the boy with the shaft so that blood sprayed through his pores in a cloud. Parzival, good lad, stood enraged on that meadow. He clutched at his javelin, and there, where helmet and vizor leave a gap above the coif, the missile pierced Ither through the eye and then the nape, so that he who was the negation of all that is perfidious fell dead.

The death of Ither of Gaheviez gave rise to women's sighs and laceration of heartfelt grief. He left them a legacy of moist eyes. Any that harboured sentiments of love for him saw her happiness routed, her gay spirit overwhelmed and escorted into the rough.*

Naive young Parzival turned him over and over. He could not tug anything off him – what a strange affair it was! Helmet-lace or knee-pieces, his fine white hands failed to loosen or otherwise twist any off. Yet he tried and tried again, this lad so little favoured with good sense.

The war-horse and the little palfrey whinnied so loudly that Ginover's page and kinsman Iwanet heard it before the walls at the moat's edge. Hearing the charger's fretting and seeing no rider in the saddle, the alert boy hastened to the scene, drawn by the friendship he felt for Parzival.

He found Ither dead, and Parzival in a child's perplexity. He quickly ran along to them, and congratulated Parzival on the honour he had won at the expense of the Lord of Cucumerlant.

* The part of the tournament field where those taken prisoner were kept.

'God reward you! Now tell me what to do. I don't know much about this. How do I get it off him and on to me?'

'I can show you that,' Iwanet proudly told fil li roy Gahmuret. The dead man was despoiled of his armour there on the field of Nantes, and it was laid upon the living, who nevertheless is still inspired by great simplicity. 'Your buskins ought not to stay beneath your armour. From now on you must wear only knightly attire.'

This did not please Parzival at all. 'Nothing my mother gave me shall ever leave my body,' said the good lad, 'for better or for worse.'

To Iwanet, who was no child, this seemed rather odd, yet there was nothing for it but to agree: he did not lose his patience with him. He encased him, over his buskins, in two jambs of gleaming steel. With them went a pair of spurs worked in gold which were attached not by leathers but silken cords. These he fastened on. Before offering him his hauberk Iwanet laced on his knee-guards. And so, suffering it with keen impatience, Parzival was armed from heel to crown.

The stout lad then demanded his quiver. 'I will not hand you any javelins: the Order of Chivalry forbids it,' said the noble page Iwanet. He girded a sharp sword on him, taught him how to draw it and commanded him never to flee. He then led forward the dead man's long-legged castilian. Scorning the stirrups, Parzival leapt fully armed into the saddle. His manly vigour is still commended today.

Iwanet further taught him how to manœuvre behind his shield and watch for his chance to harm his enemy. He pressed a lance into Parzival's hand much against the latter's will. Nevertheless 'What's this for?' he asked.

'If a man meets you in a joust you must be quick to thrust it through his shield so that the lance splinters. If you do much of that you will be praised in the hearing of the ladies.'

The story tells us that no shield-painter from Cologne or Maastricht could have portrayed him to better effect than as he sat there on his charger.

'Dear friend, my companion,' he said to Iwanet, 'I have won what I asked for. Go into the city and pay my respects to King

Arthur, and return his golden goblet to him. Tell him of the deep disgrace I suffered: a knight offended me by striking a young lady who honoured me with her laughter. Her pitiful words have moved me deeply, not merely brushing against my heart – no! the lady's undeserved sufferings are lodged at its core! Now by your companionship, feel with me in my shame. May God protect you! – I am going now. – He has power to preserve us both.'

He left Ither of Gaheviez lying in pitiful state. Ither looked so handsome for all that he was dead. Alive he was Fortune's darling. Had he met his end in chivalrous combat with a lance-thrust through his shield who would then lament a tragedy?*

He Died of a Javelin

Iwanet gathered some bright flowers to cover him, then planted the javelin-shaft above him in token of the Crucifixion. And then with seemly dignity the page forced a stick through the javelin-head to make a cross. This done, he at once went in to the city to tell news at which many a lady despaired and many a knight wept, showing his attachment through his grief. They all suffered great affliction there.

The dead man was brought in with great solemnity. The Queen rode out from the city and commanded the Monstrance to be brought and raised above the King of Cucumerlant whom Parzival had slain.

The Lady Queen Ginover spoke these expressive words of grief:

'Out and alas! This strange and dire event will shatter Arthur's noble fame! – That he who by rights should bear the palm before all at the Table Round should lie slain here in sight of Nantes! He did but acclaim his heritage and was accorded – death! When all is said, he was a member of our Household of such behaviour that ear never heard of any misdeed of his. If perfidy is wild then he was tame: from his parchment it was all erased. Now and all too soon it is my lot to inter the very Clasp on the Roll of Fame! His courteous heart – surety written and sealed above the Clasp –

---

* See p. 81, first footnote.

counselled him only the best wherever pursuit of woman's love
needs proof of manly faith and fearless will. A new and fertile seed
of grief is sown among us women!

From out thy wound lamentation issues on the air! So red were
thy locks, thy blood could not have made the fair flowers redder!
Woman's laughter thou hast squandered all away!'

Illustrious Ither was laid to rest with royal pomp. His death
pierced womankind with sighs. His armour had proved his
ruin. Simple Parzival's wish to have it had been the end of him.
Later, on reaching years of discretion, Parzival wished he had
not done it.

The lad's charger had the peculiarity that it made light of
heavy-going, hot or cold. Whether it were hoofing it over
stone or fallen tree-trunks it did not sweat from its labours on
the way. There was never any need for Parzival to narrow
its girth by so much as a single hole, even though he kept the
saddle for two days at a stretch. Fully armed, the naive young
man rode it in that one day as far as an old campaigner, minus
his gear, would never have attempted had he been asked to
ride it in two! Moreover he put it to a gallop, seldom to a trot,
and never reined him in.

Towards evening Parzival saw the pinnacles and roofing
of a tower. It seemed to him in his simplicity as though towers
were growing more and more – a whole cluster stood there
on a castle! He imagined Arthur must have sown them, and he
put it down to Arthur's sanctity, thinking him a man of many
blessings.

'My mother's men can't farm like this,' said the raw young
man. 'Of the crops she has in the forest none grow as high
as this, yet there is no lack of heavy rain.'

The lord of the castle he was now riding up to was Gurne-
manz de Graharz. Below the walls stood a spreading lime in a
green meadow perfect for length and breadth. Path and horse
conspired to lead him to where the lord of the castle and the
land was seated. Great weariness was making Parzival swing
his shield in a manner not correct – too much to the fore or
rear and in no style to earn one praise. Prince Gurnemanz was
sitting alone, while the leafy crown of the lime yielded its

tribute of shade to this captain of true courtesy. A man whose nature shunned all double-dealing, Gurnemanz received his guest as he was bound. No knight or page was in attendance there.

Prompted by youthful ignorance, Parzival was quick with his response: 'My mother asked me to seek advice of a man whose locks were grey. I will serve you in return, seeing my mother said so.'

'If you have come to seek advice, give me your good will so that I can advise you – if that is what you want.'

The noble prince cast a moulted sparrowhawk from his fist. It swung into the castle tinkling a golden bell it wore. It was a messenger, for at once a troop of handsome pages came and joined them. Gurnemanz asked them to conduct his guest into the castle and see to his comfort.

'My mother was right,' said the boy. 'An old man's words are free of guile.'

They led him without delay to where there was a throng of knights. At a place in the courtyard they all begged him to dismount. 'It was a king who commanded me to be a knight,' said the lad who was obviously naive. 'Whatever happens to me up here I'll not get off this horse!* My mother told me to greet you.' They thanked both him and her. Greetings over – the beast was weary, the man no less – they framed many an entreaty before they got him off his horse and into a chamber. 'Allow your armour to be removed and your limbs eased,' they all urged him. Whether he wanted it or no, he was soon unarmed. When those who attended him set eyes on the shaggy buskins and his fool's garb they were aghast. They retailed it to my lord with deep dismay, and he almost despaired, so pained was he. But a knight had the courtesy to say 'I declare my eyes never saw such noble progeny! His looks are such as Fortune herself would scan approvingly, allied with the pure, sweet traits of noble birth! How comes it that the very Glance of Love should be in this predicament? I shall forever regret it that I saw the Court's Delight attired in this fashion! A

---

* The primary meaning of the word for 'knight' was 'rider'.

blessing on the mother that bore him who has so many perfections! His turn-out is magnificent. Until it was removed from his comely person his armour made a splendid knight of him. I then at once observed the marks of a bloody bruise on him.'

'It was done at the bidding of some lady,' his lordship told the knight.

'Oh, no, my lord! With his manners he could never woo a lady into acceptance of his service, well favoured for love though he be.'

'Well,' said his lordship, 'let us go and see this boy whose clothes are so very odd.'

They went along to Parzival who had been wounded by a lance that was not shattered. Gurnemanz tended him so kindly that an affectionate father could not have cared for his own children better. He washed and bandaged his wound with his own hands.

Supper was now served. The stranger was in desperate need of it. After riding out from the fisherman's that morning without breakfast he was famished. His wound and the heavy armour he had bagged before Nantes spoke to him of weariness and hunger, not to mention the long day's ride from Arthur the Briton's, where they had all let him go hungry. This host asked him to sit and sup with him, and here the stranger regaled himself. He applied himself to the manger with such a will that he made a pile of provender vanish out of sight. His host took this as a joke. Loyal Gurnemanz begged him to tuck in heartily and forget his weariness.

The time came for the board to be removed. 'You are tired, aren't you?' asked his host. 'Were you up early?'

'Heaven knows, my mother was still asleep. She doesn't rise so early.' Gurnemanz laughed and led him to his sleeping quarters. He asked him to strip. This he was reluctant to do, yet it had to be. A coverlet of ermine was spread over his naked body – no woman ever bore such noble progeny.

Great fatigue and lack of sleep saw to it that he rarely turned on to his other side – that was how he waited for the dawn. The noble Prince had ordered a bath to be got ready for mid-morning at the carpet's edge near where he lay, and on the morrow so it had to be. On it they strewed roses. Though they did not raise their voices as they moved around him he woke from sleep. The charming young noble man went and sat in the tub.

Now I do not know who asked them, but some lovely girls, superbly gowned, came in with due regard for the niceties. They bathed and massaged the marks of his bruises away with their soft white hands. There was small need for him to feel lost and uncared for here, orphaned though he was of common sense! Thus he suffered his pleasure and ease. His lack of worldly wisdom was not made a butt for any unkindness on their part. Thus these modest, daring young ladies curried him down, and whatever they prattled of he said nothing. He had no reason to think it too early, for a second day shone out from them, one radiance vying with the other. And yet these two lights were quenched by his own countenance – in such matters he did not fall short.

They offered him a bath-robe but he ignored it, so bashful was he in the presence of ladies. He refused to take it and wrap it round him while they were looking on. The young ladies had to go, they dared not stand there any longer. I fancy they would have liked to see if he had sustained any harm down below, for women are such sympathetic creatures, they are always moved to pity by a friend's sufferings.

The visitor strode up to the bed. A doublet all of white lay ready for him. They threaded it with a girdle of silk and gold for his breeches. They next smoothed some hose of red scarlet* on to the fearless lad. – What a marvellous pair of legs! What a truly elegant sight! Tunic and mantle were of brown scarlet, well cut, long, and duly lined with dazzling ermine. At the front, broad trimmings met the eye – of sable, black and grey. All this the comely boy put on. It was held by a costly girdle and fastened and adorned by a precious clasp. Against it all his mouth glowed red.

His loyal host then appeared in order to welcome him,

---

* A woollen material, red or brown.

followed by a proud company of knights. This done, these gentlemen all declared they had never seen so handsome a form. They praised from their hearts the woman who had borne such progeny to the world. 'He can count on a generous response from any lady he serves to win her favour,' they asserted no less for truth than courtesy. 'A good reception and enjoyment of love are his for the asking, granted his worth is appreciated.' All paid him the same tribute, these and others who saw him in days to come.

His host took him by the hand and led him out companionably. The noble prince asked him how he had slept that night beneath his roof.

'If on the day I left my mother she had not told me to come here, I should not have survived it.'

'May God reward both you and her. Sir, you are very kind.'

Our simple warrior went to where Mass was sung to God and for his lordship. At Mass the latter taught him something that would still increase one's blessings today: to make his offering and cross himself and so punish the Devil.

After this they went to the Palace, where the table was ready laid. The stranger sat down beside his host. He did not eat his meal as though he scorned it. 'Do not be offended, sir, if I ask where you journeyed from,' said his host politely. The boy told him in all detail how he had ridden away from his mother, about the ring and the brooch, and how he had won his armour. Gurnemanz recognized the Red Knight and sighed with compassion for his tragic end. But he insisted that his guest should bear his name, calling him 'The Red Knight'.

After the board had been removed a wild spirit was tamed ...

'You speak like a child,' said my lord to his guest. 'Why do you not stop talking of your mother and turn your mind to other things? Keep to my advice, it will save you from wrongdoing.

'This is how I shall begin – allow me! You must never lose your sense of shame. If one is past all shame what is one fit for? One lives like a bird in moult, shedding good qualities like plumes all pointing down to Hell. You have a trim figure and good looks and may well be ruler of a people. If you are

95

indeed of high, aspiring race, bear this in mind: compassion-
ate the needy, ward off their distress with kindness and
generosity. Practise humility. A man of standing fallen on evil
days has to wrestle with his pride – a bitter struggle this! You
should be ready to help him. If you relieve such a man's distress
God's blessing will seek you out. Such men are in worse plight
than those who beg bread at windows.

'You must be rich and poor with discretion. A nobleman
who squanders his property does not display a noble spirit,
while if he hoards wealth to excess it will bring dishonour.

'Give moderation its due. It is clear to me that you need
counsel. Now have done with unformed ways!

'Do not ask many questions. Yet if someone has a mind to
sift you with words, you should not hold back a considered
answer that keeps straight to the point.

'You can hear, see, taste and smell: that ought to lead you
to reason. Temper daring with mercy: show me you have
followed my advice in this. When you have won a man's sub-
mission in battle, accept it and let him live, unless he has done
you mortal wrong.

'You will have to bear arms very often, but when they are
laid aside, see that you wash your face and hands. When iron
has left its rusty smear it is high time! You will then regain
your handsome looks, and women's eyes will notice it.

'Be manly and cheerful: it will enhance your reputation.
Hold the ladies in high esteem: that heightens a young man's
worth. Do not forsake their cause for a single day. These and
such thoughts should inspire a man. If you care to lie to them
you will be able to deceive many. But cunning prospers only
for a while as against noble love ... The dry wood in the
thicket snaps and crackles to accuse the prowler, and the watch-
man is roused. Many a fight breaks out in park and wasteland.
Compare this with noble love, which has its remedies for
cunning and deceit. If you earn Love's disfavour you will
surely be disgraced and suffer shame's endless torment.

'Take this lesson to heart, for I have more to say to you about
women. Man and woman are all one, like the sun that shone
this morning and what we call "day". Neither can be parted

from the other, they blossom from the self-same seed. Note that, and give it thought.'

The stranger thanked his host for his teaching with a bow. Not a word did he say of his mother aloud, though he did so in his heart, as an affectionate man may still do today.

His lordship most creditably continued. 'There is more for you to learn of knightly ways. Think how you rode up to me! I have seen many a wall on which shields were better hung than the one slung round your neck! It is not too late, let us hurry to the meadow. There you will grow more expert. Bring him his horse – mine too – and every knight his own! Let pages come as well, each with a stout new shaft!'

And so the prince rode out on to the field, where feats of horsemanship were performed. He taught his guest how to throw his mount from the gallop to full tilt with a sharp touch of the spur and thighs beating like wings, how to lower his lance to the correct angle and cover himself with his shield against his opponent's thrust – 'Like this, allow me!' he said. In this way Gurnemanz kept him from unmannerliness better than with the pliant rod that cuts the skin of wanton boys. Next he asked some dashing knights to ride a joust against him and led him to the tourneying-ground to meet one. The lad delivered his first thrust through a shield in a style all thought excessive: for he swung a sturdy knight, no mean man, back over his horse's crupper!

A new jouster was there, and Parzival had taken a stout new lance. Youth was paired in him with strength and spirit. Urged on by the blood that flowed in him from Gahmuret and the courage to which he was heir, the charming, beardless youth rode his galloper in headlong charge, aiming at the four rivets.* His host's knight failed to keep his seat and hurtled down, measuring his length on the field amid a shower of chips from shattered shafts.

In this way Parzival thrust down five of them. My lord took him and led him in again. Parzival had had the best of it at sport there; but in after-days he grew to be expert in war.

* In the boss of his opponent's shield.

The tried hands who had watched his riding declared that pluck and skill attended him. 'Now my lord will be rid of his grief and take a new lease of life. If he has any sense he will give him our lady his daughter to wife, then his sorrows will be at an end. Fortune has not forgotten him after all – amends for three dead sons has ridden up to court!'

Thus his lordship returned in the evening. Orders were given for the board to be laid and (as I heard) he summoned his daughter to table.

Now hear what my lord said to lovely Liaze when he saw the girl approaching. 'Allow this knight to kiss you and show him all respect. He has Fortune herself for guide. As to you, sir, we would require you to leave the girl her ring – if she had one. But she has none, nor brooch, either. Who would supply her with such things like the lady in the forest? *She* had someone to give her what you later chanced to acquire. There is nothing you can take from Liaze.' The stranger blushed. Yet he kissed her on her lips which were as red as fire. Liaze was charming, with a wealth of true modesty.

The table was low and long. No need for my lord to use his elbows there – he sat alone at its head! He seated his guest between himself and his daughter. Whatever the one they called 'The Red Knight' wished to eat, Liaze had to carve or cut it with her soft white hands as the host had bidden her. None was to interfere if they showed signs of growing intimacy. Well-bred girl that she was, Liaze did all that her father asked of her. She and the guest made a handsome pair.

After supper the girl withdrew at once. In this way they continued to entertain the warrior for a fortnight. But the one trouble in his heart was this: he wished for more fighting before he would warm to what are called a woman's arms. As he saw it, it was noble ambition that led to triumph in this life and the next, words that keep their truth today.

One morning he begged leave to go. He left the locality of Graharz. His host rode out with him to the open country, and then there was new heart-ache.

'In you I lose my fourth son,' said the Prince, a man of a rare depth of feeling. 'I thought I was recouped for a threefold tale of woe. Till now there had been but three. Yet now, if someone would hack my heart in four and bear each part away I would consider it sheer gain. One part for you who ride away, three others for my noble sons who died most gallantly. For such is chivalry's reward: as a horse's tail the crupper, so *its* latter end bears grief.

'One death lames all my happiness, that of my fair son Schenteflurs. Coming to the aid of Condwiramurs when she had refused to surrender land and person, he lost his life to Clamide and Kingrun, so that now my heart is riddled like a fence with sorrow's stabs. And now – too soon! – you ride away from me, wretch that I am! Oh, why cannot I die, seeing that neither my pretty girl Liaze nor my lands are to your liking!

'My second son was Count Lascoyt. Ider fil Noyt killed him, competing for a Sparrowhawk: and so I stand bare of joy. My third son was Gurzgri. Lovely Mahaute rode beside him, for her proud brother Ehkunat had given her to him in marriage. He came riding to Schoydelakurt* over against the royal city of Brandigan, and there he had to die. Mabonagrin slew him, and Mahaute lost her radiant looks. His mother died stricken with grief for him.'

The guest was alive to his host's suffering, for he had made it all so very plain. 'My lord,' he said, 'I have not yet arrived at years of discretion. But if ever I win fame as a knight such as would entitle me to sue for love, I shall ask you to give me Liaze, the pretty girl your daughter. You have told me of grief past bearing. But if, when the time is ripe, I am able to free you from sorrow, I shall not leave you to bear such a load.'

The young man took his leave of the faithful Prince and all his many retainers. For his sad Three the Prince has now been thrown a tragic Four. It was the fourth time he had proved a loser.

* The scene of the culminating episode of *Erec*.

Chapter 4

PARZIVAL rode away. He had the marks and bearing of a well-bred knight. But alas, he was pricked by many a harsh pang. His eyes were at the mercy of his heart, so that distance seemed to cramp him, space to pen him in, while all that was green seemed sere and yellow, his red armour dazzling white! Now that he had lost his youthful rawness, Gahmuret's nature claimed him, giving him no release from thoughts of fair Liaze, the gracious girl who had honoured him with friendship short of love. Whichever way his horse takes now and whether it wishes to gallop or trot he is powerless to curb it, so sad is he.

His paths through the forest led far from wayside crosses, wattled hedges and ruts cut clean by carts. He rode over much rough country where few plantains were to be seen. Hills and valleys were strange to him. An oft-quoted proverb says that a rider who loses his way will find the maul. If mighty logs have anything to do with it, here were signs of the maul past counting.

Yet he did not go far astray, for he rode straight ahead from Graharz, passing between mountains both high and wild, till he reached the kingdom of Brobarz while it was still daylight.

Then as day turned to evening he came to a torrent whose roar could be heard far away as it was thrown from rock to rock. He rode down its course – and there lay the city of Belrepeire. King Tampenteire had bequeathed it to his daughter, with whom many people are sorrowing now.

The torrent flew like bolts well feathered and trimmed when the tensed crossbow hurls them with throbbing string. It was spanned by a bridge covered with much wattle-work, at the point where it entered the sea. Belrepeire was well-positioned for defence! You know how children go on swings when they are swung for all they are worth? That is how this bridge went – though it was ropeless! Nor was it youth that made it so gay.

Sixty knights or more were stationed on the farther side with their helmets laced on and they all shouted 'Go back! Back!' Weak though they were, they raised their swords in eagerness for battle. From having seen Clamide they thought this must be he, for this man rode over the meadow towards the bridge with such a kingly air. As a result of their loud bawling at the young man, his charger shied away from the bridge however much he pricked it with the spurs. But the fearless man dismounted and led his mount over the rickety bridge. No coward would have had the spirit to ride against such strength. Moreover he had to take especial care lest his horse tumble over. Meanwhile the bawling on the other side had stopped. The knights withdrew with their helmets, shields and flashing swords and shut their Gates. They feared there were others to follow.

Thus Parzival crossed over and rode to a field of battle on which many had met their deaths pursuing knightly honour, there before the Gate by the lofty, splendid Palace. He found a ring-shaped knocker on the Gate and banged it hard. But apart from one young lady of pleasing appearance none paid any attention to his shouts. This charming girl observed the knight through a window as he stood waiting and politely said, 'If you have come here as an enemy, sir, you are wasting your time. We have suffered enough ill will by land and sea from a fierce and courageous army without your joining in.'

'Madam,' he replied, 'here stands a man who will help you if he can. A smile from you on meeting shall be my reward. I am your devoted servant.'

At this, the thoughtful girl went to the Queen and so helped him to come within the walls. This, as it turned out, relieved them of great hardship.

Thus Parzival was admitted. The populace stood in a great throng on both sides of the street. Marching in formidable array there were long ranks of slingers and foot receding into the distance and a horde of vile archers. With the same glance he took in numbers of men-at-arms with sharp, long, strong lances as yet unshattered. And, according to my understanding of the tale, many merchants stood there with battle-axes and javelins as the officers of their guilds had commanded.* They all had slack hides.

The Queen's Marshal had much ado to conduct Parzival through the crowd to the courtyard, which was well equipped for defence. Of turrets above chambers, barbicans, donjons and angle-towers there were certainly more here than he had ever seen before. From all sides knights came on horseback or on foot to welcome him. This company too were of an ashen or drab clayish complexion. My lord Count of Wertheim would have loathed being a soldier there: on their pay he could not have kept body and soul together!

Famine had reduced them to starvation. They had no cheese, bread or meat. They had given up using toothpicks and beslabbered no wine with greasy lips when drinking. Their bellies were sunken, their hips gaunt and lean and their skin lay shrivelled and shrunk over their ribs like Hungarian shagreen – famine had chased their flesh away. Very little fat dripped on to their coals. A noble man, the proud King of Brandigan, had brought them to this pass, for they were reaping the results of Clamide's wooing. No tub or can ever spilt its mead there, no plan sizzled with Trüdinger fritters† – such music had been cut short for them.

I should be a stupid man if I were to blame them for that. For where I have often dismounted and am called 'Master', at home in my own house, no mouse is ever cheered. It would have to steal its food, food which by rights none might hide from me, but of which I find not a scrap above board. All too often do I, Wolfram von Eschenbach, have to make do with such comfort.

Enough of my complaints. The story must return to the plight of Belrepeire, whose people were mulcted of happiness. Those loyal warriors led a wretched life thanks to their sterling courage. Their distress deserves your pity. I tell you their very lives are at stake if God lifts no hand to free them.

Now learn more of these wretches so deserving of your

* Or: in keeping with their status as guildsmen.
† Wassertrüdingen lies but a few miles from Eschenbach.

compassion. They received their spirited guest shamefacedly. They thought him so estimable in other respects that he should not have asked them for shelter in their plight. Yet he had no inkling of their need.

They spread a carpet on the grass where a lime had been walled in and trained to offer shade, and then the retainers unarmed him. When he had washed off all the rust in a brook his appearance was very unlike theirs – he might almost have dimmed the sun's bright radiance! They thought him now an estimable guest indeed and at once offered him a cloak to match the robe he had been wearing. Its sable trimming smelt fresh from the hunt.

'Do you wish to see our lady the Queen?' they asked. The steadfast warrior said he would much like to do so, and they walked towards the Palace to which a long flight of stairs led up.

The lovely radiance of her face, the sweet lustre of her eyes preceded the Queen in one blaze of light before she ever received him. Kyot of Katelangen and noble Manpfilyot were escorting their niece the Queen. Each was a duke, but they had renounced their swords for the love of God. Noble princes, grey-haired and handsome, they paced and, with great ceremony, conducted the lady to the middle of the stairs. Here the Queen kissed the worthy knight – the mouth of the one as red as the other's – and then she gave Parzival her hand and led him to their seats.

The ladies and gentlemen standing and sitting there had lost much strength. The Mistress and her Household had taken leave of happy times. But the dazzling beauty of Condwiramurs set her apart from the challenge of those I name now. Her bright lustre quite vanquished that of Jeschute, Enite and Cunneware de Lalant, and of those who in appraisals of feminine charms have been most commended, and even of both Isoldes. There was no denying that Condwiramurs excelled all others: she was possessed beyond all question of *le beau corps* or as we say 'a fair person'. They were useful women who gave birth to this pair sitting here together. The men and women there did nothing but gaze at them, as the two sat side by side. Parzival had found well-wishers there.

I will tell you what the stranger was thinking. 'Liaze is there, Liaze is here. It pleases God to make my sadness bearable. Liaze is here before my eyes, noble Gurnemanz's daughter.' But Liaze's beauty was as nothing compared with that of the maiden sitting here, in whom God had omitted no perfection. The lady of this land was like a rose still moist, with the sweet dew revealing from the bud its pristine glory of white and red. This gave her guest much ado; but his self-command was so entire since Gurnemanz had rid him of his folly and forbidden him to ask questions – sensible ones excepted – that he sat beside the puissant Queen without a word falling from his lips. (I say he sat close, not gingerly a way off.) Many a man more accustomed to feminine company may be tongue-tied even today.

The Queen soon began thinking 'I imagine this man looks down on me because my flesh has fallen away. – No ! He does so for a reason. He is my guest, I am his hostess, and it is I who should begin the conversation ! Since we sat down here he has given me kind looks and shown courtesy towards me. I have held back for too long. Now to end this silence.'

'My lord,' said the Queen to her guest, 'a hostess is bound to speak up. I won your salutation with a kiss of welcome, and you yourself sent in offers of service, so one of my young ladies tells me. To my deep sorrow we have not been used to such treatment from strangers. I ask you, sir, to tell me from where you have come.'

'This morning, Ma'am, I rode away from a man of flawless loyalty and left him to his sorrows, a prince named Gurnemanz, derived from Graharz. From there I rode into this country.'

'If any other had told me this,' replied the noble maiden, 'I should not have agreed that it was done in a day. For whenever a messenger of mine has ridden it, express, he has not covered the distance in two. Your host's sister was my mother. If his daughter's looks were the worse for mourning it would be no wonder. We have wept out many a bitter day with eyes that would not dry, young Liaze and I. If you hold your old host in affection, accept such entertainment tonight as we have been putting up with, both men and women. If you do, you will be partly serving him too. Now I will tell you of our trouble : we are hard put to it by famine.'

'I will send you a dozen loaves, Madam, and three hams and shoulders,' said her uncle Kyot. 'There will be eight cheeses to go with them and two kegs of wine. My brother too must help you tonight, there is need.'

'Madam,' said Manpfilyot, 'I will send you the same.'

The girl sitting there was overjoyed. She thanked them most gratefully. They took their leave and rode to their hunting lodge nearby. For these old gentlemen lived in a wild mountain gorge, unarmed, under truce from the besiegers.

Their messenger soon returned at the trot, and these enfeebled people were revived. These victuals were the grand sum of what the citizens had to nourish them! Many had already died of starvation before this bread arrived. The Queen ordered it to be shared among her debilitated people, and with it the cheeses, meat and wine, at Parzival's suggestion. As a result, scarcely a slice remained for the two of them, and this they shared without quarrelling.

These provisions were duly consumed, and the deaths of many spared by famine were averted. Then orders were given to make a bed for their guest, a soft one I can well believe. If these people were hunting-birds it could not be said that they were gorged, and this was confirmed by the dishes. All these people bore the marks of famine, all but young Parzival. He begged leave to go to bed. – You ask if his candles were penny dips? No, they were far superior. Then the handsome youth mounted a bed not designed for poverty but of a magnificence fit for a king. A carpet was spread before it. He did not keep the knights waiting there long before asking them to withdraw. Some pages removed his shoes and hose, and soon he slept – till true sorrow called him, and heart's rain from bright eyes. These quickly woke the noble warrior.

I will tell you how it came about. There was no breach of feminine decorum.* This girl of whom I am telling you was

* Those in Wolfram's audience who knew the Old French source would have been waiting for the heroine's indiscretion at this point.

chaste and constant. Distress of war and the death of dear supporters had wracked her heart so cruelly that her eyes stayed wide awake. The Queen had not come for such love as rouses what dubs maids women. She was seeking the help of a friend. She wore formidable armour: a white silken shift! What could be more challenging than a woman bearing down on a man in this fashion? The lady had thrown round her a long mantle of samite. Her step betrayed the cares that harassed her.

She left her young ladies-in-waiting and chamberlains asleep wherever they were and crept softly and noiselessly to the chamber in which those who were responsible had arranged for Parzival to sleep alone. The candles beside his couch made it as bright as day. Her way led to his bed. She knelt down before him on the carpet. So far as lovers' embraces went, both he and the Queen were dunces. The wooing and doing went thus. The maiden was unhappy and deeply embarrassed. 'Did he pull her into bed with him at all?' Alas, he has no experience of that. Yet without experience he *does* take her in *under truce* that they do not bring their appeasing limbs together. They gave little thought to that.

The girl was so utterly wretched that the tears rained down from her eyes upon young Parzival. The sound of her weeping was so loud in his ears that he woke and saw her all at once. This made him sorry – yet glad. The young man sat up and quickly asked the Queen 'Are you mocking me, Ma'am? You should be kneeling to God. Do sit down here beside me (such was his request) or lie down where I was lying, and I will make do with somewhere else.'

'If you will honour yourself and treat me with such restraint as not to struggle with me, I will lie in there with you,' she said. He agreed to these terms, and she quickly snuggled into bed.

It was still so deep in the night that not a cock was crowing. (In any case the roosts were bare: famine had shot them off their perches.) The unhappy lady asked him politely if he would hear her tale of woe? 'I fear,' she said, 'that if I tell you I shall rob you of your sleep, so much will it pain you. King Clamide and his Seneschal have laid waste all my lands and castles except for Belrepeire. My father Tampenteire died leaving me a poor orphan exposed to fearful dangers. I had at my command a large and courageous army, kinsmen, princes, vassals mighty and humble alike. Half or more of them were killed fighting in defence. How should I poor wretch be cheerful? I have now reached the point where I shall kill myself rather than yield my maidenhead and person to become the wife of Clamide, for it was he who with his own hand slew dear Schenteflurs, whose heart harboured many knightly virtues. Blossoming sprig of manly beauty, Liaze's brother, curbed all base leanings.'

At the sound of Liaze's name, her servitor Parzival was reminded of his longing. His high spirits were dashed for the love he bore Liaze. 'Could anyone do anything to solace you, Ma'am?'

'Yes, if I were saved from Kingrun the Seneschal, sir. He has thrust down many a knight of mine in regular joust. He will come again tomorrow and has visions of his master soon lying in my arms. You must have seen my Palace? Were it never so high I would pitch headlong into the fosse before Clamide should ravish my maidenhead. That is how I would cheat him of his boast!'

'Whether Kingrun be Frenchman or Briton, Ma'am,' he said, 'or from whichever land he may come, you will be defended by this my hand to the utmost of my power!'

The night drew to an end and day broke. The lady rose and, inclining her head, thanked him most gratefully. She then stole away again, and nobody there was alert enough to notice her departure but fair-skinned Parzival. He did not sleep much longer. The sun was in haste to scale the heights, its bright rays were thrusting through the clouds. Then he heard much ringing of bells. Those whom Clamide had parted from their happiness were making for church and minster.

The young man got up. The Queen's chaplain sang Mass to the honour of God and for his lady. Her guest could not help gazing at her till the benediction had been given. He asked for his armour and was well and truly armed in it. And indeed he was to prove his knightly mettle by the valiant way he fought.

Now Clamide's army was arriving with many pennants. Kingrun came spurring far in advance of the others on a horse of Iserterre, I am told. Fil li roy Gahmuret too had sallied beyond the Gates, and the prayers of the citizens went with him.

This was to be his first sword-fight. He took so wide a sweep for his charge that from the shock of his onset both horses were ungirthed. Their belly-girths snapped, and each recoiled on its quarters. Those who had bestridden them had not forgotten their swords – they found them in their sheaths. Kingrun was wounded in his arms and chest. This joust was a sad blow to the prestige he had enjoyed till this day, when his pride was quenched. He was reputed to have the strength and courage to unhorse any half-dozen knights who took the field against him. Yet Parzival's doughty sword-arm returned his blows to such effect that Kingrun the Seneschal had the bizarre impression that a mangonel was battering him with its missiles. – It was no such assault that brought him low, but a sword clanging through his helmet. Parzival hurled him to the ground and thrust his knee against his chest, and Kingrun offered him what had been offered to no other man – his surrender. Yet his adversary declined it and told him to submit to Gurnemanz.

'Oh, no, my lord! Rather put me to death. I killed his son, I took the life of Schenteflurs. God has vouchsafed you much honour. Wherever it is reported that you have proved your strength on me and had me at your mercy, people will say success has come your way.'

'I will allow you another choice,' replied young Parzival. 'Make your submission to the Queen, on whom your lord's enmity has inflicted much suffering.'

'That would mean my end. They would mince me with their swords as fine as motes dancing in a sunbeam! I have mortified many a brave man there within the walls.'

'Then take your knightly parole from this plain to the land of Britain, to a maiden who for my sake suffered what, by all that is right and proper, she ought never to have been subjected to. And tell her that whatever happens to me she will never see me joyful till I have avenged her somewhere or other where I will bore through someone's shield. Give Arthur and his wife, the two of them, my compliments – not forgetting all the Household – and tell them that I shall not return till I have wiped out the dishonour which I share with the lady who greeted me with laughter and endured such violence for it. Tell that lady I am her most humble devoted servitor.'

This command was complied with, and the warriors were seen to take leave of one another.

The citizens' champion made his way back on foot to where his mount had been caught. He was to deliver them in due course. The outer army was bewildered at Kingrun's utter defeat. Parzival was escorted into the Queen's presence. She warmly embraced him and holding him close she said 'Never in this world shall I be the wife of any man but him whom I have embraced!' She helped them unarm him and showed him all possible attention.

After his great exertion a wretched breakfast was served. The men of the fortress hurried in to swear fealty to him, declaring he must be their lord. The Queen capped this by saying that in view of his splendid victory over Kingrun he must be her lover.

Now two gleaming sails were made out from the top of the ramparts! They belonged to vessels driven smack into port by a gale. Their bottoms were laden in a way to delight the denizens – their sole cargo was food. In His wisdom God had so ordained it.

The famished crowd poured at great speed from the fortifications down towards the ships to pillage them. They could have sped like leaves before the wind, these people so lean and shrunken and scant of flesh, they had so little stuffing in their hides. But the Queen's Marshal placed the ships under his protection and forbade any to touch them on pain of the gallows. He led the merchants to the city and into the presence of his lord.

Parzival ordered them to be paid double the price of their wares, but the merchants judged it too high and so they were reimbursed for their outlay. Once again fat dripped on to the castle-dwellers' coals. Now I should love to be a mercenary there, for nobody is drinking beer: they have wine and food in plenty.

Faultless Parzival proceeded as follows. He first shared out the victuals neatly himself. He then asked the notables present to be seated. He did not wish them to gorge themselves on empty stomachs, so he gave them enough and no more, and they were pleased to follow his advice. He gave them some more in the evening, steady affable man that he was.

A question. Would they celebrate their nuptials? He and the Queen answered 'Yes'. He lay with such restraint as would not suit many women nowadays, were they so treated. Consider, that to torment a man with desire they offset their modest behaviour by dressing provocatively! In the presence of strangers they behave demurely, but their inward desires clash with their outward show. Their caresses give their lovers secret pain. But a loyal and constant man who has always used restraint knows how to spare his mistress's feelings. He thinks, as may well be true, 'I have served this lady all my days for her reward. Now she has offered me solace, and I am lying here. Once upon a time it would have been enough to be allowed to touch her gown with my bare hand. If I were now to demand possession I should be disloyal to myself to exert it. Ought I to exact this tribute and inflict deep shame on us both? At bedtime sweet airy nothings best suit a gentlewoman's nature.' It was with such thoughts as these that the Waleis lay beside his bride.

'Red Knight' though they called him he inspired little terror: he left the Queen a maiden. Yet she thought she was his wife, and for love of her handsome husband put up her hair in a fillet! Then, this virgin bride bestowed her lands and castles on him, for he was the darling of her heart.

For two days they remained thus with one another, happy in their liking, till the third night. He often thought of embracing, as his mother had advised him, and Gurnemanz too had explained to him that man and woman are all one. They entwined their arms and legs, and if you will allow me to say so he found what is sweet when near. Together they observed the old custom ever-new. They were happy, not too sad.

Now listen to how Clamide, who was approaching with powerful forces, was dispirited by the news. A page whose horse's flanks were torn by the spurs reported to him without preamble, 'On the plain below Belrepeire an encounter has taken place, quite a fierce one. The Seneschal has been defeated by a knight. Kingrun, commander of our army, is on his way to

Arthur the Briton. The mercenaries are maintaining their position below the city according to his last orders on leaving. You and your two armies will find Belrepeire well defended. Within, there is a noble knight who has no other wish than to fight. All your soldiers declare that the Queen has sent for Ither of Cucumerlant of the Table Round. His blazon came out to joust and was borne with great distinction.'

'Condwiramurs shall have me and I her and her lands!' snapped Clamide to his page. 'My Seneschal Kingrun sent me reliable news that they would soon be forced by starvation to yield the city, and that the Queen would offer me her noble love.' Ill will was all the page earned there.

The King rode on with his army, and now a knight came riding towards them who had not spared horseflesh either, and he told them the same story. Clamide's gay and martial spirits flagged. It came as a great blow to him. But then a certain prince, one of the King's men, spoke up. 'Kingrun did not fight as our champion. He fought entirely on his own account. Suppose he had been killed. Would that be any reason why two armies should lose heart – *this*, and that before the city?' He begged his lord not to despond. 'We must try again! If they have a mind to fight we shall give them plenty and put an end to their jubilation. Urge on your kinsmen and vassals and attack the city under two standards. We shall be able to make our way to them on horseback along the slope, and we shall attack the Gates on foot. I swear we shall pay them back for our defeat!'

Such was the advice given by Galogandres, Duke of Gippones. He brought those of the fortress to a sad pass. Yet *en ravanche* he met his death at their outworks, as did Count Narant, the illustrious prince from Ukerlant, and many a knight of slender means whose bodies were borne from the field. But now learn further how the citizens looked to their outer defences. They took long tree-trunks and thrust strong stakes into them, much to the torment of their assailants, for they let them down on ropes, and the logs then turned on pulleys! This had all been devised after Kingrun's defeat, before Clamide launched his attack on them. Moreover, Greek fire had come to their land with the provisions. The besiegers' engines were burnt down, their scaling-towers and mangonels – whatever had come on wheels – their *chevaux de frise*, the 'cats' in the fosses. True to its nature, fire utterly erased them.

Kingrun the Seneschal had meantime arrived in Britain and found King Arthur at Karminal, as his hunting-lodge in Brizljan was called. Here he did as Parzival had instructed him when he sent him as a prisoner, and offered his submission to Lady Cunneware de Lalant. The young lady was delighted that the man they called the Red Knight had taken up her cause so sympathetically.

The news of this event spread everywhere. The vanquished noble presented himself to the King. To Arthur and his court he then delivered the message addressed to them. Keie gave a sudden start and turned crimson. 'So you are Kingrun?' he managed to say. 'Ah me, how many Britons you have overwhelmed, my Lord Seneschal of Clamide! Though I may never win your subduer's favour, you shall profit from your high office. For we are Lords of the Cauldron, I here and you there in Brandigan. By your noblesse, help me with large pancakes to win Cunneware's good graces.'

He offered her no other amends. But let that pass, and hear how it continues where we left the story.

Clamide arrived before the walls of Belrepeire, and it came to a mighty assault. The besieged resisted the besiegers, they were in good heart and sinew. These warriors showed themselves most warlike and so made themselves masters of the field. Their sovereign Parzival fought in advance of his men. The Gates were left wide open. His arms flailed with his blows, his sword went clanging through hard helmets. Any knights he felled there met trouble enough – they were acquainted with it at the gussets of their hauberks, for the burghers avenged themselves by stabbing them through the slits, till Parzival forbade them. When they learned of his displeasure they took twenty of them alive before withdrawing from the fray.

It became abundantly clear to Parzival that Clamide and his company were declining battle at the Gates and that he was fighting in some other place. The stout-hearted youth thus made for the rough country. He spurred in a wide sweep towards the King's standard. From now on, Clamide's hire was dearly earned! Those of the city fought to such effect that their tough shields were whittled away from their grips. Parzival's was reduced to nothing by shots and blows. Small joy though the attackers might have of it, they all acclaimed him as a paragon. Their standard-bearer Galogandres, who had been giving the army a fine lead, fell dead beside his King. Then Clamide himself was in peril, so that he and his were alarmed. Clamide called off the attack. The battle-seasoned army of the city had won the advantage and glory!

Noble Parzival gave orders for the prisoners to be well cared for till the third morning. The outer army were a prey to anxiety. Then the proud, gay young lord took the captives' parole. 'Come back, good people, when I summon you,' he said. He commanded their armour to be sequestered, and they rejoined their army beyond the walls. Although those returning were flushed with wine, the Outers said 'You must be famished, poor people.'

'Don't waste your pity on us!' replied the others. 'There is such an abundance of food in there that if you camped here for a year they would maintain you as well as themselves, depend upon it. The Queen has the handsomest husband that ever won title to the Shield. He has all the marks of high descent. In his hands the honour of the whole Order of Chivalry is in safe keeping.'

When Clamide heard this he was seized with regret for all his toil. He sent in envoys to announce that whoever he might be who shared the Queen's couch 'if he is eligible for single combat and has been recognized by her as one who dares to defend both her and her lands in duel with me, then let there be a truce between the armies.'

Parzival was delighted that the embassy had been addressed to him with an eye to his fighting alone. Said the dauntless young man: 'Let my honour stand as pledge for it that no man of the inner army shall take the field for any danger I may be in.'

This truce was fixed between the fosse and the outer army. Then this bellicose pair of blacksmiths donned their armour. The King of Brandigan mounted a barded castilian called

'Guverjorz' which together with rich gifts had been sent to Clamide across Lake Uker from the north by his maternal kinsman Grigorz, King of Ipotente. Count Narant had brought it, together with a thousand men-at-arms fully equipped but for escutcheon. Their pay had been settled for two whole years ahead, if the tale informs us truly. Grigorz sent him five hundred dashing knights, each with his helmet laced ready for action and well tried in battle. Thereupon Clamide's forces had invested Belrepeire by land and sea so closely that the denizens, inevitably, suffered hardship.

Parzival now rode out to the field of the ordeal, where God was to make clear whether He wished to leave him King Tampenteire's daughter. He came on proudly, with his mount at no less than the gallop as prelude to the charge! His horse was well armed against the worst – housings of red samite were draped over its steel barding. He himself showed a red shield and red surcoat.

Clamide began the duel. He brought with him a short, uncut lance with which to unseat his man in the joust and with it took a long sweep for his charge. Guverjorz leapt headlong to the attack, and between them these beardless youths made a fine joust of it, neither missing his mark. No harder duel was ever fought by man or beast – the two chargers were steaming from their toil.

They fought till their mounts could do no more, so they dropped down beside them as one man, each bent on striking fire from helmets. There was no downing tools for them, they had work on hand! Their shields vanished in clouds of chips, as though they were playing at Tossing Feathers on the Wind! Nevertheless, the son of Gahmuret was still unwearied in any of his limbs. Then it seemed to Clamide as if the truce had been broken from the direction of the city. He asked his adversary to mind his honour and save him from mangonel-shot! Mighty blows were falling on him equal to any stones from a mangonel. But the lord of the land replied: 'I do not think you are being bombarded by mangonels. I have pledged my word against that. If you would submit to my protection *this* sling would not smash your ribs, head or thighbones.'

Clamide was succumbing to fatigue, little though he liked it. Victory won, victory lost, was being decided there for each of them. However, King Clamide first was seen in defeat, for blood spurted through his nose and ears, painting the ground red, when Parzival snatched and rammed him down. He quickly bared Clamide's head of helmet and coif, and the vanquished man sat waiting for his death-blow.

'My wife can now go free of your molestation,' said the victor. 'Learn what it is to die!'

'No, no, worthy, gallant knight! Your honour has been proved on me thirty times over. Where could you reap greater glory? Condwiramurs has cause to declare me a luckless man, while your fortunes have prospered. Your country has been saved. But as when a ship is baled or unballasted and is all the lighter for it, my power is of shallower draught, my manly zest is at an ebb. Why should you kill me? I am bound to bequeath disgrace to all my descendants. You have the glory and advantage. What need is there to do more to me? I suffer living death now that I am parted from the woman who has always encompassed me, heart and mind, in her dominion, while I have had no return. As a result, unfortunate that I am, I must yield her and her lands to you, without let or hindrance.'

Then the man who had won the victory remembered Gurnemanz's counsel that a brave and gallant man should be ready to show mercy, and followed it thus.

'I will not exempt you from taking your submission to Liaze's father,' he said to Clamide.

'Oh, no, sir, I have done him mortal wrong! I killed his son. You should not deal with me in this fashion. Schenteflurs too fought me over Condwiramurs, and if my Seneschal had not come to my aid would have killed me. Gurnemanz de Graharz sent him to Brobarz with a fine force of men: nine hundred proven knights all mounted on barded horses who acquitted themselves well in knightly exploits, and fifteen hundred men-at-arms whose equipment was complete but for the escutcheon when I met them in battle. I thought his army excessive, and in the event scarcely enough of them got back to ensure a new crop. Since then I myself have lost knights in greater number. I am now beggared of honour and contentment. What more do you want of me?'

'I will abate your fears. Go to the land of the Britons, where Kingrun has gone before you, to Arthur of Britain. Give him my respects and ask his sympathy for an insult I took away with me. A young lady laughed to see me. Nothing ever grieved me so much as when she was thrashed because of me. Tell her that it still rankles with me. Offer her your submission and do whatever she commands you – or receive your death here and now!'

'If that is the choice, I will not call it into question,' replied the King of Brandigan, 'I elect for the journey.' After swearing his oath, the man who had come to grief through his own arrogance left the field. The hero Parzival went to where his weary steed was waiting. He whose foot had never sought the stirrup leapt up without it on this occasion too and set the shavings of his shield a-swirling.

The defenders were delighted at the outcome, but the besieging army saw only cause for grief. King Clamide was aching in flesh and bone. They led him to his companions, and he sent the dead to their rest on biers. Then the foreigners left that land. Noble Clamide rode across country towards Löver.

The whole Table Round without exception were at Dianazdrun with Arthur the Briton. Unless I have lied to you, the plain of Dianazdrun must have admitted of more tent-poles than there are tree-trunks in the Spessart – with such retinue had Arthur camped for the Whitsun festival together with many ladies. Many pennants and shields, their charges unquartered, were on display there. Nowadays it would be thought a grand affair. Who could make all the stuffs for the travel-robes of such a host of ladies? Then, too, a lady was apt to think she would lose esteem if she did not have her gallant there. I would most certainly not have brought my wife to such a concourse – there were so many young bloods there! I should have been afraid of jostling strangers. Someone or other would have whispered to her that her charms were stabbing him and blotting out his joy, and that if she would end his pangs he would serve her before and after. Rather than that I would hurry away with her.

But I have been talking of my own affairs. Now hear how

Arthur's tent-ring could be told apart from the others. Matchless in their abundant gaiety, his retainers feasted in his presence: many a noble man slow to do a base deed, many a proud young lady who took jousts for arrows and shot their admirers at the enemy! And if their knights had a bad time of it whilst fighting, maybe the ladies found it in their hearts to make a kind return.

Young Clamide rode to the middle of the ring. A barded horse, a steel-cased body were suddenly before the Queen's eyes, then his helmet and shield, hacked to pieces. Then all the ladies saw it. This was how Clamide came to court. You have already heard how he had no choice in the matter. He dismounted and was much jostled by the curious throng before he came to where Cunneware de Lalant was sitting.

'Madam, are you the lady whom I must willingly serve?' he asked. 'I do so under compulsion – in part. The Red Knight sends you his humble compliments. You have his entire sympathy for the wrong that was done to you, and he further asks Arthur to make common cause with him. You were beaten because of him, were you not? My lady, I bring you my submission as commanded by him who fought with me and shall gladly honour it, if it be your wish. I was under threat of death.'

Lady Cunneware de Lalant grasped his gauntleted hand in the presence of Lady Ginover, who was sharing a platter apart from the King's. Keie was standing by the table and heard what had been said. It gave him a perceptible shock, which delighted Lady Cunneware.

'What this man has done concerning you, madam, he was forced to do,' said Keie. 'Nevertheless, someone has been imposing on him. I did what I did for the sake of courtly standards and with intent to improve your manners, for which I now suffer your ill will. However, I would advise you to have this captive unarmed. He may be bored with standing here.'

The proud young lady asked them to remove his helmet and coif, and when the one had been unlaced and the other peeled off, Clamide was quickly recognized. Kingrun darted looks of dawning recognition at him and began wringing his hands so that they snapped like dry billets. Clamide's Seneschal quickly thrust the table aside and asked his lord what had happened. He found him utterly desolate.

'I was born unfortunate,' cried Clamide. 'I have lost so fine an army that no mother ever gave suck to any man who knew a greater loss! But the loss of my army is as nothing to this: my anguish for the love which I forego so weighs me down that joy and high spirits are now strangers to me. I am growing grey for Condwiramurs! Whatever the punishment their Maker has in store for Pontius Pilate and that wretched Judas who joined the traitors with a kiss when Jesus was betrayed, I would accept their torment if only the lady of Brobarz were my wife by her consent, and I could hold her in my arms – come what might thereafter! But her love, alas, is beyond the reach of the King of Iserterre! My land and people of Brandigan must forever rue it. (My paternal cousin Mabonagrin suffered there too long!*) And now, King Arthur, compelled by a knight to do so, I have ridden to your house. You are well aware that in my country much dishonour has been done to you. Overlook it now, noble man, as long as I stay here captive! Exempt me from any displeasure it may have caused. Cunneware too, who accepted my submission when I came to her a prisoner, must also shield me from reprisal.'

Good-natured Arthur at once pronounced a pardon for those wrongs.

All got to hear, men and women alike, that the King of Brandigan had ridden to that ring. 'Come on, now, shove, shove!' – The news went round in a trice. Unhappy Clamide politely asked for a companion. 'Please commend me to Gawan, madam, if I am worthy. I know that for his part he will be willing. If he does as you ask he would honour both you and the Red Knight.' Arthur requested his nephew to give the king his company, but this would have happened in any case. Then the noble Household warmly welcomed Clamide, honourable in his defeat.

'How lamentable that any Briton should ever see you captive in his own house,' said Kingrun to Clamide. 'You were mightier

*A reference to *Erec*, in which Mabonagrin, condemned by a vow, remained in a garden with his lady until at last defeated in battle.

118

than Arthur, both in men and revenues, and you had the advantage of youth. Is Arthur now to reap the glory because Keie in his anger struck a noble princess when she, divining it in her heart, laughed, and so chose the man who is held in all truth to be the most illustrious of all? The Britons flatter themselves they have set up their laurels very high. Yet it happened without effort on their part that the King of Cucumerlant was sent back dead, and that my lord, who fought a duel with that other, owned himself beaten. This same knight overcame me too without recourse to stealth or trickery – you could see the fire leap from helmets and swords spin round in hands!'

High and low, they all agreed that Keie had misbehaved. But let us leave this and return to where we were.

The devastated land in which Parzival wore crown was made inhabitable, happiness and rejoicing were seen in it again. His father-in-law Tampenteire had left him bright jewels and ruddy gold, and these he doled out so generously that it won his people's hearts. His land was decked out with many pennants and new shields. He and his men rode many tournaments. Fearless young knight, he showed his mettle on his border, where his exploits against intruders were judged the best.

Now hear about the Queen. What more could she wish for to make her happy? The sweet young noble woman had all that heart can desire here on earth. Her love was so strong, there was no lodgement in it for infidelity. She knew her man as true. Each found it in the other. He was as dear to her as she to him. When I take the passage in hand which says they must part, their loss can only mount. I am moved to pity for that noble lady. He had delivered her land, her people and herself from great distress, in return for which she had offered him her love.

One morning he said (and many knights heard and saw it) 'If it is your wish, Ma'am, I ask leave to go and see how my mother fares. I do not know at all whether she is well or ill. I should like to go there for a short while – and also in search of adventure. If I achieve much in your service your noble love requires it.' In such terms did he ask leave to go. She loved him, so the story says, there was nothing she would deny him. He rode away from all his vassals with none for company.

119

Chapter 5

WHOEVER cares to hear where the knight is arriving whom Dame Adventure sent on his travels, can now take note of marvels unparalleled. Let the son of Gahmuret ride on. True-hearted people everywhere will wish him luck, since he is destined now to suffer great anguish, but at times also honour and joy. One thing was distressing him – that he was far from the woman than whom none was ever said by book or tale to have been more virtuous or fairer. Thoughts of the Queen began to unsettle his wits, and had he not been a stout-hearted man he must have lost them quite. His charger trailed his reins impetuously through bog and over fallen trees, for no man's hand was guiding it. The tale informs us that a bird would have been hard put to it to fly the distance he rode that day. Unless my source has deceived me, the journey he made on the day when he killed Ither with his javelin, and later when he reached the land of Brobarz from Graharz, was shorter by far.

Would you now like to hear how he is faring?

In the evening he came to a lake. Some sportsmen whose lake it was had anchored there. When they saw him ride up they were near enough to the shore to hear anything he said. One of those he saw in the boat was wearing clothes of such quality that had he been lord of the whole earth they could not have been finer. His hat was of peacock's feathers and lined inside. Parzival asked the Angler in God's name and of his courtesy to tell him where he could seek shelter for the night, and thus did that man of sorrows answer: 'Sir,' he said, 'I know of no habitation beside the lake or inland for thirty miles. Nearby stands a lone mansion. I urge you to go there. What other place could you reach before nightfall? After passing the rock-face, turn right. When you come up to the moat, where I suspect you will have to halt, ask them to lower the drawbridge and open up the road to you.'

He accepted the Angler's advice and took his leave. 'If you do find the right way there,' added the Angler, 'I shall take care of you myself this evening : then suit your thanks to the entertainment you will have received. Take care – some tracks lead to unknown country, you could miss your path on the mountainside, and I would not wish *that* to happen to you.'

Parzival set off and moved into a brisk trot along the right path as far as the moat. There he found the drawbridge raised. Nothing had been spared to make an impregnable stronghold : it stood smooth and rounded as though from a lathe. Unless attackers were to come on wings or be blown there by the wind, no assault could harm it. Clusters of towers and numerous palaces stood there marvellously embattled. Had all the armies in the world assailed it, the hurt they would have inflicted would not have ruffled the defenders once in thirty years.

A page attended to asking him what he wanted and where he had journeyed from.

'The Angler sent me here,' he answered. 'I thanked him in the hope of finding bare shelter for the night. He asked for the drawbridge to be lowered and told me to ride in to you.'

'Seeing that it was the Angler who said so, you are welcome, sir !' said the page. 'You shall be honoured and have comfortable quarters for the sake of the man who sent you here.' And he let down the drawbridge.

The bold knight rode into the fortress and on to a spacious courtyard. Its green lawn had not been trampled down in chivalric sport, for there was no vying at the bohort there, jousters never rode over it with pennants flying as they do over the meadow at Abenberg.* Zestful deeds had not been done there for many a day, for they had come to know heartfelt grief.

Parzival was not made to feel this in any way. He was welcomed by knights young and old. A crowd of very young gentlemen ran forward to take his bridle, each trying to seize it first. They held his stirrup, so down he had to come from his horse. Knights invited him to step forward and they then conducted him to his room. They unarmed him swiftly but decorously, and when they set eyes on the beardless young man and saw how

* The present-day castle of Klein-Amberg lies over two miles to the east of Wolfram's Eschenbach.

charming he was, they declared him rich in Fortune's favours.

The young man asked for water and had soon washed the rusty grime from hands and face, with the result that it seemed to them as though another day were dawning from him, with such refulgence did he sit there, the perfect image of a handsome young consort.

They brought him a cloak of cloth-of-gold of Araby, which the good-looking fellow put on – not lacing it to – which earned him many compliments.

'My lady the Princess Repanse de Schoye was wearing it,' said the discreet Master of the Wardrobe. 'It is lent to you from off her person, for as yet no clothes have been cut for you. I could decently ask it of her since, if I judge you correctly, you are a man of worth.'

'May God reward you, sir, for saying so. If you have judged me rightly I am indeed fortunate. The power of God bestows such reward.'

They filled his cup and entertained him in such a way that despite their grief they shared his pleasure. They treated him with honour and esteem. And indeed there was greater store of meat and drink there than he found at Belrepeire before delivering it from its plight.

They took his equipment away, a thing he was soon to regret when a prank took him unawares. For a man deft in speech summoned our mettlesome guest to court to join his host over-freely, with a show of anger, and for this almost lost his life at the hands of young Parzival. Not finding his splendid sword there, Parzival clenched his fist so hard that the blood shot through his nails and splashed his sleeve.

'Hold, sir!' cried the knights. 'This man is licensed to jest, however dismal we may be. Bear with him, as a gentleman. – You were merely meant to understand that the Angler is here. Go and join him – he esteems you a noble guest – and shake off your load of anger.'

They mounted the stairs to a hall where a hundred chandeliers were hanging with many candles set upon them high over the heads of the company, and with candle-dips round its walls. On the floor he saw a hundred couches with as many quilts laid over them, furnished by those who had that duty, each seating four companions and with spaces in between and a round carpet before it. King Frimutel's son could well afford it. One thing was not omitted there: they had not thought it too extravagant to have three square andirons in marble masonry on which was the element of fire burning wood of aloes. Here at Wildenberg* none ever saw such great fires at any time. Those† were magnificent pieces of workmanship!

The lord of the castle had himself seated on a sling-bed over against the middle of the fireplace. He and happiness had settled accounts with each other, he was more dead than alive. Parzival with his radiant looks now entered the hall and was well received by him who had sent him there – his host did not keep him standing but bade him approach and be seated '... close beside me. Were I to seat you a way off it would be treating you too much as a stranger!' Such were this sorrowful lord's words.

Because of his ailment his lordship maintained great fires and wore warm clothes of ample cut, with sable both outside and in the lining both of his pellice and the cloak above it. Its meanest fur would have been highly prized, being of the black-with-grey variety. On his head he wore a covering of that same fur, sable bought at great price, doubled upon itself. Around its top it had an Arabian orphrey, and at the centre a button of translucent ruby.

A great company of grave knights were sitting where they were presented with a sad spectacle. A page ran in at the door, bearing – this rite was to evoke grief – a Lance from whose keen steel blood issued and then ran down the shaft to his hand and all but reached his sleeve.

At this there was weeping and wailing throughout that

* There were several castles 'Wildenberg' in Germany: on the other hand 'Wildenberg' and 'Munsalvæsche' ('Wild Mountain') translate each other. If Wolfram intended Munsalvæsche, the reason for the greatest fires ever known there is that Saturn was at its most freezing (see pp. 249 and 434). If on the other hand, Wolfram was performing this episode at a Wildenberg, and punning on Munsalvæsche, the castle in question is most likely to have been that of the lords of Durne (Walldürn) in the Odenwald, but now called after its burg – Wildenburg.

† Doubtless the fire*places*.

spacious hall, the inhabitants of thirty lands could not have wrung such a flood from their eyes. The page carried the Lance round the four walls back to the door and then ran out again, whereupon the pain was assuaged that had been prompted by the sorrow those people had been reminded of.

If it will not weary you I will set about taking you to where service was rendered with all due ceremony.

At the far end of the Palace a steel door was thrown open. Through it came a pair of noble maidens such – now let me run over their appearances for you – that to any who had deserved it of them they would have made Love's payment in full, such dazzling young ladies were they. For head-dress each wore a garland of flowers over her hair and no other covering, and each bore a golden candelabra. Their long flaxen hair fell in locks, and the lights they were carrying were dazzling-bright. But let us not pass over the gowns those young ladies made their entry in! The gown of the Countess of Tenabroc was of fine brown scarlet, as was that of her companion, and they were gathered together above the hips and firmly clasped by girdles round their waists.

Then there came a duchess and her companion, carrying two trestles of ivory. Their lips glowed red as fire. All four inclined their heads, and then the two set up their trestles before their lord. They stood there together in a group, one as lovely as the other, and gave him unstinting service. All four were dressed alike.

But see, four more pairs of ladies have not missed their cue! Their function was that four were to carry large candles whilst the other four were to apply themselves to bringing in a precious stone through which the sun could shine by day. Here is the name it was known by – it was a garnet-hyacinth! Very long and broad it was, and the man who had measured it for a table-top had cut it thin to make it light. The lord of this castle dined at it as a mark of opulence. With an inclination of their heads all eight maidens advanced in due order into their lord's presence, then four placed the table on the trestles of snow-white ivory that had preceded it, and decorously returned to stand beside the first four. These eight ladies were wearing robes of samite of Azagouc greener than grass, of ample cut for length and breadth, and held together at their middles by long narrow girdles of price. Each of these modest young ladies wore a dainty garland of flowers above her hair.

The daughters of Counts Iwan of Nonel and Jernis of Ryl had been taken many a mile to serve there, and now these two princely ladies were seen advancing in ravishing gowns! They carried a pair of knives keen as fish-spines, on napkins, one apiece, most remarkable objects. – They were of hard white silver, ingeniously fashioned, and whetted to an edge that would have cut through steel! Noble ladies who had been summoned to serve there went before the silver, four faultless maidens, and bore a light for it. And so all six came on.

Now hear what each of them does. They inclined their heads. Then two carried the silver to the handsome table and set it down, and at once returned most decorously to the first twelve, so that if I have totted it up correctly we should now have eighteen ladies standing there.

Just look! You can now see another six advancing in sumptuous gowns, half cloth-of-gold, half brocade of Niniveh. These and the former six already mentioned were wearing their twelve gowns cut parti-wise, of stuffs that had cost a fortune.

After these came the Princess. Her face shed such refulgence that all imagined it was sunrise. This maiden was seen wearing brocade of Araby. Upon a green achmardi she bore the consummation of heart's desire, its root and its blossoming – a thing called 'The Gral', paradisal, transcending all earthly perfection! She whom the Gral suffered to carry itself had the name of Repanse de Schoye. Such was the nature of the Gral that she who had the care of it was required to be of perfect chastity and to have renounced all things false.

Lights moved in before the Gral – no mean lights they, but six fine slender vials of purest glass in which balsam was burning brightly. When the young ladies who were carrying the vials with balsam had come forward to the right distance, the Princess courteously inclined her head and they theirs. The faithful Princess then set the Gral before his lordship. (This tale declares that Parzival gazed and pondered on that lady intently who had brought in the Gral, and well he might, since it was her cloak that he was wearing.) Thereupon the seven went and rejoined the first eighteen with all decorum. They then opened their ranks to admit her who was noblest, making twelve on either side of her, as I am told. Standing there, the maiden with the crown made a most elegant picture.

Chamberlains with bowls of gold were appointed at the rate of one to every four of the knights sitting there throughout the hall, with one handsome page carrying a white towel. What luxury was displayed there!

A hundred tables were fetched in at the door, each of which was set up before four noble knights and carefully spread with white table-linen.

The host – the man crippled in his pride – washed hands, as did Parzival too, which done, a count's son hastened to offer them a fine silk towel on bended knee.

At every table there were pages with orders to wait assiduously on those who were seated at them. While one pair knelt and carved, the other carried meat and drink to table and saw to the diners' other needs.

Let me tell you more of their high living. Four trolleys had been appointed to carry numerous precious drinking-cups of gold, one for each knight sitting there. They drew the trolleys along the four walls. Knights were seen by fours to stretch out their hands and stand the cups on their tables. Each trolley was dogged by a clerk whose job it was to check the cups on to the trolley again after supper. Yet there is more to come.

A hundred pages were bidden to receive loaves into white napkins held with due respect before the Gral. They came on all together, then fanned out on arriving at the tables. Now I have been told and I am telling you on the oath of each single one of you – so that if I am deceiving anyone you must all be lying with me – that whatever one stretched out one's hand for in the presence of the Gral, it was waiting, one found it all ready and to hand – dishes warm, dishes cold, new-fangled dishes and old favourites, the meat of beasts both tame and wild ...

'There never was any such thing!' many will be tempted to say. But they would be misled by their ill temper, for the Gral was the very fruit of bliss, a cornucopia of the sweets of this world and such that it scarcely fell short of what they tell us of the Heavenly Kingdom.

In tiny vessels of gold they received sauces, peppers, or pickles to suit each dish. The frugal man and the glutton equally had their fill there served to them with great ceremony.

For whichever liquor a man held out his cup, whatever drink a man could name, be it mulberry wine, wine or ruby, by virtue of the Gral he could see it there in his cup. The noble company partook of the Gral's hospitality.

Parzival well observed the magnificence and wonder of it all, yet, true to the dictates of good breeding, he refrained from asking any question.

'Gurnemanz advised me with perfect sincerity against asking many questions,' he thought. 'What if I stay here for as long as I stayed with him? I shall then learn unasked how matters stand with this household.' While he was musing thus a page approached carrying a sword whose sheath was worth a thousand marks and whose hilt was a ruby, whilst its blade could have been a source of marvels.* His lordship bestowed it on his guest.

'Sir,' he said, 'I took this into the thick of battle on many a field before God crippled my body. Let it make amends for any lack of hospitality you have suffered here. You will wear it to good effect always. Whenever you put it to the test in battle it will stand you in good stead.'

Alas that he asked no Question then! Even now I am cast down on his account! For when he was given the sword it was to prompt him to ask a Question! I mourn too for his gentle host, who is dogged by misfortune from on high of which he could be rid by a Question.

Enough had been dispensed there. Those whose function it was, set to work and removed the tables after the four trolleys had received their loads again. And now in reverse order of entry, each lady performs her service. They again assigned their noblest, the Princess, to the Gral, and she and all the young

---

* Wolfram 'buries' this sword at the beginning of the ninth chapter, having in the meantime down-graded it in favour of Ither's sword, for which he had later devised a crucial role in the fifteenth chapter.

ladies bowed gracefully to both their lord and Parzival, and so carried back through the door what they had brought in with such ceremony.

Parzival glanced after them. On a sling-bed in a chamber, before the doors had been shut behind them, Parzival glimpsed the most handsome old man he had ever seen or heard of, whose hair I can assert without exaggeration was more silvery even than hoar-frost.

As to who that old man was, you shall learn the story later. And I shall also tell you the names of the lord, his castle and lands hereafter, when the time has come to do so, in all detail, authoritatively, and without playing on your curiosity. I shall give you the bowstring, not the bow ...

This 'bowstring' is a parable. Now you think a bow is swift: yet what it lets fly is swifter. If I have told you truly, the Bowstring stands for straightforward stories, such as people approve of. But when a storyteller takes you round about he is out to delude you. When you see a strung bow you say the string is straight, except when plucked to an angle to drive an arrow on its flight. But if one were to shoot a tale at people that is bound to weary them – for it finds no lodgement there but follows a broad path, in one ear and out of the other – one would be wasting one's efforts to assail them with it, one would then be narrating to such effect that a billy-goat or a rotten tree-stump would make a better audience!

I shall nevertheless tell you more about these sorrowful people. Parzival had ridden to a place where you never met the merry sounds of dance or bohort. These people were so wholly given up to mourning that at no time did they ever seek amusement. Wherever one sees people even of humbler station they find relief in pleasure now and again. Here there was abundance in every corner and also at court, where you have just seen them ...

'I fancy your bed has been made,' said the host to his guest. 'If you are tired, my advice is to go to bed and sleep.'

Now I should cry 'Alas!' at their leave-taking: great harm is to befall them both.

Well-born Parzival rose from the couch and stepped on to

the carpet. His host wished him good-night. The knights leapt to their feet, and some of them crowded in on the young man and quickly led him to a chamber. This was magnificently furnished and was glorified by a bed such that my poverty irks me unendingly, seeing that earth bears blossoms of such opulence. There was no poverty about that bed! A costly silken fabric lay over it with a sheen so bright, it might have been going up in flames! Parzival asked the knights to retire to their rest, since he saw no other beds there. Thus they took their leave and went. And now further kind attentions are afoot.

His countenance and the clustered lights vied with each other in shedding lustre – how could day itself be brighter? At the foot of his bed there was a couch over which a quilt had been spread, and when he sat down on it a swarm of noble pages rushed up to him and removed boots and hose from legs that gleamed white, while other well-born pages took off other of his clothes. What handsome little fellows they were! Then four dazzling young ladies came in at the door. It was their duty to see, last thing, how well the hero was being cared for and whether his bed was comfortable. Each was preceded by a page carrying a brightly burning light, so this tale informs me. Parzival, dauntless warrior, dived under the coverlet.

'You must stay awake for a while for our sakes,' said the young ladies. He won a desperate gamble with Haste itself, yet a glimpse of his white body came sweet to their eyes before he welcomed them. Moreover thoughts of his red mouth and of his being so young that not even half a bristle could be detected in his face, caused them many a pang.

Hear what these modest young ladies were carrying in their white hands. One was carrying mulberry wine, another wine of grapes, and a third clary, while the fourth discreet young lady was carrying, on a napkin dazzling-white, fruit such as grows in Paradise. This last came and knelt before him. When he asked her to be seated 'Don't confuse me,' she replied. 'If I were to do so you would not have the attention I was asked to show you.' The gentleman chatted with them very affably. He drank some wine and ate a little, after which they took their leave and went.

Parzival lay down, and the pages on their side set down his candles on the carpet. Then, seeing him asleep, they darted off.

Parzival did not lie alone. Grim toil accompanied him till daybreak. Sorrows to come sent him their harbingers where he lay sleeping, so that the anguish of the handsome youth fully equalled his mother's in her anxious dream for Gahmuret. Parzival's dream was quilted through and through at the seam with sword-blows and beyond it with many fine lance-thrusts: for in his sleep he suffered no little distress from charges delivered at full gallop. Waking, he would have suffered death thirty times over rather than this, so ill did my lord Disquiet pay him.

Oppressed by these grim matters he perforce woke up sweating in every limb. And indeed the sun was shining through the windows.

'Oh, where are the pages, seeing they are not in attendance here?' he cried. 'Who is to hand me my clothes?' With such thoughts the warrior waited for them till he fell asleep again. Nobody spoke or called there: they all remained utterly hidden. Round about mid-morning the young valiant awoke for the second time and at once sat up.

The doughty warrior saw his armour and two swords lying on the carpet. The one had been given him at his host's command. The other was of Gaheviez.

'Alas, what is the meaning of this?' he quickly asked himself. 'Clearly, I am meant to arm myself. Such anguish did I suffer in my sleep that I fancy there is toil in store for me today, now that I am awake! If the lord of this domain has been attacked I shall be glad to obey his commands and most faithfully those of the lady who so kindly lent me her new cloak. If only she wished to take a servitor! It would be fitting for me to do so for her sake, though not for her love, since to tell the truth my wife the Queen is as radiantly lovely in appearance or even more so.'

Parzival did as he should. He armed himself completely from heel to crown so that he might give as good as he got, and he girded on both swords. The noble warrior went out at the door and found his charger tethered at the stair with his shield and lance propped up against it. This was just what he wanted. But before the trusty warrior took the saddle he ran through many a room calling for the denizens, but to his boundless indignation he neither heard nor saw a single person. Roused to fury he now ran to where he had dismounted the evening before on his arrival. Here the bare earth and lawn had been churned by trampling hooves, and the morning dew lay all scattered and marred. Yelling at the top of his voice the young man raced back to his horse and with angry shouts leapt into the saddle. He found the Gate wide open. Through it ran the tracks of many horses. He waited not a moment longer but crossed over the drawbridge at a brisk trot. A page who had remained hidden pulled the cable so sharply that the end all but toppled his horse into the moat. Parzival looked back in hope of learning more.

'Damn you, wherever the sun lights your path!' shouted the page. 'You silly goose! Why didn't you open your gob and ask my lord the Question? You've let slip a marvellous prize!'

The visitor shouted that he wished to know all about it but was left without an answer. However much Parzival called to him, the page behaved as though walking in his sleep and slammed the Gate. At this disastrous juncture the page's exit is all too sudden for Parzival, who is now mulcted of his happiness – happiness that has vanished from him without trace. When he chanced upon the Gral, his joy and sorrow were staked on one throw, with his eyes,* no hand, and no dice. If trouble is now rousing him to wakefulness he has so far been unused to it, he has not known much sorrow as yet.

Parzival set out in pursuit hard on the tracks he saw. 'I imagine the men who have ridden out ahead of me are fighting manfully today in my lord's cause,' he thought. 'If they wished it, their tent-ring would be none the worse for my inclusion. I would not defect on the field but would stand by them in the thick of it and so pay for my supper and this splendid sword which their noble lord has given me, but which I wear undeserved. Perhaps they think me a coward?'

He who was the negation of all that is perfidious followed the trail of hoof-prints. How his departure from that place saddens me!

* There is a lost pun here: pips on dice are also intended.

But now the tale outdoes itself. The tracks grew ever fainter. Those riding ahead had scattered so that their trail, once broad, was now narrow. Then, to his vexation, he lost it. The young man was soon to learn news that pained him deeply.

The spirited young warrior heard the voice of a woman lamenting. The grass was still drenched in dew, and before him, seated in a linden, was a maiden, the wretched victim of her own fidelity. In her arms reclined a dead knight whose body had been embalmed. Any who saw her sitting thus without being moved to pity I should say lacked human kindness.

Failing to recognize her for all that she was his cousin on his mother's side, he turned his horse towards her. Compared with the signs of grief she had inflicted on her body all earthly fidelity was as nothing.

'Madam,' said Parzival after his greeting, 'I am very sorry to see you so distressed. If you need my help in any way I am at your service.'

She thanked him mournfully and asked him where he had come from. 'It is not fitting for anyone to undertake a journey into this wilderness, since great harm may easily befall an unversed stranger here. I have heard, and seen it too, that many have lost their lives here, finding death in armed combat. Turn back, if you value your life! But first tell me where you passed the night.'

'A mile or more back there is a castle more splendid than any I ever saw in all its varied magnificence. I rode out from it but a short while ago.'

'You should not be so ready to deceive those who trust you,' she said. 'After all, your shield is a stranger's. Riding this way from the ploughlands, though, the forest would have been too much for you. Neither timber nor stone has been hewn to make a dwelling for thirty miles around, except for a solitary castle, rich in all earthly splendours. If any seeks it out of set purpose, alas, he will not find it. Nevertheless, one sees many who attempt it. Yet when someone is meant to see the castle it must come to pass unwittingly. I presume it is unknown to you, sir. Its name is Munsalvæsche, and the broad realm which subserves the stronghold is Terre de Salvæsche. Ancient Titurel bequeathed it to his son King Frimutel – such was the warrior's name – and many laurels did he win with his strong right hand, till, impelled by the passion of love, he met his death in joust. He left four noble sons and daughters, of whom three, for all their lofty rank, live in misery. The fourth lives in humble poverty and this he does as penance in God's name. He is called Trevrizent. His brother Anfortas can only lean – he can neither ride nor walk, nor yet lie down or stand. He is lord of Munsalvæsche and is dogged by misfortune from on high. If you had made your way to that sorrowing company, sir,' she continued, 'that lord would have been rid of the suffering he has borne all this long time.'

'I saw great marvels there,' the Waleis told the maiden, 'and bevies of comely ladies.' She knew him by his voice.

'You are Parzival!' she said. 'Now tell me, did you see the Gral and his lordship all desolate of joy? Tell me the glad tidings! If an end has been put to his agony, happy you for your Heaven-blest journey! For you shall be high over all that air enfolds, creatures wild and tame shall minister to you! Majesty without confine has been assigned to you!'

'How did you recognize me?' asked the warrior Parzival.

'I am the maiden who lamented her sorrows to you once before,' she answered, 'and who told you who you are. Your mother is my maternal aunt: you have no cause to be ashamed of our relationship. She is a flower of womanly modesty that shines translucent without the dew! May God reward you for having felt such pity for my friend who lay dead to me from a lance-thrust. I hold him *here*. Now judge of the grief God gave me through him by not letting him live any longer. All manly qualities were his. His dying tormented me then, and ever since. As day has followed day, I have come to know new griefs.'

'Alas, where are your red lips? Can you be Sigune, who told me so frankly who I am? Your head has been bared of its long brown tresses. When I saw you in the Forest of Brizljan you looked very lovely despite the sorrow you bore. But now you have lost both colour and strength. Such harsh company as you have would irk me if it were mine. Come, we must bury this dead man.'

133

The tears from her eyes bedewed her clothes. Indeed, such thoughts as Lady Lunete appealed to were alien to her. For Lunete said: 'Let this man live who slew your husband. He will make ample amends to you.' Sigune desired no amends – unlike those fickle women one sees, and they are many, of whom I shall say nothing. Rather, hear more about Sigune's fidelity.*

'If anything can still give me pleasure,' she said, 'it would be this one thing: that the man of sorrows be released from living death. If you left after helping him you have earned high praise. You are wearing his sword at your waist. If you know its secret magic you will be able to fight without fear. Its edges run true. It was fashioned by the hand of high-born Trebuchet. Beside Karnant there is a spring from which the King takes his name of "Lac". The sword will stay whole for one blow, but at the second it will fall apart. If you will then take it back, it will be made whole again in that same stream, only you must take the water where it leaps from under the rock before the ray of dawn lights on it. The name of that spring is "Lac". If the fragments of that sword are not scattered beyond recovery and someone pieces them together again, as soon as they are wetted by this water, the weld and the edges will be made one again, and far stronger than ever before, and its pattern will not have lost its sheen.† The sword requires a magic spell, yet I fear you have left it behind. Yet if your lips have learned to utter it, good fortune abounding will grow and bear seed with you forever! Dear Cousin, believe me, all the marvels you ever encountered must be at your command and you can wear a crown of bliss in majesty over all the noble. You will have in plenitude all that one can wish for here on earth. There will be none so well endowed that he could vie with you in splendour! – If you duly asked the Question.'

* In Hartmann's *Iwein*, an adaptation of Chrétien's *Yvain*, Lunete advises her mistress Laudine to marry her husband Ascalon's slayer Iwein, which she does within days of the funeral.

† Despite the obvious allegory (Parzival, too, was shattered by his first blow, in Chapter 6, and pieced together again forever, in Chapter 9), Wolfram discards Trebuchet's sword before our eyes in favour of Ither's (pp. 223 and 370ff.).

'I did not ask it,' said he.

'Alas, that I have you in my vision,' said the sorrowful maid, 'since you failed so abjectly to ask! You witnessed such great marvels! – To think that you could not be bothered to ask in the very presence of the Gral! And you saw all those blameless ladies, noble Garschiloye and Repanse de Schoye, the keen-edged silver and the Bloody Lance! O what prompted you to come to me here? You dishonourable person, man accurst! You showed your venomous wolf-fangs when the canker took root in your integrity and grew apace! You should have had compassion on your host, in whom God had worked a terrible sign, and inquired about his suffering. You live, yet as far as Heaven's favour goes you are dead!'

'My dear Cousin,' he replied, 'do be a little kinder. If I have done amiss in any way I shall make amends.'

'You are exempt from having to make amends,' answered the maiden, 'since I am well aware that knightly honour and esteem vanished with you at Munsalvæsche! This is the last word you shall have from me.' Thus did Parzival go apart from her.

It was a cause of great remorse to the warrior that he had been so slow to ask the Question as he sat beside the sorrowing king. Thanks to his self-reproaches and the heat of the day, he was soon bathed in perspiration. He unlaced his helmet and carried it in his hand for the sake of the fresh air. He also untied his ventail, and his skin shone bright through rust and grime.

He now came upon a fresh trail, for ahead of him a well-shod charger had gone and a shoeless palfrey. The latter had to carry a lady along whose tracks he chanced to be riding, and now he saw her. The lady's mount had been given up to misery: you could have counted every rib through its hide. Its coat was white as ermine. It had a halter of bast attached to it and its mane swept down to its hooves. Its eyes were deep-set in large sockets. This lady's nag was altogether jaded and neglected and was often made sleepless by hunger. It was as dry as tinder. It was a marvel the beast could move at all, since it was ridden by a lady unused to grooming horses. On it was a saddle with harness, extremely narrow, from which all the bells had been torn, and with the saddle-bow broken down, and from which much else was missing. This sad, scarcely glad lady's girth was a mere rope, for which, to tell the truth, she was too well-born. Moreover, thorny branches had tattered her shift. Wherever it had been torn apart, Parzival saw numerous knotted strings, but beneath it all something gleaming – her skin whiter than swan! It was no more than a net of rags that she was wearing. Where this served as cover for her body, dazzling whiteness met Parzival's gaze. Elsewhere she had suffered from the sun. Wherever she had it from, her lips were red, their colour was such that you could have struck fire from them. From whichever quarter you might have had at her it would have been on the open side!* It would have been wrong to call her an overdressed villager,† since she had little on. Believe me, gentle people, the ill will she endured was undeserved, for she was ever-mindful of womanly virtue. I have told you a long tale of poverty. But why? This is acceptable as it is. I would rather take a person like her despite her scanty covering than some well-dressed women I know of.

When Parzival uttered his greeting a look of recognition came into her eyes. He was the handsomest man in all the lands about, and this was why she knew him at once.

'I have seen you before, to my sorrow. May God nevertheless give you more happiness and honour than you deserved of me! As a result of that meeting my clothes are poorer now than when you saw them last. If you had not approached me then, my good name would never have been questioned.'

'Reconsider, madam, whom you may be upbraiding,' he replied. 'Ever since I took shield and came to know knightly ways neither you nor any other woman has been put to shame by me – I would have dishonoured myself! Your troubles otherwise have my sympathy.'

The lady wept as she rode, so that her breasts smooth as though turned on a lathe were all bedewed. They stood high, white and round: no turner was ever so adroit that he could have made them shapelier. Lovely though she looked as she sat there, he could not help feeling pity for her. She covered herself

* The side of a mounted knight not covered by the shield.
† *vilan* 'villager'; *vil an* 'much on'.

136

with hands and arms from the gaze of doughty Parzival.

'Put my surcoat over you in God's name, my lady,' he said. 'I offer it with sincere respect.'

'If my entire happiness depended upon it beyond all question, I would not dare to touch it. If you wish to ensure that we are not killed, ride at some distance from me. Yet I should not be very sorry to die myself, my only fear is that it could go hard with you.'

'Who should take our lives, madam? Almighty God has given us them, and if a whole army were to come and seek them I should be ready to fight for us.'

'A noble warrior will be seeking our lives,' she answered. 'He is so full of fight that six of you would have your hands full. Your riding here beside me is not to my liking. Once upon a time I was that knight's wife; but now all neglected as I am I may not even be his serving-maid. – This is how he vents his anger on me.'

'Who else is here with your husband?' he asked the lady. 'I am sure that if I did as you say and ran away now you would not approve. I shall gladly die on that day when I learn what it is to run away!'

'He has nobody here but me,' answered the scantily clad duchess, 'but that brings little consolation that you will defeat him.' Only the knotted tangle and the gathering of the lady's smock remained whole. Yet in her humility she wore the glorious garland of womanly purity. – True goodness without taint was hers!

Parzival fastened his ventail across. He was set on taking his helmet into battle and moved it by its laces till his vision was right. When his charger lowered its head towards her palfrey and let out a whinny, the man who was riding ahead of Parzival and the exposed lady heard it and wanted to see who was accompanying his wife. Angrily throwing his horse clear off the path, Duke Orilus was poised for battle and stood thus ready to joust with truly manly spirit. He was grasping a lance of Gaheviez, richly painted with the colours of his blazon. The warrior's helmet was by Trebuchet, his shield had been made in Toledo in Kaylet's land, with a stout rim and boss. At Alexandria in the heathen lands a costly brocade had been woven of which this haughty prince wore a surcoat and tabard. His horse's bard of hard chain-mail had been forged at Tenebroc, and he was moved by his pride to have a precious brocade as housing over this iron covering. His jambs, hauberk and coif were magnificent though not heavy, and the fearless man was further armed in knee-pieces from Bealzenan, the capital city of Anjou. The half-naked lady who rode after him so dejectedly wore clothes that ill-matched his, she lacked the means for better. His breastplate was forged at Soissons. His warhorse had been won in a joust by his brother King Lähelin: it was from Brumbane de Salvæsche al muntane.

Parzival too was ready. He rode his horse at the gallop at Orilus de Lalander, on whose shield he descried a life-like Dragon. On Orilus's laced-on helmet another Dragon reared itself. At the same time there were numerous tiny golden Dragons on his housings and on his surcoat, they had been embellished with precious stones galore – their eyes were set with rubies !

These two intrepid heroes took wide sweeps for their charges. On neither side was challenge given: they were not bound by any treaty. Showers of new splinters flew high into the air from their lances. Had I seen such a joust as this tale tells of I should feel inclined to boast, for ridden at full tilt such a joust was joined that Lady Jeschute admitted to herself that she had never seen a finer ! She stood there wringing her hands. Wretched lady, she wished neither hero harm. Ridden thus, both mounts were bathed in sweat. Both men desired renown. The flashes from their swords as they valiantly swung them and the fire that leapt from their helmets cast a lambency over the scene. They were superlative fighting-men who had clashed here, whatever the verdict was to be for the bold and far-famed warriors. And although the steeds they had bestridden responded, they did not forbear to use their spurs, nor did they rest their bright-patterned swords. Parzival is winning commendation here for defending himself from some hundred dragons and a man. The Dragon on Orilus's helmet took a wound, and wound was added to wound. Many gems were struck from it so translucent that the sun shone straight through them. This was enacted on horseback not on foot. Lady Jeschute's favour was being fought for there with a play of swords wielded by dauntless warriors. Time and time again did they fly at one another, colliding with such shock that mail-rings left their knees in clouds even though they were of iron. If you agree, they showed their mettle.

I will tell you why one of them was angry. It was because his well-born spouse had suffered violence some time past. After all, he was her lawful guardian, so that she looked to him for protection. He imagined that her wifely feelings for him had undergone a change and that she had brought dishonour on her chaste living and her good name by taking another lover. And he made this scandal his concern. Indeed, he passed such dire judgment on her that no woman ever endured harsher treatment, short of death, and this without fault on her part. He could withhold his favour from her at any time he pleased, no one will prevent that, with wives under their husbands' jurisdiction. But Parzival, bold knight, was now demanding Orilus's favour for Jeschute with his sword. Until now I have heard people sue for favour with kind words, but here there was no question of cajolery. As I see it, both were right. May He that created the crooked and the straight avert a fatal outcome if He can resolve it. As matters stand they are harming one another.

The battle had risen to a sharp intensity, with each guarding his glory from the other. Duke Orilus de Lalander fought with all his practised skill – I doubt if any man had fought so often. He was possessed of both strength and expertise, which had brought him victory on many a field, however matters were going here. Relying on this, he clasped his arms round sturdy young Parzival, who for his part promptly took a grip, jerked him out of the saddle, swung him firmly under his arm as if he were a sheaf of oats, leapt down from his horse and rammed him over a fallen tree-trunk. Then this man, who was quite unused to such calamity, had to learn to live with defeat.

'You shall pay for having made this lady languish under your displeasure. Unless you take her back to favour you are lost!'

'That will not happen so quickly!' retorted the Duke Orilus. 'I have not yet been forced so far!'

Parzival, noble knight, gave him such a hug that a rain of blood spurted through his vizor. With this, that prince was under constraint for anything desired of him. He acted like one who does not wish to die.

'Alas, bold, strong man,' he said to Parzival, 'how have I ever deserved this extremity that I am to lie dead at your feet?'

'I shall be happy to let you live if you will return this lady to favour,' replied Parzival.

'That I shall not! – She has wronged me too grievously. She was once rich in noble qualities, but she has since diminished them and plunged me into disaster. I am otherwise willing to do whatever you wish, if you will give me life. God gave it me in the first place, but now your sword-hand is his Angel, so that I shall owe it to your glory!' Such were the words of this prince grown wise. 'I shall buy back my life right royally – my puissant brother wears a crown with mighty sway over two lands. Take whichever you like rather than cut me down. He loves me well and will ransom me in the terms I agree with you. Furthermore I will hold my duchy in fee from you. Thus your glorious reputation has gained merit from me. But, brave warrior, exempt me from being reconciled with this woman, and command me to do whatever else may bring you honour. Whatever other fate is in store for me I cannot make it up with this dishonoured duchess.'

'People, lands and possessions cannot avail you,' answered proud Parzival, 'unless you pledge me your word that you will ride straightway to Britain. There you will find a maiden who was thrashed by a man on whom I shall not forego vengeance unless she herself ask it. You are to surrender yourself to her and assure her of my humble regard – or stay here and be slain! And give Arthur and his Queen my dutiful compliments and ask them to reward my services and make amends to the young lady for her blows. Over and beyond this I intend to see this lady here reconciled and restored to your favour in all sincerity. Failing that, if you choose to cross me, you will ride away from this place as a corpse on a bier. Mark my words, and see that you turn them into deeds! Let me have your word on it, here and now!'

'If it cannot be bought with gifts,' said Duke Orilus to King Parzival, 'then I shall do as you say, since I wish to go on living.'

Meanwhile the lovely Lady Jeschute had not dared to intervene for fear of her husband. She was sorry for her 'enemy's' plight. Since he had promised to be reconciled with Lady Jeschute, Parzival let him get up.

'Madam,' said the vanquished prince, 'since my utter defeat in battle was brought to pass for your sake, come here and be kissed. My renown has suffered great loss because of you. – What of it? It is forgiven.'

With great speed the scantily dressed lady leapt from her palfrey on to the grass, and although the blood from his nose had dyed his mouth red, she kissed him, such being his command.

Without more ado the two knights rode with the lady to a hermit's cell in the rock-face. There Parzival saw a reliquary with a painted lance propped nearby. The name of the hermit was Trevrizent.

Now Parzival did a charitable deed. He took the relics and swore on them, administering his oath to himself in these terms: 'If I have any worth – whether I myself possess worth or not, any who see me with the Shield will rank me among the Knighthood, and as the Office of the Shield informs us, the virtue inherent in its Order has often won high renown and indeed its name remains a lofty one today! – may I forever be disgraced in this life and my fame be brought to naught; and that these words are fact let my prosperity stand surety in the eyes of Him Whose hand is highest (God according to my creed); and let me be mocked and damned in this life and the next through His power, if this lady did amiss when I chanced to tear her brooch from her, when I also bore off other gold! I was a young fool – no man – not yet grown to years of discretion. Weeping copiously and bathed in perspiration, she had much to put up with in her wretchedness. I tell you she is an innocent woman. I except nothing from this oath, may my honour and hopes of bliss be pledge for it! By your leave, she shall be innocent! Here, give her back her ring. Thanks to my youthful ignorance her brooch was thrown away.'

The good knight accepted the gift. Wiping the blood from his lips he kissed the darling of his heart. He also covered her nakedness. Thrusting the ring on to her finger again the illustrious Prince Orilus draped her in his wide surcoat of magnificent brocade, torn as it was by mighty blows. – Never have I seen ladies wear tabards so tattered in battle, nor were tournaments ever cried on, or lances broken by them – *anywhere*! The Good Squire and Lämbekin would get up a joust more ably.* And so the lady's sorrows were assuaged.

Prince Orilus turned to Parzival again. 'Knight,' he said, 'your oath so freely offered gives me much joy and little sorrow. The defeat I have suffered in battle has brought me back my happiness. Now I can make amends to this lady with honour after banishing her from favour. When I left the sweet woman all alone what could she do to prevent anything untoward? Only, since she mentioned your good looks, I fancied there might have been an affair behind it. But now – may God reward you! – she stands cleared of infidelity. It was not as a gentleman that I treated her when I rode out into young timber skirting the Forest of Brizljan.'

Parzival laid hold of the lance from Troyes there and took it away with him. (It had been forgotten and left there by Dodines's brother 'Wild' Taurian.) Now tell me how and where they can pass the night, these warriors of the tormented shields and helmets, their hacks and gashes plain to see.

Parzival took leave of the lady and her lover, at which this prince grown wise invited him to join him in camp beside his fire, but it was of no avail, however much he pressed him. So it was here that those knights parted company.

The story tells me further that when the illustrious Prince Orilus repaired to his pavilion where some of his people were, they were all overjoyed to see him reconciled with the Duchess, now shedding happiness all round her. No time was lost in unarming Orilus, who then washed the blood and grime from himself. He took the graceful Duchess, led her to the place of re-

---

* The reference, whether literary or unliterary, remains obscure.

union and ordered two baths to be prepared for them. Then Lady Jeschute lay beside her lover all in tears: for joy and not for sorrow, as still happens with good women today. And indeed there is the proverb that tear-filled eyes make sweet lips.

To this I shall add that great affection is marked by both joy and sorrow. If one were minded to set Love's nature on the scales and weigh it, it would always have these ups and downs.

And now they celebrated their reunion right royally, believe me! First each went to a bath. You could see twelve comely maidens in attendance on her. These had been taking care of her ever since she had gained her dear husband's displeasure for no fault at all, so that however scantily clad she had been riding by day, she had always had bed-clothes by night. They bathed her happily.

Now will you kindly give ear to how Orilus learned of a journey King Arthur was making? A knight was there saying 'I saw a thousand pavilions, or more, pitched on a broad meadow. The noble, puissant King Arthur, Lord of all the Britons, lies encamped not far from here with a bevy of ravishing beauties! They are a mile away, rough riding. There is also a great uproar of knights there. They have camped all along the Plimizœl on both banks.' Hearing this, Orilus sprang out of his bath, and he and Jeschute busied themselves thus. The sweet gentle lovely woman also quickly stepped from her bath to his bed, and there sorrow found its cure. Her limbs deserved better covering than she had been long wearing. In close embrace, the love of the princess and prince grown wise attained the very summit of joy.

The young ladies now attired their mistress – one *had* to admire her gown! – and her husband's armour was brought for him. They sat on their bed gaily eating birds caught with the fowling-stick.* Lady Jeschute received no few kisses. The giver? Orilus.

A handsome palfrey, strong and of even gait, was led on for the noble lady. Its bridle was fine, as was the saddle into which they lifted her, for she was to ride out with her dauntless husband. His war-horse was soon caparisoned just as when he rode it to battle. The sword with which he had fought that day was

*A cloven pole for trapping birds.

slung from the front saddle-bow. Armed from heel to crown, Orilus strode to his charger and in full sight of the duchess leapt into the saddle. On leaving with Jeschute he ordered his retinue back to Lalant. Only the one knight was to lead the pair to Arthur, and he asked his people to wait for him.

When they came near enough to Arthur to see his pavilions little short of a mile downstream, the prince sent the knight back who had been showing them the way. And now Orilus had lovely Lady Jeschute for his retinue and no other.

Honest, affable Arthur had repaired to a meadow after supper and had his noble Household seated around him, and it was up to this same ring that true-hearted Orilus came riding. His helmet and shield were so badly scarred that their ornamentation could no longer be discerned, such blows had Parzival dealt him.

The gallant man dismounted and gave Lady Jeschute the reins. A crowd of pages ran towards him, and he and she were at the centre of a great press.

'We must take care of your horses,' they said. Orilus, worthy knight, laid the ruins of his shield on the grass and at once inquired after the lady of whom he had come in search.

They showed him where the highly commended Lady Cunneware de Lalant was seated, whereupon he advanced in full armour into the presence. The King and Queen welcomed him, and he thanked them, then at once offered his submission to his comely sister. She would have recognized him easily by the Dragons on his surcoat but for one doubt that perplexed her.*
'You are a brother of mine,' she said, 'either Orilus or Lähelin – but I shall accept the submission of neither! If I ever had any request to make, you were always both at my service. If I were to feud with you and betray my upbringing, it would be "Mate!" to my affection.'

The prince knelt before the girl. 'You are right,' said he. 'I am your brother – Orilus. The Red Knight has compelled me

* Orilus's vizor is down, and Cunneware cannot see her brother's face. The state of heraldry in the centrifugal Holy Roman Empire of the day was so chaotic that confusion between a senior brother (King Lähelin) and a cadet (Duke Orilus) was possible.

to submit to you as the price of my life. Receive my surrender: then my vow will have been duly discharged here.'

With her white hands enfolding his she received the pledge of the knight who bore the Dragon, and set him free. When this had been done, he stood up and said: 'The bond that unites us requires me to make public complaint, and I am bound to do so. Fie! Who was the man that struck you? I shall always feel the pain of the blows you suffered! When the time comes for me to avenge them I shall make it clear to any who cares to witness it that I, too, was greatly wronged by it. Moreover, the boldest man a mother ever bore – he calls himself the Red Knight – will make common cause with me. My lord King, my lady Queen, he sends you his obedience through me, and further to my sister especially. He asks you to requite his humble duty and make amends to this girl for her blows. Had the dauntless knight known how close she and I are, and how keenly I feel the wrong she suffered, I should have got off more lightly.'

The animosity of the knights, ladies and others towards Keie as they sat there beside the Plimizœl reached a new intensity. Gawan and Jofreit fiz Idœl and the captive King Clamide, of whose defeat you have already heard, and many other distinguished men whose names I could easily name but for my wish to avoid long-windedness, began to elbow their way to the front. Their attentions were suffered with courtesy. Lady Jeschute was brought in still seated on her palfrey, and King Arthur and his Queen duly welcomed her, after which there was much kissing among ladies.

'I knew your father Lac, the King of Karnant, to be so estimable a man that I deplored your sad state from the moment I learnt of it,' Arthur told Jeschute. 'And indeed you are so personable that your lover ought to have spared you. Did not your dazzling charms win you the Prize at Kanedic? Your far-famed beauty brought you the Sparrowhawk and you left Kanedic with the bird riding your fist. However much Orilus has wronged me, I would not have wished you to be unhappy, nor ever shall, anywhere. I am glad you are back in favour and that after your most painful experience you are dressed as a lady should be.'

'May God reward you, Sire,' she answered. 'Your words only

enhance your reputation.' And Cunneware de Lalant at once led Jeschute and her lover away.

To one side of the King's ring above a brook which took its rise there, yet on level ground, stood Cunneware's pavilion, and above it it seemed as though a Dragon were holding half of the entire button in its claws! The Dragon was tethered to four guy-ropes as if it were alive and on the wing and were carrying the pavilion off into the upper air!* Orilus thereby knew her tent, since his device was the same. Under its cover he was unarmed. His sweet sister honoured him and saw to all his needs, as she well knew how.

Everywhere Arthur's retainers were saying that the Red Knight's courage had taken glory for companion and they did not say so in whispers.

Keie asked Kingrun to wait on Orilus in his stead, and the man he asked was well able to do so, for he had long held such office at Clamide's court in Brandigan. The reason why Keie relinquished serving Orilus was that he had been prompted by his ill-luck to thrash that prince's sister too energetically with his stave. It was his sense of propriety that made him yield this service, for indeed the noble maiden had still not forgiven him his lapse. Nevertheless, he made ample provision of food, and Kingrun set it down before Orilus.

Cunneware, versed as she was in all commendable accomplishments, carved for her brother with her soft, white hands, while Lady Jeschute of Karnant ate delicately, as women do. King Arthur did not omit to call where the two were sitting companionably at supper.

'If you are having a poor meal here this evening it is far from my intention, for you never sat at a table where the host entertained you with a better will and such complete sincerity. My lady Cunneware, look after your brother well. And now God bless you and good night!'

Arthur retired to his rest, and Orilus was bedded in such fashion that his lady Jeschute had the friendly care of him till day broke.

* Dragon-standards in the form of wind-socks were being revived from Roman times.

Chapter 6

WOULD you care to hear how King Arthur had left his castle at Karidœl and then his country altogether?

Following the advice of his retainers he had ridden for eight days with notables of his land and other territories in search of the man who styled himself the Red Knight and who had done him the honour of saving him from a grave predicament by slaying Ither with his javelin and had also sent Clamide and Kingrun to Britain and to his court in particular. He wished to invite the Red Knight to the Table Round as a Companion. It was with this in mind that Arthur was riding in quest of him, yet on these explicit terms: all who were concerned with the Office of the Shield, be they rich or poor, had promised Arthur on oath with formal handshake that they would refrain from all jousting unless they first had his leave to fight.

'We must ride through many lands that are well able to strike back at us with martial exploits. We are bound to see lances upraised and at the ready. But if you are then going to dash ahead of one another like unruly hounds loosed by the huntsman, that would not meet my wishes. I mean to quell any such commotion! Yet if there is no avoiding battle I shall help you, depend on my valour for that!'

Now you have heard what they vowed. Would you now like to hear where Parzival the Waleis has got to?

A heavy fall of snow had descended on him during the night. Yet according to what I heard it was not the time for snow.* All that was ever told of Arthur, the man of the merry month of May, happened at Whitsun or at blossom-time in Spring. Think of all the gentle breezes they waft at him! Thus the tale is of contrasting colours here, it is chequered with that of snow.

One evening Arthur's falconers rode out from Karidœl to the

---

* It was Michaelmas, see p. 433.

Plimizœl to hunt, when they had a stroke of ill-luck. They lost their best falcon. She had darted away from them and landed in the forest. It was due to overfeeding that she had thus forsaken the lure. That night she lodged near Parzival where the forest was known to neither, and both were freezing cold. When Parzival made out first light he saw his path ahead snowed under. From there he rode over much rough country strewn with boulders and fallen trees, and all the while the bright sun was climbing higher. The trees, too, began to thin out and let in the light, till – with Arthur's falcon following all along – he made his way to open country, where a solitary tree-trunk lay felled. Some thousand geese had settled here, when suddenly there was a great cackling. With one fell swoop she was in among them, the falcon, and had struck one of the geese there to such effect that it barely got away under a branch of the fallen tree: it was too badly hurt to seek the heights. From its wound three red tears of blood fell upon the snow. These were to cause Parzival much distress.

This came from his loyal attachment. For when he saw the drops of blood on the white, white snow he asked himself, 'Who has set his hand to these fresh colours? Condwiramurs, these tints may truly be likened to your complexion! It is God's will to give me untold happiness in finding your counterpart here. May the hand of God be praised, and all His creatures! Condwiramurs, here lies your bright image! The snow lending its white to the blood, the blood reddening snow – Condwiramurs! Your fair person is reflected here, I'll not excuse you the comparison!' The hero set two drops against her cheeks, the third against her chin, just as they had chanced to fall. The love he cherished for her was the true which never wavered. In this way he became lost in thought till he fell into a trance. Mighty Love held him enthralled, so sharply did longing for his wife assail him. For the Queen of Belrepeire was mirrored in these colours, her presence bereft him of all awareness.

Thus he sat motionless in the saddle as though asleep. And who do you think came running towards him? Cunneware's servant-lad had been sent on an errand to Lalant, when he glimpsed a much-gashed helmet and a shield that had been hacked to pieces in the service of his own lady! A knight in full panache had halted there with upraised lance, ready to joust by the look of him.

The lad returned to where he had come from. Had he recognized Parzival as his lady's knight in time he would not have begun such a hue and cry over him. As it was, he called out the retinue and set them on to him, meaning to do him harm as though he were an outlaw. He thereby lost all claim to being thought courtly. Yet no matter, his lady, too, was flighty.*

'Shame, shame, shame on you!' shouted the boy, 'Shame on you, you knaves! Are Gawan and other of these knights, and Arthur the Briton himself accounted men of high renown?' In such terms did this serving-lad call to them. 'The Table Round is disgraced! The enemy has run through your guy-ropes!'

At this a·great hubbub arose among the knights. They began to ask everywhere if feats of arms were being done. They then learnt that a lone man was waiting outside in readiness to joust, and no few regretted the promise which Arthur had received from them.

Ever lusting for battle and at such speed that he walked not a step, Segramors ran forward with great bounds, for wherever he suspected there was fighting he had to be shackled, otherwise he would mix in. The Rhine is not so wide at any point that if he were to see fighting on the farther shore he would pause to try whether his bath were warm or cold, but, gallant knight, he would plunge straight in! The young man came hot-pace to court in Arthur's ring, where the noble King lay fast asleep. Segramors ran in under the guys, burst through the door of the pavilion and ripped off a sable coverlet from those who lay blissfully asleep beneath it, so that they had no choice but to wake up and laugh at his unmannerliness.

'My lady Queen Ginover,' said he to his kinswoman, 'we are so well related, people know far and wide that I look to you for favour. Now help me, Ma'am, and arrange with your husband Arthur for me to be allowed to break the first lance in an adventure that has presented itself.'

* Since Cunneware's behaviour in Wolfram's poem is the opposite of flighty, it seems that he is playing on a bawdy etymology of her name.

'You gave me your word that you would follow my wishes and keep a check on your impetuousness,' said Arthur to Segramors. 'If you deliver a joust here many others will quote it as a precedent and want me to let them sally out to enhance their reputations. In this way my fighting-strength would fall away. We are approaching Anfortas's men, who are based on Munsalvæsche and defend the Forest by force of arms. Since we do not know its position we might easily have our hands full.'

But Ginover pleaded with Arthur with success that delighted Segramors. When she had won leave for him to attempt the adventure he all but died for joy. It would have gone against the grain for him to have yielded to another his share of imminent glory in this affair.

The proud, beardless youth and his charger were armed. Segramors rois sallied out at the gallop over young timber, his mount leapt over the tall bushes. Numerous golden bells jingled on the horse's trappers and on the man. You could have flown him into a thicket at a pheasant – had anyone had to trace him quickly he would have found him by the music of his bells!

And so the rash warrior rode out to meet him who had been sold into Love's bondage. Segramors challenged him before dealing any blow, whether with sword or lance. But Parzival sat there lost to the world, thanks to those spots of blood and imperious Love, who also robs me of my senses and sets my heart in turmoil. (Alas, a lady is doing me violence! And if she continues to oppress me thus and never comes to my aid, I shall hold her responsible and abandon the hopes I placed in her.) But now listen to how those two met and parted company.

'You comport yourself, sir,' said Segramors, 'as though you were pleased that a king lies encamped here in force. However trivial this may seem to you, you will have to give him satisfaction or I shall lose my life. You have ridden too near in search of combat. But I will ask you as a courtesy to surrender to me, otherwise you will get what you deserve, at once, and be brought hurtling down on to the snow! You would do better to yield with honour while you can.'

Parzival remained silent for all Segramors's threats: Mistress

Love assigned other cares to him! Bold Segramors wheeled his charger away from him with intent to deliver a joust – and the castilian too on which Parzival sat oblivious turned away, with the result that Parzival lost sight of the blood. His gaze was deflected and his renown enhanced accordingly. For when he saw those droplets no more, Mistress Reason restored him to his senses.

Segramors rois was now full upon him. Parzival lowered the stout, tough, gaily painted lance of Troyes which he had found at the hermit's cell. He took Segramors's thrust through his shield, but his own was so aimed that that noble warrior was forced to quit the saddle, while the lance which brought him down nevertheless stayed whole. Without even asking his name, Parzival rode back to the blood-drops. No sooner had his eyes come to rest on them than Mistress Love wound him in her toils again. Not a word did he utter of any kind, since he was at once bereft of his senses.

Segramors's castilian trotted back to its manger. If its rider too wished to find rest somewhere he would have to stand up, whereas most people lie down to do so (as you have often heard tell). What ease did he find in the snow? I myself should hate to lie there. Losers always meet with mockery, Heaven sides with the fortunate.

The army were encamped near enough to be able to see Parzival sitting motionless at the same spot as before. He had had to concede victory to Love, who had even vanquished Solomon.

Not long after these events Segramors returned to his companions, and whether they received him well or ill, doled out much abuse without favour to one and all.

'You have often heard that chivalry is a game of hazard and that men have fallen in joust before. Even sea-going ships can founder. But let me never assert that he would have dared to face me, had he recognized my shield. This I do resent in this man who is still willing to joust out there. He otherwise deserves much praise.'

Bold Keie promptly brought the King the news that Segramors had been unhorsed and that a tough fellow was waiting outside as eager to joust as ever. 'My lord,' said he, 'I should regret it always if he were to leave us, fleshed at our expense. If you value me this far, let me explore what he is after, in view of his waiting there with lance erect in sight of your wife. Unless a stop is soon put to his provocation I shall quit your service, for the Table Round has been disgraced. His manly courage feeds on our prestige. Now give me leave to fight. Even if we were all deaf and blind you should forbid it him, it is high time!'

Arthur gave Keie leave to fight.

The Seneschal was armed. He intended to clear a whole forest of lances, jousting with the newly arrived stranger. The latter, however, bore Love's great burden which snow and blood had laid on him. It would be a sin were anyone to add to his troubles. Love too wins small credit for having planted her sceptre above him in token of her sway.

Mistress Love, why do you cheer an unhappy man with such short-lived joy? For swiftly do you slay him. Is it seemly in you, Mistress Love, to overthrow manly sentiment and stout-hearted aspiration so utterly? In how short a space do you win the victory over noble and base alike and every thing on earth that is at war with you! Truly beyond all doubt we must concede your might. Mistress Love, you have one merit and no others: Mistress Affection keeps you company. Else would your rule be sadly wanting!

Mistress Love, with old ways ever-new you foster disloyal ties. You snatch their good name from many women; you prompt them to take lovers over-near of kin. Under your suasion many a lord has wronged his vassal, vassals their lords, friends their companions: thus do your ways lead to Hell. Mistress Love, you should be ashamed that you inure the body to such craving as will bring the soul to torment. Mistress Love, since you have power to age the young in this fashion when youth is in any case so brief, your works bear the cast of perfidy.

This discourse would ill beseem any other than one who has never known your solace. Had you helped me more I should not be so laggard in your praises. You have marked me up short and diced my enamoured glances away,* so that I have lost my trust in you. My sufferings have meant very little to you. But you are too well-born for me ever to indict you in my puny anger. The goad you apply is so sharp, the burden you lay upon my heart so heavy.

With what skill Sir Henry of Veldeke appraised his Tree regarding your nature! – If only he had gone on to tell us how to keep you! For in showing how to win you he split off mere slivers of the whole.† The treasure-trove of many a young fool is ruined by his ignorance: whatever I have learned or have yet to learn of this, I make it a reproach to you, Mistress Love, who are a padlock on our reason. Neither shield nor sword, nor swift charger nor lofty fortress with stately towers avails against you: you overpower all our opposition. On land and in the sea, whether it swim or fly, what can elude your onslaught?

Mistress Love, it was violence on your part, too, when the brave knight Parzival, inspired by loyal affection, fell into a trance, all because of you. The sweet and lovely, noble Queen of Belrepeire sent you to him as a messenger. You also took the life of her brother Kardeiz son of Tampenteire. If such is the tribute you exact, lucky I, who have had nothing of you – unless you are going to grant me better solace!

I have spoken for us all. Now hear how matters went in the tale.

Valorous Keie sallied forth in full knightly panoply as one lusting for battle, and King Gahmuret's son gave him battle well and truly! All ladies with knights in thrall must now wish him luck, for she is a woman who has reduced him to such straits that Love has lopped his wits from him. Keie refrained from levelling his lance at the Waleis until he had hailed him.

'Sir, since it fell to you to insult the King, if you will be guided by me – and I fancy it is in your best interest – you will

---

*A double pun on 'eyes' = 'pips' and 'edges' = 'dice' is lost here.

† In his *Eneide* (an adaptation of the *Roman d'Eneas*, itself a medievalizing adaptation of Virgil's *Aeneid*), the Limburger Heinrich von Veldeke tells of Eneas's masterly wooing of Dido beneath a tree, not in a cave as in Virgil.

put yourself on a leash and let yourself be led into his presence. There is nothing you can do to escape me, since I shall lead you to court by force in any event, in which case you will be roughly received.'

Love's oppression constrained the Waleis to silence. Keie raised his lance and gave Parzival's head such a thwack with it that his helmet rang. 'Wake up!' he said. 'Your sleeping arrangements here are without bed-linen. I have other things in mind for you – I shall bed you in the snow. If the beast that bears sacks to the mill were thrashed as I shall thrash you he would rue his sluggishness.'

Mistress Love, give heed! If you ask me, it is to your dishonour that this is being done. In such circumstances a peasant would be quick to say 'Be this done as to my lord!'* Parzival, too, would complain if only he could speak. Mistress Love, let the noble Waleis avenge himself! For I do not doubt that *this* guest* *would* avenge himself if your dread dominion and bitter oppression would let him.

Keie charged at him hard and forced his horse round, with the result that the Waleis lost sight of his bitter-sweet pain, the image of his Queen of Belrepeire, I mean the particoloured snow, whereupon Mistress Reason returned a second time and gave him back his senses. Keie put his horse to the gallop and came on with intent to joust. As they reached full tilt they lowered their lances. Exactly where he had measured it with his eyes, Keie delivered his joust through the Waleis's shield and opened a veritable window in it. But this assault was paid back to him, for Keie, Seneschal to King Arthur, was brought down by the counter-stroke on to the fallen trees where the goose had got away, with the result that man and beast were in dire trouble together – the man was wounded, the horse was dead. In this fall, between the saddle-bow and a boulder, Keie's right arm and left leg were broken. His girth, saddle and bell-harness all snapped under the weight of this charge. Thus the stranger avenged two beatings: a maiden had suffered the one

*A sly dig, through quotation, at Wolfram's great contemporary the poet Walther von der Vogelweide, who had been a recent visitor at the court of Thuringia.

because of him and he himself had had to abide the other.

Parzival, uprooter of all that is perfidious, was prompted by his loyal affection to find the three blood-drops on the snow that had robbed him of his wits. His thoughts concerning the Gral and this semblance of the Queen both afflicted him sorely, but now Love weighed heavier in the scales. 'Love and sorrow break stout hearts' – and is it to be wondered at? Both could well be called 'pain'.

Brave people ought to lament Keie's plight, for his courage urged him with much spirit into many battles.

It is alleged far and wide in many lands that Keie had the manners of a ruffian, but my story frees him from this charge. He had his due share of honour. However little one may wish to agree with me, Keie was a loyal and courageous man, such is my declared opinion. And I will tell more of him. King Arthur's court was the goal of many strangers, noble and ignoble alike, who sought it out, yet Keie was not impressed by those who were out to deceive with a show of fine manners. On the other hand, those who were truly well-bred and genuinely companionable he always served and honoured.

I own that Keie was a critical observer.* In order to protect his lord he displayed much asperity, sorting out imposters and dishonest folk from the honest – he came down on their misbehaviour like a hail-storm, with a sting even sharper than a bee's. Believe me, it was people of this sort who perverted his good name. He knew manly loyalty when he saw it and reaped much spite from the rest. Prince Hermann of Thuringia, I have weighed certain inmates of your court who would go better by the name of 'outmates'.† You could have done with a Keie, seeing that your true generosity has brought you so mixed a following, here a vile rabble, there a noble throng. That is why Sir Walther had to sing 'Good day, both base and worthy!'‡ Yet when one sings in this style, the dishonest are honoured by it. Keie would not have asked him to do so, nor

* Seneschals were responsible for the security of castles.
† Compare the assessment of Walther von der Vogelweide: 'Whoever suffers from ear-ache, take my advice and avoid the court of Thuringia.'
‡ The song of which this must be the opening line has not survived.

Sir Henry of Reisbach.* But now listen to further marvels of what was happening there on the meadow beside the Plimizœl.

Keie was fetched at once and carried into Arthur's pavilion. Many knights and ladies who were his friends expressed their sympathy. My lord Gawan too appeared at his bedside.

'Unhappy day!' cried Gawan. 'Alas that this joust was ever ridden which made me lose a friend!' Thus passionately did he lament for Keie.

'My lord,' said the irascible man, 'are you sorry for me? This is the way old women should yammer. You are my sovereign's nephew: would that I could serve you now according to your pleasure. While God still gave me the use of my limbs I was not slow to fight much in your cause, and I would go on doing so if that might be. Now stop your wailing and let me nurse the pain. The noble King your uncle will never again find a Keie like me. You are too well-born to be my avenger. But had you lost a finger out there I should have gambled my head against it, believe you me. Pay no attention to my taunts. *That* man who, far from fleeing at the trot or the gallop, waits out there, knows how to settle matters brusquely. On the other hand, there is no lady's hair at court so fine and fragile that would not be stout enough to tie up your hand from battle. Men who show such meekness honour their mothers too: yet from their fathers they should have mettle. Take after your mother, lord Gawan. Blanch at the flash of swords and be soft where men are hard!'

In this way the illustrious knight was attacked on the open side, with words. He could not pay back in kind, as happens with well-bred men whose lips are locked by modesty such as is unknown to the shameless.

'Wherever hack or thrust was aimed at me I fancy I was never seen to blanch, had anyone watched my colour,' Gawan said to Keie. 'You have no cause for anger: I have always been at your disposal.'

Lord Gawan, noble knight, left the pavilion, called for his horse, and minus both sword and spurs, leapt into the saddle.

* An otherwise unknown contemporary of Wolfram's.

He rode out and found the Waleis, whose wits were in pawn to Love. The shield he was carrying was holed in three places by lance-thrusts aimed by champions, for Orilus too had gouged it. And so Gawan rode up to him, neither galloping nor charging, for he wished to discover amicably who had given battle there.

Gawan spoke words of greeting to Parzival but they passed him by – inevitably, since Mistress Love was displaying her power over Herzeloyde's son. Uncounted kinship* and vulnerability to Love inherited from his father's and mother's lines had made him all oblivious. Little did the Waleis take in of what my lord Gawan had said to him.

Thereupon 'My lord,' said King Lot's son, 'since you refuse me a greeting you mean to employ force? But I am not so faint-hearted that I shall not question you otherwise. You have put the King's vassals and kinsmen to shame, and his royal person too, and brought disgrace on us all. Yet if you will follow my advice and accompany me into his presence I will win you his pardon so that he overlooks the offence.'

Threats and entreaties were lost on King Gahmuret's son. Gawan, the glory of the Table Round, had had experience of such trouble. He had come to know it rudely when he stabbed a knife through his palm under Love's dominion and that of a noble woman's friendship. She who saved him from death was a queen, when after a great joust Lähelin had him at his mercy. The sweet gentle lovely woman had offered her own head as pledge! Reine Inguse de Bahtarliez was the faithful lady's name.†

'What if Love is now oppressing this man as once me,' my lord Gawan mused, 'and his loyal heart has had to yield to her?' He took note of where the Waleis was looking and followed the direction of his gaze. He then flung a cape of Syrian silk lined with yellow cendale over the blood-drops.

When the drops were covered by the cape and Parzival could see them no more, the Queen of Belrepeire restored his senses

---

* Father and mother were not reckoned as relations, cf. p. 420.
† The episode alluded to has not survived in Arthurian romance.

to him, though she kept his heart with her there. Now be pleased to hear what he said.

'Alas, my lady and wife,' he said, 'who has robbed me of your presence? Did I with deeds of arms ever win your noble love, a crown and country? Was it I who freed you from Clamide? – Among those giving you aid I found moans and groans and many bold hearts fraught with sighs. A mist before my eyes has now stolen you away from me in broad daylight, how, I do not know! – Oh where is the lance I brought with me?' he continued.

'You shattered it in a joust, sir,' replied my lord Gawan.

'On whom?' asked the worthy knight. 'You have neither shield nor sword here: what honour could I have won from you? Though I have to suffer your mockery you may perhaps show more respect later. I have managed to keep my seat when jousting once or twice, you know. If I do not clash with you the world is still wide enough for me to go out and reap both toil and fame, and abide both joy and tribulation.'

'The words addressed to you', replied my lord Gawan, 'were friendly and transparent, not murky like still waters. I desire no more than I am ready to deserve. A king and a host of knights lie encamped here, and with them many fair ladies. If you will let me ride with you I will give you company on our way to them. I shall see to it that none attacks you.'

'Thank you, sir. You speak fair, and I shall try to deserve it. Since you offer me your company, tell me, who is your lord or who are you?'

'I name a man "my lord" from whom I have much revenue, and I shall proceed to name some. He has always been pleased to honour me as a knight. King Lot took his sister to wife, and it was she who brought me into the world. Whatever God has bestowed on me has been dedicated to that man's service. They call him King Arthur. My name too is far from hidden, it is not hushed up anywhere. Those who know me call me Gawan. Both I and my name are at your service, if you will do me so much honour.'

'Are you Gawan?' he asked. 'What small credit I shall gain from being well received by you, for I have always heard it said of you that you receive everybody well! I can only accept your kindness on a footing of reciprocity. Now tell me, whose tents are they that have been pitched there in such number? If Arthur has indeed camped there I must say to my sorrow that I cannot meet either him or the Queen with honour, so far as I am concerned. Before that happens I must pay back a thrashing that has saddened my life ever since, and this is the story. A noble maiden greeted me with laughter, and because of me the Seneschal thrashed her so soundly that splinters rained down as from a tree-felling.'

'That has been roughly avenged,' said Gawan. 'His right arm and left leg were broken. Ride this way and see his horse and this boulder. The shivers of your lance about which you were asking are lying here in the snow.'

Seeing that this was so, Parzival pursued it further. 'I am taking your word for it, friend Gawan, that this is the same man who put me to shame,' he said. 'On this understanding I will ride with you anywhere you please.'

'I shall not treat you to lies,' replied Gawan. 'Now Segramors, too, a great fighting-man whose feats have always received especial praise fell under your lance-thrust here. You achieved that before Keie was downed. You have gained much honour from the pair of them.'

The Waleis and Gawan rode off together. Inside, a great concourse on horseback and on foot offered Gawan and the Red Knight a noble welcome, as their sense of propriety required of them. Gawan then made for his pavilion. Lady Cunneware de Lalant (whose guy-ropes bordered on his) was delighted. It was with joy that the damsel received her knight who had avenged the wrong Keie had done her. She took her brother and Lady Jeschute of Karnant, and Parzival saw them approaching hand in hand. Through the grime of his armour his face showed clear as though dewy roses had been blown there. No sooner had he been unarmed than, espying the ladies, he leapt to his feet. Now hear what Cunneware said.

'Welcome, first to God and then to me, seeing how you have kept your manly ways. I had refrained from ever laughing till my heart told me who you were – at which Keie took my happiness away by beating me. But you have avenged it fully. I would kiss you if that were not too high an honour for me.'

'I should have lost no time in claiming that today, had I dared,' answered Parzival, 'for your welcome has given me much pleasure.'

She kissed him and made him sit down, then sent a young lady for some fine clothes already cut from a brocade of Niniveh, which her prisoner King Clamide was to have worn. These the girl brought, but she told her apologetically that the cloak had no lace. Thus, ceremoniously, Cunneware drew out a ribbon from next her own white thigh and threaded it in for him. With her permission he washed away the grime and there emerged a young man red of mouth and fair of skin. And when the gallant knight was robed he was seen to be proud and handsome. All who set eyes on him truly declared that he was adorned with graces beyond all other men's, such praise did his appearance compel.

Parzival's clothes became him well. Cunneware closed the neck with a brooch of green emerald, yet she gave him more – a costly and splendid girdle, an orphrey on whose surfaces were many animals made up of precious stones, with a ruby for clasp. And how did this beardless youth strike the eye when the girdle had been tied? The tale says 'well enough'!

Those present wished him well, and all who saw him, men or women, held him in high esteem.

After King Arthur had heard Mass, they saw him approaching a way off with men of the Table Round, of whom none had ever lent a hand to perfidy. They had already heard that the Red Knight had gone to Gawan's pavilion, so Arthur the Briton was making his way there.

Antanor – the one who had been beaten black and blue – ran ahead of the King all the way till he found the Waleis. 'Was it you who avenged me and Cunneware de Lalant?' he asked him. 'They say that Keie has lost much glory to you. His threats are now at an end. Little do I fear his blows now, his right arm is too weak to do its work for him!'

But for a lack of wings Parzival bore the marks of an angel that had blossomed out on this earth. Together with his nobles,

Arthur welcomed him amiably, and indeed all who saw Parzival there felt abounding good will towards him. Their hearts assented with 'Yes!', none said 'No!' when appraising him, so enchanting were his looks.

'You have given me both pain and pleasure,' Arthur told the Waleis. 'You have brought me and sent me greater honour than I have received from any other man. I should still not have deserved it had you gained no other merit than that of restoring the Duchess Lady Jeschute to favour. Keie's misdemeanour too would have been atoned for had I talked with you before.' Arthur told him what request he wished to make to him and why he had ridden to those parts and through other country besides. Then all joined in entreating Parzival to pledge chivalric companionship to each Member of the Table Round individually. Their entreaty was not unwelcome to Parzival, indeed he had reason to be pleased, and so he complied.

Now lend an ear and judge whether the Table Round succeeds in keeping its Ordinances this day! For its President, Arthur, had a rule that knights should not dine in his presence at court on any day on which Dame Adventure had passed it by.

It must be said to the credit of the Table Round that Adventure is favouring them now. And so, although the Table was left behind in Nantes, its ceremonial was transferred to the flowery mead where tents and bushes offered no hindrance. King Arthur has commanded it in honour of the Red Knight, whose noble fame was thus rewarded there. A brocade of Acraton, which had been brought from far-away heathendom, had been devised to this effect: it had not been cut square but round, like the Table Round itself, since their courtesy dictated it, with no man claiming a seat of honour opposite the King, and so with all seats equally honourable. Arthur further commanded that noble knights and ladies should be on view in the ring. Those who were thought highly of, maidens, married women and men, took their repast there.

Lady Ginover appeared with a bevy of fair ladies, and with her many noble princesses all dazzlingly lovely: for the ring had been made so ample as to allow numerous ladies to sit beside their gallants without jostling or discord.

Loyal Arthur led the Waleis by the hand, and Cunneware, freed from her sorrows, accompanied him on the other side. King Arthur looked at the Waleis, and you shall hear what he said.

'I will bid my old spouse* kiss your handsome self,' said Arthur. 'You have no need to ask a kiss of anyone here, since you have ridden out from Belrepeire where the supreme goal of all kissing resides! Yet there is one thing I should like to beg of you – that if I should ever visit you in your own home you will pay me back this kiss.'

'I shall do entirely as you wish, there and in other places,' replied the Waleis. And now the Queen stepped a short way towards Parzival and welcomed him with a kiss.

'I forgive you in all sincerity for having bereaved me,' she said. 'Such sorrow did you give me when you took King Ither's life.' From this reconciliation the Queen's eyes grew moist with tears, since Ither's death brought pain to women.

King Clamide was seated over towards the bank of the Plimizœl, and Jofreit fiz Idœl was sitting beside him. The Waleis was asked to sit between Clamide and Gawan. My source gives me as its assessment that no man suckled at a mother's breast ever sat in this ring whose noble mien belied him less than Parzival's; for the Waleis brought the glow of youth and strength with him. When you looked at him closely you had to admit that many a lady has viewed herself in a glass more dim than his mouth. I will tell you of the skin that covered his chin and cheeks. – His complexion would serve as tongs, for it would grip a woman's constancy so that her innate fickleness could be whittled down to nothing! I refer to women who forsake their lovers and forget the ties that joined them. Parzival's dazzling looks were thus a bond of feminine constancy! Where he was concerned, their fickleness vanished. Their gaze received him loyally, and he passed through their eyes into their hearts.

Men and women alike wished Parzival well, and he enjoyed their esteem – till sighs and groans put a term to it. For now

* The best M S. and some others lack 'old'. If 'old' is Wolfram's own, it goes with his lack of warmth towards Ginover because of her infidelities in other Arthurian romances.

came a maiden of whom I must speak, one praised for integrity, but whose manners were quite crazy. Her news brought pain to many.

Now hear how this damsel rode. She was mounted on a mule as high as a castilian, a dun, with its nostrils much incised and with marks of the searing-iron such as proclaim the galled steeds of Hungary. Great care had gone into the making of her costly bridle and harness. The beast's gait was not open to cavil. She herself did not look like a lady. Oh why did she have to come? Whatever the cause, she was there, and there was nothing to be done about it. She brought suffering to Arthur's Company.

She was so talented that she spoke all languages – Latin, Arabic and French. She was on easy terms with such learned matters as dialectic and geometry, and she had mastered astronomy. Her name was Cundrie, her nickname 'The Sorceress'. Her mouth suffered from no impediment, for what it said was quite enough. With it she flattened much joy upstanding.

In appearance this learned damsel did not resemble those whom we call fine people. This hail-storm so destructive of happiness had donned a fine fabric of Ghent such as bridal gowns are made of, bluer even than azure and made up into a travelling cloak well cut in the French fashion. On the underside next her body there was good brocade. A hat of peacock-feathers from London, lined with cloth-of-gold – the hat was new, its ribbon not old – hung down over her back.

Her news was a bridge, it carried grief across joy. She snatched away the merriment of that company there.

A plait of her hair fell down over the hat and dangled on her mule – it was long, black, tough, not altogether lovely, about as soft as boar's bristles. Her nose was like a dog's, and to the length of several spans a pair of tusks jutted from her jaws. Both eyebrows pushed past her hair-band and drooped down in tresses. In the interests of truth I have erred against propriety in having to speak thus of a lady, yet no other has cause to complain of me.

Cundrie's ears resembled a bear's. Her rugged visage was not such as to rouse a lover's desire. In her hand she held a knout, the lashes of which were of silk, the stock of ruby. This fetching sweetheart had hands the colour of ape-skin. Her finger-nails were none too transparent, for my source tells me that they looked like a lion's claws. Seldom (or never?) were lances broken for her love.

Thus it was that this fount of sorrow, oppressor of joy, came riding into the ring as she made her way to their lord. Lady Cunneware de Lalant was sharing a platter there with Arthur, while the Queen of Janfuse* was paired with Ginover.

King Arthur was seated there in high state. Cundrie rode on into the Briton's presence and addressed him in French, and though I am to tell you in German, her announcement does not please me too well.

'Fil li roy Utepandragun, what you have done here has put you and many Britons to shame! The pick from every land would be sitting here in high honour had not some canker spoilt the vintage of their fame! – Now that Perfidy has joined it the Table Round has been destroyed! King Arthur, you once stood high above your peers for glory, but your ascendant fame now plunges down! Your prestige, which used to go by leaps and bounds, *hobbles* at the rear! Your praises are declining from their zenith! Your high name stands revealed as counterfeit!

'The mighty reputation of the Table Round has been maimed by the presence at it of Lord Parzival, who moreover wears the insignia of knighthood. You call him "The Red Knight" after the man slain at Nantes. Their two lives were not alike – lips never told of any knight so perfect in his qualities as Ither.'

Leaving the King, Cundrie now rode to the Waleis. 'In causing me to deny my salutation to Arthur and his Retinue,' said she, 'you have divorced me from my custom. A curse on your fair looks and manly limbs! Were peace and conciliation mine to bestow, you would go begging for them! You think me monstrous, yet I am less monstrous, far, than you! Now explain to me, Lord Parzival, how it came about that when the Sorrowful Angler was sitting there, joyless and despondent, you

* Ekuba, dragged in as a trailer for Feirefiz, who was begotten in the next chapter in order of composition, that is, Chapter 1.

164

failed to free him from his sighs! He made the load of grief he bore apparent to your eyes. O heartless guest! You ought to have had compassion on his sufferings. May your mouth be as empty – I mean of your tongue – as your heart is void of feeling! In Heaven, before the seat of the Most High, you are assigned to Hell as you will be assigned here on earth, if noble people come to their senses. You ban on salvation, curse on felicity, you disdainer of flawless fame! For where manly honour counts, you are timid, and as to noble esteem you are so far gone that no physician can cure you. If someone will administer the oath, I will swear on your head that no man of your looks was ever more perfidious. You feathered hook,* you viper's fang! Did not your host present you with a sword you never deserved? By your silence you acquired great sin. You are the sport of Hell's guardians. You man devoid of honour, Lord Parzival! Moreover, you saw the Gral carried into your presence, the keen knives of silver and the Bloody Lance! You ender of joy, donor of sorrow! Had you thought of asking there at Munsalvæsche, your Question would have brought you more than Tabronit, city of fabled wealth in heathendom, could give. Feirefiz Angevin, whose manly courage never failed him – that same courage possessed by him that was father to you both – won the queen of that country with fierce deeds of arms! – Your brother has a quite marvellous peculiarity, for believe it or not, this son of the Queen of Zazamanc is mottled black and white! – And with that my thoughts return to Gahmuret from whose heart the tares of perfidy had been weeded out. Your father took his name from Anjou and left you qualities that ill accord with your deeds, for you are dead to honour. Had your mother ever misbehaved I should easily be persuaded you are not his son. But no, her constancy proved a cause of suffering to her. You must believe good things of her, and that your father was versed in manly loyalty and was indeed a gaping trap of high renown! His was a rollicking nature. The heart within his breast was great, his spleen was small. He was a creel, no,

---

* Probably the first reference, and a disapproving one, to fly-fishing in a European vernacular. Medieval German gentlemen did not fish.

an entire rapacious fish-weir, the dauntless man was adept in catching fame! But your renown has now proved false. Alas, that it was ever made known by me that Herzeloyde's child has strayed thus from the path of fame!'

Cundrie abandoned herself to grief. She wrung her hands and wept, with the tears falling fast on each other as great sorrow pressed them from her lids. It was goodness of heart that taught this damsel how to lament her woe. And now she turned to their lord again and announced new matters.

'Is there some worthy knight here whose manly heart yearns for renown and for exalted love as well? I know of four queens and four hundred young ladies, a delight to see. They reside at Schastel marveile. Compared with what one could achieve there, with its noble prize of lofty love, all other adventures are vain! Though the journey will give me much discomfort I intend to be there tonight.'

Without asking leave to go, the unhappy damsel rode from the circle. Many a backward look did she cast through her tears. Now hear the last words she spoke.

'Acme of sorrow, ah Munsalvæsche! Alas, that none will console you!'

Cundrie the Sorceress, sour yet proud, has mortified the Waleis. How could the promptings of a brave heart and truly manly breeding help him now? Nevertheless, he has a further resource, a sense of shame that reigns supreme over all his ways. His deeds were free of all that deserves the name of falseness, since a sense of shame is rewarded in the end by esteem and, when all is said and done, is the soul's crowning glory and a virtue to be practised above all others.

The first to weep because that odd creature Cundrie the Sorceress had denounced the brave knight Parzival was Cunneware. And heartfelt grief brought tears to the eyes of many a noble lady you could then see weeping there.

Cundrie, source of their laments, had ridden away. But now a high-spirited knight comes riding up. His armour from feet to head-guard they rated as of the finest quality – his crest and other adornments were magnificent, and his charger and his person were armed as befits a knight. He found them here in the ring all desponding, men, women and maidens. He rode towards them, hear in what terms.

His heart was proud, yet fraught with sorrow. I will explain this double state. His pride sprang from manly courage, his sorrow from mortal wrong. He rode to the confines of the ring. Did they form a jostling crowd round him? A throng of pages darted towards him to welcome the noble man, but both he and his escutcheon were unknown to them. He did not remove his helmet, and, unhappy man, carried his sword in his hands, covered in its sheath.* He asked after two men – 'Where are Arthur and Gawan?' – and the boys pointed them out to him.

And so in his costly surcoat adorned with gleaming brocade he went through the broad ring. He halted before the lord of the Round Assembly, and these were his words.

'God preserve King Arthur, and his vassals and the ladies! I offer my humble greetings to all I see here. Only to one do I deny my good will, and he shall never have it. For I wish to live in his enmity. Whatever enmity he can muster, blow for blow, *this* enemy shall requite his enmity! Let me name the man I mean. Alas, poor me, that he left such a gash in my heart! The sorrow I have from him is too great! I mean Lord Gawan here, who has done many glorious deeds and won himself high renown. Yet he was in the grip of infamy when his ambition took him to the lengths of slaying my lord in the act of greeting! It was Judas's kiss that inspired him with that thought! It pains a myriad hearts that my lord suffered bitter death by murder! If Lord Gawan denies this charge let him make answer in single combat on the fortieth day from now in the presence of the King of Ascalun in the capital city of Schanpfanzun. I summon him to appear there armed and ready to do battle with me. Unless he defect from the Office of the Shield I would remind him further of what he owes his helmet and the whole code of chivalry. Chivalry is endowed with two rich revenues: a true sense of shame, and noble loyalty. These bring renown, now as in the past. If Lord Gawan desires to share the company of

*A symbolic gesture implying that his mission has to do with the execution of justice.

those of the Table Round over there, he must not behave in shameless fashion. For were a traitor to sit at it, it would breach its constitution. But I am not here to rail. Believe me, since you have heard it, I demand not abuse but battle, whose price is nothing short of death or life with honour, if fortune so decide.'

The King sat mute and ill at ease. He then answered the charge in these terms.

'Sir, he is my nephew on my sister's side. Were Gawan dead I would myself fight the duel rather than leave his bones uncleansed of the charge of treachery. But if fortune pleases, Gawan's own hand shall make it plain to you in battle that his conduct is honest and true, and that he has never been guilty of treachery. If perhaps some other man has wronged you, do not bruit Gawan's shame abroad in this fashion without cause. For if he becomes reconciled with you by establishing his innocence, you will have slandered him enough in this short space to have harmed your own good name in the eyes of the discerning.'

Dashing Beacurs, Lord Gawan's brother, leapt to his feet. 'Sire,' said he impetuously, 'it is mine to stand as surety at whatever place of combat is appointed for Gawan! It rouses me mightily that he should be called a traitor! If you persist in accusing him, address yourself to me – I am his surety and will fight the duel in his stead. When high repute, such as beyond all cavil Gawan enjoys, is brought low, it cannot be settled with words!'

Beacurs then went to where his brother was sitting and, falling on his knees, pleaded with him as you shall hear.

'Remember, brother, that you have always helped me to attain honour. To spare you all the trouble, let *me* be your hostage and champion. If I survive the ordeal, you will have undying glory of it.' And he continued to entreat him for the sake of his brother's renown.

'I have enough sense, brother, not to grant your brotherly request,' replied Gawan. 'I do not know why I must fight, nor do I much care for duelling, so I should be loth to deny you were it not that I should be dishonoured.' Beacurs begged and implored him.

The stranger had not moved from his place. 'I am being offered battle by a man I never heard of,' he interposed. 'I have nothing to seek in that quarter. If he be strong, brave, handsome, loyal and mighty in full measure, he may stand surety all the better: I have no quarrel with him. The man for whose sake I have embarked on this wrangle was my lord and kinsman. Our fathers were brothers who never failed one another. There is no crowned head whom my birth would not fully entitle me to call to account in single combat, and on whom I might not undertake vengeance. I am a Prince of Ascalun, Landgrave of Schanpfanzun – Kingrimursel by name! If Lord Gawan cares for his honour he will have no recourse but to come and fight a duel with me there. I guarantee that none shall molest him throughout the land, bar me alone: outside the duelling-ring I faithfully promise him peace. May God preserve all whom I now leave, save one – he himself well knows why.'

With these words the illustrious man departed from the Vale of Plimizœl.

As soon as Kingrimursel had named himself, upon my soul, was he not recognized! The noble reputation of this seasoned prince was far-flung, and all agreed that Lord Gawan had cause to fear the duel opposite the tested manhood of the great baron now riding away from them. Moreover, sad feelings had prevented many from duly honouring him, since, as you have heard, news had come to court such as might easily cause a stranger to be left without a welcome from his host. From Cundrie, too, they had learned Parzival's name and lineage: that a queen had given birth to him; and how the Angevin had won her.

'I well recall,' said many a man, 'that he won her below the walls of Kanvoleiz galloping at full tilt in a series of splendid charges, and that he earned the heavenly girl with dauntless courage. The much-fêted Ampflise, too, had tutored Gahmuret so that he became a courteous knight. Now all Britons should rejoice that this hero has come to us where his reputation, like Gahmuret's before him, is known to be well-founded. True Nobility was ever his yoke-mate!'

To Arthur's company that day both joy and lamentation had come, such a chequered existence was the lot of the warriors there. They rose to their feet round the whole ring and gave way to measureless sorrow. Men of high esteem hastened over to where the Waleis and Gawan were standing together and consoled them as best they could.

It seemed to the high-born Clamide that *he* had lost more than any there and that his pain was much too keen. 'Even though you visited the Gral,' he said to Parzival, 'I must say in all seriousness that whatever has been narrated about the wealth of Tribalibot in heathendom and the Mountains of Caucasus, too, not to mention the splendour of the Gral itself, all this would not recompense me for the mortal pain I got below Belrepeire! Ah, wretched, ill-fated man that I am! – And it was you who parted me from my happiness! Now here is Lady Cunneware de Lalant. This noble Princess for her part is set on doing your bidding to the point where she will let no man serve her, rich though her reward might be. She may nevertheless be tired of having me here as her prisoner all this long time. If I am ever to know happiness again you must help me. See to it that she honours herself so that her love makes part-amends to me for what you made me lose when I missed the pinnacle of bliss! But for you, I would surely have attained it. So now help me to this girl.'

'That I will,' replied the Waleis, 'if she courteously grants a request. I should be glad to make amends to you, since the lady who you say is a cause of sorrow to you is mine – I refer to lovely Condwiramurs.'

The infidel lady of Janfuse, Arthur and his Queen, Cunneware de Lalant and Lady Jeschute of Karnant came over to console Clamide. What more was there to do? They gave him Cunneware, for he was suffering torments of love for her. In return he gave her his person, her head a crown.

Having witnessed this, the infidel lady of Janfuse addressed the Waleis. 'Cundrie named a man to us,' said she, 'of whom I fully approve as your brother. His sway reaches out far and wide. The powers of two kingdoms subserve him fearfully on land ways and at sea. The lands of Azagouc and Zazamanc are altogether mighty. Apart from the Baruc's riches (wherever they are fabled of) and Tribalibot, your brother's wealth is beyond compare. His skin has a most marvellous sheen, for in outward appearance he is remote from all other men – he shows both black and white! On my way here I passed through one of his lands, and he would gladly have turned me from my journey. He tried but did not succeed. I am the daughter of his mother's maternal aunt! As to him, he is an august monarch! Let me tell you further marvels of him. Jousting with him no man ever kept his saddle. His renown is of the highest worth. No person ever suckled was so magnanimous as he. His ways are the very negation of all falsity. In exploits done for ladies' sakes, Feirefiz Angevin became inured to hardship. However strange it was for me here, I came for new experience and to learn about Adventure. Now you bear the marks of heavenly favour to the glory of all Christendom, if helped by noble conduct, seeing one can truthfully ascribe to you handsome looks and manly ways. And strength and youth go with them.'

This discerning infidel lady, who was also very rich, had acquired the facility of speaking excellent French, and the Waleis answered her in these terms.

'May God reward you, madam, for consoling me so kindly. Yet I am not released from doleful feelings, as I shall explain. I cannot show my pain as it makes itself known to me when many a one, ignorant of my griefs, misbehaves towards me and subjects me to mockery, too. I shall never own myself happy till I have seen the Gral, whether the time be short or long. My thoughts impel me to that goal, from which nothing shall sever me till the end of my days. If, having followed the precepts of my education, I am now to hear people twitting me, then Gurnemanz's schooling may have had some flaws. For the noble man instructed me that I should refrain from asking questions overfreely and to be always on my guard against unmannerliness. Now I see many worthy knights standing here. Pray advise me, gentlemen, how to win your good will. Dire execution has been done on me here with words, nor do I reproach any whose favour I have lost because of that. But if I gain distinction in days to come, then treat me according to my deserts. I am in great haste to take my leave of you. Whilst my reputation flourished you all gave me your company. I now declare you free till I have gained that thing the lack of which has seared my verdant joy! Great sorrow will attend me such as brings heart's rain to eyes, seeing that I, alas, left *how many?* lovely maidens up at Munsalvæsche, and so was cast out from true happiness. For whatever marvels men have storied of, the Gral has more! Its lord drags out a wretched life. – Helpless Anfortas, what help was it to you that I was at your side?'

They cannot stand here any longer, they must now take leave of one another. The Waleis told Arthur the Briton and his knights and ladies that he desired their kind leave to go, but this found favour with none, for in my opinion they were all very sorry to see him ride away in such despondency.

Arthur solemnly promised him that if his country were ever again reduced to such straits as Clamide had brought it to, he would treat the affront as if done to himself, and he added that it vexed him that Lähelin had wrested two kingdoms from Parzival. Amid many protestations of their devotion the warrior left them, impelled by deep sorrow.

Lady Cunneware, lovely girl, took the dauntless knight by the hand and led him away. Then my lord Gawan embraced him. 'It is plain to me,' said the brave knight to the mettlesome warrior, 'that you will not escape fighting on your journey. May God then grant you a favourable outcome, and may He help me too to go on serving you as I would wish. May God in his power grant me this!'

'Alas, what is God?' asked the Waleis. 'Were He all-powerful – were God active in His almightiness – he would not have brought us to such shame! Ever since I knew of Grace I have been His humble servitor. But now I will quit His service! If He knows anger I will shoulder it. My friend, when your hour of combat is at hand, let a woman join issue in your stead, let her guide your hand! Let the love of one whom you know to be modest and given to womanly virtues watch over you there. I do not know when I shall see you again. May all my good wishes be fulfilled for you!'

Their parting gave them Despondency as a harsh neighbour to live with.

Lady Cunneware now led him to her pavilion and called for his armour. Then, arming the son of Gahmuret with her soft fair hands, 'It is my duty and my privilege,' she said, 'since thanks to you the King of Brandigan has asked for me. Deep concern for your noble person causes me many a sad sigh. When I find you defenceless against sorrow, your cares prey on my happiness.'

Parzival's war-horse was now ready in its housing, and his troubles were to begin in earnest. For his part the handsome warrior was clad in shimmering steel, every piece of the highest quality, while his tabard and his surcoat were adorned with gems. When only his helmet remained to be laced on, he kissed lovely young Cunneware – this is what the tale told me of her. Then there was a sad farewell between these two who were so dear to one another.

Gahmuret's son rode away. Now whatever marvels have been told until now, let no one draw comparisons till he has heard what Parzival does later, which path he chooses and where his journey leads him. Let those who shun knightly combat not think of him meanwhile if their proud spirits so persuade them.

Condwiramurs, how often the memory of your lovely person will be evoked! What marvellous exploits will be laid at your feet! From now on the Office of the Shield will be pursued by Herzeloyde's child with the Gral as his mark, and indeed he was co-heir to it.

Many of Arthur's retainers then set out with the arduous ambition of seeing an adventure where four hundred damsels together with four queens were held captive in Schastel marveile. Whatever befell them there they may keep it, I do not begrudge it them: where ladies' rewards are concerned I lag behind.

'I failed to come up to the mark there,' Clias the Greek openly admitted. 'The Turkoyt* thrust me over my crupper, to my shame. Nevertheless, he named me four ladies there who are entitled to wear crowns. Two of them are old, two still very

* Florant of Itolac.

173

young. Of these, one is called Itonje, the second is Cundrie;* the third lady is Arnive and the fourth Sangive.' The knights all wished to see this with their own eyes, but their journeys did not unveil it, for, willy-nilly, they were discomfited there. For my part I deplore it but little, since when men endure hardship for women it may bring them happiness, yet sorrow too can tip their scales right down, such is often Love's way with her reward.

Lord Gawan too made himself ready to appear before the King of Ascalun as one able to champion his own cause, and many Britons with many women, both married and unmarried, mourned it. They lamented the warlike excursion that took him away from them. The Table Round was now orphaned of its glory.

Gawan gave his close attention to the wherewithal of victory. Certain merchants had brought some shields on their sumpters, old, firm and well seasoned – little did he care what they looked like! And though they were not for sale, Gawan was given three of them. True stalwart that he was, he then acquired seven chargers picked for their fitness for battle, and from his friends he received a dozen keen lances from Angram hafted with stout bamboos from a swamp in heathen Oraste Gentesin.

Gawan then took his leave of them and set out with dauntless courage. Arthur would hold back nothing from him, he made him gifts most costly and sumptuous: gleaming gems, red gold and many sterlings of silver.

Gawan's fortunes were now trundling towards cares and perils.

Young Ekuba – I mean the puissant infidel lady – went to embark on her ship. Then the gathering dispersed from the Plimizœl in all directions. Arthur repaired to Karidœl, but not before Cunneware and Clamide had taken their leave of him, followed by the illustrious Prince Orilus and Lady Jeschute of Karnant, who nevertheless sojourned in the meadow for three more days with Clamide, since he was celebrating his nuptials. The wedding-feast was yet to be arranged and indeed it took place later in his own country on a larger scale. Many knights,

* Gawan's sister. Not Cundrie the Sorceress.

gentlefolk struggling against poverty, remained in Clamide's train and *all* the strolling entertainers, since his munificence demanded it of him. These he took with him to his own land, where his goods and chattels were doled out among them to his great credit. There was no fobbing them off with lying excuses!

At Clamide's request, Lady Jeschute rode to Brandigan in the company of her darling Orilus. This was done in honour of Lady Cunneware the Queen, for Orilus's sister was crowned there.

Now I am sure that any intelligent woman who reads this, granted she be sincere, will truthfully agree with me that I have succeeded in narrating better on the subject of women than I once sang of a certain lady.* Queen Belacane was without fault and she was free of all falsity when a dead king was laying siege to her. Then Herzeloyde's dream left a veil of sighs round *her* heart. Consider Lady Ginover's plaint on the day of Ither's passing. Further, I was grieved by the pity of it that the King of Karnant's daughter, the Lady Jeschute, famed for her modest ways, should have been so paraded and put to shame. What a basting Cunneware had when gripped by her hair! But these two have been vindicated, their humiliation has turned to high esteem.

Now let a man who is adept in romancing and skilled at joining and separating couplets take this story and end it. I myself would gladly tell you more, were lips borne by other feet than dangle in my stirrups to command it.†

* See p. 68.
† Wolfram's Lady Patroness. See also the last words of the poem.

Chapter 7

THIS story will now rest for a while with one who never did a shameful deed – with Gawan, famed as a man of worth. For this tale takes friendly note of many beside or beyond its hero Parzival. Those who laud their darling to the skies all the time lack words to praise another. A poet who commends his hero with an eye for truth needs approval to encourage him, otherwise, whatever he said, it would be as a house without a roof. Who will retain a sensible utterance if not men of judgment? If you ask me, lying tales would be better left out in the snow with no host to care for them, so that those who spread them as truth would hurt their mouths – then God would have dealt with them to the liking of worthy poets whose honesty makes them take pains. When a noble patron allies himself to those who crave such corrupt works he must do so from lack of discernment. Had he a sense of shame he would desist, that is the course he should follow.

Gawan, upright man, was so circumspect in his valour that his fame never suffered hurt from cowardice. On the field of battle his heart was a stronghold which loomed high above the fray – in the mêlée all saw him! Friend and foe alike declared that his shout rang clear as he pursued honour, glad though Kingrimursel would have been to deny it him with his challenge.

Now Gawan, brave knight, had taken leave of Arthur I do not know how many days past, and having emerged from the forest was crossing a valley with his retinue when, from the rise at the far side, a fearsome sight came into view that only redoubled his courage. All too plainly the warrior saw an army led by many banners and marching in grand style.

'It is too far for me to escape back into the forest,' he thought. He told his squires quickly to saddle a charger which Orilus had given him. It was called 'Gringuljete of the Red Ears' and had been presented to him without his asking for it in any way.

176

It was from Munsalvæsche and had been captured by Lähelin on the shores of Lake Brumbane – he had thrust a knight over its crupper so that he fell dead from the wound, as Trevrizent was later to divulge.

'When a man loses heart and turns tail before he is attacked, it is too quick for his good name, as I see it,' Gawan mused. 'I will go straight up to them, whatever comes of it. In any event, most of them have seen me. There is bound to be some way out.'

He dismounted as though to make a halt. The contingents of those riding in company there were beyond count. Gawan saw many well-cut tunics and shields with markings altogether strange to him, nor did he know their pennants.

'I am a stranger to this army,' said noble Gawan, 'for they are quite unknown to me. If they wish to make a quarrel of it, I vow I will deliver them a joust with my own hand before I turn away!'

And now they had girthed Gringuljete who had been urged on to the attack in many a tight corner such as was intended for him here. Gawan saw innumerable helmets magnificently adorned with their crests, whose wearers' pages for their bitter sport were carrying thousands of new white lances overpainted in various colours making known their lords' devices. Gawan fil li roy Lot also saw a terrible welter of mules carrying paraphernalia and a train of well-laden waggons hastening to their quarters. The sutlers followed after in indescribable confusion – how could it be otherwise? 'Ladies' were not wanting either: some were wearing their twelfth girdle as gage for their favours. No queens they, these drabs were what you call 'soldiers' sweethearts'. There, too, were a crowd of vagabonds both young and old, their limbs weary from trudging. Some would have better graced the gallows rather than swell the ranks of an army and dishonour worthy people.

The army which Gawan had waited for had either ridden or marched past. This was because any that had seen him standing there had imagined him to be one of their number. No prouder company of knights ever marched, on this side of the sea or on the other. They were in high spirits.

Racing hard on their tracks came a well-bred squire with a

riderless war-horse at his saddle-bow. He was carrying a brand new shield and was spurring his nag unmercifully on both flanks in haste to join the fray. His clothes were of excellent cut.

Gawan rode up to this squire and after duly greeting him asked whose retinue it was.

'Sir, you are mocking me,' replied the squire. 'Had I earned such a cruel snub from you by some discourtesy I should have been dishonoured less by any other misfortune I had suffered! You and the others are better acquainted than I, so why ask me? These matters are better known to you a thousand times!'

Gawan denied that he had recognized any of those who had ridden past and proffered many oaths to support it. 'My travels are a disgrace to me, since I cannot truly say that I have ever seen any of these knights before, wherever my services were needed.'

'Then, sir, I have behaved badly. I should have answered you in the first place. My better judgment failed me. Now pronounce on my fault and deal with me as you will. Then I shall gladly tell you. But first let me apologize for my rudeness.'

'By your embarrassment – which does your manners credit – tell me who they are, young sir.'

'The man now marching ahead of you, whose warlike advance nothing can withstand, is King Poydiconjunz. Duke Astor of Lanverunz is with him. Also marching there is a blackguard whom no woman freely favoured. He wears the crown of outrage, and is named Meljahkanz. Any pleasure he ever had of woman, married or otherwise, was had by force. He should be put to death for it. He is Poydiconjunz's son and is set on doing feats of arms. And indeed the valiant man performs them often and resolutely. But what is the use of his being brave? A sow will defend her farrow if she has it trotting beside her! I never heard any man praised whose courage was not paired with decency, and many will agree with me.

'Sir, listen to a remarkable thing, and let me tell it from start to finish. Behind you, King Meljanz of Liz, spurred on by his unmannerliness, is bringing a great army. He has succumbed to pride and anger and acted for no other cause than misconceived love.

'My lord,' continued the courteous squire, 'I will tell you the story, since I witnessed it all. King Meljanz's father summoned the great nobles of his land to his death-bed. The forfeit for his brave life was not redeemed, so he had to surrender to Death! In these sad circumstances he commended handsome young Meljanz to all present. Then, privately, he chose one of his greatest princes, a man of proven loyalty and free of all guile, and asked him to bring up his son. – "Upon him, now, you can authenticate your loyal love," he said. "Ask him to show honour to both strangers and familiars, and should any needy man desire it, bid him let the man share in his possessions." In such terms was the boy commended to them.

'Duke Lyppaut put into effect all that his lord the King Schaut had asked of him on his death-bed. No tittle of it lapsed, in the sequel it was all discharged down to the last item.

'Duke Lyppaut took the boy with him. At home he had children of his own whom he loved and rightly still does – a daughter judged fully ripe to take a lover, called Obie, and her sister Obilot. It is Obie who has caused us this trouble.

'One day things came to the point where the young King asked her to reward his attentions. She cursed his poor wits and asked what fancies he was indulging, and why he had taken leave of his senses. "If you were old enough to have excelled on occasions when honour is to be won amid the grim dangers of battle, crouched behind your shield, your helmet laced on your head, for five full years of your life and had then returned to place yourself at my command and only then had I said yes to your desire, I should have granted you too soon. You are as dear to me – who denies it? – as Galoes to Annore, who found death later, after losing him in a joust."*

'"I do not like to see you so enamoured, madam, that you vent your rage on me. If true love is to receive its due, mercy has its place beside devotion, when all is said. When you disdain my overtures you go too far, my lady. You have outrun yourself. I should have thought it would stand in my favour that your

* See pp. 51 and 56.

father is my vassal and holds his castles and lands from me."

' "Let any whom you enfeoff deserve it of you!" she said. "The mark I have set myself is higher. I do not wish to hold a fief from anyone! My freedom fits me for any crown worn by mortal head!"

' "Your pride has been puffed up by things you have been told!" he retorted. "Your father has put you up to this and will have to make amends to me for wronging me. I shall bear arms here to such effect that there will be some hacking and thrusting – tournament or battle, no few lances will be shattered!"

'In high dudgeon he left the girl. The retainers deplored this outburst, and Obie, too, regretted it. Faced with this untoward happening, blameless Lyppaut declared he would stand trial, and offered other and ample amends. Whatever the rights and wrongs of the case, he demanded justice of his peers at a diet attended by Princes, and protested his innocence of the charges. He urgently sought his sovereign's grace and favour: but Meljanz's anger had put checkmate to all happy thoughts.

'It was not Lyppaut's way suddenly to seize his lord, since he was Meljanz's host, as indeed loyal men still avoid such acts today. Misled by faulty judgment, the King went away without asking leave. His squires – princes' sons in attendance on him – showed their distress in floods of tears. Having tutored them faithfully and denied them nothing that goes to make a noble style of living, Lyppaut has nothing to fear from them, apart from my lord Lisavander, Burgrave of Beauvais in France, whom Duke Lyppaut nevertheless treated well. These squires all had to break with Duke Lyppaut with due formality on assuming the Shield of Knighthood, since today many princes and other squires besides were invested by the King.

'The army that marched ahead is commanded by a man inured to hard fighting, King Poydiconjunz of Gors. Many well-armed chargers follow him. Meljanz is his paternal nephew. The young man and his senior are both given to arrogant deeds. Let blackguardry care for its own!

'Thus anger plays so prominent a part in this affair that these two kings plan to besiege Bearosche, where ladies' favours will have to be striven for by the breaking of many lances, with thrusts exchanged at full tilt! The defences of Bearosche are so formidable that had we twenty armies, each larger than those we have, we should be forced to leave it unreduced! I have made this foray unbeknown to the army in the rear and have slipped away from my fellow squires with this shield – the very first he ever had! – in the hope that my lord can take a joust through it in headlong charge!'

The squire glanced back and saw his lord coming up fast behind with three mounts and twelve white lances abreast of him. I fancy none was deceived as to his intentions, namely to race beyond the vanguard and claim the first joust – so my tale informs me.

'By your leave, I must go, sir,' said the squire to Gawan, and he turned to rejoin his lord.

And now what would you wish Gawan to do, if not take a closer look at these events? Yet he was in a very painful quandary.

'If I am to look on while others fight and not take part myself,' he mused, 'the renown I have gained would be extinguished. But if I go there to fight and fail to come away, then, truly, the high esteem I enjoy among men will tumble down. I shall certainly not let this happen, but on the contrary fight my promised duel.' He was between two interlocking pressures: were he to stay it would go hard with his journey to the duel, while on the other side he could not ride past these armies! – 'May God preserve my manly vigour!' he cried and rode in the direction of Bearosche.

Lying before him with its town was a castle so fine that none was ever better housed than Lyppaut. Adorned with its towers this queen of fortresses met his eye with dazzling beauty. The army was already encamped on the meadow below, where Gawan could see many rings of splendid tents. Pride was added to pride there, for soon he made out strange pennants in great profusion, and outlandish camp-followers of all sorts.

With anguish for blade, Gawan's indecision cut him plane-like to the heart. He rode straight through the camp. Although their guys were hard up against each other, this army covered a great area. Gawan observed how they were quartered and what each group was about. To those who hailed him with 'Bien sey venuz!' he answered 'Gramerzi!' Together at one side lay a great company of men-at-arms from Semblidac and near them, but apart, horse-archers of Kaheti. Who loves a stranger? Gawan, son of King Lot, rode on with none inviting him to stay, and thus he made for the town.

'If I am to be a snapper-up of battlefield débris,' he thought, 'I shall be better insured against loss up in the town rather than down here among the besiegers. I seek no gain other than to keep what is mine without forfeiting my luck.'

Gawan rode towards a Gate, only to be vexed by measures the denizens had taken, for they had walled up all the Gates and armed all their towers, with each and every battlement manned by a marksman with crossbow, leaning forward in readiness to shoot. They were all set on the handiwork of war. Gawan nevertheless rode up towards the castle-hill. Unfamiliar though the place was to him, he continued as far as the fortress, where his gaze lit on a bevy of noble ladies; for the chatelaine herself had gone up on to the Palace with her daughters, that dazzlingly lovely pair, to watch events outside. Soon Gawan could catch what they were saying.

'Who is this coming along now?' they asked.

'What sort of cavalcade is this?' asked their mother the Duchess.

'Mother, that is a merchant,' the elder daughter darted in.

'But they have his shields with them.'

'Lots of merchants do.'

'You are accusing him of what never happened!' interposed the Duchess's younger daughter. 'You ought to be ashamed, sister. *He* never ranked as a merchant! He's such a handsome man, I'm going to have him for my knight! He can serve me and ask for my reward, and I'll give it him, seeing that he pleases me!'

Gawan's squires noticed a lime and some olives standing below the castle-wall and thought it a lucky find. What else would it please you they should do? King Lot's son alighted where he found the coolest shade, and his chamberlain quickly fetched a quilt and a mattress. On these the proud knight sat him down, while above him a profusion of women were reclining. His clothes and armour were unloaded from the sumpters, then the squires who had accompanied him installed themselves beneath the other trees.

'Daughter, what merchant could bear himself so stylishly?' asked the mother Duchess. 'You should not attack him in this way.'

'She has let her bad manners get the better of her on other occasions,' said young Obilot. 'She was haughty towards King Meljanz of Liz when he sued for her favour. *Damn* such sentiments!'

'I don't care how he bears himself – the man sitting out there is a huckster!' cried Obie, in the grip of anger. 'He will do a good trade here. Your "knight's" panniers are so well guarded, silly sister, it's clear he means to be his own watchman!'

Every word they said reached Gawan's ears. But let us leave this matter where it stands and listen to events in the town. A navigable river flowed past it under a great bridge of stone. On the far side, where the field was free of the enemy – not the side they had occupied – a marshal rode up briskly and set up his quarters over a wide space in the meadow at the bridgehead. His lord duly arrived, together with others who had been detailed to go there. And if you have not heard who it was came riding to the Duke's aid and was loyally to fight for him, I will tell you. – His brother Duke Marangliez had joined him from his lands of Brevigariez! Two other brave knights had come for love of him, the noble King Schirniel, who wore crown in Lirivoyn, and Schirniel's brother, who wore his in Avendroyn.

When those within the fortress saw help approaching, they judged those measures mistaken which they had all favoured before.

'Alas, that it has ever befallen Bearosche to have its Gates walled up!' lamented Duke Lyppaut, 'for when I serve as a knight against my liege lord, my good manners have passed their prime! His gracious favour would stand me in better stead and place him in a better light than his fierce hostility. What would a lance-thrust aimed by him through my shield look like? – Or if my sword should gash my noble sovereign's?

If any lady in her right mind were to applaud *that* she would be behaving too frivolously by far. Now, granted I held my lord in my dungeon, I should feel compelled to free him, to go with him and place myself in his, and in whatever way he thought fit to punish me I should accept it. Notwithstanding, I have cause to thank God that I am not the King's prisoner, seeing that his anger is such that he does not refrain from besieging me! Now give me your wise advice,' he said to those in the Castle, 'as to how to cope with this harsh situation.'

'If you could have had the benefit of your innocence, matters would not have come to this,' many men of good judgment agreed. They earnestly advised him to throw open the gates and ask the best knights to ride out and offer battle.

'We can use that tactic rather than fend off Meljanz's two armies from the battlements. Those who have come with the King are squires for the most part. We shall easily gain a hostage from among them such as has always quelled great anger. Performing knightly exploits here the King may feel inclined to moderate his anger and refrain from exerting duress on us. After all, open combat will suit us better than that they should prise us out from the Walls. But for Poydiconjunz's forces – he leads the hard core of their chivalry – we should be sure to take the fight to their tent-ropes. What we most have to fear are the captive Britons under Duke Astor, whom you can see here in the forefront. His son Meljahkanz is also there. Had Gurnemanz been his tutor he would have stood in very high repute. Even so one sees him in the ranks of battle. To offset these we now have strong reinforcements.'

You have heard their advice in full, advice which the Duke put into action. He removed the masonry from the Gates, and the defenders, with steadfast courage, began to march out into the open. – Here there was a joust, there another! – The main body of the outer army, too, moved towards the town in spirited fashion.

The vesper-skirmish went well. On both sides there were companies beyond number and varied cries of pages, some of whom, believe me, were shouting there in Scots or Welsh! The fighting between the knights here was without prior agreement of ransoms, they were swinging their limbs in deadly earnest!

Those who sallied out from the besieging army were mostly squires. They did many noble deeds, yet the defenders bound them against forfeits as peasants deal with trespassers at harvest-time. No one too young to have been given costly gifts by his lady could have worn finer clothes than they. To single out Meljanz, I heard it said that his caparison was excellent, and he himself was in great spirits astride a handsome castilian which Meljehkanz had acquired when he thrust Keie over the crupper to such a height that he was left hanging from a branch for all to see.* Since Meljahkanz had won it in fair fight, Meljanz was entitled to ride it here. And indeed, Meljanz's achievements stood out above the rest. His every thrust was framed in Obie's eyes up in the Palace, to which she had repaired to view the scene.

'Just look, sister,' she said. 'Truly, my knight and yours are acquitting themselves unequally. Yours is of the opinion that we should lose both Rock and Castle. We must find some other defence.' Such taunts did the younger have to bear.

'He can make it good. I still believe he has courage that will save him from your gibes! He must address his attentions to me, and I will make him happy. Since you say he is a merchant, he can chaffer for my recompense!'

Gawan listened attentively to their bickering but (as was only seemly) sat through it without a sign as best he could. Death alone can rob a pure heart of its modesty.

The great army led by Poydiconjunz lay quiet. Only one young nobleman, the Duke of Lanverunz, was in action, together with all those of his tent-ring. Then the old campaigner Poydiconjunz rode up and took various knights away with him, for the preliminary skirmish with all its wounds and bruises was over, bravely fought for love of noble ladies.

Poydiconjunz then asked the Duke of Lanverunz, 'Have you no thought to wait for me when you go fighting for your own vainglory? Is that your idea of a fine exploit? When noble Laheduman and my son Meljahkanz go into action, and I my-

* The incident is narrated in Hartmann von Aue's *Iwein*.

self, then you could see some fighting indeed, if you are any judge of it! I shall not leave this field till I have given us all our bellyful of fighting, or until every man and woman in this castle come out and surrender to me!'

'Your royal nephew preceded us, Sire, with all his army of Liz,' replied Duke Astor. 'Should your own army have busied themselves meanwhile with sleeping? Is that what you taught us to do? Then, when it is time to fight, I shall sleep! – I am good at sleeping when others are in the thick of it! But believe me, had I not appeared, the defenders would have gained the advantage and got the credit, so I saved you from disgrace. Put your anger by, in God's name! More was won than lost by your people – if Lady Obie will but own it.'

All Poydiconjunz's anger was now centred on his nephew Meljanz. Notwithstanding, that worthy youth brought back a shield holed by many lance-thrusts, which called for no regrets for his new-fledged reputation. And now let us turn to Obie.

Obie did not spare her ill will towards Gawan, who had done nothing to deserve it. Set on humiliating him in public, she sent a page to where he was sitting.

'Greetings over, ask him if his horses are for sale,' she said, 'and whether he has any fine stuffs in his panniers that he would wish to trade. We women will buy them all without haggling.'

When the boy approached Gawan he met with an angry reception. The lightning which flashed from Gawan's eyes struck terror into his heart, he was so utterly cowed that he failed to ask a word of what his mistress had charged him with.

Gawan on the other hand was not tongue-tied. 'Off with you, riff-raff!' he said. 'If you come a step nearer you will have my fist in your face more times than you can count!'

The page went – or did he run? Now hear what Obie was about.

Obie asked a young gentleman to speak to the Burgrave of the town, whose name was Scherules. 'You are to ask him to do me a favour and act with vigour. Under the olives by the moat there are seven war-horses. These he is to take and the other valuables, too. A merchant there is out to swindle us – ask the

Burgrave to put a stop to it. I rely on his boldness to seize the lot without payment, and indeed he shall keep it without reproach.'

'I am here to protect us from fraud,' answered Scherules. 'I will go and see.' He rode up to where the ever-courageous Gawan was seated, and as he ran his eyes over the whole man, the mould of his arms and either hand, Scherules could find no trace of inferiority in him, but on the contrary a fair countenance, a broad chest and an altogether handsome knight.

'My lord,' said he, 'you are a stranger here. What a lack of discernment on our part to leave you without lodgement! How very remiss of us. Now I myself shall be your groom, and my people, my effects, all that I call mine I shall place at your disposal. No guest ever came riding to a host more at your service!'

'Thank you, my lord,' replied Gawan. 'Though as yet I have done nothing to deserve it, I gladly accept your invitation.'

Scherules was widely commended for his qualities, and his good heart prompted him to say 'Since it has fallen to me, I shall be your guarantor against loss. Should the besiegers try to rob you I shall be fighting at your side.' Turning to all the pages there he added with a smile 'Load on all your gear! We are going down to the plain.'

Gawan went with his host.

Obie now has to send a minstrel-woman to her father, to whom she was well known, with a message telling him that a counterfeiter was on his way. – 'His goods are fine and costly. Since my father has crowds of mercenaries serving for horses, silver and clothes, ask him as he is a true knight to make this man's goods their next payment. There's enough to put seven men into the field.'

The woman repeated to the Duke all that his daughter had intended for him. Those engaged in warfare have always been forced to lay hand on costly prizes. The need to pay his mercenaries pressed heavily on honest Lyppaut, so that he at once concluded 'I must acquire these stores peaceably or otherwise', and set out after him.

Riding back, Scherules met Lyppaut and asked him where he was going in such haste.

'I am on the tracks of a swindler. I have been told he is a coiner.'

Gawan was innocent. It was all because of the spare mounts and other equipment he had with him. Scherules had to laugh.

'My lord,' he said, 'you are mistaken. Whoever told you this – man, maid or woman – was lying. My guest is innocent, you must gain another opinion of him. If you will but hear the truth, he never owned a die, or wore a trader's money-bag. See how he bears himself, listen to the way he speaks! I left him in my own house, where, if you are any judge of knightly ways, you will be bound to agree that he's one of the right sort! *He* never resorted to trickery. Whoever does violence to him under this head, and were he my own father or a child of mine – *any* who vents his spleen on him, whether my kinsman or my brother – will have me to contend with! I intend to protect him and save him from unprovoked attacks, wherever, my lord, I may do so with your gracious favour. I would rather retire from the chivalric life into sackcloth, and flee to a place so remote from my noble origins that none would know me, than that you should bring shame upon yourself by mishandling him. It is more fitting that you should give a kind welcome to all who come here after learning of your trouble than that you should rob them. You should rid yourself of any such thought.'

'Show him to me,' replied the Duke. 'No harm can come of that.' And he rode to where Gawan was. The two eyes, one heart, that Lyppaut had brought with him told him that this stranger was handsome and that his manners were informed by truly manly qualities.

When true liking has made one suffer the pangs of heartfelt love (such love is known by the heart's being forfeit to true Love, so utterly mortgaged and sold!) no lips can ever recount in full what miracles Love can work. Whether in man or woman, heartfelt Love often impairs a lofty understanding. Obie and Meljanz's love was so true and entire that the young man's anger deserves your sympathy. Obie was hurt so deeply by his riding away in a huff that she lost her composure and flew into a passion, too! Thus Gawan, though in no way to blame, had to bear the brunt of her displeasure, together with others

188

who had to endure the siege with her. Obie's lapses from lady-like behaviour were now frequent. Her modest ways were interlaced with anger, so that whenever she saw a fine figure of a man it stuck in her eyes like a thorn; for her heart told her that it was Meljanz who had to be far and away the best! 'If he makes me very unhappy,' she thought, 'I must suffer it gladly for his sake. I love the noble darling young man more than anything else in the whole world! Feelings deep down within me drive me to it!'

Even now Love occasions much anger – so do not reproach Obie!

Now hear what Obie's father said on coming face to face with Gawan, and how he welcomed him to his domain.

'My lord,' he began, 'your coming is auspicious. I have travelled widely, but my eyes have never been so charmed by what they saw. This day of your advent shall console us in our predicament, since it has power to console!' He invited Gawan to join in the fighting. 'If you are not fully equipped let us supply what is missing. If you wish, my lord, join my detachment.'

'I should be willing to do so,' answered noble Gawan, 'since I have weapons and stout limbs, only there is a truce on my fighting till an agreed term. Were the odds for or against you I would gladly make common cause with you. But, sir, I must forego it till a duel that concerns me has been fought. My honour has been staked in it at such a price that if I am to be accepted in noble society I must redeem my pledge in combat or die in the attempt – that is why you see me on the road.'

To Lyppaut this was grievous news. 'Sir,' he said, 'I beg you of your nobility and gracious breeding to hear my innocence. I have two daughters whom, since they are mine, I love. Whatever God has given me in them I will live with it in contentment. Lucky me, ever to have known the sorrow they bring me! But one daughter bears sorrow in common with me, though in unequal shares: for my lord hurts her with love and me with want of love. As I see it, my lord intends to do violence to me because I have no son. Well, then, I am more attached to daughters, so what of it, if I have to suffer for it? I count such pain among my blessings. As to warfare, although a daughter may not wield a sword she is just as effective, provided her father choose with her, for with her modest ways she can catch him a spirited son – that is what I'm setting my hopes on!'

'May God grant you your desire!' said Gawan.

Lyppaut renewed his entreaties.

'In God's name, my lord, do not pursue it,' answered King Lot's son. 'As you are a man of breeding do not ask me to break my word. Yet there is one thing I will do for you: before evening is out I will tell you what I have resolved.'

Lyppaut thanked him and left immediately. In the courtyard he met Obilot and the Burgrave's little daughter flicking rings.*

'Where have you come from, daughter?' he asked.

'I am on my way down, father. I'm sure *he*'ll do as I ask – I'm going to ask the stranger to be my Knight-servitor!'

'I am sorry to be telling you, daughter, that he has said neither yes nor no. Pursue it to a successful conclusion!' Off she sped to find the stranger.

As Obilot entered his room Gawan leapt to his feet and after welcoming the sweet child sat down beside her and thanked her for championing him when he was being maligned.

'If ever a knight suffered pangs for such a little lady I am in the throes because of you!' said he.

'Heaven knows, sir,' prattled the lovely child, 'you are the first man with whom I ever had a tête-à-tête. If I may do so without hurt to modesty and decorum, I shall be pleased. For my governess told me "Speech is the outer garment of the mind.' My lord, prompted by direst pain I have a request for you and me, and by your leave will name it. And even if you think any the worse of me, I shall have kept within proper bounds, since in asking you I ask myself. For truly, you and I are one, though the terms "maid" and "man" are two. Now I have asked both you and me; so if you send me away, shame-faced, with a refusal, sir, your good name will have to answer to your courtesy, since I am a damsel seeking refuge in your mercy. If it be your pleasure, my lord, I offer you love with all

* Or possibly: playing at morra.

190

my heart. If yours are manly ways, I am sure you will not fail to serve me who am so worthy to be served. Though on his side my father is asking kinsmen and other friends to aid him, do not let that be a reason for not rendering service to us both for my reward alone.'

'Madam,' he replied, 'the music of your lips will part me from my honour. You should be no friend to perfidy. My honour has been put most grievously to pawn. Unless it be redeemed I am dead. Yet, granted I were to devote my thoughts and attentions to winning your love, you would have to be five years older before you could bestow it, only then would you be ripe for love.' And he remembered how Parzival had placed greater trust in women than in God. Parzival's advice spoke into Gawan's heart as though it were her angel, and he promised the little lady that he would bear arms for her. 'Let my sword be in your hand,' he went on, 'and if anyone wishes to joust with me, *you* must ride to the attack and fight there in my stead. People will see *me* doing battle there, but it is *you* who must be fighting for me.'

'That does not scare me at all,' she answered. 'I shall be your shield and your defence, your heart and your firm faith, now that you have freed me from doubt. When misfortune threatens, I shall be your guide and friend, the roof sheltering you from the hail-storm, affording you sweet repose. My love shall fence you about with peace, and bring you luck when you are faced with danger so that your courage will surely defend you "down to the chatelain" as they say. But I am your chatelain and chatelaine and shall be at your side in battle. If you only put your faith in that, neither fortune nor courage will forsake you.'

'Madam,' replied Gawan, 'since I live at your command I will have your love and the benefit of your encouragement.' Meanwhile her little hand reposed between his hands.

'And now, my lord, let me go,' she said, 'for I must not be found wanting. How would you fare without my guerdon? I am far too fond of you to let that happen. I must go and busy myself about a love-token. When you wear it no man's fame will overtower yours.'

After many protestations of their devotion, the girl and her playmate went away, while Gawan, their guest, acknowledged their complaisance with bow upon bow. 'When you grow up,' he said, 'were the forest to bear as many lances as it now bears trees, it would be a meagre harvest for you two. If, young though you are, you hold such sway over a man and keep your charm till you come of age, desire for your love in days to come will teach knights' hands to shatter shields indeed!' And off the two girls went as happy as could be.

'Tell me, my lady,' said the Burgrave's little daughter, 'what are you thinking of giving him? Seeing we have nothing but dolls, if mine are any prettier than yours, let him have them, I shan't mind, we shan't quarrel about that.'

Duke Lyppaut had ridden half-way up the castle-hill when he saw Obilot and Clauditte walking up ahead of him. He asked them to stop.

'Father,' cried young Obilot, 'I never needed your help so much as now! Tell me what to do about it – the knight has granted my request!'

'You shall have whatever you want if I have it, daughter. O happy we, that our loves bore such fruit! The day you were born was an auspicious one!'

'Then I'll whisper what is troubling me, and then please tell me what to do.'

Lyppaut asked to have her lifted in front of him on to the saddle.

'What is to become of my playmate?' she asked.

The Duke had a number of knights in attendance, and these vied with one another as to who was to take Clauditte. It would have been to the liking of each one of them, for Clauditte was a pretty child, too. In the end she had to be given to someone.

As they rode up, the father said to his daughter 'Obilot, tell me about your troubles.'

'I have promised the foreign knight some love-tokens. I must have been out of my mind. What is the use of living if I have nothing to give him, now that he has offered to be my Servitor? If I have no gift for him I shall blush for shame. – No young woman ever so doted on a man!'

'Rely on me, daughter,' answered Lyppaut. 'I shall provide you with the wherewithal. Since you wish to have him serve you I will give you something to bestow on him, if your mother should fail to help you. Heaven grant I reap some advantage from it! Proud nobleman that he is, what hopes I set on him! Though as yet I had exchanged no word with him, I saw him last night in my dreams!'

Lyppaut and his daughter Obilot went in to the Duchess.

'My lady,' said he, 'provide us with what we need. – My whole being shouted for joy that God had given me this child to save me from vexation!'

'What do you wish to have from my effects?' asked the mother Duchess.

'Granted you wish to let us have them, madam, Obilot needs a finer set of clothes. With so illustrious a man aspiring to her love and so well disposed to serve her and asking for her love-token, she feels fully entitled to have them.'

'That charming, excellent man?' asked the girl's mother, 'You mean the stranger on a visit here, whose glance is dazzling as May sunshine?' And being not unversed in such matters she ordered samite of Ethnise to be fetched. With it they also brought uncut rolls of brocade of Tabronit from the land of Tribalibot. The infidel weave many such intricate tissues with red gold of Caucasus on pure silk.

Lyppaut promptly ordered a gown to be cut for his daughter. Whatever the quality of the material, the poorest or the finest, he would have let it go without regret. As it was, they cut a brocade stiff with gold on the little lady's body, leaving one arm bare. – The sleeve was removed, since it was destined for Gawan!

Such was Obilot's ceremonial gift: brocade of Nourient imported from distant heathendom. It had touched her right arm but had not been sewn to her gown, not a thread had been twisted for it. This sleeve Clauditte took to handsome Gawan, and at the sight of it his cares vanished away! Choosing one of his three shields he nailed it on at once. No longer did he despond. Nor did he fail to express his gratitude, but bowing profusely blessed the path taken by the young lady who had welcomed him so kindly and in such charming fashion made him so happy.

The day had drawn to an end and it was night. On both sides there were great forces composed of many excellent valiant knights. Had the Outer Army not been so vast, the Inners would have done a deal of fighting. Yet not being given to faint-heartedness they marked out their forward defences by the bright moon. Before daybreak they had constructed a dozen spacious redoubts, walled and ditched against attack, each with three barbicans for mounted sorties.

Duke Kardefablet's marshal took over four Gates, and his army was seen there in the morning ready for combat and full of fight. As to the mighty Duke, he went into action like a true knight. Lyppaut's wife was his sister, and he himself was of stouter heart than most warlike men who continue to fight when the odds are against them, and so was often in trouble on the field. His army had marched into the fortress during the night. He had come a long way, for he was not the man to shun a fierce encounter. He strongly defended four Gates.

At Lyppaut's request all the troops on the far side of the bridge marched over into Bearosche before daybreak – Jamor's men had ridden over ahead of them. By dawn, each Gate was formidably manned: they had been entrusted to such as would assure it! Scherules chose a Gate which, together with Gawan, he did not mean to leave unguarded. The voices of some allies – I fancy it was the pick – could be heard complaining that there had been fighting in their absence and that the vesper-skirmish had passed off without their jousting. Yet such complaints were unfounded, unlimited jousts were to be had by any who cared to ride out and find them.

The streets were deeply scarred by horse-tracks. Many pennants of men riding in could be glimpsed in the moonlight, and helmets magnificently adorned whose wearers longed to take them into battle, and gaily painted lances innumerable. A Regensburger taffeta would not have been rated highly on the level ground below the walls of Bearosche, for many tabards were seen there of far more gorgeous stuffs.

Night did as it has always done, and a new day marched in

behind it, announced not by the carolling of larks but something altogether more warlike – the clang of jousters colliding! There was such an ear-splitting sound of shattering lances, you would have said the clouds were bursting. Here the youthful army of Liz was clashing with the men of Lirivoyn and with the King of Avendroyn, while the splendid jousts they gave and took popped and crackled like chestnuts thrown on the fire! Oh, how the strangers rode on that meadow and how the Inners took them on!

For the good of their souls thus at risk and their heavenly salvation, a priest read a mass for Gawan and the Burgrave. He chanted it to the glory of God and themselves. Their honour was soon to be enhanced, for this was the nature of the rite. This done, they rode to their defences. Here, their redoubt was manned by many worthy knights, Scherules's men, who were giving a good account of themselves.

What more can I tell? Haughty Poydiconjunz rode up in such strength that, running your eye over his formations, you could not have visualized a forest of spears more dense had each bush of the entire Black Forest been a shaft! He marched up with six pennants, and to meet them battle was joined thus early in the morning. Trumpets rang out with a resounding crack like dreadful thunderclaps, and their blare was accompanied by hard-working drummers. If stalks of grass were trampled down here and there, I was not to blame. Of such ruinous trampling under innumerable horses' hoof-prints, the vineyard at Erfurt still tells the tale.*

And now the Duke Astor was attacking those of Jamor. As lance was whetted on lance, many noble men lost their seat and were swept over the cruppers on to the field, so keenly did all contend, to the shouting of many strange war-cries. No few steeds were trotting round empty-saddled with their riders simply standing there – I fancy these had taken a toss.

Gawan now observed that the field was fully woven, with

* Wolfram's patron, the Landgrave Hermann of Thuringia, with his Bohemian allies besieged the Emperor Philip in Erfurt in the summer of 1203.

friends threaded among foes. He, too, measured his course into the attack. It was not easy to keep him in sight – Scherules and his men did not spare their mounts, you know, yet Gawan forced the pace till it hurt! Oh, the knights he thrust down there and the stout lances he shattered! If this man from the Table Round had not had his strength from God, we should be asking glory for Gawan. Amid all that clanging of swords he cared not a rap for either army, not for that of Liz nor for that of Gors, against which he had set his hand. He captured many mounts from both, galloped them to his host's standard and asked if anyone wanted them. Many answered 'Yes!' They were all enriched by his companionship.

At this point a knight rode up who was not given to sparing lances any more than he. Lysavander of Beauvais and courtly Gawan clashed together with the result, that, taking a fall over his charger's quarters, the young Burgrave reposed upon the flowers! This I do deplore for the sake of the young squire who had ridden in such courtly style the day before and explained to Gawan what lay behind this action. He now dismounted and bent over his lord. Recognizing him, Gawan returned the horse he had seized and, I am told, the squire thanked him with a bow. But see how Kardefablet himself stands there in the field after a joust by Meljahkanz head on! And now with cries of 'Jamor!' and fierce blows from their swords his men snatch him up! Matters grew tight there, with little room for man-œuvre, as shock succeeded shock. Helmets rang loud in their wearer's ears. Taking his company with him, Gawan delivered a mighty charge, and in a trice with his host's colour-squadron had thrown a ring round his grace of Jamor, spilling knights all over the turf. Believe it if you will, for apart from what my story tells, I have no witnesses.

Laheduman Count of Muntane now advanced against Gawan, and a fine joust was fought – with the result that mighty Laheduman measured his length on the field in his horse's tracks and, for all his proud name as a noble warrior, pledged surrender to Gawan with a handshake. Duke Astor was then fighting at the front next the redoubts, and charge followed on charge as they did battle. There were shouts of 'Nantes!,

Nantes !', King Arthur's war-cry, since there were many Britons there, unwilling exiles, and mercenaries from Erec's land of Destrigales, all stubborn fighting-men whose prowess was much in evidence. Their commander was the Duke Lanveranz. These Britons had been captured from King Arthur in a battle on Mount Cluse in the course of a great assault; but they were giving such a good account of themselves that Poydiconjunz should have set them free. Wherever they sought battle they shouted 'Nantes !' in their old style, such being their hereditary war-cry. Already the beards of some were turning grey. On helmet or shield each Briton showed a Dragonlet, a charge derived from the coat of Ilinot, Arthur's noble son. How could Gawan hold back sighs of heartfelt grief on seeing this device? He recognized this escutcheon clearly, and his eyes filled with tears at the dolorous memory of his cousin's death. He therefore left these men of Britain to fight on in that meadow and refrained from attacking them, an obligation of friendship still acknowledged today.

Instead, Gawan made for Meljanz's army. Here the defenders were acquitting themselves in a way deserving high praise, yet owing to the great odds against them, courage did not suffice them to hold their ground, so that they had retreated towards the moat. One knight, whose armour was red all over, assailed the Inners time and time again. He was styled 'Sir Nameless', for nobody knew him there.

I shall tell you as I was told it. This knight had joined Meljanz three days past, with the outcome that those of the fortress had cause to regret this aid which he had decided to give to Meljanz. Meljanz had supplied him with twelve squires from Semblidac to attend him in jousts and massed charges, yet however many lances they handed up to him he smashed them all ! Following up his thrusts, his mount charged the others' with a mighty clang of armour ! Indeed, this knight captured King Schirniel and his brother there, and more, he claimed Duke Marangliez's surrender ! These three were the spear-head. Nevertheless, their people resisted stubbornly.

King Meljanz himself was fighting there. And all (whether Meljanz had been a friend or done them mortal wrong) had to admit that rarely had so young a man acquitted himself better than he. The firm shields that he clove and the stout lances he shattered into clouds of tiny splinters, as charging squadron interlocked with squadron! His spirit was so great that he *had* to seek battle, though to his annoyance none could give it him fully till he fronted Gawan.

From his squires, Gawan took one of the twelve spears of Angram which he had acquired on the Plimizœl. Meljanz's cry was 'Barbigœl!' from his capital city of Liz. Gawan aimed his thrust with care, and the tough cane shaft from Oraste Gentesin, passing clean through Meljanz's shield and lodging in his arm, taught him the meaning of pain – a magnificent blow! Gawan sent Meljanz flying with his thrust, while his own rear saddle-bow was severed, so that, plainly, the two warriors found their feet behind their horses! Doing as best they could, they fought on with swords. They threshed more than enough to have satisfied two yokels, each carried the other's sheaf, and these they flailed to pieces. Moreover, Meljanz had to drag a spear that was sticking in his arm, and the sweat and blood were making him hot. Then all of a sudden my lord Gawan plucked him into the Brevigariezian's barbican and put pressure on him to surrender, which he was willing to do, though had the young man been unwounded none would have learned so soon that he would knuckle under, one would have been forced to spare him *that* much longer.

The lord of that land, Prince Lyppaut, was not found lacking in courage when the King of Gors attacked him. Both man and beast suffered cruelly there from arrowfire when the horse-archers of Kaheti, masters of attack-and-retreat, and the men-at-arms of Semblidac began to apply their skills, forcing the defenders to consider by what means they could keep the enemy from their outposts. The Inners deployed archers-on-foot: their redoubts were now as well guarded as anywhere today where men do their best.* Worthy men who lost their lives there were rudely apprised of Obie's anger, for her childish petulance was

---

* The Inners have been forced to deploy archers, abominated by the Knighthood and prohibited by the Church, to meet the ruthless use of horse- and other archers by the Outers.

a source of hardship to many. What had Duke Lyppaut done to deserve this? – His lord the old King Schaut would never have inflicted this on him.

The squadrons were now growing weary, yet Meljahkanz was still hard at it. You ask if his shield was intact? Not a hand's breadth remained! Duke Kardefablet then chased him far afield.

The two teams had come to rest against each other upon that flowering mead.

My lord Gawan appeared upon the scene, with the result that Meljahkanz found himself in greater trouble than when noble Lanzilot, incensed at Queen Ginover's being held captive, closed and fought with him after crossing the Bridge of Swords, and won her back in battle.*

Lot's son wheeled into the charge. What could Meljahkanz do but urge his mount on with spurs? Their joust was seen by many people. You ask 'Who was it lying there behind his horse?' It was he whom the man from Norway had lowered on to the meadow. Numerous knights and ladies witnessed the encounter and sang Gawan's praises. – The ladies had a clear view of it as they looked down from the Palace. Meljahkanz was trampled, many horses that did not live to crop young herbage again were driven to water through his surcoat, blood rained down on him! (Horses died that day as though by a pestilence, much to the vulture's gain.) Finally, Duke Astor recovered Meljahkanz from the men of Jamor, and with that the game was done.

Who rode with the greatest distinction and deserved their ladies' favour with their prowess? I could not judge their claims. Were I to name them all for you I should be a very busy man. For the Inners, great feats were performed by the knight who fought for young Obilot, and for the Outers, by the Red Knight. These two took the palm above all others beyond question.

When the guest of the Outer Army realized that no thanks for his service would be forthcoming from his captain, who had been led in a prisoner, he rode to his squires and addressed his

* An incident in the *Lancelot* of Chrétien de Troyes and an amanuensis.

own prisoners, the King of Avendroyn, Schirniel of Lirivoyn and Duke Marangliez.

'You have surrendered to me, gentlemen,' he said. 'As to me, I have suffered the misfortune that the King of Liz has been taken. So bend your efforts to releasing him, if he is to profit thus far from my good offices.' And exacting a well-phrased oath to the effect that they were either to redeem Meljanz or find the Gral for himself, he let them ride to the town. But they could not at all tell him where the Gral resided, except that a King Anfortas had the care of it.

In answer to this declaration the Red Knight said 'If nothing can come of my request, ride to Belrepeire, surrender yourself to the Queen and tell her that the man who fought Kingrun and Clamide for her sake is consumed with longing for the Gral and of course again for her love. I pine without end for both. Now tell her that I sent you to her. May God preserve you, stout warriors!'

They took their leave of him and rode in.

'We need have no fear as to our winnings,' the Red Knight told his squires. 'Take all the horses that were captured, only leave one for me. – As you see, mine is badly wounded.'

'My lord,' those good squires replied, 'thank you for helping us along so very generously. We are made for life!'

He selected one for his journey, Ingliart of the Short Ears, who had strayed away from Gawan while he was capturing Meljanz. The Red Knight had seized the beast, and many shields were holed in consequence.

He took leave and went on his way, leaving them fifteen unwounded chargers or more. The squires thanked him warmly and begged and implored him to stay: but his was a more distant goal. The charming man took a direction where great comfort was not to be had – battle was his one desire! I fancy no man of his day ever did so much fighting.

The Outer Army all marched to camp to rest their limbs.

Inside the fortress, hearing that Meljanz had been captured, Duke Lyppaut asked how it had come about. It was a happy turn of events for him and was to stand him in good stead later.

Gawan now removed the Sleeve from his shield most carefully

lest he tear it: he was aiming at greater glory.* He gave the Sleeve to Clauditte pierced and hacked though it was at its middle and end, and asked her to take it to Obilot.

When the girl saw it she was overjoyed! Her white arm had been left bare, and she quickly fastened it over. Each time she passed her sister she asked 'Who did this?' and Obie was stung to anger by this prank.

The knights were now driven to their rest by sheer exhaustion. Scherules took Gawan and Count Laheduman and he saw other gentlemen there whom Gawan had captured single-handed that day on the field which had seen so many massed assaults. The lordly Burgrave seated them all as befitted their knightly status. Weary though he and his squadron were, they remained standing till Meljanz had dined: he was at pains to see that the King should be well entertained.

This struck Gawan as excessive. 'If it please the King you should be seated, my lord host,' he said discreetly, impelled by his sense of decency to intervene. But his host declined his suggestion.

'My lord the Duke is the King's liege man,' said he. 'Had it pleased the King to accept it of him, he would have rendered this service in person. My lord has absented himself from tact, being out of favour. If God should ever mend this friendship we shall carry out all his commands.'

'During my whole stay under your roof your courtesy has been so unfailing that I have never lacked your guidance,' replied young Meljanz. 'Had I heeded your advice more, earlier on, I should be a happy man today. Now help me, Count Scherules (for I know I can rely on you in this matter) with regard to my lord who holds me captive here, and Lyppaut, my second father, who I pray will show his considerateness towards me. Both will be open to your advice. Had his daughter not made a fool of me I would never have lost Lyppaut's love. She did not behave as a lady.'

'There will be such a peace-making here,' said Gawan, 'as only death shall sever.'

* Or possibly: it was too precious to him (to tear). Gawan was to gain the 'greater glory' of reconciling Obie and Meljanz through Obilot.

201

At this moment the prisoners the Red Knight had taken came up into the royal presence and explained what had happened. When Gawan learned their adversary's coat-of-arms and to whom they had surrendered and their answer concerning the Gral, he concluded that Parzival was at the bottom of it and with bowed head rendered up thanks to Heaven that God had not let them engage in their battle-ardour that day. Their discreet silence as to their identity had seeen to it that neither was named; nor did any recognize them there, though elsewhere they were well known.

'Sire,' said Scherules to Meljanz, 'if I may request you, deign to see my lord. Assent to advice offered by friends on both sides and put your anger by.'

This met with general approval, and so, at the invitation of Prince Lyppaut's Marshal, the Inner Army of the town ascended to the hall in which the King was held prisoner. Then Gawan took Count Lahedamun and his other captives who had joined them and asked them to transfer to his host Scherules the paroles he had won from them that day. Thus they all went up to the Palace at Bearosche as promised. The Burgravine presented Meljanz with a magnificent suit of clothes and a lady's veil as sling for his arm, which Gawan had run through with his lance.

Gawan sent a message through Scherules to his lady Obilot to say that he would like to see her and assure her for all to hear that he would be her life-long Servitor, and then take his leave of her. 'And say I will make over the King to her and ask her to consider how she can so dispose of him that her conduct will be praised.'

Meljanz heard these words. 'Obilot will grow to be the flower of all womanly virtue,' he said. 'If I am to be her prisoner it will solace my heart to live here under her protection.'

'Learn this concerning her,' replied noble Gawan. 'It was she, no other, who took you prisoner, and she alone shall have the honour I reaped by it!'

And now Scherules rode up to court, where ladies both married and single together with their menfolk were all so attired that they could well dispense with mean and shabby clothes on that occasion. All who had given their parole out on the field rode to court with Meljanz. Here, Lyppaut and his wife and daughters, all four, were seated. The captives entered and went up to them, with Meljanz pacing at Gawan's side. The master of the house ran to greet his lord, while those in the Palace pressed in eagerly as he received his enemy and friends.

'If it is not too great a condescension, your old friend – I mean my wife the Duchess – would wish to welcome you with a kiss.'

'I should much like to be welcomed with a kiss by two ladies I see here,' said Meljanz to the master. 'With the third I cannot claim to be at peace.'

At this the two elder women wept. But Obilot was delighted. They received the King with their kiss and two other beardless kings besides, together with Duke Marangliez. Gawan, too, had to be kissed and take his lady in his arms. He pressed the pretty child to him in an access of loverly affection as though she were a doll!

Turning to Meljanz he said 'You pledged yourself my prisoner. I free you from your parole. Now surrender yourself here, for perched on my arm is the giver of all my joys. You are to be her prisoner!'

Meljanz stepped forward to do as he was bidden. The girl drew Gawan close to her and, strange though it all was, submission was done to Obilot, with many knights to witness.

'My lord King,' said little Obilot, 'if my knight is a merchant as my sister claimed so provokingly, it was wrong of you to surrender to him!' She then commanded King Meljanz to transfer to her sister Obie the homage done to herself. 'You must take her as your mistress to the glory of chivalry, and she must cherish you as her lover and lord always. I shall accept no excuse on either side.'

It was God himself that spoke through her young mouth: her command was obeyed on both sides.

And now Love with her great artistry, working with deepest loyalty, fashioned their affection as new. Obie's hand slipped from her cloak and took Meljanz by the arm. With her red lips she kissed the place where the lance had passed and the tears from her bright eyes rained down on it. Who was it that made her so bold with all those people looking on? It was Love, ancient ever-young.

All Lyppaut's wishes had come true, for never had such happiness befallen him. Since God had not spared him the honour he now called his child 'Sovereign Lady'.

As to how the wedding festivities went, ask those who received largesse there. And where they all rode off to, whether to a life of ease or battle, I cannot tell in full. I was told that Gawan took his leave in the Palace, to which he had climbed to say farewell. At this, Obilot burst into tears. 'Take me with you,' she cried. But he denied the sweet child her wish. Her mother could scarce tear her away from him. He then said farewell to them all.

Many times did Lyppaut assure him of his humble devotions, for he had grown very fond of Gawan, whose proud host Scherules now insisted on riding out with the brave knight in company with all his men.

Gawan's path led towards a forest, and Scherules sent huntsmen with food to go with him for a long stretch. Then the noble warrior Scherules took leave of him. Yet Gawan will be delivered up to sorrow.

Chapter 8

No matter who had come to Bearosche, Gawan had outshone them all on both sides, lone man that he was, although, unrecognized for all his red armour, one knight was seen outside whose fame was flaunted high. Gawan had his full share of honour and good fortune.

But now the time is at hand for the duel to which Gawan had been challenged though innocent. The forest he had to pass through, were he not to quit the contest, was broad and deep, and he had lost his steed Ingliart of the Short Ears, than which the Moors in Tabronit never galloped a better. The forest was of uneven growth – coppices here, bare patches there, some of such size as would scarce take a tent. Keeping a sharp look-out he saw cultivated land, Ascalun by name, and here he asked all the passers-by to direct him to Schanpfanzun, to reach which he had crossed so many ranges, traversed so many marches. And now the stranger saw a castle – with what splendour did it shine! – and to this he made his way.

Now listen to a strange tale, and as I tell it help me lament the great trouble that is to befall Gawan. My listeners, quick or slow of understanding, I appeal to your companionship: join me in sympathy with him!

Alas, I should say no more. But no, let him sink on, who has sometimes had cause to thank Fortune, but has now plunged down towards hardship!

This castle had been reared with such magnificence that when Eneas came upon Carthage (where Lady Dido forfeited her life for love) it did not seem more lordly. What palaces did it house, how many towers stood there? (Acraton had no few, which, apart from Babylon, had the broadest limits, so the infidels assert.) The walls around it and where it marched with the sea were so lofty that it feared no assault or hostility, however vehement.

Below it lay a wide plain some miles in length. Lord Gawan was passing through when five hundred knights or more came riding towards him, all in gay clothes of elegant cut, though one outshone the rest.

Their falcons were hunting the crane or whatever took flight before them, so my tale informs me. King Vergulaht was riding a tall horse of Spain. His aspect was like the sun shining through night. Mazadan had sent his lineage out before the mountain at Famurgan – Vergulaht was of that fairy race. Any who took note of the King's appearance would have thought he was looking at high May when flowers most abound. With the King shedding his lustre thus in his direction, Gawan concluded he must be a second Parzival, bearing the traits of Gahmuret when, as has been told, Gahmuret rode in to Kanvoleiz.

To elude pursuit, a heron swerved into a swamp, driven by an onrush of falcons. Going to the aid of his birds, the King missed his way across and got a wetting. As a result, he lost his horse and all his clothes as well, yet he freed his falcons from their trouble. The royal falconers took these forfeits. But were they within their rights? Yes, it was their due, they were entitled to them and must be left with what is theirs. Someone lent him a horse, and he yielded up his own. They hung another suit of clothes on him – the others were his falconers' winnings.

To this scene Gawan now came riding, and see! – They did not fail to receive him better than Erec was received at Karidœl when he returned to Arthur from his battle. He was accompanied by Lady Enite, who restored his happiness after the dwarf Maclisier with his lash in full sight of Ginover had cruelly torn his skin, which led to the duel fought in the spacious ring at Tulmeyn for the Sparrowhawk, where, to save his life, Ider fil Noyt had to offer his surrender . . .* But let that rest and listen to this tale.

I doubt if you ever heard of a finer welcome. But alas, the son of noble Lot will be rudely quit of his debt. If it is your

* Wolfram here gives the bare bones of the opening sequence of *Erec*, see p. 412.

wish I will stop short and tell no more, but turn back, lest I sadden you.

– Yet kindly listen to how a clear mind was muddied by others' duplicity. If I continue with this tale along its true course you will join me in my laments.

'My lord, I judge it best for you to ride in,' said King Vergulaht. 'I will deny you company now if you will allow it; though if you do not wish me to ride on, I will leave what I am about.'

'It shall be as you please, Sire,' replied noble Gawan, 'it is only right that you should. Do so with all my heart, I shall not be offended.'

'There, sir, is Schanpfanzun in full view,' said the King of Ascalun. 'My young sister is in residence. Of all the traits praised for beauty she has her full share. If you care to see it as a stroke of fortune she will be charged with entertaining you till I come. I shall be with you sooner than I intended, though once you have seen my sister you will be happy to wait for me and not mind if I stay longer.'

'I look forward to seeing both you and her, though great ladies have always passed me by with their estimable entertainment,' was proud Gawan's answer.

The King sent a knight to the castle with a message telling the young lady to take such good care of Gawan that hours would seem fleeting minutes. Gawan rode to where the King had commanded him.

Even now I shall pass over this distressful affair, if you wish. No, I shall tell on.

The road (not to mention a horse) took Gawan towards the Gate where the Palace ended. An architect could speak better than I on the stoutness of this building: yet here stood the best fortress ever called 'earthly mansion'. Its compass was hugely vast.

Now let us leave praising this castle, since I have much to tell you about this young lady who was sister to the King – here, too, questions of 'build' are much to the fore, on which I shall pass seemly judgement. If she had beauty it became her well, and if she had a good heart it tended to a noble nature, with the result that in her ways and temperament she resembled the Margravine* whose ample form often loomed over the Marches from Heitstein.† Lucky man who should judge of her charms in a tête-à-tête! Believe me, he would find better entertainment there than elsewhere.

I am entitled to comment on ladies as my eyes discern them. But where my remarks are well intentioned they need the restraint of your good breeding. Now let honest decent people hear this tale! I am not concerned with the dishonest, who with threadbare penitence have forfeited paradise, so that their souls are doomed to suffer Wrath.

Gawan rode up to the courtyard outside the Palace to keep the rendezvous arranged for him by the King, who was to dishonour himself by his treatment of him. The knight who conducted him to court led him in to where the handsome Princess Antikonie was seated. If feminine repute is to be had in the market, Antikonie had bought a great store; she had no truck with falsity and so was praised for her modest ways. Alas that the wise man of Veldeke‡ died so soon – he could have praised her better!

While Gawan took stock of the maiden, the messenger approached her and passed the King's message in full, after which the Princess did not forbear to say 'My lord, come here. You shall be my tutor in decorum. Now command and instruct me. For if I am to entertain you it must be just as you say. Since my brother has commended you to me so favourably I will receive you with a kiss, if protocol allows it. Now bid me kiss you or no, as you judge fit.' And she rose most courteously at his coming.

'Madam,' replied Gawan, 'your lips are so apt for kissing that I must be welcomed with a kiss.' Her mouth was hot, full and red. Gawan presented his own to it, and a kiss was given and taken such as is not customary between strangers.

The noble guest now sat down beside the well-tutored

* Elizabeth, sister to Duke Ludwig I of Bavaria and since 1204 widow of Berthold of Vohburg.
† A castle near Cham on the Bavarian frontier towards Bohemia.
‡ See p. 153, second footnote.

maiden. There was no want of conversation on either side, both charming and sincere. They found ever-new ways of framing them – he his entreaties, she her denials, so that Gawan grew deeply distressed and implored her to be kind. The girl answered as I shall tell you.

'If in other ways you are a gentleman you will consider this enough. To please my brother I have treated you so well that Ampflise did not treat Gahmuret better, short of sharing a couch. (My integrity would bring the scale down hard were she and I to be weighed.) For, sir, I do not know who you are. Yet after so short a time you seek my love.'

'My flair for genealogy tells me and I shall tell it you, madam, that I am my father's sister's brother's son. If you are inclined to have mercy on me do not hold back on grounds of birth: mine is so well up to yours as to be equal, making a perfect match.'

No sooner had a maid poured out for them than she was gone. Other ladies who had remained sitting there remembered they had things to do and went. The knight who had brought Gawan in had also left. Seeing the whole company gone Gawan reflected that a very small eagle may take the great ostrich.

He thrust his hand beneath her cloak and I fancy stroked her soft thigh – this only sharpened his torment. The man and the maid were so hard-pressed by desire that if malevolent eyes had not espied it a thing would have been done that both were intent on. Look, their bitter grief is approaching them! A knight, hoary with age, entered suddenly. Recognizing Gawan, he named him and gave the alarm.

'Out and alas, was it not enough for you to slay my lord without having to ravish his daughter here?'

Men have always heeded the alarm, and custom was honoured there and then.

'Madam, what shall we do?' Gawan asked the young lady. 'Neither of us has any weapons to speak of. If only I had my sword!'

'Let us take refuge up in that turret outside my room and there defend ourselves,' replied the noble young lady. 'Perhaps matters will take a better turn.'

Knights ran here, merchants there. She soon heard the rabble coming from the town. She took her friend Gawan to the turret, where he was soon to suffer much hardship. She implored the crowd to desist, but, what with the din and uproar, none took notice. Set on coming to blows they pressed towards the door before which Gawan had taken his stand and was now denying them entry. From the wall he tore a great bolt that was used to bar the turret, and at every flourish his bad neighbours and their men fell back. The Princess ran this way and that in search of some weapon to use against the treacherous throng, till, at last, spotless maid, she found a set of chessmen and a board, huge and beautifully inlaid. This she brought Gawan to fight with. It was hung up by an iron ring, which Gawan gripped as he took it. On this square shield much chess had been played, but now it was badly hacked away.

Hear about the lady, too. The pieces were large and heavy. Yet king or rook, she hurled them at the enemy. And it is narrated that whoever was hit by her throws was toppled, despite himself. The puissant Princess acquitted herself there like a true knight, she was seen fighting at Gawan's side with such spirit that the huckstresses at Dollenstein* never fought better of a Shrovetide, except that they do it as a frolic and exert themselves without cause. If one were asked to judge of their modesty, women who begrime themselves with armour forget their nature, unless loyal affection inspires them. In Schanpfanzun, Antikonie was made to know sorrow, and her pride was humbled. As she fought, she shed copious tears. But she gave clear proof that affection between lovers is steadfast.

But what was Gawan doing? When he had the leisure to look closely at this maiden, her mouth, eyes, nose, – I doubt if you ever saw hare on spit more neatly shaped than she, here and there, 'twixt hips and breast (her form was *made* to kindle love's desire), nor did you ever see ant more finely jointed where her girdle rested – the sight inspired manly courage in her companion. She stood firm with Gawan in their predicament. The surety specified was his very life, there was no other stipulation.

* A village in the Altmühl.

When he caught sight of the maiden he thought little of his enemies' attacks, and many lost their lives as a result.

But now King Vergulaht arrived and saw the warlike force doing battle with Gawan. Short of wishing to deceive you I cannot gloss over the fact that he is about to disgrace himself in respect of his noble guest, who is making such a stout defence here. Lord and host though he was, the sovereign did a deed that makes me sorry for King Gandin of Anjou – that his most noble lady daughter* should have borne a son who commanded a treacherous company, his own, to wage fierce war!

Gawan had to pause till the King was armed. This done, Vergulaht advanced to battle. Gawan was forced to give ground, but did so without dishonour. He was pressed back under the turret-door.

But look! Here comes the very man who had challenged him to single combat in Arthur's presence! The Landgrave Kingrimursel dug his nails through skin and scalp, he wrung his hands at Gawan's plight, since it was *his* word that had been pledged that Gawan should be immune from any bar one man. Were they young or old, he drove them all back from the turret, which the King had ordered to be pulled down.

Kingrimursel shouted up to where he could see Gawan. 'Stout knight, grant me a safe passage to join you there! I mean to share your hardships as your comrade in this extremity! If I fail to preserve your life, the King must kill me first!' Gawan gave him a safe-conduct, and the Landgrave ran up to join him. At this, the besiegers grew uncertain, for Kingrimursel was Burgrave there. Old and young, they fought in gingerly fashion, so that Gawan, followed by Kingrimursel, ran out into the open – the one was as gallant as the other.

The King exhorted his men. 'For how long are we going to suffer at the hands of these two men? My cousin here has taken it upon himself to save this man who has done me a wrong he should more fittingly avenge, had he the courage!'

Prompted by loyal feelings certain men among them chose a spokesman to the King.

* Flurdamurs, see p. 215.

'Sire, if we may speak out, there are many here who would not lift a hand against the Landgrave. May God lead you to courses we can better accept from you. Were you to slay your guest, public esteem would turn against you, you would heap shame upon yourself. Then, as to the other man in breach of whose safe-conduct you unleash this quarrel, he is your kinsman! You should refrain. You will be execrated. Now give us a truce for as long as the day lasts and let it continue overnight. You will still be able to put into execution any conclusions you have arrived at, whether it bring honour or obloquy. Free of all guile, my lady Antikonie stands there beside him all in tears. If this does not move you, seeing that one mother bore you, then consider, Sire, as a man of discretion, it was yourself sent him in to the girl. Even if none had granted him a safe-escort, his life should be spared for her sake.'

The King allowed a truce till he had taken further counsel as to how to avenge his father. (Yet Gawan was innocent; another man had done the deed. For it was proud Ehkunat who had run him through with his lance when he was leading Jofreit fiz Idœl towards Barbigœl after capturing him beside Gawan. It was all because of Ehkunat that the present crisis had arisen.)

When the truce had been agreed, the men quickly left the scene of battle and returned to their quarters. Princess Antikonie clasped her cousin tight and showered kisses on his lips for rescuing Gawan and saving himself from a shameful deed. 'You are my true cousin – it is not in you to do amiss because of anyone!'

If you care to listen I shall now acquaint you with something I mentioned earlier, namely that 'a clear mind has been muddied'. A curse on the assault that Vergulaht made at Schampfanzun, for such leanings were not inborn in him through his father or his mother. The good youth endured torments of shame whilst his sister the Princess upbraided him. It was thus that the noble young lady was heard appealing to him.

'Lord Vergulaht, had it pleased God that I should be a man and wear sword and follow the calling of the shield, you would have lost your urge to fight here. But I was an unarmed girl, except that I *did* bear shield, one with an honourable device, which I shall name if you will deign to hear it: Seemliness and Modesty, coupled with Steadfastness. This I interposed to guard my knight, whom you had sent up to me. I had no other protection. Although you are now mending your ways, you treated me very badly, if we women are to be paid due respect. I have always heard it said that whenever it chanced that a man sought refuge with a woman, the gallant pursuers, if bred to truly manly ways, should call off their attack. Lord Vergulaht, the flight of your guest to me in fear for his very life will bring deep disgrace to your name!'

Next to speak was Kingrimursel. 'When on the meadow at Plimizœl I gave Lord Gawan safe-conduct to your country, I placed my trust in you. Your word was pledge that were he to venture this far I on your behalf should guarantee that one man and no other should engage him. My lord – and I call my peers to witness – your actions have diminished me! We reject this infamy! If you do not know how to treat your great lords with due consideration, *we* shall diminish the Crown! If you have any decency you must own that your kin extends to me. Though I were your kinsman only through some furtive armour, rash man, you would have gone too far! After all, I am a knight in whom no falseness has been found to this day! May I earn the distinction so to die! – I trust to God it may be so, for which I send my hopes of Paradise into His presence to plead! Indeed, wherever it is rumoured that Arthur's nephew had come to Schanpfanzun under my escort, and people – be they of France or Britain, Burgundy, Galicia or Punturteis – hear of Gawan's peril, any renown I have will perish instantly. His desperate battle will cramp my fame, broadcast my infamy. This would cut my happiness at the root and put my honour to pawn!'

After this speech one of the King's men stood forward that went by the name of Liddamus. Kyot himself names him so.*
Now Kyot laschantiure was the name of one whose art compelled him to tell what shall gladden no few. Kyot is that noted Provençal who saw this Tale of Parzival written in the heathen-

* It is here, as a lead-in to the revelations of the following chapter, that Wolfram springs his surprise on his audience of an alleged source for his story other than Chrétien's *Perceval*. See p. 427.

213

ish tongue,* and what he retold in French I shall not be too dull to recount in German.

'What is this man, who slew my lord's father and so nearly dishonoured him, doing in his Palace?' asked Prince Liddamus. 'If my lord is a true nobleman he will avenge it here with his own hand and so let one death requite the other. I deem the penalties equal.'

Now see the pass to which Gawan has come! Now indeed did he know its dangers!

'Men who are so quick with their threats should hasten to battle,' said Kingrimursel. 'Whether you attack at close range or in the open, you are easily fought off. Lord Liddamus, I fancy I shall save this man from you, and that even if he had done you unimaginable wrong you would leave it unavenged! Your tongue has run away with you. One is justified in believing that you were never seen at the front, but on the contrary were so averse to battle that you were the first to flee. You have the further accomplishment that when your comrades were pressing on to engage, you always drew off like a woman! The crown of any king who relied on your advice would sit askew. I myself would have faced the brave warrior Gawan in the duelling-ring. I had resolved that our combat should take place here, had my lord the King been pleased to allow it. But now he bears my hostility with the load of his own misdeeds. I had hoped better things of him. Lord Gawan, give me your hand on it that you will be ready to account for yourself in single combat a year hence if it so happens that my lord will spare your life here – I will give you battle then. I challenged you beside the Plimizœl. Let our combat be at Barbigœl in the presence of King Meljanz. I shall have cares enough to wind a wreath of them till the time set to meet you in the ring. There your manly right hand shall acquaint me with care's true nature.'

Gallant Gawan complied with this request and gave his polite assurance. And at once Duke Liddamus spoke up again and delivered himself of a shrewd speech in the hearing of all. He said – for speak he had to – 'Wherever I go to war and either

* Arabic is undoubtedly intended, see p. 232, third footnote.

engage in battle or seek flight when things turn against me, my lord Landgrave, you pronounce as you can best judge of me whether I am a craven among cravens or cover myself with glory! Even though I shall never receive your pay, I stand very well with myself. If you are going to play Lord Turnus,' the mighty Liddamus went on, 'then let me be Lord Tranzes,* and censure me, *if* you know why, and do not get above yourself! Though you may rank highest among my peers the Princes, I too am a sovereign lord: I hold many fortresses throughout Galicia right over towards Vedrun.† Whatever harm you or any Briton sought to inflict on me there, I should not bring one fowl to coop for fear of you. A knight has arrived here from Britain whom you have challenged to a duel. Now avenge your lord and kinsman, but leave me out of your quarrel! If someone has slain your uncle, whose vassal you were, settle it with him! I did not harm him, nor do I imagine any will say I did. I am duly re-conciled to his loss: his heir duly wears his crown and is exalted enough to be my overlord. Queen Flurdamurs bore him. His father was Kingrisin and his grandfather King Gandin, and, to be even more precise, his maternal uncles were Gahmuret and Galoes. Unless I were plotting to harm him I could honourably take my lands in fee from him. Let them fight who wish, though I do like to hear the outcome. Let proud ladies reward those who win battle-honours – for my part I will not be deluded by love of anyone into exposing myself to undue harass-ment. Why should I play Wolfhart?‡ My path to battle is moated, my keenness for prey hooded. Though you should never forgive me for it, I would rather do as Rumolt* did, who offered advice to King Gunther when he was leaving Worms for Hunland – he asked him to toast long slices and twirl them in the cauldron!'†

* Ultimately Virgil's Drances, of the Æneid, XI, ll. 122ff.; cf. page 153, second footnote.
† Identified with Pontevedra on the coast of Galicia.
‡ A young berserker-type in the *Nibelungenlied* (see Penguin Classics, Chap. 38).
* Lord of the Royal Kitchen in Worms in the *Nibelungenlied*.
† Cf. *Nibelungenlied*, pages 185ff. Wolfram is either elaborating or quoting a different version.

'You speak as many of us have been accustomed to hear from you all your days. You are advising me to do what I myself am set on, and you claim you would do what a cook advised the Nibelungs, who blithely set out for where vengeance was wreaked on them for what had been done to Sivrit. I shall teach Gawan direst revenge, else he must slay me!'

'I quite agree,' said Liddamus. 'But even if I were to be given here all that his uncle King Arthur possesses, and the Indians, too, as they have it in their lands, and if it were made over to me without condition, I would give it up rather than fight. Now you keep the glory men accord you. Myself, I am no Segramors who has to be bound lest he fight. Yet I am well received by the King as I am. Sibeche* never drew sword and was always among those who sought flight: nevertheless people had to come to him cap in hand. Though he never hacked sword through helmet he received many great gifts and mighty fiefs from Ermenrich. My skin will never be shredded for your sake, Lord Kingrimursel, such is my firm resolve in your direction.'

'Have done with your wrangling!' said King Vergulaht. 'It displeases me in both of you that you are so free with your tongues. I am too near for you to raise your voices in this fashion, it beseems neither me nor you!'

This all took place in the Palace, to which his sister had come. At her side stood Gawan and many another worthy man.

'Now take your companion with you,' the King told her, 'and the Landgrave, too. Those who wish me well, come with me and help me weigh up what is best to be done.'

'Add your plighted word to the scales!' said his sister.

The King now goes to council. The Princess has taken her cousin and her guest, with Anxiety as third. She clasped hands decorously with Gawan and led him to where she had in mind. 'If you had not escaped, every land would have suffered loss,' was what she said to him. The son of noble Lot was walking hand in hand with her, and well might he be glad to do so! And soon she and the two men entered her chamber. Yet thanks

---

* The treacherous counsellor of King Ermenrich in heroic poems of the Dietrich (Theoderic) Cycle.

to the ministrations of her chamberlains the room remained empty of all others but for the bevy of radiant young ladies in attendance there. Here the Princess courteously entertained Gawan, for whom she cherished tenderest feelings. The Landgrave was with them meanwhile, but did not come between them. Nevertheless, I am told the noble maiden was in great fear for Gawan's life. And so the two were with the Princess in her boudoir till day gave way to night and it was time for supper.

Slender-waisted young ladies served wine, mulberry and clary, and for fine dishes pheasant, partridges, choice fish and wastel-bread. Gawan and Kingrimursel had emerged from great peril, and since it was the Princess's pleasure they fell to accordingly, as did others who wanted anything. Antikonie herself carved for them, an honour which embarrassed these gentlemen. Of all the kneeling cup-bearers there not one broke his points, for you see they were young ladies in what we still regard as their flower. I should not be surprised had they already changed their state, as a new-moulted falcon his plumes – I would not rule out this notion.

Now before the council breaks up, hear what advice was given to the King of the land. He had summoned experienced men, and they had come to his council. Certain of them had voiced their opinions to the best of their understanding, then examined it from many angles, and the King, too, bade them listen to what he had to say.

'Not a week past I was involved in a passage of arms,' he said. 'I had ridden out into the Forest of Læhtamris in search of adventure when a knight reaped too much honour from me – for without pausing he thrust me headlong over the crupper! He then made me promise to win the Gral for him. Were I to die over it, I must keep the promise he wrested from me. Advise me on this: there is urgent need. My best shield against death was that I gave him my hand on what I told you of. He is magnificent for courage and spirit! The warrior further commanded me that if I had not won the Gral when a year had passed, I should without shift or subterfuge betake myself to her who wears crown by common acclaim in Belrepeire, to Tampenteire's daughter, and that as soon as my eye lit on her I should own myself her captive. He sent her the message by me that if he were in her thoughts, his happiness would be the more; and that he it was, time past, who had delivered her from King Clamide.'

When they had heard of this affair, Liddamus spoke up once more.

'By the good leave of these lords I shall now speak: and for their part let them discuss it. Let Lord Gawan here stand in for what the other man wrung from you, beating his wings as he is over your fowling-stick! Ask him to swear to you in the presence of us all that he will win the Gral for you. Then let him ride away from you free of further molestation and strive to gain it. Were he to be slain under your roof we should all have cause to rue the shame. Now pardon him his misdeeds and win back your sister's love. He has endured great hardship here and must now choose a path that leads deathwards. For in all the lands girt by the sea there never was a house so well defended as Munsalvæsche! Wherever it lies, the way that leads there is roughened by strife. Leave him at his ease this night. Tell him our decision in the morning.' The councillors all assented, and so Gawan kept his life.

Overnight, so I am told, the warrior was given the most comfortable of quarters. Then after Mass had been sung and the morning was well advanced, there was a great press of nobles and of commoners in the Palace. The King did as he had been counselled. He summoned Gawan with intent to force him to no other course than as you yourselves have heard.

Now see where the handsome Princess Antikonie is leading Gawan together with her cousin and no few others of the King's men! She was conducting him into the royal presence hand in hand. Her head was adorned by a garland, yet her lips robbed the flowers of their splendour, since not one of them was so red! When she graciously bestowed a kiss upon a knight he was fired to shatter *forests* of lances!

We should welcome sweet, modest, true-hearted Antikonie with praises, for her conduct was such that her good name was never overrun by calumny. All who ever learned of her high repute would wish that it should stand unclouded by murky slander. Her constancy, lambent as balm,* was clear and far-sighted as a falcon's eyes urged on by a noble keenness.

'Brother,' said this sweet, felicitous young lady with all decorum, 'I bring you the knight whom you yourself asked me to take care of. Treat him well for my sake. Do not let it vex you, but think of a brother's love, and do it without regret. Manly integrity will become you better than that you should endure universal hatred, and mine – given I could hate. Teach me how to quell it!'

'I shall do so if I can, sister,' answered the charming, noble young man. 'Now you yourself advise me. You think that Wrong-doing has swooped between me and Nobility and driven me from Reputation? Were that so, how could I be your brother? For if all crowns subserved me I should renounce them at your bidding. To be hated by you would be my worst affliction. I care nothing for happiness and public esteem except as you instruct me. Lord Gawan, I have a request. You came riding to us in pursuit of renown. Now for the sake of this renown help me win my sister's forgiveness for my shortcoming. Rather than lose her affection I would overlook the mortal wrong you did me, provided you gave me your word that from now you will put your sincere endeavours to winning the Gral for me!'

This reconciliation effected, Gawan was sent forthwith to do battle for the Gral. Kingrimursel, too, forgave the King, who had lost his allegiance for breaching his safe-conduct. This was transacted in the presence of the Princes, where the swords of Gawan's squires were hanging – the squires had been separated from them during the fracas, with the result that not one of them was wounded. A man of influence in the town had begged a truce for them, then taken them and put them into prison. And now, were they Frenchmen or Britons, or from whichever land they hailed, sturdy squires and little pages, they were freed and brought to dauntless Gawan. When the pages saw him there was much embracing. Each of them clung to him in tears –

* Balsam burned with a steady glow in vessels of glass. Compare those at the Gral Ceremony, p. 125.

tears of pure affection. Count Liaz fiz Tinas from Cornwall was with him there, and another noble page attended him, Duke Gandiluz fiz Gurzgri – Gurzgri who lost his life because of Schoydelakurt where many ladies knew bereavement.* Thus Liaze was this page's aunt. His mouth, eyes and nose were Love's true kernel. All took delight in gazing at him. In addition to these two there were six other little pages. In birth, all eight young gentlemen could not be faulted, they were of high lineage. They loved him for kinship's sake and served him for his hire – distinction was the reward he gave them, and good treatment otherwise.

'Bless you, my dearest kinsmen!' said Gawan to his pages. 'I am persuaded you would have grieved for me had I been slain here!' And one could well imagine they *would* have grieved, in such a wretched state were they. 'I was very anxious on your account,' he said to them. 'Where were you when they were attacking me?' They told him, and all spoke truth. 'A merlin, a moulted one, escaped while you were sitting with the Princess, so we all ran out after it.'

Those who were standing or sitting there were taking close stock of Lord Gawan, and they judged him a gallant, well-bred man. He now asked leave to depart, which the King granted, together with the whole company with the one exception of the Landgrave. The Princess took these two and Gawan's young gentlemen and led them to where they were waited on by bevies of young ladies who would not be gainsaid, but politely saw to their needs.

When Gawan had breakfasted – I am telling you just as Kyot told it – deep attachment found vent in bitter sorrow.

'Madam,' said Gawan to the Princess, 'if I have any discernment and God preserve me, I shall be bound to devote my knight-errantry and chivalric aspirations to the service of your womanly virtue always. A happy fate has taught you to vanquish falsity, so that your honour outweighs all other! May fortune grant you her blessings! My lady, I ask leave to depart. Give it me, and let me go. May your breeding preserve your reputation!'

* See p. 99, footnote.

220

His departure filled her with sorrow, and many lovely girls wept in sympathy with her. 'Had I been able to do more for you, my happiness would have risen above my grief,' said the Princess with sincerity that was not feigned. 'As it was, no better terms were to be had for your acquittal. But believe this, whenever you are hard-pressed and your knightly calling has cast you among a host of bitter cares, I wish you to know, my lord Gawan, in victory or defeat, my heart will be there with you.'

The noble Princess kissed Gawan on the mouth. He was sadly out of spirits to be riding away from her so abruptly. If you ask me, it distressed the two of them.

Gawan's pages had seen to it that his horses had been brought to the courtyard before the Palace beneath the shade of the Castle Lime. The Landgrave had been joined by his following, so I heard, and rode out with Gawan beyond the town. Gawan courteously asked him to give himself the trouble of conducting his retinue as far as Bearosche. 'Scherules resides there, and they are to ask him themselves for an escort to Dianazdrun, where some Briton or other living there will take them to my lord, or to Queen Ginover.'

Kingrimursel promised to do so, and the gallant knight said goodbye. His charger Gringuljete was soon armed, and so was my lord Gawan. He kissed his kinsmen the pages and his noble squires, too. His vow impelled him Gralwards, and alone now as he was he rode to meet perils fantastic.

Chapter 9

'OPEN!'

'To whom? Who is there?'

'I wish to enter your heart.'

'Then you want too narrow a space.'

'How is that? Can't I just squeeze in? I promise not to jostle you. I want to tell you marvels.'

'Can it be you, Lady Adventure? How do matters stand with that fine fellow? – I mean with noble Parzival, whom with harsh words Cundrie drove out to seek the Gral, a quest from which there was no deterring him, despite the weeping of many ladies. He left Arthur the Briton then: but how is he faring now? Take up the tale and tell us whether he has renounced all thought of happiness or has covered himself with glory, whether his fame has spread far and wide or has shrivelled and shrunk. Recount his achievements in detail. Has he seen Munsalvæsche again and gentle Anfortas, whose heart was so fraught with sighs? Please tell us – how it would console us! – whether *he* has been released from suffering? Let us hear whether Parzival has been there, he who is your lord as much as mine. Enlighten me as to the life he has been leading. How has sweet Herzeloyde's child, Gahmuret's son, been faring? Tell us whether he has won joy or bitter sorrow in his battles. Does he hold to the pursuit of distant goals? Or has he been lolling in sloth and idleness? Tell me his whole style of living.'

Now the adventure tells us that Parzival has ranged through many lands on horseback and over the waves in ships. None who measured his charge against him kept his seat, unless he were compatriot or kinsman – in such fashion does he down the scales for his opponents and, whilst making others fall, raise his own renown! He has defended himself from discomfiture in many fierce wars and so far spent himself in

222

battle that any man who wished to lease fame from him had
to do so in fear and trembling.

The sword which Anfortas gave Parzival when he was with
the Gral was shattered in a duel. But the virtues of the well
near Karnant and known by the name of Lac made it whole
again. That sword helped him in winning fame. He sins who
does not believe it.*

The story makes it known to us that Parzival, brave knight,
came riding to a forest – I cannot say at what hour – where
his eyes fell on a new-built cell through which ran a fast-flowing
stream. It was reared with one end above the water. The fear-
less young knight was riding in search of adventure – and God
was graciously disposed towards him! He found an anchoress
who for the love of God had dedicated her maidenhood and
given up all joy. The seed of woman's sorrow blossomed from
her heart ever-anew, though fed by love that was old. Schion-
atulander and Sigune! – These two did he find there. The
young warrior lay buried inside, while above his tomb she led
a life of pain. Duchess Sigune never heard Mass: her life was
one long prayer on bended knee. Her full, hot, red lips were
withered and blenched now that joy of this world had deserted
her. No maiden ever endured such affliction. For her laments
she needed solitude.

For the sake of the love that had died with this prince
without his having enjoyed her, she now loved him dead as he
was. Had she become his wife, Lady Lunete would have been
slow to offer her the rash advice she gave to her own mistress.†
Even today one can often see a Lady Lunete ride in to give
counsel out of season. When a woman shuns amorous ties out-
side the marriage-bond during her husband's life-time both for
the sake of their partnership and her own decency, he has been
blessed with treasure beyond price, as I see it. No restraint
becomes her so well, and I am ready to testify, if wanted. If
he dies, let her do as her circumstances guide her. Then if she

* On this hastily improvised 'burial' of Anfortas's gift-sword, see p. 127,
footnote.

† See p. 134, second footnote.

223

still maintains their honour she would not wear so fair a garland were she to seek pleasure at the dance.

But why do I speak of pleasure in face of the suffering to which Sigune's love condemned her? I had better drop the subject.

Parzival rode up to the window over fallen trees – there was no path – nearer than he would have wished, since he merely wanted to discover his bearings in the forest. He asked for an answer there.

'Is anyone inside?'

'Yes!' answered Sigune.

Hearing a woman's voice he promptly threw his mount round on to the untrodden grass. He reproached himself and felt a stab of shame, not to have dismounted at once. He tethered his horse firmly to the branch of a fallen tree and hung his pierced and battered shield on it, too. Then the bold yet modest man ungirt his sword and laid it aside as courtesy required and went to the window in the wall to ask what he wanted to know.

That cell was empty of joy, bare of all light-heartedness. Great sorrow was all he found there. He asked her to come to the window. The pallid young lady courteously left her prayers and rose to her feet. And still he had no inkling who she was or might be. Under her grey cloak next her skin she was wearing a hair-shirt. Her lover was Great Sorrow, who laid her Gaiety down and roused many sighs from her heart.

The maiden came politely to the window and received him with a gentle greeting. She was holding a psalter in her hand, on which the warrior Parzival espied a little ring she had kept, despite her rigours, for true love's sake. Its gem-stone was a garnet that darted its rays through the window like fiery sparks. Her wimple showed bereavement.*

'There is a bench by the wall outside, sir,' she said. 'Pray be seated, if you have leisure and inclination. May God who rewards honest greetings reward you for bestowing yours on me!'

---

* Sigune may be wearing a widow's head-dress.

The knight accepted her suggestion and went and sat down at the window, with the request that she, too, be seated within.

'I have never before sat here in the presence of a man,' said she.

The knight began to question her about her régime and sustenance. 'It is inconceivable to me, madam, how you can lodge here in this wilderness so far from any road, and how you nourish yourself, since there is no cultivation anywhere around you.'

'My nourishment is brought to me from the Gral by Cundrie la surziere punctually every Saturday evening, this is how she has arranged it. Well provided for with food as I am, I have little anxiety on that score – would that I were as content in other ways!'

Parzival fancied she was lying and might well deceive him further. 'For whose sake are you wearing your ring?' he asked banteringly through the window. 'I have always heard it said that anchoresses and anchorites should refrain from having love-affairs!'

'If your words had power to do so you would make me an imposter. If ever I learn fraud, point it out, if you happen to be there! Please God, I am free of all deceit. It is not in me to thwart truth! I wear this engagement-ring for the sake of a dear man,' she went on, 'of whose love I never took possession by any human deed: yet my maiden's heart impels me to love him. Here inside, I have the man whose jewel I have worn ever since Orilus slew him in joust, and I shall give him love through the joyless days that remain to me. It is true love that I shall bestow on him, for he strove to win it in chivalric style with shield and lance till he died in my service. I am a virgin and unwed: yet before God he is my husband. If thoughts could produce deeds, then I have no hidden reservation that could impede my marriage. His death wounded my life. And so this ring, token of true wedlock, shall assure my safe passage to God. The torrent welling up from my heart and through my eyes guards my steadfast love.* There are

* In an obscure image Wolfram may be thinking of a stronghold moated on one or both flanks by a torrent.

two of us in here. Schionatulander is one, I am the other.'

Hearing this, Parzival realized she was Sigune and was deeply affected by her sorrow. In haste he bared his head from his coif before addressing her again. The young lady then glimpsed the fair skin gleaming through the rust and recognized the gallant knight.

'You are Parzival! Tell me, how have you fared with regard to the Gral? Have you at last got to know its nature? Or what turn has your quest now taken?'

'I have forfeited much happiness in that endeavour,' he told the well-born maiden. 'The Gral gives me no few cares. I left a land over which I wore a crown, and a most lovable wife, too, than whom no fairer person was ever born of human kind. I long for her modest, courteous ways, and often pine for her love – yet even more for that high goal as to how to see Munsalvæsche and the Gral! For this has not yet come to pass. Cousin Sigune, unacquainted with all my many sorrows as you are, it is very unjust of you to treat me as your enemy.'

'All cause I had to censure you, cousin, shall be forgiven,' said the girl, 'for you have indeed forfeited much happiness after neglecting to ask the Question that would have brought you high honour, when gentle Anfortas was your host and your good fortune. A Question would have won you all the heart can wish for: but now perforce your happiness turns tail on you, and your high spirits limp behind. Your heart has made Care its familiar that would have remained a stranger had you asked to be told.'

'I acted as an ill-starred man,' he said. 'Dear cousin, give me your advice. Remember that we are blood-relations and tell me for your part how matters stand with you. I should mourn your sorrows, did I not bear a greater load of suffering than ever any man bore. My burden threatens to crush me.'

'May the hand of Him to Whom all suffering is known succour you! – What if you should prove so lucky that a track should lead you to where you can see Munsalvæsche, with which, so you tell me, your whole happiness is bound up! Cundrie la surziere rode away from here quite recently. I am sorry I did not ask her whether she was going to Munsalvæsche or to some other place. When she comes here her mule always stands over there, where the spring gushes from the rock. I advise you to ride after her. Most likely she will not be riding ahead of you so fast that you could not soon catch up with her.'

The warrior at once took his leave and set out along the fresh track. Cundrie's mule had gone that way: but tangled undergrowth baulked him of the path which he had chosen, and so the Gral was lost a second time, and his happiness utterly dashed. Had he arrived at Munsalvæsche, he would assuredly have done better with the Question than on the earlier occasion you know of.

Now let him ride on. Where is he to go?

A man came riding towards him, bare-headed but wearing a sumptuous tabard above his shining armour. Indeed, but for his head, he was fully caparisoned. He advanced against Parzival at speed.

'Sir,' he said, 'it displeases me that you beat a track through my lord's forest in this fashion. I shall give you a reminder such as you will regret. Munsalvæsche is unaccustomed to having anyone ride so near without fighting a desperate battle or offering such amends as those beyond our forest call "death".'

In one hand he carried a helmet whose attachment was of silver cords and a keen lance-head helved on a new shaft. In high dudgeon the warrior laced his helmet level on to his head. His threats and his bellicosity were soon to cost him dear, yet all unaware he made ready for the joust.

Parzival, too, had shattered many lances no less fine. 'Were I to ride over this man's crops nothing could save me, how should I escape his wrath? As it is, I am only trampling his wild bracken. Unless my arms and hands fail me, I shall ransom my passage without his binding me.'*

On both sides they gave free rein for the gallop, then drove with the spur and pulled their mounts into full tilt – and of neither did the thrust miss its mark! Parzival's high chest had

* Trespassers on the harvest-field were bound with straw and released only on payment of a ransom, see p. 185.

braved many lance-thrusts, while, guided with zest and skill, his went cleanly and accurately to where the other's helmet-lace was knotted. He struck his man at the spot where you hang your shield at tournaments, with the result that the Templar* from Munsalvæsche rolled from his saddle down a deep gulley in the mountain-side so far that his couch knew no rest. Parzival followed his joust through with his horse racing ahead so that it pitched down and smashed its bones. He himself gripped a bough of a cedar with both hands – now do not account it a disgrace in him that he hanged himself without an executioner! – then caught firm rock beneath him with his feet. Down below him his charger lay dead in the thick under-growth. The other knight was making all speed to safety up the farther side of the gulley. Had he been intending to share any gain won from Parzival, as matters turned out, the Gral back home had more to offer!

Parzival climbed back again. The reins of the horse which the other had left behind were dangling down, and it had stepped through them and was waiting as though told to do so. When Parzival had taken his seat in the saddle he had lost nothing but his lance; but in view of what he had found he was reconciled to the loss. If you ask me, neither the mighty Làhelin, nor proud Kingrisin, nor King Gramoflanz, nor Count Lascoyt fiz Gurnemanz ever rode a better joust than that in which this war-horse was won.

Parzival then rode on with no notion of where he was going, but in such direction that the Company of Munsalvæsche did not come into conflict with him. It grieved him that the Gral kept so aloof from him.

If anyone cares to hear it I will reveal to him how Parzival fared thereafter. But I shall not number the weeks during which Parzival rode seeking adventure as before.

One morning a light mantle of snow lay on the ground, yet of a depth that would make us shiver today. This was in a great forest. And now an old knight came towards him, beside

* See p. 438.

whose grizzled beard his skin shone clear. His wife was as grey-haired as he. Over their bare bodies they both wore coarse grey cloaks on their pilgrimage to and from Confession. His daughters, two young ladies most pleasing to the eye, went in the same habit, as their chaste hearts prompted them. All went barefoot. Parzival saluted the grey knight as he came on. (His counsel was to bring Parzival good fortune, later.) He had all the appearance of a lord. Ladies' lap-dogs ran along beside them. Other knights and squires, many of them young and beardless, were walking on this pilgrimage, meekly and decorously, their pride subdued.

Parzival, noble warrior, had cared for his person so well that his magnificent caparison was in all ways worthy of a knight. In such splendid armour did he ride that the clothes of the grey man riding towards him were quite outshone. With a tug at the reins he quickly turned his horse aside from the path. He questioned the good people on their journey and was answered with gentle speech. Yet the grey knight reproached him that the Holy Season had given him no cause to ride unarmed or walk barefoot in observance of the Day.

'My lord,' replied Parzival, 'I have no knowledge whatever as to when the year begins or the number of the passing weeks or of what day of the week it is. – This is all unknown to me. I used to serve one named "God" till it pleased Him to ordain such vile shame for me. Told to look to Him for help, I never failed Him in devotion: yet there is no help for me there.'

'Do you mean God born of the Virgin?' asked the grey knight. 'If you believe in His Incarnation and His Passion for us this Day which we are now observing, this armour ill beseems you. Today is Good Friday, in which the whole world can rejoice and at the same time mourn in anguish. Where was greater loyalty seen than that shown by God for our sakes when they hung Him on the Cross? If you are of the Christian faith, sir, let this traffic afflict you: He bartered His noble life in death in order to redeem our debt, in that Mankind was damned and destined to Hell for our sins. Unless you are a heathen, sir, remember what Day this is. Ride on along our tracks. Not too far ahead there sits a holy man; he will advise you and allot penance for your misdeed. If you show yourself contrite, he will take your sins away.'

'Why are you so unfriendly, father?' asked his daughters. 'With the foul weather we now have, how can you venture to give him such advice? Why don't you take him to where he can warm himself? However splendid his arms look in their casing of steel, we fancy they must be very cold! Though there were three of him, he would freeze! You have tents nearby, and rough-woollen shelters, and if King Arthur were to call on you, you would keep him well supplied with victuals. Now do as a good host should, and take this knight away with you!'

'My daughters speak truly, sir,' said the grey-haired man. 'Every year, in all weathers, as the Day of His Passion approaches, Who gives sure reward for our devotions, I set out from a place nearby through this wild forest. I will gladly share with you the poor fare I have brought with me on this holy observance.'

The young ladies eagerly entreated him to stay and earnestly assured him that he would be an honoured guest. When Parzival looked at them he saw that although their lips were dry from frost they were red, full and hot, out of keeping with the Sorrows of that Day. If *I* had some petty score to settle with them I should be lothe to waive my due, but would take a kiss if they wished to make it up again. When all is said, women will always be women. They will subdue a mettlesome man in a trice, they have brought it off repeatedly. Parzival listened to the charming invitations assailing him from all sides, from father, mother and daughters, and thought 'If I stop I would nevertheless not wish to go along with this company. These girls are so lovely that it would be wrong for me to ride beside them with all of them walking. It would be more fitting if I left them, seeing that I am at feud with Him Whom they love with all their hearts and look to for help but Who has shut me out from His succour and failed to shield me from sorrow.'

Parzival answered them at once. 'My lord and lady,' he said. 'Give me leave to go. May you prosper and enjoy abundant happiness! As to you young ladies, may your courtesy be rewarded for wishing to make me so comfortable. You must allow me to go.' He inclined his head, and they theirs. They could not hide their regret.

Herzeloyde's child rides on. His manly discipline enjoined modesty and compassion in him. Since young Herzeloyde had left him a loyal heart, remorse now began to stir in it. Only now did he ponder Who had brought the world into being, only now think of his Creator and how mighty He must be. 'What if God has such power to succour as would overcome my sorrow?' he asked himself. 'If He ever favoured a knight and if any knight ever earned His reward or if shield and sword and true manly ardour can ever be so worthy of His help that this could save me from my cares and if this is His Helpful Day, then let Him help, if help He can!'

He turned back in the direction whence he had ridden. They were still standing there, saddened by his departure, for they were loyal-hearted people. The young ladies followed him with their eyes, while he in turn confessed in his heart that they pleased his eyes – for their bright looks declared them beautiful.

'If God's power is so great that it can guide horses and other beasts and people, too, then I will praise His power. If the wisdom of God disposes of that help, let it guide my castilian to the best success of my journey – then in His goodness He will show power to help! Now go where God chooses!' He laid the reins over his horse's ears and urged him on hard with his spurs.

The beast made for Fontane la Salvæsche, where Orilus had received the oath. This was the abode of the austere Trevrizent, who ate miserably many a Monday and no better all through the week. He had forsworn wine, mulberry and bread. His austerity imposed further abstinence: he had no mind for such food as fish or meat or anything with blood. Such was the holy life he led. God had inspired this gentleman to prepare to join the heavenly host. He endured much hardship from fasting. Self-denial was his arm against the Devil.

From Trevrizent, Parzival is about to learn matters concerning the Gral that have been hidden. Those who questioned me earlier and wrangled with me for not telling them* earned nothing but shame. Kyot† asked me to conceal it because his source forbade him to mention it till the story itself reached that point expressly where it *has* to be spoken of.

The famous Master Kyot found the prime version of this tale in heathenish‡ script lying all neglected in a corner of Toledo. He had had to learn the characters' A B C beforehand without the art of necromancy. It helped him that he was a baptized Christian – otherwise this tale would still be unknown. No infidel art would avail us to reveal the nature of the Gral and how one came to know its secrets.

There was a heathen named Flegetanis who was highly renowned for his acquirements. This same physicus was descended from Solomon, begotten of Israelitish kin all the way down from ancient times till the Baptism became our shield against hellfire. He wrote of the marvels of the Gral. Flegetanis, who worshipped a calf as though it were his god, was a heathen* by his father. – How can the Devil make such mock of such knowledgeable people, in that He Whose power is greatest and to Whom all marvels are known neither does nor did not part them from their folly? For the infidel Flegetanis was able to define for us the recession of each planet and its return, and how long each revolves in its orbit before it stands at its mark again. All human kind are affected by the revolutions of the planets. With his own eyes the heathen Flegetanis saw – and he spoke of it reverentially – hidden secrets in the constellations. He declared there was a thing called the Gral, whose name he read in the stars without more ado. 'A troop left it on earth and then rose high above the stars, if their innocence drew them back again.† Afterwards a Christian progeny bred to a pure life had the duty of keeping it. Those humans who are summoned to the Gral are ever worthy.' Thus did Flegetanis write on this theme.

* This must have been on the occasion of the performance of Chapter 5.
† See p. 213 and footnote.
‡ Doubtless Arabic.
* Muslim.
† The Neutral Angels, see pp. 240, 396 and 436.

The wise Master Kyot embarked on a search for this tale in Latin books in order to discover where there may have been a people suited to keep the Gral and follow a disciplined life. He read the chronicles of various lands in Britain and elsewhere, in France and Ireland; but it was in Anjou that he found the tale. He read the truth about Mazadan beyond a peradventure – the account of the latter's whole lineage was faithfully recorded there – and on the distaff side how Titurel and his son Frimutel bequeathed the Gral to Anfortas, whose sister was Herzeloyde on whom Gahmuret begot a son to whom this tale belongs, and who is now riding along the fresh tracks left by the grey knight that met with him ...

Despite the snow on the ground Parzival recognized a spot where once upon a time dazzling flowers had stood. It was at the foot of an escarpment where, with his manly right hand, he had made Orilus relent towards Lady Jeschute, and Orilus's anger had evaporated. But the tracks did not let him stop there: Fontane la Salvæsche was the locality towards which his journey tended. Parzival found its lord at home, and he received him.

'Alas, sir,' said the hermit, 'that you should be in this condition at Holy-tide. Was it some desperate encounter that forced you into this armour? Or had you no fighting to do? – In which case other garb would have been seemlier if your pride permitted it. Pray dismount, sir – I fancy you will have no objection – and warm yourself beside the fire. If thirst for adventure has brought you out with an eye to winning Love's reward and it is True Love you favour, then love as Love is now in season, and in keeping with the Love of this Day! After that, serve women for their favour. But please do dismount, if I may invite you.'

The warrior Parzival alighted at once and stood before him with great courtesy. He told him of the people who had pointed out the way and how they had praised his guidance.

'Sir,' he said, 'guide me now: I am a sinner.'

In answer to these words the good man said: 'I shall give you guidance. Now tell me who directed you here to me.'

'Walking towards me in the forest, sir, there came a grey-haired man. He saluted me kindly, as did his retinue. That same honest person sent me here to you, and I rode along his tracks till I found you.'

'That was Gabenis,' said his host. 'He is versed to perfection in noble ways. The Prince is a Punturteis, the mighty King of Kareis married his sister. No fruit of human body was ever purer than his daughters who came walking towards you in the forest! The Prince is of royal line. He visits me here each year.'

'When I saw you standing in my path, were you at all afraid as I rode up to you?' Parzival asked his host. 'Did my coming irk you?'

'Believe me, sir,' replied the hermit, 'bears and stags have startled me more often than man. I can tell you truly: I fear nothing of human kind, since I, too, possess human ability. If you will not think me boastful, I declare I never fled the field; nor am I innocent of love. My heart never knew the villainy of turning tail in battle. While I bore arms I was a knight like you and strove to win the love of noble ladies. From time to time I paired chaste with sinful thoughts. I lived in dazzling style to win a lady's favour. But I have forgotten these things. Give me your bridle. Your horse shall rest at the foot of that cliff. Then, soon, we shall go and gather some young fir-tips and bracken for him – I have no other fodder. Nevertheless we shall keep him in good fettle.'

Parzival made as though to prevent him from taking the bridle.

'Your good manners do not permit you to struggle with your host short of lowering themselves,' said the good man. And so Parzival yielded the bridle to his host, who then led the horse beneath the overhanging rock where the rays of the sun never came – a wild stable indeed! A waterfall gushed down through it. A weak man would have been hard put to it, wearing armour where the bitter cold could strike him in this fashion. His host led Parzival into a grotto, well protected from the wind and with a fire of glowing charcoal which the stranger could well put up with! The master of the house lit a candle, and the warrior removed his armour and reclined on a bed of straw and ferns, while all his limbs grew warm and his skin shone clear. No wonder he was weary from the forest, since he had ridden along few roads and passed the night with no roof over his head till day-break, and many another, too. But now he had found a kind host.

There was a coat lying there. The hermit lent it him to put on and then took him to another grotto, where the austere man kept the books he read. An altar-stone stood there bare of its cloth, in keeping with the Good Friday rite. On it a reliquary could be seen which was instantly recognized – Parzival had laid his hand on it to swear an unsullied oath on the occasion when Lady Jeschute's suffering was changed to joy, and her happiness took an upward turn.

'I know this casket, sir,' said Parzival to his host, 'for I once swore an oath on it when passing by. I found a painted lance beside it. Sir, I took that lance and was told later that I advanced my reputation with it. I was so absorbed in thoughts of my wife that I lost my self-awareness. I rode two mighty jousts with it – I fought them both in utter obliviousness! Honour had not yet deserted me. But now I have more cares than were seen in any man. Kindly tell me, how long is it since the time I took the lance from here?'

'My friend Taurian left it behind,' replied the good man. 'He told me he missed it, later. It is now four-and-a-half years and three days since you took it.* If you care to listen I will reckon it out for you.' And from his psalter he read him the full count of the years and weeks that had elapsed in the meantime.

'Only now,' said Parzival, 'do I realize how long I have been wandering with no sense of direction and unsustained by any happy feelings. Happiness for me is but a dream: I bear a heavy pack of grief. And I will tell you more. All this time I was never seen to enter any church or minster where God's praise was sung. All I sought was battle. I am deeply resentful of God, since He stands godfather to my troubles: He has lifted them up too high,† while my happiness is buried alive.

* See p. 432.
† As though children from the font.

If only God's power would succour me, what an anchor my happiness would be, which now sinks into sorrow's silt! If my manly heart is wounded – can it be *whole* when Sorrow sets her thorny crown on glory won by deeds of arms from formidable foes? – then I set it down to the shame of Him who has all succour in His power, since if He is truly prompt to help He does not help me – for all the help they tell of Him!'

His host sighed and looked at him. 'Sir,' he said, 'if you have any sense you will trust in God. He will help you, since help He must. May God help both of us! You must give me a full account, sir – but *do* sit down first! Tell me soberly how your anger began so that God became the object of your hatred. Yet kindly bear with me while I tell you He is innocent, before you accuse Him in my hearing. His help is always forthcoming.

'Although I was a layman I could read and indite the message of the Scriptures: that to gain His abundant help mankind should persevere in God's service, Who never wearied of giving His steadfast aid against the soul's being plunged into Hell. Be unswervingly constant towards Him, since God Himself is perfect constancy, condemning all falsity. We should allow Him to reap the benefit of having done so much for us, for His sublime nature took on human shape for our sakes. God is *named* and *is* Truth, He was Falsity's foe from the Beginning. You should ponder this deeply. It is not in Him to play false. Now school your thoughts and guard against playing Him false.

'You can gain nothing from Him by anger. Anyone who sees you hating Him would think you weak of understanding. Consider what Lucifer and his comrades achieved! As angels they had no gall: so where in God's name did they find the malice that makes them wage ceaseless war, whose reward in Hell is so bitter? Astiroth and Belcimon, Belet and Radamant and others I could name – this bright heavenly company took on a hellish hue as the result of their malice and envy.

'When Lucifer made the descent to Hell with his following, a Man succeeded him. For God made noble Adam from earth. From Adam's body He then broke Eve, who consigned us to tribulation by not listening to her Maker and thus shattered our bliss. Through birth these two had progeny. One son was driven by his discontent and by vainglorious greed to deflower his grandmother. Now it might please many to ask, before they understood this account, how this is possible? It nevertheless came to pass, and sinfully.'

'I doubt that it ever happened,' interposed Parzival. 'From whom was the man descended by whom, according to you, his grandmother lost her maidenhead? You ought never to have said such a thing.'

'I will remove your doubts,' his host replied. 'If I do not tell the unvarnished truth you must object to my deceiving you! The earth was Adam's mother, by her fruits Adam was nourished. The earth was still a virgin then. It remains for me to tell you who took her maidenhead. Adam was father to Cain, who slew Abel for a trifle. When blood fell upon the pure earth her virginity was gone, taken by Adam's son. This was the beginning of hatred among men, and thus it has endured ever since.

'There is nothing in the whole world so pure as an honest maiden. Consider the purity of maidens: God Himself was the Virgin's child. Two men were born of virgins: God Himself took on a countenance like that of the first virgin's son, a condescension from His sublimity. With Adam's race there began both sorrow and joy, for he whom all angels see above them* does not deny our consanguinity, and his lineage is a vehicle of sin; so that we, too, have to bear our load of it. May the power of Him Who is compassionate show mercy here! Since His faithful Humanity fought faithfully against unfaithfulness you should put your quarrel with Him by. Unless you wish to forfeit your heavenly bliss admit penance for your sins. Do not be so free of word or deed – let me tell you the reward of one who slakes his anger in loose speech. He is damned by his own mouth! Take old sayings for new, if they teach you constancy. In ancient times the vates Plato and Sibyl

* After the Harrowing of Hell, Christ took the souls of the Patriarchs with him, so that it could be assumed that Adam, representing Man, already sits in the choir above the angels.

the Prophetess truly foretold beyond all error that a surety would come to us for greatest debts. In His divine love He that is highest of all released us in Hell* and left the wicked inside.

'These glad tidings tell of the True Lover. He is a light that shines through all things, unwavering in His love. Those to whom He shows His love find contentment in it. His wares are of two sorts: He offers the world love and anger. Now ask yourself which helps more. The unrepentant sinner flees God's love: but he that atones for his sins serves Him for His noble favour.

'He that passes through men's thoughts bears such Grace. Thoughts keep out the rays of the sun, thoughts are shut away without a lock, are secure from all creatures. Thoughts are darkness unlit by any beam. But of its nature, the Godhead is translucent, it shines through the wall of darkness and rides with an unseen leap unaccompanied by thud or jingle. And when a thought springs from one's heart, none is so swift but that it is scanned ere it pass the skin – and only if it be pure does God accept it. Since God scans thoughts so well, alas, how our frail deeds must pain him!

'When a man forfeits God's benevolence so that God turns away in shame, to whose care can human schooling leave him? Where shall the poor soul find refuge? If you are going to wrong God, Who is ready with both Love and Wrath, you are the one who will suffer. Now so direct your thoughts that He will requite your goodness.'

'Sir, I shall always be glad that you have taught me about Him Who leaves nothing unrewarded, whether virtue or misdeed,' said Parzival. 'I have spent my youth in care and anxiety until this day and endured sorrow for the sake of loyalty.'

'Unless you do not wish to divulge them, I should like to hear your sins and sorrows,' replied his host. 'If you will let me judge of them I might well be able to give advice you could not give yourself.'

---

* Wolfram here seems to merge the just pagans of the pre-Christian era with good Christians of the new age.

'My deepest distress is for the Gral,' replied Parzival. 'After that it is for my wife, than whom no fairer creature was ever given suck by mother. I languish and pine for them both.'

'You are right, sir,' said his host. 'The distress you suffer is as it should be, since the anguish you give yourself comes from longing for the wife that is yours. If you are found in holy wedlock, however you may suffer in Purgatory, your torment shall soon end, and you will be loosed from your bonds immediately through God's help. You say you long for the Gral? You foolish man – this I must deplore! For no man can win the Gral other than one who is acknowledged in Heaven as destined for it. This much I have to say about the Gral, for I know it and have seen it with my own eyes.'

'Were you there?' asked Parzival.

'Indeed, sir,' was his host's reply.

Parzival did not reveal to him that he, too, had been there, but asked to be told about the Gral.

'It is well known to me,' said his host, 'that many formidable fighting-men dwell at Munsalvæsche with the Gral. They are continually riding out on sorties in quest of adventure. Whether these same Templars reap trouble or renown, they bear it for their sins. A warlike company lives there. I will tell you how they are nourished. They live from a Stone whose essence is most pure. If you have never heard of it I shall name it for you here. It is called "Lapsit exillis"*. By virtue of this Stone the Phoenix is burned to ashes, in which he is reborn. – Thus does the Phoenix moult its feathers! Which done, it shines dazzling bright and lovely as before! Further: however ill a mortal may be, from the day on which he sees the Stone he cannot die for that week, nor does he lose his colour. For if anyone, maid or man, were to look at the Gral for two hundred years, you would have to admit that his colour was as fresh as in his early prime, except that his hair would grey! – Such powers does the Stone confer on mortal men that their flesh and bones are soon made young again. This Stone is also called "The Gral".

* Or some such Latin or pseudo-Latin name, see p. 431ff.

'Today a Message alights upon the Gral governing its highest virtue, for today is Good Friday, when one can infallibly see a Dove wing its way down from Heaven. It brings a small white Wafer to the Stone and leaves it there. The Dove, all dazzling white, then flies up to Heaven again. Every Good Friday, as I say, the Dove brings it to the Stone, from which the Stone receives all that is good on earth of food and drink, of paradisal excellence – I mean whatever the earth yields. The Stone, furthermore, has to give them the flesh of all the wild things that live below the aether, whether they fly, run or swim – such prebend does the Gral, thanks to its indwelling powers, bestow on the chivalric Brotherhood.

'As to those who are appointed to the Gral, hear how they are made known. Under the top edge of the Stone an Inscription announces the name and lineage of the one summoned to make the glad journey. Whether it concern girls or boys, there is no need to erase their names, for as soon as a name has been read it vanishes from sight! Those who are now full-grown all came here as children. Happy the mother of any child destined to serve there! Rich and poor alike rejoice if a child of theirs is summoned and they are bidden to send it to that Company! Such children are fetched from many countries and forever after are immune from the shame of sin and have a rich reward in Heaven. When they die here in this world, Paradise is theirs in the next.

'When Lucifer and the Trinity began to war with each other, those who did not take sides, worthy, noble angels, had to descend to earth to that Stone which is forever incorruptible. I do not know whether God forgave them or damned them in the end:* if it was His due He took them back. Since that time the Stone has been in the care of those whom God appointed to it and to whom He sent his angel. This, sir, is how matters stand regarding the Gral.'

'If knightly deeds with shield and lance can win fame for one's earthly self, yet also Paradise for one's soul, then the chivalric life has been my one desire!,' said Parzival. 'I fought

* See p. 232 and last footnote.

240

wherever fighting was to be had, so that my warlike hand has glory within its grasp. If God is any judge of fighting He will appoint me to that place so that the Company there know me as a knight who will never shun battle.'

'There of all places you would have to guard against arrogance by cultivating meekness of spirit,' replied his austere host. 'You could be misled by youthfulness into breaches of self-control. – Pride goes before a fall!' Thus his host, whose eyes filled with tears as he recalled the story he was now to tell in full.

'Sir, there was a king who went by the name of Anfortas, as he does today,' he said. 'The agony with which he was punished for his pride should move you and wretched me to never-ending pity! His youth and wealth and pursuit of love beyond the restraints of wedlock brought harm to the world through him. Such ways do not suit the Gral. In its service knights and squires must guard against licentiousness: humility has always mastered pride. A noble Brotherhood lives there, who by force of arms have warded off men from every land, with the result that the Gral has been revealed only to those who have been summoned to Munsalvæsche to join the Gral Company. Only one man ever came there without first having been assigned.* *He had not reached years of discretion!* He went away saddled with sin in that he said no word to his host on the sad plight in which he saw him. It is not for me to blame anyone: but he will be bound to pay for his sin of failing to inquire about his host's hurt. For Anfortas bore a load of suffering, the like of which had never been seen. Before this man's visit, King Lähelin had ridden to Brumbane. Here the noble knight Lybbeals of Prienlascors had waited to joust with him, and by joust had met his death. Lähelin led the warrior's charger away, thus plainly despoiling the dead.

'Sir, are you Lähelin? In my stable there is a horse of the same coat as those belonging to the Gral Company. The horse comes from Munsalvæsche because its saddle shows the Turtle-dove, the device which Anfortas gave for horses when happi-

* Because of Parzival's immaturity, Providence had announced, but not assigned him.

241

ness was still his, though their shields have always borne it. Titurel handed it down to his son King Frimutel, who, brave knight, was displaying it when he lost his life in a joust. Frimutel loved his wife so dearly that no wife was ever loved more by husband, I mean with such devotion. You should renew his ways and love your spouse with all your heart. Follow his example – you bear him a close resemblance! He was also Lord of the Gral. Ah, sir, from where have you journeyed? Kindly tell me from whom you are descended.'

Each looked the other in the eyes.

'I am the son of a man who, impelled by knightly ardour, lost his life in a joust,' Parzival told his host. 'I beg you to include him in your prayers, sir. My father's name was Gahmuret, and by birth he was an Angevin. Sir, I am not Lähelin. If I ever stripped a corpse it was because I was dull of understanding. However, I did this thing, I confess myself guilty of the crime. I slew Ither of Cucumerlant with my sinful hand, I stretched him out dead on the grass and took what there was to take.'

'Alas, wicked World, why do you so?' cried his host, saddened by this news. 'You give us more pain and bitter sorrow than ever joy! So this is the reward you offer, such is the end of your song? Dear nephew,' he went on, 'what counsel can I give you now? You have slain your own flesh and blood. If you take this misdeed unatoned to the Judgment into the presence of God and He judges you with strict justice, it will cost you your own life, since you and Ither were of one blood.* What payment will you make Him for Ither of Gaheviez? God had made manifest in him the fruits of true nobility which enhanced life's quality. All wrong-doing saddened him who was the very balm of constancy! All obloquy of this world fought shy of him, all that is noble made its way into his heart! Worthy ladies ought to hate you for the loss of his lovable person. His service of them was so entire that when they saw the charming man their eyes shone. May God have pity on it that you were ever the cause of such distress! Add to that,

* See the Glossary of Personal Names, under 'Ither'.

your mother, my sister Herzeloyde, died of anguish for you!'

'Oh no, good sir!' cried Parzival. 'What are you saying now? Were that so and I were Lord of the Gral it could not console me for what you have just told me! If I am your nephew, do as all sincere people do and tell me straight: are these two things true?'

'It is not in me to deceive,' answered the good man. 'No sooner had you left your mother than she died – that was what she had for her love. You were the Beast she suckled, the Dragon that flew away from her. It had come upon her as she slept, sweet lady, before giving birth to you. I have a brother and a sister living. My sister Schoysiane bore a child and died bearing that fruit. Her husband was Duke Kyot of Katelangen, who henceforth renounced all happiness. His little daughter Sigune was entrusted to your mother's care. Schoysiane's death afflicts me utterly – how could it fail to? Her womanly heart was so virtuous, it might have been an ark afloat on the flood of wantonness! A sister of mine is as yet unwed and keeps her chastity. She is Repanse de Schoye and has charge of the Gral, which is so heavy that sinful mortals could not lift it from its place. Her brother and mine is Anfortas, who was Lord of the Gral by heredity and so remains. Alas, happiness lies far beyond his reach, apart from his firm hope that his sufferings will earn him bliss eternal! Things came to this sad pass in a way scarce short of marvellous, as I shall tell you, nephew. If you have a good heart you will be moved to pity by his sorrows.

'When my father Frimutel lost his life, his eldest son was summoned to the Gral as King and Lord Protector both of the Gral and its Company. This was my brother Anfortas, who was worthy of the Crown and its dominion. At that time we were still quite small. But when my brother approached the age at which the first bristles begin to show, Love assailed him, as is her way with striplings – she presses her friends so hard that one may call it dishonourable of her. But any Lord of the Gral who seeks love other than that allowed him by the Writing will inevitably have to pay for it with pain and suffering fraught with sighs.

'As the object of his attentions my lord and brother chose a lady whom he judged of excellent conduct – as to who she was, let it rest. He served her with unflinching courage, and many shields were riddled by his fair hand. As knight-errant the charming, comely youth won fame so exalted that he ran no risk of its being surpassed by any in all the lands of chivalry. His battle-cry was "Amor!", yet that shout is not quite right for humility.

'One day – his nearest and dearest did not at all approve – the King rode out alone to seek adventure under Love's compulsion and joying in her encouragement. Jousting, he was wounded by a poisoned lance so seriously that he never recovered, your dear uncle – through the scrotum. The man who was fighting there and rode that joust was a heathen born of Ethnise, where the Tigris flows out from Paradise. This pagan was convinced that his valour would earn him the Gral. His name was engraved on his lance. He sought chivalric encounters in distant countries, crossing seas and lands with no other thought than to win the Gral. As a result of his prowess, our happiness vanished. Yet your uncle's prowess must be commended too. He carried the lance-head away with him in his body, and when the noble youth returned to his familiars his tragic plight was clear to see. He had slain that heathen on the field – let us not waste our tears on *him*.

'When the King returned to us so pale, and drained of all his strength, a physician probed his wound till he found the lance-head and a length of bamboo shaft which was also buried there. The physician recovered them both. I fell on my knees in prayer and vowed to Almighty God that I would practise chivalry no more, in the hope that to His own glory He would help my brother in his need. I also foreswore meat, bread and wine, and indeed promised that I would never again relish anything else that had blood. I tell you, dear nephew, parting with my sword was another source of sorrow to my people. "Who is to be Protector of the Gral's secrets?" they asked, while bright eyes wept.

'They lost no time in carrying the King into the presence of the Gral for any aid God would give him. But when the King

244

set eyes on it, it came as a second affliction to him that he might not die. Nor was it fitting he should after I had dedicated myself to a life of such wretchedness, and the dominion of our noble lineage had been reduced to such frailty.

'The King's wound had festered. None of the various books of medicine we consulted furnished a remedy to reward our trouble. All that was known by way of antidotes to asp, ecidemon, ehcontius, lisis, jecis and meatris* – these vicious serpents carry their venom hot – and other poisonous snakes, all that the learned doctors extract from herbs by the art of physic – let me be brief – were of no avail: it was God Himself who was frustrating us. We called in the aid of Gehon, Phison, Tigris and Euphrates, and so near to Paradise from which the four rivers flow that their fragrance was still unspent, in the hope that some herb might float down in it that would end our sorrow. But this was all lost effort, and our sufferings were renewed. Yet we made many other attempts. We obtained that same twig to which the Sibyl referred Aeneas, to ward off the hazards of Hell and Phlegethon's fumes, not to name other rivers flowing there. We devoted time to possessing ourselves of that twig as a remedy, in case the sinister lance that slays our happiness had been envenomed or tempered in Hellfire: but it was not so with that lance.

'There is a bird called Pelican. When it has young it loves them to excess. Instinctive love impels it to pick through its own breast and let the blood flow into its chicks' mouths. This done, it dies. We obtained some blood of this bird to see if its love would be efficacious, and anointed the wound to the best of our ability: but it helped us not at all.

'There is a beast called Monicirus,† which esteems virginal purity so highly that it falls asleep in maidens' laps. We acquired this animal's heart to assuage the King's pain. We took the carbuncle-stone on this beast's brow where it grows at the base of its horn. We stroked the wound with it at the front, then completely immersed the stone in it: but the wound

* The translator must not deny the reader the pleasure of hunting these reptiles.
† The Monocerus or Unicorn.

kept its gangrened look. This mortified the King and us.

'We then took a herb called trachonte* – it is said to grow from any dragon that is slain and to partake of the nature of air – in order to discover whether the revolution of the Dragon† would avail against the planets' return and the change of the moon, which caused the pain of the wound: but the sublime virtue of this herb did not serve our purpose.

'We fell on our knees before the Gral, where suddenly we saw it written that a knight would come to us and were he heard to ask a Question there, our sorrows would be at an end; but that if any child, maiden or man were to forewarn him of the Question it would fail in its effect, and the injury would be as it was and give rise to deeper pain. "Have you understood?" asked the Writing. "If you alert him it could prove harmful. If he omits the Question on the first evening, its power will pass away. But if he asks his Question in season he shall have the Kingdom, and by God's will the sorrow shall cease. Thereby Anfortas will be healed, but he shall be King no more."

'In this way we read on the Gral that Anfortas's agony would end when the Question came to him. We anointed his wound with whatever might soothe it – the good salve nard, whatever is decocted with theriac, and the smoke of lign-aloes: yet he was always in pain. I then withdrew to this place. Scant happiness is all my passing years afford me. Since then a knight rode that way, and it would have been better had he not done so – the knight I told you of before. All that he achieved there was shame, for he saw all the marks of suffering yet failed to ask his host "Sire, what ails you?". Since youthful inexperience

* A dragon-wort.

† In view of its position so near to the Pole Star, the constellation Draco can scarcely be intended. It has been suggested that Wolfram rather has in mind the progression through the zodiac of the 'Dragon's Head' and 'Dragon's Tail' (points where the lunar orbit intersects the plane of the ecliptic or the terrestrial orbit). Chaucer, *Astrolabe*, ii, 4, lumps the 'Tail of the Dragoun' together with Saturn and Mars as 'wykkid' when in the house of the ascendant. Wolfram was in any event drawing on the magic of etymology. The Head and Tail of the Dragon are said to be a Muslim, not a Classical conception.

saw to it that he asked no Question, he let slip a golden opportunity.'

The two continued their tales of woe till shortly before noon.

'Let us see to our nourishment,' said Parzival's host. 'Your mount is quite unprovided for. Nor can I feed us unless God assigns us the wherewithal. Smoke never rises from my kitchen! You will have to put up with it today and for as long as you stay with me. If only the snow would let us, I would teach you the herbary. God grant that it soon thaws! Meanwhile, let us gather some yew-tips. I imagine your horse often fed better at Munsalvæsche. Neither you nor your beast ever came to a host who would fend for you more willingly, if food and fodder were available!'

They went out to forage, with Parzival attending to the fodder, while his host grubbed up roots for them. With this they had to content themselves. The host did not forget his Rule, for of all the roots he dug up he ate not one before nones, but hung them with care on the bushes and went looking for more. (Many was the day when he failed to find the place where his food was hanging, and fasted to the glory of God.)

These two companions did not omit to go to the brook to wash their roots and herbs. No laugh echoed from their lips. Each washed his hands. Parzival set a bundle of yew-twigs before his horse. They then returned to their fire and lay down on their palliasse. There was no question of other courses being fetched for them – the kitchen was bare, there was neither stew nor roast! Moved by the loyal affection which he felt towards his host, Parzival shrewdly judged that he had eaten with greater contentment here than when Gurnemanz was tutoring him, or when so many dazzlingly beautiful ladies had passed before him at Munsalvæsche where he was feasted by the Gral.

'Nephew,' said his wise and honest host, 'do not scorn this food. You would not easily find a host who wished you a good meal more heartily than I.'

'Sir,' replied Parzival, 'may the Grace of God avoid me if any other entertainment I received tasted better!'

Had they forgotten to wash their hands after any of the fare served up here, it would not have harmed their eyes, as they say fishy hands do. I assure you for my part you could have gone hawking with me, were I a hunting-bird, I would have soared from the fist with ravening keenness, fed on such tiny morsels – you would soon have seen me in flight! But why do I mock these good people? I am misbehaving again! Now you have heard what had made them poor in happiness from having been so rich, often going cold, seldom warm. – They suffered deepest sorrow for pure love's sake, naught else. And they had their reward for their affliction from the hand of God, who had taken the one into His Grace and was now taking the other.

Parzival and the good man got up and went to where the horse was stabled.

'I am very sorry you have to endure such hunger,' said the host to the animal in a sad tone of voice, 'because of the saddle on your back bearing Anfortas's escutcheon.'

While they attended to the horse they found cause for new lamentations.

'My dear lord and uncle,' said Parzival to his host, 'if shame would let me reveal it I would tell you of a sad misfortune that befell me. I beg you of your courtesy to pardon my misdeed – after all, my loyal heart has sought refuge with you. I have erred so greatly that if you assent to my being punished for it, farewell to consoling hope: I shall never be freed from sorrow. You should deplore my youthful folly whilst giving me loyal aid. The man who rode to Munsalvæsche and saw all the marks of suffering and who nevertheless asked no Question was I, unhappy wretch! Such is my error, my lord.'

'What are you saying now, nephew?' exclaimed his host. 'Seeing that you have denied yourself success in so masterly a fashion, we two must let happiness slide and together fasten on grief! The five senses that God gave you shut off their aid from you – how they betrayed your compassion then, when faced with Anfortas's wound! Yet I will not deny you my advice. You must not grieve to excess, but grieve and cease grieving in measure! Human nature has a wild, perverse strain. Some-times youth affects wisdom, and if on the other hand age

pursues folly and clouds a life once clear, you could say white-
ness has been sullied and the young green has wilted that could
have rooted and borne noble fruit. Could I restore the lusty
green and so nerve your heart that you would win honour and
not despair of God, then your achievement would be so glorious
as to rate as full amends!* God Himself will not abandon you,
I counsel you in His name.

'Now tell me, did you see the Lance at Castle Munsalvæsche?
We knew from the wound and the summer snow that the
planet Saturn had returned to its mark. Never before had the
frost caused your dear uncle such pain as then. They had to
place the Lance in the wound – one pain relieved the other –
and so it was reddened with blood. The advent of certain
planets which stand so high one above the other and which
return at different speeds, gives the denizens here great sorrow;
and the change of the moon, too, is bad for the wound. At
these times which I have named, the King can find no peace.
The intense frost torments him, his flesh grows colder than
snow. Since the venom on the spear-head is known to be hot,
it is laid on the wound at those times. It draws the frost from
his body and round the Lance, as icy glass which none could
remove by any means till the wise Trebuchet fashioned two
knives of silver that cut it without more ado – a charm engraved
on the King's sword told him the trick of it. Many people will
tell you that asbestos wood does not burn: but when fragments
of this glass flew on to it, a fiery flame leapt up! – What
miracles this poison can perform, seeing that asbestos itself
took fire from it!

'The King is unable either to ride or walk or even to lie
down or stand – he *reclines* – he does not sit – his awareness
fraught with pain that mounts at the moon's change. There is
a lake called Brumbane on to which he is taken so that the
stench from his gaping wound shall be quelled by the
fragrant breezes. He calls it his sporting day. However much
he may catch, racked by such agony, back at home he will

* For not winning the Gral.

249

need more! From this a rumour went the rounds that he was a fisherman. He had to endure this story,* though, sad, unhappy man, he had no salmon or lamprey for sale.'

'I came upon the King at anchor on the rippling lake,' Parzival was quick to reply. 'I imagine it was to catch fish or for some other pastime. I had journeyed many miles that day after leaving Belrepeire at mid-morning, so that by evening I was anxious as to where I should find shelter. My uncle then provided it for me.'

'You rode along a dangerous path through alert look-outs,' said his host. 'Each is so well manned that no ruse of war would help anyone against their sorties. Till now any who rode against them took a perilous turning, for they stake their lives against others' and give no quarter. Such penance are they given for their sins.'

'Yet I rode up to the King on that occasion without being engaged,' said Parzival. 'That evening I saw his Palace filled with grief – how could they find such contentment in it? For no sooner did a squire run in at the door than the Palace rang with lamentation. He bore a shaft towards all four walls, helved with a point all red with blood, at the sight of which the Company were overwhelmed with grief.'

'Nephew,' said his host, 'never before or since has the King been in such pain as when the planet Saturn thus announced its advent, for it is its nature to bring great frost. Laying the Lance on the wound as had been done before failed to help us, so this time it was thrust into the wound. Saturn mounts so high that the wound sensed it before the other frost that followed: for the snow, however easily, fell only on the second night in Summer's unabated splendour. While the King's frost was being warded off in this way his people were in the depths of misery.

'They were subject to grief, such is its pay,' said the austere Trevrizent. 'The Lance which had cut them to the very heart took their happiness away! The sincere outpouring of their grief renewed the doctrine of the Baptism!'

* See p. 165, footnote.

'I saw five-and-twenty maidens of excellent bearing standing there before the King,' Parzival told his host.

'God ordained concerning the Gral that it should be kept by virgins ministering before it. The Gral chooses lofty servitors, thus knights are appointed to guard it endowed with all the virtues that go with chastity. The advent of the high planets brings grief to the denizens, young and old. God has maintained his wrath against them overlong. – When shall they be able to welcome happiness?

'Nephew, I will tell you something you can well believe. Fortune often faces those of Munsalvæsche with win-and-lose. They receive handsome children of high degree: but if a land should lose its lord, and its people see the hand of God in it and ask for a new lord from the Gral Company, their prayer is granted. Moreover, they must treat him reverentially, since from that moment on he is under the protection of God's blessing. God sends the men out in secret but bestows maidens openly. You must rest assured that King Castis sued for Herzeloyde's hand, and that your mother was given to him to wife with due ceremony, but that he was not destined to enjoy her, since death laid him in his grave before. Yet with all due form he had already made over to your mother Waleis and Norgals with their cities of Kanvoleis and Kingrivals. That King was not to live longer: on his way back to his country he laid him down and died. Herzeloyde thus became queen over two lands, in which Gahmuret won her. As I say, maidens are given away from the Gral openly, men in secret, in order to have progeny (as God can well instruct them), in the hope that these children will return to serve the Gral and swell the ranks of its Company. Those knights who are resolved on serving the Gral must forego woman's love. Only the King may have a spouse in wedlock, and those others whom God has sent to be lords in lordless lands. By serving a lady for her love I transgressed this commandment. My fresh and comely youthfulness and the quality of a noble lady prompted me to ride out in her service, in the course of which I fought many fierce battles. Strange and wild adventures were so much to my liking that I seldom tourneyed. Her love brought delight into my heart, and I often took the field for her sake. The great passion she inspired in me drove me to seek deeds of arms in wild and distant regions. I bought her love by fighting Christian and heathen alike. The reward she had to give I thought was sumptuous! Such was my life in the three continents of Europe, Asia and deep into Africa for the sake of that noble lady. When I wished to engage in fine jousting I rode past Gauriun. I have also broken many lances at the foot of Famurgan's mountain and ridden many fine jousts at Agremontin, below its mountain, where if you issue your challenge on one side fiery men sally forth, whereas on the other the jousters you see are not on fire. And when I had ridden past the Rohas* in search of adventure a company of noble Slovenes rode out in counter-challenge. I had sailed from Seville all round the sea towards Celje, passing out from Aquilea through Friuli. Alas, that I ever saw your father, whom I was fated to meet in Seville! When I marched in, the noble Angevin had found quarters ahead of me. The journey he made to Baghdad will never cease to distress me, for he was slain in a joust there. This is what you were telling me about him earlier: in my heart I shall always lament it.

'My brother is rich in possessions. He often sent me out in secret magnificently caparisoned, and when I left Munsalvæsche I took his seal with me and brought it to Carcobra where the Plimizœl forms a lake, and so to the sea of Barbigœl. On the strength of Anfortas's seal the Burgrave there made me a lavish provision of squires, and trappings for jousting in wild parts and other chivalric expeditions. I had to arrive there unaccompanied, and on my return I left my whole retinue with him before setting out for Munsalvæsche.

'Now listen to me, dear nephew. When your worthy father saw me for the first time in Seville he at once claimed me as the brother of his wife Herzeloyde, though he had never seen my face before! And indeed, there was no gainsaying that none was more handsome than I, then a beardless youth. When Gahmuret came to my quarters I swore many oaths, informal

* The Rohitscher Berg in the Saangau, Styria.

ones, denying what he had said. But he pressed me so hard that I confided my secret to him, to his great delight.

'Gahmuret gave me some treasures of his, and my return gift pleased him. My reliquary, which you saw the time before and which is greener than clover, I had cut from a precious stone the excellent fellow gave me. He left his maternal kinsman* with me as squire, Ither, King of Cucumerlant, whose honest heart saw to it that no trace of falsity was in him. Unable to delay our journeys any longer we were forced to part company. Gahmuret went to join the Baruc, and I made my way to the foot of the Rohas. Arriving there from Celje I tourneyed on three successive Mondays. I thought I had fought well there. I then rode at my best pace into the broad Gandine,† after which your grandfather Gandin is named. Ither was well known there. The place lies where the Grajena flows into the Drau, a river that bears gold.‡ There Ither found love, since there he met your aunt on your father's side, the lady of that land. It was Gandin of Anjou* who had made her Queen. Her name was Lammire, her land Styria. Those who wish to follow the calling of the shield must traverse many lands.

'Now I am moved to grief for my red squire, for whose sake Lammire honoured me highly. You are of the same stock as Ither, yet ignoring the ties of blood you raised your hand against him. But God has not forgotten them, He can trace them again. If you mean to lead a life of trust towards Him you must atone to Him for this. I tell you in sorrow: you have two great sins. You slew Ither; and you must lament your mother's death. Because of the great love she bore you she did not survive your going away and leaving her. Now do as I advise: do penance for your misdeeds and have a care for your

* This relationship is not substantiated elsewhere in the text. Either the term used is an error or intended vaguely; or (more likely) it is thrown in impromptu to support the idea soon to be voiced that Parzival killed a near kinsman in Ither, with whom he is otherwise related only through his great-great-great-grandfather Mazadan.

† Candin, now Haidin.

‡ Both Haidin and the confluence of Grajena and Drau (Drava) are near Pettau (Ptuj).

* See p. 429.

253

ending, so that your toil here on earth earns you peace for your soul above.'

And now his host went on gently questioning him. 'Nephew, I still have not heard from where this horse came to you.'

'I won this horse in battle, sir, when I rode away from Sigune after talking with her at her cell. I thrust a knight head-long from the saddle and led his horse away. The man was from Munsalvæsche.'

'Did the man survive to whom it belongs by right?' asked his host.

'Sir, I watched him make off and found his mount beside me.'

'If you are for robbing the people of the Gral in this fashion, yet believe you will win their friendship, your mind is riven with contradictions.'

'I took it in fair fight, sir. Let whoever accounts that a sin in me first consider the circumstances. I had already lost my own. Who was the maiden that carried the Gral?' Parzival continued. 'She lent me her cloak.'

'She is your aunt on your mother's side, nephew,' replied his host, 'and if the cloak was hers she did not lend it you to boast of. She was fondly hoping you would be lord there, the Gral's and hers, not to mention mine. Your uncle gave you a sword, too, with which sin came to you, since with a ready tongue in your head you unfortunately asked no Question. Let that sin rest with the others – it is time we went to bed.' No mattresses or bolsters were fetched for them: they went and lay down on the straw that had been scraped together, you remember, a couch well below the mark for men of such high birth.

In this style Parzival stayed there for a fortnight. His host cared for him as I shall tell you: herbs and roots of necessity were their best fare. Parzival endured this hardship for the sake of the glad tidings, for his host took away his sins and nevertheless counselled him as a knight.

One day Parzival asked him 'Who was the man lying before the Gral, his silvery hair contrasting with his clear skin?'

'It was Titurel,' his host replied. 'He is your great-grandfather through your mother. He was the first to whom the Pennant of the Gral was commended, to defend it as his fief. He suffers from a laming disease named podagra and is helpless, though he never lost his colour, since he gazes on the Gral so often that he cannot die. They have him, bedridden as he is, to advise them. As a young man, he was always riding out across fords and meadows in search of jousting.

'If you wish to make something fine and truly noble of your life, never vent your anger on women. Women and priests are grouped together as unarmed: but God's blessing is outstretched over the clergy alone. The latter you should serve faithfully in hope of a good ending: you must place your trust in the clergy. Nothing you see on earth is like a priest. His lips pronounce the Passion that nullifies our damnation. Into his consecrated hand he takes the highest Pledge ever given for debt. When a priest so guards his conduct that he can perform his office chastely, how could he lead a life more holy?'

This was their day of separation.

'Give me your sins!,' said Trevrizent with all solemnity. 'I shall vouch for your penitence before God. And do as I have instructed you: let nothing daunt you in this endeavour.'

They took their leave of one another. Elaborate how, if you wish.

Chapter 10

W E are approaching strange tales such as can empty us of joy and bring high spirits: they have to do with both.

The term of one year was past, and the judicial combat which the Landgrave had been accorded on the Plimizœl after its transference from Schanpfanzun to Barbigœl, had been settled and King Kingrisin left unavenged. Vergulaht had confronted Gawan there, but the assembled company had noted their kinship, which irresistibly quashed the duel. Moreover it was Count Ehkunat that bore the guilt of the deed of which Gawan had been accused. Thus Kingrimursel cleared brave Gawan of his suit.

Thereupon Vergulaht and Gawan each went his separate way in search of the Gral, setting out at the same hour. It was a quest that would require them to deliver many attacks, for whoever desired the Gral would have to make his way to glory sword in hand – only thus is glory to be striven for.

As to how the ever-blameless Gawan fared since he set out from Schanpfanzun and whether his excursion involved him in fighting, let them tell who saw it. But he will certainly be going into battle soon.

One morning lord Gawan came riding up to a green meadow. There he glimpsed a shield which had been holed by a lance-thrust, and then a palfrey harnessed for a lady, with costly bridle and saddle. The beast had been tethered to the shield, which was hanging from a bough.

'Who can this woman be,' he mused, 'that is of such warlike bearing as to use a shield? If she decides to attack me, how shall I defend myself? I fancy I shall be able to acquit myself if I dismount. Granted there is jousting on foot and if she will wrestle that long, she may actually bring me down, whether I

win favour or disfavour for it! Though she were Lady Camilla*
herself, who won renown with deeds of arms below Laurente,
and were Camilla in full vigour as she rode there and were
now to challenge me I would nevertheless try her mettle!'

The shield, moreover, was badly gashed, and as Gawan rode
up he surveyed it. A window had been carved in it by the entry
of a broad spear-head – in this way does battle paint a shield!
Who would pay the blazoners if their colours were like this?

The trunk of the tree was very thick. Behind it on the clover
sat a disconsolate lady. She had forgotten all joy, so intense
was her grief. As Gawan rode round the tree towards her he
saw a knight lying in her lap. This was the cause of her great
sorrow.

Gawan was forthcoming with his greeting, and the lady
acknowledged with a bow. Her voice struck him as hoarse,
worn out by shrieks of woe. My lord Gawan now dismounted.
The man who lay there had been run through, and he was
bleeding internally. Gawan asked this knight's lady whether
he were alive or in his death throes.

'He is still alive, sir,' she answered, 'but I don't think it will
be for long. God has sent you to sustain me. Now give me
your honest advice – you have seen more trouble than I. Show
me that you mean to aid and comfort me!'

'I shall do so, madam,' he replied. 'I could save this knight's
life, and I undertake to cure him absolutely if only I had a
tube, so that you would see him and hear him alive again for
many a day. His wound is not a fatal one, it is simply the
blood pressing on his heart.' Gawan then took a branch from
the tree, peeled off the bark to make a tube and – no ignoramus
he where wounds were concerned – inserted it into the knight's
body through the lance-wound. He then told the lady to suck
it till the blood flowed towards her, whereupon the warrior's

* The Volscian battle-maiden of the eleventh book of the *Æneid*, known
to Wolfram either from the *Roman d'Énéas* or Heinrich von Veldeke's
German adaptation of it, or from both. The *Roman* speaks of the 'city
of Laurente', but classical scholars are not satified that there ever was a
city of 'Laurentum', for *Æneid* VIII, 1, can be otherwise interpreted.

strength surged back to him so that he regained the power of speech, and spoke. Seeing Gawan bending over him, he thanked him warmly, said it redounded to his credit that he had brought him out of his swoon and asked him if he had come to Logroys in pursuit of chivalry.

'I myself was roving from far-off Punturteis and wished to seek adventure here. But I shall always regret having ridden so near. And if you have any sense, you, too, will hold aloof. I never dreamt it would come to this. Lischois Gwelljus has gravely wounded me, he set me down behind my horse with a mighty joust delivered with great impact through shield and body. Then this good lady helped me to this place on her palfrey.' He implored Gawan to stay, but Gawan said he wished to go to the scene where this hurt had been inflicted.

'If Logroys lies so near and I can overtake the man outside its walls he will have to answer to me, for I shall ask him what he had against you.'

'Do nothing of the sort,' replied the wounded man. 'I can tell you the whole story. It is no children's outing to that place! Rather should I call it mortal danger.'

Gawan bound the knight's wound with the lady's kerchief, then uttered a charm over it and commended them both to God's care. He found their tracks all bloody, as though a stag had been shot there. This kept him from riding astray. Soon he saw fair Logroys, praised and honoured by many people.

The structure of the castle was splendid! With its path ascending in spirals the castle-hill resembled a top, so that when a simple person saw it from a way off he thought it was all spinning round! People claim of that fortress even now that no assault could match it and that it went in little dread of any malice brought to bear on it. All round the castle-hill ran a palisade of cultivated trees – figs, pomegranates, olives, as well as vines and other productive plants, all growing in abundance. Gawan had ridden all the way up the path, when, looking down, he saw a sight that gladdened yet pained his heart.

From the rock there leapt a spring, beside which – and this did not displease him – was a fair lady. He gazed at her with delight despite himself, she was the fairest flower of all feminine beauty. Except for Condwiramurs, no lovelier woman was ever born. She was of radiant charm, shapely, refined. Her name was Orgeluse de Logroys, and the story tells of her that she was a lure to love's desire, sweet balm to a man's eyes, windlass to his heartstrings.

Gawan offered her his salutation. 'If I may alight by your good leave, madam, and if I see you disposed to have me in your company, my great sorrow will yield to joy, no knight would ever have been so happy. I am destined to die with no woman ever having pleased me more!'

'What of it? – This is no news to me,' said she, looking him up and down. And her sweet lips went on to say, 'Don't overpraise me or you may well reap disgrace from it. I don't want every Tom, Dick or Harry mouthing his judgments at me. If all were free to praise me – the discerning and the undiscerning, the crooked and the straight – that would bring small credit. How should my praises then excel all others'? I mean to guard them so that only the discerning use them. I have no idea who you are, sir. It is time you left me, but you shall not escape *my* judgment: you are near my heart, but right outside, not in! If you desire my love, what have you done to deserve it of me? Many a man who persists in gaping at what wounds his heart, bowls his eyes so wildly that he could hurl them more gently with a sling! Trundle your wretched desires at other loves than mine. If you are a man who serves for love, if thirst for adventure has brought you out to do deeds of arms to win a lady's favour, you will find no reward in me! Dishonour is what you can earn here, if I'm to tell you truly!'

'Madam,' said he, 'you *do* tell me truly, my eyes *are* a danger to my heart! For they have dwelt on you to such effect that I must truthfully declare I am your prisoner! Treat me as a proper woman should. However much it irks you, you have locked me in your heart! Now loose or bind! You will find me so minded that if I had you where I wanted you I should gladly suffer Paradise!'

'Now take me with you,' she answered. 'If you wish to share any gain you win from me with your love-suit, you will only end by regretting your disgrace. I should like to know whether you are a man who dares to endure battle for my sake. Yet, if honour is dear to you, refrain. If I may advise you further, and if you were to do as I say, you would seek love in some other quarter. For if you desire my love, you will be disappointed of both love *and* joy! So if you take me away with you, great trouble will beset you later.'

'Who can have love without deserving it?' asked my lord Gawan. 'If I may tell you my opinion, a man sins who carries off love without deserving it. A man who is eager to win a noble love must serve for it before and after his requital.'

'If you want to serve me,' was her reply, 'you must lead a life of combat. Yet all you will get will be dishonour! I do not need the service of a coward. Go along that path (it is no road) across the little high bridge into the orchard and see to my palfrey. There you will find a crowd of people dancing, and hear them singing love-songs and playing on tabors and flutes. However much they insist on escorting you, pass straight through them to where my palfrey stands and untether it. It will then follow you.'

Gawan leapt down from his charger. He was then in a great quandary as to how his mount should wait for him. There was nothing beside the spring on which to tether it. He wondered if it would be seemly of him to expect the lady to hold it, and whether he could decently ask her.

'I can read what is troubling you,' she said. 'Leave this horse with me. I'll hold it till you come back. But my service will do you little good.'

My lord Gawan then took the horse's bridle. 'Hold it for me, my lady!' he said.

'I see you are a fool,' she retorted. 'Your hand has rested there! I'll not lay hold of it.'

'Madam, I have never grasped the lower end,' said this aspirant to love.

'Very well, I will receive it,' she said. 'Now make haste and bring me my palfrey. As to our travelling in company, your wish is granted.'

To Gawan this seemed a happy gain. He left her and

hastened over the bridge and in at the gate, where he saw a dazzling bevy of ladies and many knights-bachelor, singing and dancing.

The sight of Gawan thus magnificently caparisoned saddened those of the orchard, for they were loyal-hearted people. Standing, reclining or sitting in their pavilions, there was not one who did not voice his sorrow. A number of knights and ladies who deplored this affair said – and said it again – 'With her deceitful ways My Lady plans to entice this man into great toil. Alas, that he consents to her bidding with so sorrowful a prospect!' Many a worthy man went up to him and embraced him in token of friendly welcome. He then approached the olive where the palfrey was standing. Its bridle and harness were many marks in worth. Leaning on his staff beside it stood a knight with an ample beard, well braided and grey. He bewailed and bewept Gawan's coming for that horse, yet received him with kind words.

'If you are open to advice you will let this palfrey be. However, nobody here will stand in your way. Yet if you have always done what is wisest you will leave this horse alone. A curse on My Lady for this way she has of causing so many fine men to lose their lives!'

Gawan replied that he would not desist.

'Then alas for what will follow!' said the venerable grey knight. He then untied the palfrey's halter. 'There is no need to wait any longer,' he said, 'just let this palfrey follow you. May He Whose hand made the sea all briny succour you in your need! Take care lest My Lady's beauty make a mock of you, for with her sweetness goes much sourness, as in a hailstorm lit by sunshine.'

'May it rest in God's hands!' replied Gawan. He took his leave of the grey-haired man and of some others, here and there, to the mournful cries of all. The palfrey followed him along a narrow path out through the gate and up on to the bridge. There he found the mistress of his heart, who was also Lady of that land. Although his heart sought refuge with her she brought much suffering to it.

She had pushed the fastenings of her wimple from under

her chin up on to her head. When one finds a woman thus she is ready for combat and may well have a mind for sport. – What other clothes was she wearing? If I were thinking of going over her attire, her dazzling looks would absolve me from the task.

As Gawan approached the lady this is how her sweet lips greeted him: 'Welcome back, you goose! If you are set on serving me, no one will ever have lugged such a load of folly around as you! What good cause you would have not to do so!'

'Though you are angry to begin with, you will receive me into favour in the end,' he answered. 'Though you upbraid me now, you will have the honour of giving satisfaction later. Meanwhile I shall render you service till you feel inclined to reward me. I shall hand you on to this palfrey if you so desire.'

'I did not ask you to do so,' she retorted. 'Let your unattested hand reach for a meaner forfeit!' Turning away she leapt from the flowers on to her horse and told him to ride on ahead. 'What a pity it would be,' she went on, 'if I were to lose so estimable a companion! May God lay you low!'

Now those who will be advised by me should not malign her. Let nobody's tongue run away with him till he knows the full charge, and has learnt the state of her feelings. I, no less, would have a bone to pick with this lovely woman. Yet however she has misbehaved towards Gawan in her ill humour, and to whatever she may subject him later, I exonerate her on all counts!

Puissant Orgeluse went not as a good companion, for she came riding towards Gawan in such a fury that, in his shoes, I should have had small hope of release from my cares through her! The two now rode off to a heath gay with flowers. Here Gawan espied a herb whose root he declared good for wounds. The noble man alighted, dug up the root and remounted, while the lady did not forbear to remark 'If my companion is adept in both medicine and chivalry and learns how to hawk boxes of salves and pills he will be able to make a good living.'

'I rode past a tree beneath which lay a wounded knight,' said Gawan. 'If I still find him there this root should heal him and restore his strength.'

'I should like to see that,' said she. 'Perhaps I could learn some skill in medicine.'

A squire came riding after them in great haste to deliver a message he had been entrusted with. Gawan was about to stop and wait for him when he was struck by his monstrous appearance. – The proud squire was called Malcreatiure, and Cundrie la surziere was his comely sister. He was the spit image of her, except that he was a man. Like hers, his two fangs jutted out like a wild boar's, not a human being's. On the other hand, his hair was not so long as that which dangled over Cundrie's mule, but short and sharp as a hedgehog's coat. Such people grow in the land of Tribalibot beside the River Ganges, from dire mischance. For, having knowledge from God, our father Adam named all things wild and tame. He divined the nature of each, and the revolutions of the seven planets, too, and their innate powers. He furthermore perceived the virtues of all herbs and their individual properties. When his daughters reached the age of child-bearing, Adam counselled them against intemperateness. Whenever a daughter was with child he never failed to impress on her most earnestly that she should avoid numerous herbs that would deform human offspring and so dishonour his race – 'except for those which God allotted to us when He sat down to His work of making me,' said Adam. 'My dear daughters, do not be blind as to where your happiness lies!'

Those women – do you wonder? – did according to their nature. Some were prompted by their frailty to do the deed on which their hearts were set, with the result that to Adam's bitter sorrow Mankind was corrupted. Yet Adam never despaired in his purpose. Queen Secundille, whom with her lands Feirefiz had won with deeds of chivalry, had many such people in her realm since ancient days whose appearance was deformed and no denying it – wild, outlandish features did they display! Secundille was told of the Gral, that there was nothing so splendid on earth and that it was in the care of a King Anfortas. This struck her as very strange, since many rivers washed into her lands not sand but precious stones, and she had vast mountain-chains of gold! 'How shall I gain knowledge of this man to whom the Gral is subject?' she wondered. She sent him costly gifts, a pair of human wonders, namely Cundrie and her fair brother, and in addition, I do swear, more treasure than one could ever buy – you would never find it up for sale! Gentle Anfortas, who as you know had a magnanimous nature, sent Orgeluse de Logroys this courtly squire. Well-marked features, the outcome of woman's intemperate desire, set him apart from other human kind.

This kinsman of the herbs and planets bawled at the top of his voice at Gawan, who had waited for him on the path. And now Malcreatiure rode up on a wretched nag that was limping on all fours and stumbled and fell from time to time. (Lady Jeschute was riding a better horse that day when Parzival made Orilus receive her back to favour, lost through no fault of hers.)

'Sir!' said Malcreatiure angrily, and looking hard at Gawan. 'If you are a knight you might in decency have refrained! You strike me as a fool, taking my lady away with you in this fashion. You will win high praise if you can fend off the correction in store for you. But if you are a man-at-arms, staves shall so tan your hide for you that you might well wish it were otherwise.'

'My knightly person has never suffered such rude correction. It is the mob of good-for-nothings, incapable of giving a manly account of themselves, who should be thus thrashed – hitherto I have gone free of such punishment. But if you and my lady wish to offer me insults, it is you alone who will have to enjoy what you would rightly call my anger. However frightful your appearance I can easily dispense with your threats.'

Gawan then seized him by the hair and flung him from his nag to the ground, from where the estimable, sapient squire looked up at him most timidly. Yet his hedgehog's bristles avenged him, cutting Gawan's hand so deeply that it was red with blood all over.

The lady laughed to see it. 'I love to see you two quarrelling like this,' she said.

They set out with the squire's mount trotting beside them till they reached the place where the wounded knight

264

was lying. Gawan loyally bound the herb on to the wound.

'How did you fare since leaving me here?' asked the wounded man. 'You have brought a lady with you who is bent on harming you. It is all her doing that I am so badly hurt. In Av'estroit mavoie she involved me in a sharp joust at the risk of my life and property. If you wish to stay alive, let this deceitful woman ride away and have nothing more to do with her. Judge from my condition where her counsels lead! But I could recover completely if I could find a place to rest. Help me to that, good man.'

'Ask any help of mine you care to name,' replied my lord Gawan.

'Not far from here there is a hospital,' said the wounded knight. 'If I could get there soon I could rest for quite a while. We have my companion's sturdy little horse standing here all this time – hand her up and set me behind her.'

The well-born stranger untethered the lady's palfrey from its branch and was in the act of leading it to her when the wounded man shouted 'Keep away! – Why are you in such haste to have me trampled?' Thus Gawan brought it to her a longer way round. At a hint from her man, the lady followed Gawan at a slow and gentle pace. Gawan hoisted her on to her palfrey – and in that instant the wounded knight leapt on to Gawan's castilian. It was ill-done, if you ask me. Profiting from their sinful deed, that knight and his lady rode away.

Gawan gave vent to his annoyance, but the lady found more to laugh at in this prank than any pleasure he had from it. Now that he had been robbed of his horse her sweet lips uttered these words: 'I took you for a knight. Soon after, you turned surgeon. And now you are reduced to footman. If anyone can make a living by his skill you can certainly trust your wits! Do you still desire my love?'

'Yes, my lady,' answered Gawan. 'If I could have your love it would be dearer to me than all else. There are none that dwell on earth – crowned heads, *all* who wear a crown and win honour and joy! – but that if I were to be offered the choice between all their possessions and you, my discerning heart would bid me leave their wealth to them! It is your love that

I wish to have. If I cannot win it, may I be seen to die a bitter death! You are laying waste your own. If I was ever free, you must now have me as your bondsman: I judge this your indisputable right. Now whether you call me knight or squire, peasant or footman, with the mockery you have subjected me to and the scorn you pour on my service, you burden yourself with sin. Were I to profit from my service you would have done with your jibes. Though they never vexed me, they nevertheless lower your worth.'

The wounded man rode back to them. 'Are you Gawan?' he asked. 'If you ever borrowed anything of me it has now been paid back in full! Remember when you overpowered me and took me prisoner in a tough encounter and led me home to your uncle King Arthur? He saw to it that I ate with the hounds for a month on end!'

'Are you Urjans?' Gawan countered. 'I do not deserve any harm you wish me now, for I won the King's pardon for you. They were ignoble thoughts that moved you, with the outcome that you were excluded from the Order of Knighthood and declared an outlaw for denying a maiden her inviolability and the protection of the law. King Arthur would have punished you with the gallows had I not spoken up for you.'

'Whatever happened there, here you are now. You have heard the saying from before your time that if a man saved another from death that other would be his enemy ever after. I act as one who has his wits about him. It is more fitting that a babe should cry than a man whose beard has grown. I intend to keep this horse for myself.' And he spurred hard and rode away from him, much to Gawan's annoyance.

'It happened thus,' he told the lady. 'At that time Arthur was in the town of Dianazdrun, attended by many Britons. A lady had been sent to his country on an embassy. As to this outsider, he had come out for adventure. He was a guest there, so was she. Yet his low thoughts prompted him to struggle with the lady against her will but at his pleasure. Her cries reached the court, the King raised a hue and cry at the top of his voice. It happened at the skirt of a forest, and thither we all hastened. I rode far ahead of the others and picked up the villain's tracks. It was as my prisoner that I led this man back into the King's presence. The maiden rode back with us in a piteous state because one who had never been her Servitor had taken her chaste maidenhead. Nor had he added anything to his fame as a knight by attacking her, defenceless. She had found my lord, true-hearted Arthur, beside himself.

' "This damnable outrage should move us all to pity! Alas that the day ever dawned by whose light this violence was done and, moreover, within the jurisdiction proclaimed as mine, and where I am still judge today! You would be well advised to take an advocate and bring a plaint," he said, turning to the lady, who did not hesitate to follow his suggestion.

'By now a great company of knights were assembled there. Urjans, the prince from Punturteis, stood before Arthur of Britain with his life and honour at stake. The fair plaintiff advanced to where rich and poor alike could hear her and with accusing words petitioned the King in the name of all womankind and of maidenly honour to take her shame to heart. She further entreated him by the traditions of the Table Round and her having been sent to him as an envoy, that if he were the acknowledged judge there he should judge of the wrong she had suffered with due process of law. She begged the entire Company of the Table Round to apprise themselves of her rights, since she had been robbed of what could never be restored to her – her pure, chaste virginity – and that they should all join in asking the King for his judgment and speak on her behalf.

'The guilty man (to whom I accord small honour) took an advocate who defended him as best he could; but his defence was vain. Urjans was condemned to die with loss of honour, they were to twist a withy for him to die in without shedding his blood. In his dire need he appealed to me and reminded me that to save his life he had surrendered to me. I feared that, were he to lose his life there, all my honour would be gone. Urging that the plaintiff herself had witnessed the manly vengeance I had exacted for her, I asked her as a good-hearted woman to calm her angry feelings, since she had to put down what he had done to her, to her radiant, seductive beauty. "For if ever a man grew desperate from serving a lady," I told her, "and she helped him in the sequel, honour that help now and let yourself be turned aside from anger." I begged the King and his vassals that if I had ever done him any service he should bear it in mind and merely by letting the knight live, ward off the disgrace that would dog me. I entreated his consort the Queen to help me by the love that binds blood-relations; for the King had reared me since childhood and in my attachment I had always sought refuge with her. And this she did. She had a private word with the young lady, and his life was saved, thanks to the Queen. Nevertheless, he had to suffer torment. He was cleared in the following way, such was the atonement he was faced with. He ate out of one trough with the hounds, leader or lymer, for four weeks. In that way the lady was avenged. And this, madam, is his revenge on me!'

'His vengeance will go awry,' said Orgeluse. 'I am unlikely ever to show you favour, but he will be so rewarded for it before he quits my domain that he will account it a disgrace, seeing that the King did not avenge the deed in the land where the lady suffered it, and it has come into my jurisdiction! You are both subject to my command, yet I do not know who you are. He will be brought to battle – for the lady's sake alone, and not at all for yours! Gross misdemeanours should be punished with thrusts and blows.'

Gawan went along to Malcreatiure's nag and caught it with only a light leap. The squire now came up with them, and the lady told him in the heathen tongue all she wanted done up there in the Castle. Now indeed Gawan's peril is approaching.

Malcreatiure went off on foot. Gawan then took a closer look at the young gentleman's jade and concluded that it was too frail for fighting. The squire had taken it from a peasant before coming down the slope, and now Gawan had to make do with it as charger – he had no alternative but to accept this quid pro quo.

And now she addressed him thus (I fancy with malicious intent): 'Tell me, won't you ride on?'

'I shall set out from this place in full accord with your advice,'* replied my lord Gawan.

'You will wait a long time for that!' she retorted.

'But I am serving you just to win it!' he countered.

'I think you a fool to do so! Unless you give it up you will have to avoid jolly people and turn moper. You will always have fresh troubles.'

'I am engaged in your service, whether I have joy or trouble of it, for your love told me to wait on you, riding or walking.'

Standing beside the lady he looked his war-horse up and down. Its stirrups of bast were of poorest quality for a fast joust, and there were times when the stranger had had a better saddle. He did not mount because he feared his foot might rip the whole saddle-harness apart. The nag had a hollow back, so that if he had leapt up on to it, it would have caved in altogether, a thing he had to avoid at all costs. In times past he would have jibbed at such a procedure; but now he led the beast and carried his shield and lance!

The lady who was the source of so much pain to him laughed heartily at his cruel ordeal, and when he tied his shield to the horse, she asked 'Have you brought some merchandize to sell in my country? Whom do I have to thank for a doctor and a marketeer? Look out for the customs along the road – some of my tax-gatherers will strip you of your good humour!'

He found her well-salted jibes so acceptable that he did not mind what she said, since whenever he looked at her he was quit of any pain she caused him. In his eyes she was May-time in person, a blossoming that outshone all things bright – sweetness to his eye, yet also bitterness to his heart. Since a man could both lose and find his joy in her and a remedy for happiness that languished, it made him at all times free and closely tied.

* There is a double entendre in the original. The concealed meaning, on which Orgeluse picks and which Gawan bandies back, is: 'after you have freed me from my desire'.

Many of my authorities assert that Amor and Cupid and also Venus, mother of those two, inspire love in people with arrows and with fire. Such love is malign. But if true fidelity dwells within one's heart, one will never be free of love, one will know joy and sometimes sorrow. Benign love is true fidelity. Cupid, your dart misses me always, as does Lord Amor's spear. If you two have power over love, and Venus, too, with her searing torch, the pangs you inflict are unknown to me. If I am to say I know true love, it can come to me only through fidelity.

If I had the wit to help anyone against Love, I am so fond of Gawan that I would help him without payment. When all is said, it is no disgrace to him that he now lies fettered by Love, or that Love, destroyer of stout defences, has him in a turmoil. He was always so well able to defend himself, his defence so much that of a man of worth, that it ought to be given to no woman to harass his warlike person.

Ride nearer, Lord Love-tyranny! You tear at Joy with such might that her place is pitted with holes, and Sorrow beats herself a path there! Indeed, Sorrow's tracks grow so broad that had her march gone elsewhere than straight into Heart's Zest, I should have deemed it Joy's advantage!

If Love is set on misbehaving, I judge her too old to do so. Or, when she inflicts pain on a lover's heart, does she blame it on her tender years? I could condone wantonness in her youth more readily than if she misbehaved in old age. She has been the source of much trouble: to which of her two aspects shall I set it down? If, thanks to youthful promptings, she intends to lapse from her old and settled ways, she will soon lose her reputation. The matter should be explained to her more clearly. The love I prize is pure and limpid, and all men and women of discernment will agree. Where tender feeling responds to its like, transparent and untroubled, and neither demurs when Love locks their hearts with ever-faithful love, such love is high above all other.*

Glad though I should be to fetch him away, Gawan cannot

* Conventional love-service for a high-born lady, with an often frustrating inequality between the lovers, was called 'high love'.

escape Love's making him unhappy. So of what use is it if I interpose, however much I say? A man of worth should not fend off Love, if only because Love must help to save him. Gawan had to toil because of Love: his lady rode, he trudged on foot.

Orgeluse and the brave knight were entering a great forest, and still he had to walk. He led the nag towards a tree-stump, took the shield he had laid on the beast and which he carried in pursuance of his chivalric calling, slung it round his neck, and mounted. The nag barely managed to take him forward to the ploughland on the far side. There he made out a castle, and his heart and eyes confessed they had never known or seen this castle's like. Its whole circuit was magnificent – towers and palaces abounded in that fortress! Nor could he help seeing many ladies at its windows, four hundred of them or more, among them four of illustrious race.

A causeway with very heavy going led to a broad, fast-flowing, navigable river, and he and his lady rode towards it. Beside the quay there was a meadow where much jousting was done. The fortress loomed above the river.

Gawan, brave warrior, espied a knight who had never been one to spare either shield or lance. 'If you will bear me out,' said puissant Orgeluse haughtily, 'I do not break my word. I told you so often that you would reap great dishonour here. Now defend yourself if you can – nothing else will save you! The man advancing there will throw you down with his strong right arm to such effect that if your breeches get torn somewhere or other you will be embarrassed because of the ladies sitting up above and looking on. Supposing they were to glimpse your shame ... ?'

The master of the ship crossed over at Orgeluse's bidding and, to Gawan's sorrow, she went aboard. 'You will not be joining me here on board!' the well-born puissant lady shouted back at him angrily. 'You stay out there as a pledge to fortune!'

'Why are you in such a hurry to leave me, my lady?' he called after her despondently. 'Shall I never see you again?'

'The honour of my letting you see me again may yet befall

you, but I fancy not so very soon.' Such were her parting words.

And now Lischois Gwelljus rode up. If I were to tell you that he flew, I should be deceiving you with such an expression. But short of that he moved at such a pace over the green meadow as did credit to his charger, which showed a great turn of speed.

'How shall I await this man?' Gawan asked himself. 'Which of the two would be the more advisable: on foot, or on this little nag? If he plans to come at me full tilt, not checking his charge, he will ride me down. Then what can his horse expect but to take a tumble over my nag? If he then offers me battle with the two of us on foot, such being his wish I will give it him, even though the lady who has involved me in this fight should never smile on me!'

Nothing could avert it now, the man coming on was as gallant as the man awaiting him. Gawan prepared for the joust and set his lance forward on the wretched saddle-cloth of felt. Their two thrusts were delivered so accurately that the impact shattered both lances, and the warriors lay on their backs, just as Gawan had planned it – the man with the better mount had come a cropper, with the result that both he and my lord Gawan were couched upon the flowers! You ask what they did next? They leapt up, sword in hand, each athirst for battle. There was no sparing of shields, for these were so carved up that little remained above the grips – shields always bear the brunt of battle! – and you could see sparks and flames leap up from their helmets! Whichever God allows to gain the victory, you can account him a lucky man, since he will first have to cover himself in glory. They stuck it out so long on the broad expanse of that meadow that two smiths, however strong their limbs, would have tired from dealing so many mighty blows, so hard did they strive to win renown. Yet who should praise them for fighting for no cause, other than that Fame should smile on them, rash men? They had no issue to decide, no grounds for holding their lives so cheap. Each could protest to the other that he had seen no wrong.

272

Gawan had learnt to wrestle and pin down his man after throwing him. When he went in under his opponent's sword and grappled with him, he could force him to do what he wanted. Since he had been forced to defend himself, he gave a formidable account of himself. The noble, spirited man seized the gallant young knight, who was also endowed with manly strength, and quickly threw him beneath him.

'Now surrender, knight, if you wish to live!'

Lischois lying there beneath him was ill-prepared to meet his demand, since he had never been accustomed to surrender. It seemed very strange to him that any should have the strength to wrest from him what had never been exacted before, namely an oath extorted in defeat such as he himself had often wrung from others. However the affair had turned out here, in the past he had received many surrenders which he was not inclined to trade further, in lieu of which he offered his life, declaring that whatever should come of him he would never give his parole under duress, but rather treat with death.

'Does victory rest with you, now?' asked the supine warrior. 'She was mine as long as God willed it and I was vouchsafed the glory. Now let your noble hand make an end of it! When knights and ladies learn that I whose renown soared so high have been defeated – before this news bereaves my friends it would be better I should die!'

Gawan demanded his surrender: but Lischois's whole desire was set on his life's ending in a swift death. 'Why should I kill this man?' Gawan asked himself. 'If he would obey me in all else I should let him go unharmed.' And he tried to gain his assent to such terms, but Lischois would not give it.

Gawan let the warrior rise without pledge of surrender. And now each of them sat among the flowers. Gawan had not forgotten his discontent at having such a wretched nag. It occurred to him in his prudence that he should mount and set spur to Lischois's charger till he had made trial of its ways. The horse was well caparisoned for battle: above his housings of mail there was a second covering of brocade and samite. Having won the horse in a chance encounter, why should he not ride it now that it fell to him to do so? He mounted and

273

was delighted with the beast's long leaps as it gathered pace.

'Is it you, Gringuljete,' he asked, 'whom Urjans got from me with a perfidious request? – He would know how to name the deed that dishonoured him. Who has equipped you so splendidly since then? If it is really you, God (Who often puts an end to sorrow) has returned you to me most graciously.' He dismounted and saw a device, the Gral's escutcheon in the shape of a Turtle-dove, branded on the horse's forearm. Riding it, Lähelin had slain the knight of Prienlascors. This horse then came to Orilus, who gave it to Gawan on the meadow by the Plimizœl.

The good man's spirits that had been so despondent now rose high again, except that he was oppressed by great sadness and the loyal devotion he felt towards his lady, who nevertheless heaped scorn on him. – His thoughts chased him in pursuit of her. Meanwhile, proud Lischois dashed to where he saw his sword lying which Gawan, worthy knight, had torn from his grasp. And now many ladies saw them fight a second battle. Their shields were so far gone that each left his lying where it was and made haste to engage without them – both came on at once, ready to give an account of themselves like stouthearted men. Bevies of ladies were sitting at the windows in the Palace above and watching the duel unfolding before their eyes. And now indeed their fury was renewed! Each was of such high birth that it would have irked his reputation to accept defeat from the other. Their swords and helmets suffered severely, since these were their shields for warding off death. I fancy that any who witnessed the fighting of these warriors would have judged them very hard put to it.

The tactic of the charming young Lischois Gwelljus was this: his lofty heart inspired him to bold, courageous deeds with many a swift sword-stroke – time and time again did he leap away from Gawan and return to press his attack. Gawan's constant purpose was thus: 'If I can hug you close to me,' he thought, 'I shall pay you back in full.' You could see flashes of fire there, and again and again swords raised on high by valiant hands. They were now manœuvring each other to the side, to the fore and behind: but the execution they did was unnecessary, they could have let the matter rest without fighting. Then my lord Gawan seized him and threw him by sheer strength beneath himself. – May I be spared such loving embraces, they would prove too much for me!

Gawan demanded his surrender, but Lischois beneath him was as unwilling to give it as in their first bout.

'You are wasting your time,' he said. 'Rather than surrender I offer my life. Let your noble hand make an end of whatever fame I knew, for I am accurst in the eyes of God who is oblivious of my glory! For love of Orgeluse the noble Duchess many worthy men have had to yield their fame to me, so that you can inherit much fame by slaying me.'

'Truly, I should not do so,' thought King Lot's son, 'for were I to slay this bold warrior for no cause, Fame would cease to smile on me. It was love of Orgeluse, the same that torments and harasses me, that has driven him to attack me – why shouldn't I let him live for her sake? If she is destined to be mine, he will be powerless to avert what fortune has bestowed on me. Had she witnessed our battle it is my belief that she would have to give me credit for knowing how to deserve love. For the Duchess's sake I will spare your life,' said Gawan.

They were now aware that they were very tired. Gawan let him get up, and they then sat down well apart from one another.

The master of the ferry came ashore carrying a moulted grey merlin on his fist as he walked towards them. It had been determined as his lawful fief that when knights jousted on that meadow he should have the loser's horse and bow to the hand of him who had won the victory and noise his fame abroad. In this way the flowery mead was made to yield him revenue. Such was his best hidage, or when his merlin tore into a crested lark. He had no other tilth, this seemed ample estate to him. He was of knightly descent and of excellent breeding. He went up to Gawan and politely asked for his due from the meadow.

'I have never been a tradesman, sir, and you can well spare me your toll,' said brave Gawan.

275

'My lord,' replied the master of the ferry, 'so many ladies saw you win a glorious victory here that you will have to concede my rights. Give me my lawful due, my lord. For did you not win this horse for me in regular joust with renown untarnished when you thrust this man down, who was truly acknowledged supreme until this day? Your victory – for him a blow from on high – has taken away his happiness, while great fortune has befallen you.'

'He thrust me down,' Gawan answered, 'though I made up for it later. Since one has to pay you tax on a joust, let him discharge it. There is a little nag, sir, which he won from me in battle. Take it if you will. The man that shall dispose of this war-horse is myself! It will have to carry me away though you never gained another. You talk of right. If you want right on your side you could never agree to my leaving on foot. I tell you I should regret it too keenly if this horse were yours. Early this morning it was still mine beyond all challenge. If you want an easy ride you had rather mount a hobby! Orilus the Burgunjoys gave it me for my own, but Urjans the prince from Punturteis stole it from me for a while. You would sooner get a she-mule's foal! But I can favour you in another way: since you value him so highly, in lieu of the horse you are now asking for, take the man who rode it against me – I don't care if he likes it or not.'

The ferryman was delighted. 'I have never seen so rich a gift,' he said, with laughter on his lips, 'if it were fitting for a man to accept it. But, sir, if you will guarantee it to me, my demand has been exceeded! Truly, he has always been of such resounding reputation that I would not have taken five hundred swift strong chargers for him, since that would have been unseemly in me. If you intend to make me rich, act as a true knight – if it lies within your power deliver him into my cog. I should then say you knew how to do a handsome deed!'

'I shall deliver him over to you as a captive both on to and off your cog till he stands inside your door,' answered the son of King Lot.

'Then you shall be well received,' said the ferryman bowing

assiduously in token of his gratitude. 'My dear lord,' he continued, 'honour me further by condescending to spend the night in comfort under my roof. No greater honour ever befell any of my fellows who ply the ferry. – It will be accounted a most felicitous event for me if I entertain a man of such worth.'

'I ought to ask for what you have desired. I am overcome by a great weariness which makes it imperative for me to rest. It is the way of her at whose command I suffer this hardship, to turn sweet to bitter, to make the heart poor in joy but rich in cares. – Hers is no fair reward! Alas, Loss, inseparable from the finding of her, you weigh down my left breast, here, that always was uplifted when God gave me joy! The heart that lay beneath it, has, I fancy, vanished away! Where shall I find solace? Must I endure such grief for love's sake all unaided? If she is a true-hearted woman, she who has such power to wound me ought to make me happy.'

Hearing him thus oppressed by love and grappling with its cares, the ferryman addressed him: '"Sad today, glad tomorrow" – this is the rule here below, both out in the meadow and in the forest, and everywhere where Clinschor is lord, and neither courage nor cowardice can contrive to alter it. Here is a thing of which you may well be unaware. – This whole land is one great marvel, and its magic holds night and day! If a man has courage, luck can help him. But, sir, the sun is very low, and you should come aboard.' The ferryman urged him to do so.

Gawan led Lischois away with him and on to the water, and the warrior was seen to comply patiently and without demur, while the ferryman followed with the charger. And so they crossed over to the other shore.

'Be host in my house,' the ferryman asked Gawan. Indeed the house was such that Arthur need never have built a better at Nantes where he often had his residence. Gawan escorted Lischois inside while the master and his household did the honours. 'See to the comfort of my lord here!' he at once commanded his daughter. 'You two go together. Now see to his every need, we have received great benefactions from him.' Gringuljete he commended to the care of his son.

The girl did as she was bidden most courteously, and Gawan accompanied her to an upper chamber whose pavement was strewn with fresh-cut rushes and gaily coloured flowers. The sweet girl now unarmed him.

'May God reward you,' said Gawan. 'I am acutely embarrassed, madam, and had you not been told to do it by the master of the house, I should say you were showing me too much attention.'

'I am waiting on you more to win your favour, sir,' she answered, 'than for any other reason.'

A son of Gawan's host, a squire, brought in a pile of soft cushions and bolsters and set them beside the wall opposite the door, then a carpet was laid before it. Gawan was to sit here. Next the squire skilfully spread a coverlet of red cendale over the bed, and a couch was made for the host, after which another squire set table-linen and bread before it, all as the master had bidden them. They were followed by the lady of the house, who on seeing Gawan welcomed him warmly. 'You have made us rich who were poor,' she said. 'Our good fortune is awake and smiles on us!'

Gawan's host now entered, and water was brought in. After he had washed, Gawan uttered a wish. He asked his host for company. – 'Let this young lady dine with me.'

'There has never been any word of her dining with lords or of sitting so close beside them – she might easily put on airs! Yet this favour is but one of many kindnesses you have done us. – Daughter, do everything he asks, I give my full approval.'

The sweet girl blushed with confusion, but did as the master had commanded. Lady Bene sat down beside Gawan. His host had reared two sturdy sons besides, and his merlin having caught three crested larks on the wing, he told the boys to go together and serve up all three of them to Gawan, together with a sauce. The girl was mindful to cut tasty morsels for Gawan and lay them on white wastel-bread with her fair hands, and this she did with excellent breeding.

'You should send one of these roasted birds over to my mother, sir, since she has none,' she said.

Gawan told the comely girl that he would gladly do her will in this or any other thing she might ask him. And so a lark was sent to the lady of the house, who acknowledged Gawan's gesture with many polite bows, while his host, too, voiced his thanks. After this, one of the latter's sons brought in purslane and lettuce dressed with vinegar. (If consumed for any length of time such provender is not highly recommended for building up one's strength, nor does one have a good colour from it. Yet the colour one gets from what one slips into one's mouth speaks true, whereas colour laid on above one's skin has never won resounding praise. If you ask me, it is the woman whose heart is perfect in constancy that wears the best lustre.)

Had Gawan been able to nourish himself on good will alone, he would have thriven there; for no mother could ever have wished her child better than wished him this host whose bread he was eating. When the board had been removed and the mistress of the house had left, bedding and pillows were brought up and placed for Gawan. One item was a bed of down in a cover of green samite, not of the better sort, but imitation. A quilt was spread over the bed especially for Gawan's comfort – it was made of brocade, but without the gold thread brought from far-off heathen lands, and quilted over palmat-silk.* Over this, soft bed-clothes were drawn – a pair of sheets of snowy linen. They laid a pillow on them and a spotless new ermine cloak such as young ladies wear.

The master asked leave before going off to bed, and I was told that Gawan was left alone there with the girl for company. Had he desired anything of her I fancy she would have granted it him. But Gawan needs to sleep if he can. May God preserve him when the new day dawns!

* A soft flock-silk used in mattresses, Lat. *palmatium*, *palmacium*, apparently more widely known in Germany, both north and south, than in England in those days.

Chapter 11

GREAT weariness shuttered Gawan's eyes. He slept thus till he awoke early next morning. One wall of his chamber had a number of glazed French windows, one of which stood open towards the orchard. Into this he went to see what he could see, to breathe the fresh air and listen to the birds singing. He had not sat there for long before he recognized the Castle he had seen the evening before, when undergoing his adventure, and the many ladies in the Palace, of whom no few were very beautiful. And he marvelled that these ladies should choose to be awake instead of sleeping, since it was still early twilight.

'I will go to sleep again for their sakes,' he thought and went back to bed. His blanket was the girl's cloak that covered him. You ask if he was wakened? No, his host would have been displeased. But now the girl broke her slumber where she lay at her mother's feet and went to her guest to offer him company. But he was fast asleep. So, ever mindful of her service, the lovely girl sat down beside the bed on the carpet. I cannot say that I ever see an apparition of this sort gliding in to me of an evening or a morning.

After some time Gawan awoke. He looked at her and laughed. 'God preserve you, young lady,' he said, 'for cutting short your sleep like this for my sake and inflicting hardship on yourself quite beyond what I deserve.'

'I wish to be without your service,' said the lovely girl, 'I crave nothing but your gracious favour. My lord, command me. I shall do whatever you say. All who live with my father, my mother and her children, shall always have you for their lord – you have done us so much kindness!'

'Have you been here long?' he asked. 'Had I known of your coming sooner I should have liked to ask you some questions, provided you would not have minded answering me. Yesterday, and this morning, I saw many ladies high above me. Please tell me who they are.'

The young lady was startled. 'Do not ask that, sir!' she said. 'I shall never tell you! I cannot tell you anything about them. Though I know, I am bound to silence. Do not be offended with me, ask me about something else – that is my advice if you will take it.'

Gawan asked her again and again and pressed his question concerning all the ladies he saw sitting up there in the Palace. But the loyal girl wept bitterly and showed every sign of grief.

While it was still very early her father joined them. He would have let it pass and not upbraided him had the comely girl been forced to something or other and there had been a rough-and-tumble; for the modest girl was behaving as though there had been, and was sitting near the bed. Her father made no bones about that. 'Don't cry, daughter,' said he. 'When things of that sort happen in fun, though at first they may arouse anger, it is soon forgiven and forgotten.'

'Nothing has happened here,' said Gawan, 'other than what we are ready to own openly. I asked this girl a question, but she thought it would lead to my undoing and begged me to refrain. If you do not mind, let me deserve it of you, dear host, that *you* kindly tell me about those ladies up there. Never in any land did I ever hear of any place where so many superb women wearing such dazzling fillets were on display together.'

'In God's name do not ask!' cried his host, wringing his hands. 'My lord, there is anguish surpassing all other there!'

'Then I have reason to deplore their distress,' replied Gawan. 'Tell me why my question displeases you, host.'

'Sir, it is because of your manly spirit. If you cannot forbear to ask, you are bound to question me further, and this will bring sorrow to your heart and sadden me and all my children who have been born to serve you.'

'You *must* tell me!' answered Gawan. 'If you withhold it from me and leave me uninformed, I shall learn how matters stand there, nevertheless.'

'I cannot help being very sorry indeed, my lord, that you insist on asking,' said his faithful host. 'I will lend you a shield, now arm yourself for battle. You are in Terre marveile, and Lit marveile is here. My lord, the perils up at Schastel marveile have never yet been attempted. Your life is hastening deathwards! If you have known adventure before, whatever your past feats, that was child's play compared with this! Calamity is coming your way.'

'I should be very sorry if I were to ride away from these ladies in comfort without exerting myself,' replied Gawan, 'and without trying to learn more about them. I have heard of them before, and now that I have come so near, for their sakes I shall not shirk the challenge!'

'No hardship can be compared to that man's who has to endure this adventure,' this host told his guest in tones of heartfelt grief, 'for it is sharp and terrible! Believe me, my lord, I am no deceiver.'

The illustrious Gawan ignored the other's fears. 'Now advise me as to this battle,' said he. 'By your leave and please God I shall achieve knightly exploits here. I shall be glad of your advice and instruction always. But it would be very wrong of me simply to ride away, sir. Friends and enemies alike would think me a coward.'

At this, his host's unhappy protests were redoubled, since such sorrow had never befallen him before. He turned to Gawan and said: 'If God makes it manifest that you are not to die, you will be lord of this land. If you have the strength to release all the ladies held captive here, and numerous men-at-arms and noble knights too, you will be accorded such renown as no knight ever won till now, and God himself will have honoured you well. Then you will be able to lord it happily over many dazzling beauties from many lands. But who would set it down to your dishonour were you to leave these parts as matters stand, now that Lischois Gwelljus has surrendered his renown to you? Sweet youth, how well he deserves this salute! For he has done many deeds of arms, his chivalric exploits are performed with great spirit! Apart from Ither of Gaheviez, the Almighty never thrust so many fine qualities into a man's heart. Yesterday my ship ferried over the man who slew Ither below the walls of Nantes. He gave me five war-horses, God bless him, that had been ridden by dukes and kings. Whatever booty he won from them will be narrated at Belrepeire, since he made them his sworn prisoners. His shield bears the scars of many jousts. He was riding here in quest of the Gral.'

'Which way did he go?' asked Gawan. 'Tell me, host, being so near, did he learn the nature of the Adventure?'

'He did not learn it, sir. I took good care not to mention it to him. – I should have opened myself to blame had I done so. If it had not occurred to you to ask of your own accord, you would never have been apprised by me of what's to do here – mighty sorcery fraught with terror! If you will not be wooed from your purpose and you lose your life, it would be the greatest sorrow that ever befell me and my children. But if you win the victory and become lord of this land, my penury will be at an end, for I know your generous hand will raise me up to affluence. If your lot is to survive, your victory here can win joy without sorrow. Now arm yourself against great hardship!'

Gawan was still without weapons and armour. 'Bring me my equipment,' he said, and it was his host who carried out the order. But the one who armed him from his feet upward was the sweet and lovely girl. His host went to fetch his charger. On one of his walls there hung a thick, tough shield – it saved Gawan's life, later – and this was brought to him together with his horse.

And now the master of the house had the forethought to come and stand before him and say: 'I will tell you how you must comport yourself when faced with those deadly perils. You must carry my shield, which is neither hacked nor pierced, for I never fight – so how should it suffer any harm? When you arrive up at the Castle, sir, there is one thing that can help you with your horse. A huckster sits before the Gate. – Leave your mount with him outside. Buy something of him, no matter what. He will guard your charger all the better for it if you leave it as an earnest. And if you are not prevented, you will be glad of your horse.'

'Am I not to ride in on horseback?' asked my lord Gawan.

'No, sir. All those radiant ladies will stay hidden from your sight: the hour of peril is at hand! You will find the Palace deserted. – Great or small, you will find no living thing there. May the Grace of God be with you when you enter the chamber which houses Lit marveile! If the crown and all the treasure of the Mahmumelin* of Morocco were set against that Bed and its bed-posts, they would not fetch their price! As you lie on it, it will be your lot to suffer what God has in mind for you. May He manifest a joyful outcome! Remember, sir, if you are a worthy knight, never to part company with this shield or with your sword. For just as you are thinking that your great trial is over, it will take on the colour of serious fighting!'

When Gawan had mounted, the girl's spirits faltered, while all those present gave way to unrestrained laments.

'God willing, I shall not be slow to reward you for your loyal service in entertaining me like this,' Gawan assured his host. He then took leave of the maiden whose great sorrow was only natural. Now he rode off, while they stood weeping here. And if it is your wish to hear how Gawan fared there, I shall tell you all the more willingly.

I shall tell you as I heard it. Arriving before the Gate, Gawan found the Huckster. The latter's Booth was not empty, for in it, up for sale, lay goods that would make me wild with joy, had I such treasure! Gawan rode up to him and dismounted. He had never seen such magnificent wares as it was his lot to see there. The Booth was made of samite, square, high and capacious. And what did it hold for sale? Were there any question of buying it, the Baruc of Baghdad could not have met the cost of what lay in that Booth, nor the Catholicus of Hromgla. Moreover, in the days when Bysance still had its treasure,† its Emperor could not have paid for it, not even if the other two had helped him – of such rare worth was that Merchandise!

* The *Amīru 'l-mu'minīn*, 'Commander of the Faithful'.
† That is, until 1204, when the knights of the Fourth 'Crusade' looted it.

Gawan greeted the Huckster. When he saw the marvels on sale there he asked to be shown some girdles or clasps, in keeping with his modest means.

'Truly', said the Huckster, 'I have been here for years on end without any other than noble ladies venturing to inspect the contents of my Booth. If yours is a manly heart this shall all be yours. It was brought from far-off lands. If you are bent on winning fame and have come here in quest of adventure, and if success attends you, you can easily come to terms with me. – Then all my wares will be yours! Continue on your way, and God's will be done! Was it Plippalinot the Ferryman who showed you the way here? Many ladies will laud your coming to this land if you release them. If you wish to go after adventures leave your charger here. If you will leave him to me I will take care of him.'

'I should be glad to leave him to you, if it is not beneath you. But your wealth affrights me, for never since I first sat up on him did he have such an opulent groom!'

'Sir,' replied the Huckster pleasantly, 'what more shall I say? I myself and all my goods will be yours if you come through alive here. Who would have a better right to my allegiance?'

Gawan's dauntless courage inspired him to march on on foot. As I told you before, the Castle he saw before him was vast, with each of its flanks stoutly fortified. If any had a mind to harm it, it would not care *that* much in thirty years! Enclosed within its walls was a meadow – but the Lechfeld extends farther! Many towers loomed above the battlements. The story tells us that when Gawan looked at the Palace its whole roof resembled peacock's feathers, so gaily coloured was it and such that neither rain nor snow could mar its lustre. Inside, the Palace was embellished and adorned, its window-shafts well fluted and bearing lofty vaulting. In alcoves lay couches past number, here and there, each on its own and draped with luxurious quilts of many kinds. Sitting on them had been ladies who had taken care to withdraw. Thus Gawan, on whom the advent of their joy, their day of·bliss depended, was not received by them. If only they could have seen him, what greater pleasure could they have had? Not one was allowed to do so, despite his wish to wait on them. It was not of their doing.

My lord Gawan walked up and down as he surveyed the Palace. In one of the walls – don't ask me on which side – he saw a wide-open door, in the chamber to which it led he was either to win glory or die in the attempt. He entered. Its pavement shone smooth and clear as glass. Upon it stood that fabulous Bed: Lit marveile! Below, clasped by the bed-posts they carried, four balls* of glowing ruby finely rounded ran swifter than the wind! I must praise this pavement for you. Devised by Clinschor to his taste, it was of jasper, chrysolite and sardine. With his subtle lore he had brought the artifice applied to it from many lands.

The pavement was so glassy that Gawan could hardly find purchase for his feet. He went at a peradventure. And as often as he made a step, the Bed moved on from where it was. The heavy shield he was carrying and which his host had commended to him so earnestly began to irk him. 'How shall I get at you?' he wondered. 'Are you set on dodging away from me? I shall teach you, if I can pounce on top of you!' At that moment the Bed stood still in front of him. He took a flying jump and landed plumb in the middle. No one will ever hear again of the speed at which that Bed went crashing from side to side! Not one wall did it spare, but hurtled against each so that the whole Castle echoed with its thuds.

In this way Gawan rode many a mighty charge. If all the thunder that ever roared had been in that room and all the trumpeters there ever were, from the First to the Last, and they were blowing for their hire, there could not have been a more ear-splitting din. Although he was abed, Gawan had to stay awake. What did the warrior do? He was so overwhelmed by this clamour that he pulled his shield up over him. He lay still and left his fate in the hands of Him Who has power to help nor ever wearied of it when men in dire need have known how to seek it of Him. When trouble manifests itself to a wise and stout-hearted man he appeals to the Almighty, Whose

* Or: discs.

hand bears aid in abundance, and Who will succour him. This is what happened to Gawan too. He asked Him to Whose power and goodness he had always ascribed his own renown, to watch over him now. The crashing and blaring ceased the moment the Bed came to a halt at the very centre of the pavement equidistant from the four walls. This was the signal for even greater peril for him. Five hundred slingstaves had been primed to throw by subtle arts, and their cast was aimed at the Bed on which he lay. The shield was so tough that he felt their impact but little – hard, round pebbles they were – though it was holed in several places.

The hail of pebbles was now over. Never had he endured so violent a bombardment! And now five hundred crossbows or more were tensed to shoot, and one and all were trained straight on the Bed. Any used to torment of this sort will know what bolts are like! It was not long before their whirrs had died away. Whoever has an eye to his comfort should fight shy of a bed of this sort, he would be given no comfort there: from the ease Gawan had found in *that* Bed young men could turn grey, yet his heart and hand did not tremble. The bolts and pebble-stones were far from having missed him, he was all cut and bruised through his chain-mail.

Gawan was now hoping that his troubles were over, but he still had to win fame by fighting. For at that instant a door opened opposite him through which came a brawny rustic, horrible to see, clad in a smock, bonnet and baggy breeches made from the skin of a water-beast. In his hand he held a club whose bulge was thicker than an ewer. He made for Gawan, which was not at all to Gawan's liking, rather was he put out at his coming.

'This fellow has no armour,' he reflected. 'He is incapable of defending himself from me.' Gawan sat up as if none of his limbs were aching. The other retreated a step as though about to withdraw.

'You need have no fear of me!' he shouted angrily nevertheless. 'All the same, I shall see to it that something happens to you from which you will lose your life. That you are still alive is due only to the power of the Devil, but even if he has saved you here, nothing can prevent your dying. This I shall bring home to you as soon as I have left.' And the rustic went back into the room.

Gawan cut the shafts of the crossbow bolts from his shield with his sword – they had all forced their way clean through it and struck his mail with a clang. He then heard a roar as though twenty drums were being beaten for a dance. In his firm courage, whose integrity had never been gashed or scarred by real fear, Gawan wondered 'What is going to happen to me now? I could claim to have enough trouble as it is. Is there more in store for me? I must see to my defence.' And as he looked towards the rustic's door, a mighty lion, tall as a horse, leapt out from it. Not given to running away, Gawan gripped his shield by its thong, and the better to defend himself leapt down on to the pavement. This huge and mighty lion had been made terrible by hunger, but he was to reap little advantage from it. He pounced angrily at the man. Lord Gawan stood on guard. The lion all but snatched his shield away with its first lunge, since its paw went through it, claws and all! Never before has a beast struck its paw through such toughness! Gawan prevented it from tearing his shield from his grasp by hewing off its leg at a stroke, with the result that the lion was now prancing on three legs, leaving the paw of the fourth wedged in the shield. The beast's blood gushed out so copiously, spreading this way and that, that Gawan could not take a firm stance. Time and time again did the lion leap at the stranger and bare its fangs with many a snort. If it had been trained to devour good people as its fare I should not like to be its neighbour. Fighting him for his life Gawan, too, was equally averse to such a prospect.

Gawan had wounded the lion so gravely that the whole chamber was wet with its blood. And now it sprang at him in a fury to pluck him under itself. But Gawan stabbed it through the breast to such a depth that his sword was buried to the hilt, at which the lion's rage abated, for it stumbled and fell down dead. Gawan had fought and overcome his great peril. His next thought was 'What is best for me now? I don't want to sit here in this blood. This Bed too dashes around so

madly that I must take good care not to sit or lie in it, if I
have any sense.'

Now Gawan's head was in such a whirl from the slingstones
and bolts, and his wounds were beginning to bleed so copiously
that his gallant strength forsook him and he fell down in a
swoon. His head was pillowed on the lion, and his shield had
fallen beneath him. If he had ever had strength and intelligence
they had been ravished from him now, so roughly had he been
assailed. All his senses had given him the slip! His pillow was
unlike the one which charming, clever Gymele of Monte
Rybele laid under Kahenis's head and on which he slept his
glory away!* Glory, however, was racing towards *this* man,
for you have heard in full how he was bereft of his senses and
lay swooning, and how it all arose.

Unseen eyes observed that the chamber-floor was bedewed
with blood. Both Gawan and the lion seemed dead. A comely
young lady-in-waiting peeped timidly down from a high
window, and her bright face paled at the sight. This young
woman was so appalled that her senior, the wise Arnive, wept
at her news – Arnive, whom I still honour for warding off
death and saving him.

Arnive went to the scene to look, and when she too had
peeped down she was unable to tell whether it was to be days
of future happiness or never-ending grief. She feared the
knight was dead – a thought which much distressed her –
for Gawan was lying on the lion and had no other couch. 'I
shall be mortified if your loyal courage has lost you your noble
life,' she said. 'If you have found death here for the sake of us
poor exiles, your goodness will move me to pity always,
whether you be young or old, since it was a loyal heart that
prompted you.'

Seeing the warrior lying there in such sad state she said to

* An allusion to a recension of *Tristan* more archaic than that of Thomas
(see Penguin Classics), possibly the French rather than the German
Tristrant of Eilhart von Oberge of *c.* 1175. Here, Gymele slips a magic
pillow beneath Kahenis's head that will send him instantly to sleep, so
that she can meet Isold's command that she sleep with him, yet preserve
her honour.

all her ladies: 'You ladies that are Christians, call on God for His blessing!' She sent two young ladies there with orders to tiptoe in and bring her news, before withdrawing, as to whether he were dead or alive: such was her bidding to these two. You ask if either of these lovely girls was weeping? *Both* were weeping, I assure you, moved by true sorrow, when they found him lying there in this plight, his shield awash with his blood. They examined him to see if he lived.

One of them with her fair hand unlaced and removed his helmet and then his ventail, revealing flecks of foam on his red lips. She now looked intently to discover whether he were still breathing or she were deceived by the semblance of life: for the issue was in doubt. On his surcoat there were two Dragonlets cut in sable such as Ilinot the Briton had displayed with great lustre – he who had gathered glory enough in his young life. Of this fur the girl plucked a tuft and held it beneath his nose and watched closely to see if it stirred, however slightly, in response to his breathing.

Breathing *was* detected there. And at once she told her fair friend to fetch some clear water, and this the latter quickly brought her. The girl delicately inserted a slender finger between his teeth and gently poured in some water, in driblets, not too much, till suddenly he opened his eyes. He thanked the charming girl most gallantly. 'I am sorry you had to find me lying in this ill-bred fashion,' he said. 'I should judge it a kindness on your part if you would not let this go any further. I rely on your courtesy to dissuade you.'

'You lay and are lying as one who has covered himself with glory!' they declared. 'You have gained such renown here that you will grow old in contentment. Victory is yours today! Now assure us poor people that the state of your wounds is such that we can share your joy.'

'You must aid me if you wish to see me live,' he answered. He then asked the young ladies, 'Let someone skilled in such matters examine my wounds. But if I have to fight again lace on my helmet and go – I intend to defend myself!'

'You are exempt from further fighting,' they replied. 'Let us stay with you, sir, except that one of us must go and be

rewarded by four queens for the news that you are still alive!
They will also have to make ready for you comfortable lodge-
ment and pure medicaments, and tend you faithfully with
ointments such as will soothe your bruises and heal your wounds
with gentle efficacy.'

Thus one of the girls nimbly raced away to bring the news
to court that the warrior was alive. 'And in such vigour that,
God willing, he will bring us abundant happiness! But he is
in great need of attention.'

'Thank God!' they said, one and all.

The wise old Queen ordered a bed to be made ready and a
carpet to be spread before it in front of a good fire. For the
bruises and wounds she obtained unguents most rare, in-
geniously concocted. She then commanded four ladies to go
and receive his armour. They were to remove it from him
tenderly and take good care not to put him to the blush.

'Take a roll of silk to screen you and unarm him behind it.
If it is possible for him to walk, allow it, otherwise carry him
to where I shall be seeing to the bed he is to lie in. If his
battle passed off without a mortal wound I shall soon restore
him to health. But if any of his wounds is of a fatal kind,
this would cut across our rejoicing, for then we too would be
slain and have to endure a living death!'

This was duly done. Lord Gawan was unarmed and led
away from that place and given aid by those who knew how.
His wounds were of the number of fifty or more, but the
bolts had not forced their way through his chain-mail to any
depth, since he had slung his shield in front of him. The old
Queen took dittany* and warm wine and a piece of blue
cendale and with it wiped the gore from his wounds, when
there was some, and bandaged him so well that he recovered.
As to the bruises on his head, where you could see his helmet
had been dented by missiles, raising bumps, she made them
disappear by a combination of skill and potent salves.

'I shall soon bring you relief. Cundrie la surziere is kind
enough to come and see me often. She acquaints and sup-

* See p. 322, second footnote.

plies me with whatever is efficacious in medicine. Ever since
the time when Anfortas was afflicted, and they enlisted aid for
him, this salve helped him stay alive – it was brought from
Munsalvæsche!'

When Gawan heard Munsalvæsche named, he was pleased,
imagining himself to be near it. 'You have got my senses back
into me that had taken leave of me, Ma'am,' honest Gawan
told the Queen. 'My pain, too, is abating. Any strength or
sense that are mine, your servant owes to you entirely.'

'We must all exert ourselves loyally to woo your favour,
sir,' she said. 'Now do as I say and do not talk much. I am
going to give you a herb that will send you to sleep: that will
do you good. You should not desire food or drink before
nightfall. In this way you will recover your strength. Then I
shall come to you with food, so that you will be able to hold
out till morning.'

She placed a herb in his mouth, and he fell asleep at once.
Then carefully she tucked him in. In this way, he who was
so rich in honour, so poor in shame, slept through the day
and lay soft and warm. Now and again as he slept, a cold
shudder ran over him, and he wheezed and sneezed, all by
virtue of the salve. There was a great company of ladies, some
going, others coming, of noble, radiant appearance. With her
authority old Arnive let it be known that none was to raise
her voice as long as the hero slept. She also commanded the
Palace to be locked, with the result that no man-at-arms or
castle-dweller learnt the news till the next day. Then fresh
cause for sorrow was to befall those ladies.

The warrior slept thus till evening. The Queen judged
it time to remove the herb from his mouth. He awoke needing
something to drink, and the experienced lady told them to bring
some in, and nourishing food as well. He sat up and ate cheer-
fully. With the many ladies standing there in his presence
he had never been waited on more nobly, so decorously did they
minister to him. My lord Gawan scrutinized them closely,
these, those and yonder: his longing for lovely Orgeluse
had of course returned to him. For in all his life, when as
sometimes his love had been requited, or love had been

denied him, no woman had ever moved his heart so deeply.

'My lady,' said the dauntless warrior to his nurse, the old Queen, 'it offends my sense of propriety – you may think me too demanding – if these ladies are to go on standing before me. Ask them to go and sit down, or have them eat with me.'

'Sir, there will be no sitting down by any one apart from me. They would have cause to be ashamed if they did not lavish their attentions on you, since it is to you we all look for our happiness. Yet, sir, if we have any sense, whatever you say will be done.'

Those noble ladies of high degree adhered to their standards of conduct – they served him with right good will – and sweetly begged him to let them stand till he had supped, with none of them sitting down. When this was done, Gawan laid himself down to sleep.

Chapter 12

IF anyone now were to disturb Gawan's repose when he has such need of it I should say he would incur much guilt. As the story has testified, Gawan has taxed himself sorely and under great duress advanced his fame in all directions. Noble Lanzilot's sufferings on the Bridge of Swords and the ensuing battle with Meljahkanz were as nothing against Gawan's perils, as were the exploits told of the proud and mighty King Garel, who so gallantly threw the lion from the palace at Nantes and fetched the knife that was to cause him such suffering in the marble pillar.* Were a-mule to be loaded with all those deadly bolts which brave Gawan allowed to be sent whirring at him according to the dictates of his manly heart, the beast could not have carried them. Neither the Ford Li gweiz prelljus† nor Erec's winning of Schoydelakurt from Mabonagrin‡ inflicted such agony, nor the sequel to proud Iwan's insistence on pouring water on the Marvellous Stone.* If all these trials were added together, Gawan's suffering would outweigh them in the judgment of those who can discriminate.

But what suffering have I in mind? If you do not think it too early I will name it for you explicitly. Orgeluse entered the inmost thoughts of dauntless Gawan, ever-strong in true courage. But how was it possible for a woman of her stature to be hidden in so small a place? She came by a narrow path into Gawan's heart, with the result that the suffering she brought banished all his aches and pains. After all, it was but a tiny cell that housed so tall a woman, to whom his waking

* The story alluded to has not survived. A Garel is featured elsewhere in *Parzival* as a minor figure of the Table Round.
† Where Gawan himself is to face a severe test in this same chapter of *Parzival*.
‡ Narrated in Chrétien's *Erec* and in Hartmann's adaptation.
* Narrated in Chrétien's *Yvain* and Hartmann's adaptation *Iwein*.

thoughts were dedicated in unfailing constancy. Let no one laugh that a woman can discomfit so redoubtable a fighting-man in this way! God in Heaven, what does it mean? – It is Mistress Love venting her ill humour on one who has covered himself in glory! Yet she found him resolute and formidable in battle. It ought to have been beneath her to use force on a sick and wounded man: he ought to benefit from having been vanquished by her perforce, while still unscathed.

Mistress Love, if you wish to cover yourself in glory let it be told to you that this fight can bring you no honour. Gawan has always lived his life in accord with your gracious commands, as did his father Lot before him. His family on his mother's side have always recognized your authority all the way down from Mazadan, whom Terdelaschoye took to Famurgan, where you aroused his passions. As to Mazadan's descendants, we have heard many times that you spared not one. Ither of Gaheviez bore the impress of your seal, and wherever he was mentioned if only by name in the hearing of ladies, not one was ashamed to acknowledge Love's power. So consider those who saw him! – They really knew what it was to love! His death has denied you much observance.

Now drive Gawan to his death as you drove his cousin Ilinot, whom, as a sweet youth fled from his father's land in childhood, your power compelled to strive for Florie of Kanadic as his noble mistress! Then a stranger to his own country, he was reared by that same queen. Loading him with Love's burden, Florie chased him beyond her frontiers and, as doubt-less you have heard, he was found dead in her service.* Gawan's line have often been assailed by heartfelt anguish because of love. I shall name you other of his kinsmen who have been afflicted by it. Why did the blood-tinged snow torment faithful Parzival? – It was his wife, the Queen, who caused it. You planted your foot on Galoes and Gahmuret to such effect that you consigned them to their biers. Noble young Itonje, Gawan's lovely sister, bore King Gramoflanz love that was perfect in its constancy. Mistress Love, you doled out

* This reference has not been traced.

harassment to Surdamur through her love for Alexander.*
It did not please you to excuse any of the relations Gawan ever
had, neither these nor others, from rendering service to you,
Mistress Love. And now you are bent on winning glory from
him! You ought only to pit your strength, bringing it to bear
on those who are well and fit, and let Gawan live, weakened
by wounds as he is. Many a man sings about love whom Love
never oppressed as much as Gawan. Now I ought to hold my
tongue – let the love-poets lament the state of him of Norway
after surviving the Adventure, when Love's all too savage
hail-storm broke on him in his helplessness!

'Alas,' he said 'that I ever saw these beds! The one wounded
me severely, the other has redoubled my thoughts of love!
The Duchess Orgeluse must have mercy on me if I am to stay
a happy man.' He tossed and turned so with impatience that
some of his bandages burst, in such anguish did he lie there.
But see, day broke and was shining down on him who had
waited for it in such discomfort. He had in the past endured
many a sharp sword-fight with greater ease than this time
when people rest. If there is any love-poet who boasts suffering
equal to Gawan's, let him, fit and well as he is, be mangled
by crossbow-bolts – that will perhaps make him smart as much
as his old love-pangs!

Gawan was burdened with love and other troubles. And now
day shone out so brightly that the rays cast by his bright candle
were much foreshortened. The warrior sat up. His underlinen
was stained by his wounds and armour, but a doublet and hose
of fine buckram had been laid out for him, an exchange he
was glad to accept, and also a sleeveless robe of marten and a
jerkin of the same fur, and then, to go above these, a rare
tissue sent all the way from Arras. A pair of roomy summer
boots also stood there. All these new clothes he donned. And
then my lord Gawan passed through the chamber-door and
walked up and down till he came to the Palace, which was so
magnificent that he had never set eyes on anything fit to

* Gauvain's sister Soredamur and Emperor Alexander of Bysance were
the parents of Cligés in Chrétien's romance of that name.

compare with it for splendour. At one side of the Palace a spiral staircase, vaulted and moderately broad, ascended through the whole height of the Palace and beyond. It carried a splendid Pillar not made of rotten wood but strong and burnished and so tall that Lady Camilla's sarcophagus might fittingly have rested upon it.* Clinschor had brought this towering master-piece from Feirefiz's lands. It was as round as a tent. The skill that went to make it would have surpassed the understanding of Master Geometras, had he set his hand to it; for it was contrived with subtle arts. The windows were adorned with diamond and amethyst, topaz and garnet, chrysolite and ruby, emerald and sardine – the tale would have us know – and they were as high as they were broad, while, overhead, the ceiling was in the same style as the window-columns. Yet there was not one column among these that could compare with the great Pillar in their midst. Its wondrous nature is told by the story.

Alone as he was, Gawan mounted this watch-tower with all its costly gems in order to survey the scene and discovered such great marvels as he never wearied of gazing at. It seemed to him as though each land was revealed to him in the great Pillar, that they were whirling round and the huge mountains clashing with one another. He saw people in the Pillar, riding and walking, this man running, that one standing. He sat down in an oriel the better to examine this marvel.

And now old Arnive came with her daughter Sangive and two of Sangive's daughters. All four came towards Gawan who, seeing them, leapt to his feet.

'You ought still to be asleep, sir,' said Queen Arnive. 'You are too badly wounded to do without rest, if further trials are in store for you.'

'My lady and mistress physician,' answered Gawan, 'your help has so restored me in body and mind that, given life, I shall be your servant.'

'If I am right in thinking you have acknowledged me as your mistress,' said the Queen, 'my precept is that you should

* Wolfram here alludes to a fanciful extension of *Æneid*, XI, 845 ff., by the poet of the *Roman d'Eneas*, in which Heinrich von Veldeke (Henrik van Veldeken) followed him in *Eneide*.

kiss these three ladies. By so doing you will not demean your-self, for they are of royal line.'

Pleased to comply, Gawan kissed those lovely women, San-give, Itonje and sweet Cundrie.* Gawan sat down with the four. His gaze wandered from one to the other of the handsome pair of girls, but the image of a woman who dwelt within his heart compelled him to admit to himself that their lustre was as a misty day compared with hers – such beauty did he find in Orgeluse, Duchess of Logroys, towards whom his feelings were driving him.

Well, Gawan had been presented to all three ladies, who were nevertheless so dazzling that a heart which had known no pain before might easily have been cut by it. He asked his 'mistress' to tell him the nature of the Pillar there.

'Sir,' said she, 'ever since I first came to know it, this stone has shone out day and night over the countryside to a distance of six miles on all sides. All that takes place within that range can be seen in this Pillar, whether it be on land or water. It is the true tell-tale of bird and beast, strangers and foresters, foreigners and familiars – all these have been reflected in it! Its lustre extends over six miles and it is so solid and whole that no smith, however adroit, could flaw it with his hammer. It was taken from Queen Secundille in Thabronit, without her leave, I fancy.'

In the Pillar at that moment Gawan saw people riding – he could make out a knight and a lady. The lady he thought very lovely. The man and his horse were fully armed, his helmet was adorned with its crest. They rode in great haste through the causeway on to the meadow. Gawan was the object of their sortie. They came, taking the same path through the marsh as that taken by proud Lischois, whom Gawan had defeated. The lady was conducting the knight ceremoniously by the bridle, and this knight's one desire was jousting. Gawan turned away with redoubled pain. He thought the Pillar had deceived him. But then he saw Orgeluse de Logroys and a courtly knight

* Not to be confused with Cundrie la surziere, whose name is pro-nounced differently in the original.

approaching the quay beside the meadow. Like hellebore, swift
to act, pungent in the nostrils, the Duchess stung his eyes as
she pressed through into his heart. A man helpless in the face
of love – alas, such a one is Gawan! Seeing this knight
approaching, he addressed his mistress-physician.

'There is a knight riding up, Ma'am, with lance raised,
intent on seeking combat – and indeed he shall find what he
seeks! Since fighting is what he wants I shall give it him.
But tell me, who is the lady?'

'She is the lovely Duchess of Logroys,' was her answer.
'Whom is she out to harm now? She is attended by the
Turkoyt, of whose dauntless spirit one has heard so often. With
his lance he has earned renown enough to make three lands
illustrious. You must avoid battle with this formidable man
now, for it is much too early for you to fight, you are too badly
wounded. And even if you were in full health and vigour you
ought to decline battle with him.'

'You say I am to be lord here,' said my lord Gawan. 'When
a man comes so close in search of combat and offers battle with
all my honour at stake, I must have my arms and armour,
Ma'am.'

This gave rise to much weeping on the part of the four
ladies. 'You must not fight at all if you wish to enhance your
fame and fortune,' they said. 'Were you to lie slain at his feet,
our distress would reach new depths. But even if you were to
escape death at his hands, with you in your armour the wounds
you have already would prove fatal. Thus, either way, we
should be delivered up to death.'

Gawan had these troubles to contend with – you may care
to hear what was oppressing him? He had taken the noble
Turkoyt's coming as an affront. In addition, his wounds were
giving him much ado. And Love was giving him very much
more – not to mention the sorrow of the four ladies, whose
sincerity was plain to him. He begged them not to weep and
then asked for his horse, sword and armour, and those beaut-
eous, noble ladies conducted him back. He asked them to pre-
cede him down to where the other ladies were assembled who
were so sweet and lovely. Here Gawan was soon armed for his

sortie under the gaze of bright eyes wet with tears. This was done secretly lest any should get to hear of it, apart from the chamberlain, who had had his charger dressed. Gawan tiptoed out to where Gringuljete was standing, but he was so badly wounded that he carried his gappy shield there only with great difficulty.

Gawan mounted his war-horse and then turned away from the Castle towards his faithful host, who never crossed him in any of his wishes. He gave Gawan a stout lance, untrimmed. – He had retrieved many such, outside on his meadow. Then my lord Gawan asked to be taken over immediately, and Plippalinot ferried him to the other side, in a pontoon, to where the proud and noble Turkoyt stood. The latter's reputation was entirely without blemish, and he enjoyed the high renown that all who had engaged him in joust had taken a toss and landed behind their mounts – with such thrusting had he defeated all who had ridden out against him in pursuit of honour. Moreover the noble warrior had trumpeted it out that he intended to acquire high fame with lance alone, without the sword, or let his good name perish; and that if any reaped the glory of unhorsing him he would be found unarmed and would surrender to his vanquisher. All this Gawan learnt from Plippalinot, stake-holder of the joust, who took forfeits on these terms: that in those jousts in which one man fell and the other kept the saddle he should receive without either's resenting it the loss of the one and the other's gain, that is, the horse, which he, Plippalinot, should then lead away. He did not care how much they fought, and left it to the ladies to say who had distinguished or disgraced himself – they had many opportunities of seeing such contests.

Plippalinot told Gawan to sit firm, led his horse ashore and handed him his shield and lance. And now the Turkoyt rode up at the gallop like a man well versed in measuring his joust, neither too high nor too low, while Gawan advanced to meet him. Gringuljete of Munsalvæsche answered Gawan's rein and wheeled towards the meadow.

Come on, now! Let them joust! King Lot's son rode up like a man, no tremor in his heart. Where are helmet-laces knotted?

– It was there that the Turkoyt's lance-thrust landed! Gawan caught him in another place – through his vizor – and at once it was clear who had brought the other down! Gawan had received the other's helmet on his short, stout lance, so off rode helmet and here lay this man who had always been the very flower of excellence till he covered the grass in this fashion, his magnificent accoutrements vying with the flowers in the dew. Gawan then rode up to him and forced him to surrender.

The ferryman claimed the horse. It was his due, and who denies it?

'You might well exult that the mighty lion's paw has to follow you round in your shield – if that were any reason!' said lovely Orgeluse in order to vex Gawan once again. 'And now you imagine you have distinguished yourself because these ladies have seen the outcome of this joust. We must leave you to your raptures! You can dance for joy at being let off so lightly by Lit marveile, despite which your shield is battered as though you had been fighting! No doubt you are too badly wounded for the rough-and-tumble of battle, that would hurt you too much! – Take that on top of "Goose"! You may prize your shield, pierced by so many bolts that it is holed like a sieve, for giving you something to boast of. At present you may well wish to flee discomfort – *take that*! I tweak your finger! Ride up to the ladies again, for how dare you contemplate battle such as I would provide, *if* your heart wished to serve me for love?'

'Madam,' he answered the Duchess, 'if I have any wounds they have been helped here and now. If your readiness to help a man can be reconciled to the favour of accepting my service, there would be no danger so formidable but that I would not be found serving you in despite of it!'

'I shall allow you to ride in my company to fight further battles in pursuit of honour,' said she, making the proud and noble Gawan very happy indeed. He sent the Turkoyt away with his host Plippalinot, with a message to the comely ladies up in the Castle to treat him with great respect.

Although the two chargers had been urged to full tilt with the spur, Gawan's lance had remained whole, and so he took it with him on leaving the bright meadow. Many ladies wept at his setting out and leaving them. 'The man on whom we have pinned our high hopes has chosen a lady who is balm to his eyes yet a thorn to his heart,' Queen Arnive lamented. 'Alas, that he should now be following the Duchess Orgeluse towards Li gweiz prelljus! This bodes ill for his wounds!' Four hundred ladies gave way to lamentation while he rode off to win renown. Any distress he suffered from his wounds was banished by the radiance of Orgeluse's looks.

'You must get me a garland from the twig of a certain tree,' she said. 'If you will give it me I shall praise your exploit, and then you may ask for my love.'

'Madam, wherever that twig may be,' he replied, 'which can win me such high renown and bliss that I may acquaint you with my passion in the hope that you will favour me, I shall cull it unless death prevents me!'

However gay the flowers in that meadow, they were as nothing beside the brightness shed there by Orgeluse. She was so deep in Gawan's thoughts that his former sufferings gave him no trouble now.

Thus leaving the Castle behind her, Orgeluse rode on with her guest along a broad, straight road for some two miles until they came to a magnificent forest of tamarisk and brazil, as willed by Clinschor whose forest it was.

'Where shall I break the twig for the Garland that will mend my happiness, now so full of holes?' He ought to have swung her down, as has often happened since to many a fine lady.

'I shall show you where you can assert your claim to prowess,' she said. They rode over the fields towards an escarpment till they saw the tree of the Garland. 'Sir,' she then said, 'that tree is tended by the man who robbed me of my happiness. If you fetch me down a twig of it no knight would ever have won such high renown for love's sake as a lady's Servitor.' Such were the words of this duchess.

'I shall go no further. If you intend to ride on, may it rest in God's hands! There will be no need to drag matters out, urge your mount to one spirited leap from here and you are

302

over Li gweiz prelljus.' She halted on the meadow, and Gawan rode on.

Gawan now heard the roar of a torrent which had cut a broad, deep bed for itself, barring the way. Yet the gallant, noble warrior set spur to his horse and drove him forward … The animal landed with only his forelegs on the far side, and so the leap ended in a spill, at which (though it may surprise you) the Duchess wept. The current was fast and strong, and Gawan exerted his great strength, but was weighed down by his armour. He then saw a branch of a tree that had taken root in the river and this the mighty man seized, since he wished to go on living. His lance was floating beside him, so the warrior grabbed it and climbed up on to the bank.

Meanwhile Gringuljete was swimming, now partly above water, now submerged. Gawan turned to help him. The beast had drifted so far downstream that Gawan could have done without having to run after him, burdened with heavy armour and weakened by many wounds as he was. But a whirlpool now drove his mount towards him, and he reached him with his lance at a point where heavy rains had carved out a broad gulley through the steep slope. Here the river-bank was breached, saving Gringuljete; for with his lance Gawan edged him so near to the shore that he was able to grasp his bridle. And so my lord Gawan hauled his charger on to the meadow, where, safe and sound, the beast shook himself. Gawan's shield had not been lost either, and after girthing his horse he took possession of it. If there are any who do not protest at all his sufferings, let it rest. He had much to endure, since Love it was who willed it. – Dazzling Orgeluse was driving him on his gallant way towards the Garland.

The tree was so well guarded that had there been two Gawans they would have had to yield up their lives in the attempt to win the Garland which King Gramoflanz kept. And nevertheless Gawan culled it.

The river was called the Sabins, and it was a rough toll Gawan gathered when he and his mount splashed into it!

However radiant Orgeluse's looks, *I* would not take her love on such terms, I know where to draw the line.

When Gawan had broken the twig and set the Garland on his helmet, a handsome knight in the very prime of life rode up to him. His arrogant spirit was such that however much a man might have wronged him he declined to do battle with him unless he were one of two or more. His heart was so proud and lofty that whatever any one man did to him he let it rest without contention. Fil li roy Irot, that is, King Gramoflanz, offered Gawan a good morning.

'Sir,' he said, 'I have not let this Garland go entirely. I should have withheld my greeting had there been two of you who had not forborne to take a twig from my tree in this fashion in hope of making a name for themselves. They would have had to defend themselves! But like this it is beneath my notice.'

For his part too Gawan would have been disinclined to fight with him, for the King had ridden out unarmed – rather was the illustrious warrior carrying on his noble fist a moulted sparrowhawk which Gawan's charming sister Itonje had sent him. His royal head was shaded by a peacock-feather hat from Sinzester, and the mantle he wore was of grass-green samite lined with gleaming ermine and cut so that its points on either side brushed the ground. The fine ambler which carried the King was of moderate height but strong enough and not lacking in marks of beauty. It had been brought from Denmark by land (unless it was by sea). The King rode quite defenceless, since he wore no sword.

'Your shield declares you have been fighting,' said King Gramoflanz, 'there is so little left of it. – Lit marveile has fallen to you, you have endured the adventure which should have awaited me, except that subtle Clinschor has always set me a peaceful precedent and that I am at war with a lady who with her beauty has won true love's victory. Her anger against me is unabated, and indeed she has overriding cause: I slew her noble husband Cidegast in the company of three others. I then abducted Orgeluse and offered her a crown and all my lands: yet her heart has vented its hostility on all my offers to subserve her. I kept her for a whole year subject to my entreaties, yet failed to win her love, I must tell you with deep sorrow. It is clear to me that she has offered you her love, since you are here to encompass my death. Now had you brought another with you, you could have taken my life, or both of you would have died – thus much would you have got for your trouble. My heart is set on other love, where help depends on your favour, now that you are lord of Terre marveile, for your prowess has won you glory. If you feel kindly disposed, help me with a young woman for whom my heart suffers pangs. She is King Lot's daughter. Of all the women in the world none ever gained such cruel power over me. I have her love-token here. So convey to the handsome young lady there the assurance of my devotion. I am persuaded she is well disposed towards me, since I have faced the dangers of battle for her sake. After mighty Orgeluse vehemently and explicitly denied me her love, any renown I have since won, with pleasure or with pain, was brought to pass by Itonje. To my sorrow I have never set eyes on her. But if you will console me with your help, deliver this little ring to my sweet and lovely lady. You will be entirely exempt from battle here unless your numbers are greater, that is, two or more. Who would set it down to my credit if I were to kill you or force your surrender? I have never agreed to fight on such terms.'

'I am a man well able to give an account of himself,' replied my lord Gawan. 'If you have no wish to win the fame of slaying me, for my part I shall gain none for having culled this twig; for who would give me any great credit for slaying you, unarmed as you are? So I will bear your message. Give me the ring and let me convey your humble duty and tell your doleful tale.'

The King thanked him profusely, and Gawan continued: 'Since it is beneath your dignity to fight me, tell me who you are, sir.'

'Do not think any the worse of me if I divulge my name,' answered the King. 'My father was named Irot, and he was slain by King Lot. I am King Gramoflanz. The integrity of my lofty spirit decrees that I shall never fight with one man whatever the wrong he has done me, except a man called Gawan, whom I have heard so highly praised that I should like to meet him in battle to avenge my sorrows. For his father treacherously slew my father in the very act of greeting. I have enough to seek in that quarter. But now Lot has died, and Gawan has won pre-eminence in fame such as no other knight of the Table Round can match. The day on which I do battle with him will surely come.'

'If you mean to do so to please your friend – assuming that she is one –' replied the son of noble Lot, 'while you accuse her father of such a low-down trick and would gladly kill her brother too, then she is a wicked young woman not to protest at such behaviour on your part. If she had filial and sisterly feelings she would shield both father and brother and seek to wean you from this hostility. How seemly would it be for your father-in-law to have committed an act of treachery? If you have not exacted vengeance upon yourself for having imputed treachery to him, a dead man, his son will not be disheartened or deterred from doing so! If he cannot count on his pretty sister's good offices, he will hazard his own person in this affair! Sir, my name is Gawan. Whatever my father has done to you, avenge it on me, for he is dead! To shield him from calumny I will stake in single combat any honour life has brought me!'

'If you are he with whom I stand in lasting feud, your noble nature both gladdens and saddens me,' said the King. 'There is something about you that pleases me, namely that I am to fight with you. For your part a great honour has befallen you, in that I have conceded to you alone that I shall meet you in single combat. And it will enhance the glory of both if we invite noble ladies to witness it. I shall bring fifteen hundred, and you too have a resplendent company at Schastel marveile. For your complement bring your uncle King Arthur from the Land called Löver. Do you know the town of Bems-on-Korcha? – His following are all there. He can arrive here in a week from now in gay pomp. I myself shall appear on the field at Joflanze on the sixteenth day from today to exact payment for this Garland.'

306

The King invited Gawan to accompany him into the town of Rosche Sabins. 'You will find no other bridge.'

'I shall go back the way I came,' replied Gawan. 'I shall do as you ask in all else.'

They pledged their word that they would come to the duelling-ground at Joflanze with knights and ladies to do single combat with one another at the time and on the terms laid down.

And so Gawan took his leave of that noble man. With a light heart he gave his horse free rein – he was wearing the Garland as crest! – and far from wishing to check his mount he spurred him towards the gorge. Gringuljete timed his leap so well and made such ample allowance that Gawan did not come down. The Duchess now rode up to where he had alighted on the grass to girth his horse and quickly dismounted opposite him, then, puissant lady, threw herself at his feet.

'My lord, I never deserved the hardships I asked you to undergo,' she said. 'Truly, your trials afflicted me with such heartfelt suffering as a faithful woman must feel for her dear friend.'

'If it is true, madam,' he said, 'that no hidden malice lurks in what you are saying to me, you are on the way to getting a good name. Do not doubt that I know this much: if Knighthood is to be given its due, you have wronged it! The Office of the Shield is so sublime that whoever practised it correctly never let himself be made a mock of. Madam, if I may say so myself, all who have seen me engaged in chivalry have had to concede my competence: yet several times since you first met me you have maintained the contrary. But no matter: receive this Garland. By your dazzling looks, you must never again offer a knight such insults! If I am to be the butt of your mockery I would rather be without love.'

'My lord,' said the lovely Duchess amid a flood of tears, 'when I tell you of the distress that weighs on my heart you will grant that mine is the greater sorrow. Let any I have slighted have the courtesy to pardon it. I cannot lose more happiness than I lost in peerless Cidegast! My fine handsome charming lover! Inspired by desire of true honour, his renown was so illustrious that mortal men, whoever they were, had to concede him fame unsurpassed by any other. He was a fount of quality, untouched by any falsity, his youth fecund of excellence. Pressing up from darkness he had unfolded towards the light and thrust his fame so high that it could be reached by none whom baseness had power to weaken; indeed it grew so high from his heart's seed that all other was overshadowed by it. How does swift Saturn run his course high above all other planets ... ? My paragon of a husband – for I can truly call him so – was as faithful as the unicorn, a creature maidens should lament, since it is for his love of purity that he is slain. I was his heart, he my life. I lost him, and am a woman fraught with loss. He was slain by King Gramoflanz, from whom you bring this Garland. My lord, if I have used you ill it was because I wished to put to the test whether you were of such worth that I should offer you my love. I am well aware that I said things which offended you; yet it was to try you out. Now graciously set aside your anger and pardon me once and for all like the very gallant knight you are. I compare you to gold that has been purified in the fire – your spirit has been purged. The man whose harm I sought through you and whom I still hope to harm has done me mortal wrong.'

'Unless death forestall me, madam,' replied my lord Gawan, 'I shall acquaint that king with such desperation as will check his arrogance! I have pledged my word to ride and meet him in single combat shortly – then indeed we shall tax our manhood! My lady, I *have* pardoned you. If you would be so civil as not to frown on my uncouth suggestion, I should advise what would be much to your honour as a woman and what *noblesse* enjoins. We are now alone. – Madam, grant me your favour.'

'I have never warmed to a mail-clad arm,' she answered. 'But I will not dispute that at some time you may claim the reward you have deserved. I shall mourn all your sufferings till you are well again and your various wounds and lesions are healed. I will go up to Schastel marveile with you.'

'Then you are making me a very happy man,' said this

ardent lover as, gathering the lovely woman firmly to him, he lifted her on to her palfrey. (She had thought him unworthy of such a favour when he had met her beside the spring and she had addressed him so forwardly.)

Gawan rode happily on, but she could not restrain her tears till he joined her in her sorrow and asked her to say *why* she was weeping and begged her in God's name to forbear.

'I must complain to you,' she said, 'of the man who slew noble Cidegast, causing sorrow to grope into my heart where happiness had dwelt whilst I still enjoyed his love! I am not so far reduced that I have not since sought to harm that king at great cost, with many sharp jousts aimed at his life. What if you were to give me the help that would avenge me and make good the grief that has given edge to my sufferings! To encompass Gramoflanz's death I accepted service offered by a king who was lord of earth's most precious treasure. Sir, his name is Anfortas. In the name of love I received from him the merchandise of Thabronit which still stands at your Gate and could only be had for a fortune. In my service this king suffered a disaster that ruined my whole happiness. Instead of giving him love I was forced to seek new griefs – he was wounded in my service! Anfortas's wound brought me equal or greater sorrow than Cidegast had power to give me. Now tell me, how am I, poor woman, with my faithful heart, to keep my reason in the face of such afflictions? My mind does give way, now and then, when I think of him lying there so helpless – the man I chose to console me for the loss of Cidegast and to avenge him. Now hear me pronounce by what means Clinschor acquired the rich Merchandise at your Gate.

'After comely Anfortas, sender of the gift, had been turned away forever from love and its ecstasies, I went in dread lest I be put to shame. For Clinschor has the art of necromancy at his beck unfailingly, so that he can bind men and women with his spells. Of all the worthy people on whom his eye falls not one does he leave without trouble. And so I gave him my precious Merchandise in order to be left in peace, and on these terms: that I should seek the love of the man who had faced and achieved the Adventure; but that if he would not favour me the Merchandise should revert to me. – In such terms did those present swear. As matters stand, it shall be our joint possession. I was hoping to bring Gramoflanz down with this ruse, but unfortunately this has not yet come about – had *he* gone for the Adventure he would have met his death!

'Clinschor is subtle and urbane. For the sake of his prestige he lets me have my famous retinue engage in deeds of arms with lance and sword throughout his lands. Every day of every week of the year I have special detachments on the watch for haughty Gramoflanz, some by day, others by night, at such great cost have I planned to harm him. He has fought many battles with them – what is it that shields him all the time? I steadfastly plotted his death. I allowed many to serve me for love who, though too wealthy to accept my pay, were otherwise well disposed towards me – yet without promise to requite them. No man ever saw me whose service I could not have had, bar one who wore red armour. He put my retinue in great jeopardy, since he undid them to such effect, riding up to Logroys, that he strewed them on the ground in a way that gave me little pleasure. Five of my knights pursued him to a place between Logroys and your landing-stage: he discomfited them all on the meadow and gave their mounts to the ferryman. After he had defeated my people, I rode after the warrior myself and offered him my lands and person. He replied that he had a wife more beautiful and one he held more dear. I was piqued by what he said and asked him who she might be. "She whose looks are so radiant is called the Queen of Belrepeire. My own name is Parzival. I do not want your love: the Gral bids me seek other troubles." With these wrathful words the fine warrior rode off. Tell me, please, was it wrong of me to offer the noble knight my love with an eye to avenging my bereavement, and has it cheapened my love?'

'My lady,' said Gawan to the Duchess, 'I know the man whose love you desired to be of such merit that had he chosen you to be his lover your worth would have suffered no loss from him.'

Courteous Gawan and the Duchess of Logroys looked full into each other's eyes.

They were now riding so near that they were seen from the Castle in which Gawan had achieved the Adventure.

'If I may request it, my lady,' said he, 'please withhold my name – the knight who rode off with Gringuljete named it. Do as I request, and if anyone asks you, say "I don't know who my companion is, since he was never named to me!".'

'Since it is your wish that I should not name it,' said she, 'I shall gladly withhold it.'

Gawan and the beauteous lady turned in towards the Castle. The gentlemen there had now heard that a knight had come, had endured the Adventure, overcome the lion, and later brought the Turkoyt down in regular joust. Gawan meanwhile was riding through the meadow towards the landing-stage and was now visible to those on the battlements. Then men mounted on swift Arab chargers came riding out from the Castle hot-pace, raising a great din, all displaying fine pennants. Gawan thought they meant to fight.

Seeing them come from the distance, Gawan turned to the Duchess and asked, 'Is that troop on its way to attack us?'

'They are Clinschor's company,' she said, 'and have awaited you scarce able to contain themselves; but now they have set out with joy to receive you. It must not incur your displeasure, since their happiness bids them do so.'

Plippalinot and his proud and lovely daughter had now crossed in a pontoon. The girl walked a long way over the meadow towards Gawan and received him joyfully. He in turn saluted her, and she kissed his stirrup and foot and then welcomed the Duchess. She took the horse by the bridle and asked the man to dismount. Gawan and the lady went to the vessel's bows where a carpet and quilt lay ready, and there at his request the Duchess sat down beside him. The ferryman's daughter was prompt to unarm him, and I have heard that she even brought her cloak – the one which had covered him that night when he had lodged with them – and indeed it was most opportune now. Thus Lord Gawan donned her cloak and his own surcoat while she took his armour away.

Only now, as they sat side by side, could the lovely Duchess study his face.

Sweet Bene brought in a brace of larks, a rummer of wine and two white wastel-loaves on a napkin white as could be. The fowl had been caught on the wing by the merlin you remember. They were able to serve themselves with water if they wanted to wash their hands, and indeed they both did so. It filled Gawan with joy that he was to dine with the woman for whose sake he was ready to suffer pleasure and hardship. When she presented the rummer which her lips had touched, the thought that he was to drink after her brought him new joy. His unhappy feelings began to lag behind as his high spirits raced ahead. The sight of her sweet mouth, her fair skin, chased him away from his cares at such a pace that the pain of his wounds was forgotten.

The ladies were able to observe this entertainment from the Castle above. Many noble knights had come to the landing-place on the other bank and they performed their bohort with all punctilio. On this side, Gawan thanked the ferryman and his daughter for the meal they had so kindly provided, as did the Duchess for her part.

'What came of the knight who delivered the joust yesterday as I was riding away?' asked the thoughtful Duchess. 'If someone defeated him did it end with his living or dying?'

'I saw him alive today, my lady,' said Plippalinot. 'He was given me in exchange for a horse. If you want to free him, let me have Swallow, which belonged to Queen Secundille and was sent to you by Anfortas. If that Harp can be mine, the Duke of Gowerzin goes free!'

'The man sitting here has power to bestow or withhold that Harp and other wares with his own hand, if he so wishes,' she replied. 'Let him decide. If ever I was so dear to him, he will ransom Lischois, Duke of Gowerzin, for me here and that other prince of mine, Florant of Itolac, who commanded my watch by night. I valued him so highly as my Turkoyt that I could never rest happy while he was sad.'

'You shall see both of them free before nightfall,' Gawan promised the lady. They then decided to cross to the farther bank, where Gawan again handed the fair Duchess on to her palfrey.

Many noble knights received them here, and as they turned in towards the Castle their escort began to ride with zest, and to display such skill as did full honour to the bohort. What more can I say – other than that noble Gawan and the shapely Duchess were welcomed to Schastel marveile in a style that might well content them? You can account him a lucky man that such good fortune ever came his way. Arnive now led him to his chamber to rest, and those who were skilled in such matters gave attention to his wounds.

'I need a messenger, Ma'am,' said Gawan to Arnive. A young lady-in-waiting was sent and she came back with a squire who was as manly and discreet as is given to a squire to be. The youth swore on oath that whether his mission turned out well or ill, he would not divulge the message to anyone there or in any other quarter than where he was instructed to deliver it. Gawan, son of King Lot, asked for ink and parchment. He wrote elegantly with his own hand. Into the Land of Löver he sent to Arthur and his Queen his humble duty and the assurance of his unflawed fealty, and went on to say that if he had won through to any renown this would perish, unless they helped him in his need by recalling the bond of loyalty and bringing their retinue to Joflanze together with a company of ladies; and that for his part he would come and meet them there to take part in a judicial combat in which his whole honour was at stake. He further informed Arthur that the terms agreed for the duel required the King to come with all due pomp. Lord Gawan then went on to ask the whole court, ladies and knights alike, to consider their loyalty towards him and advise the King to come – this would enhance their honour. He sent all those worthies his respects and told them of the straits his duel placed him in.

This letter bore no seal. His own well-known hand was sufficient authentication.

'Now delay no longer!' Gawan commanded his servitor. 'The King and Queen are at Bems-on-Korcha. Accost the Queen early of a morning and do whatever she tells you. And keep this well in mind: say nothing of my being Lord here. Nor must you let them know at all that you are a retainer here at court.'

The squire was in haste to be gone. Arnive tiptoed after him and asked where he was off to and the nature of his errand.

'I am to tell you nothing, Ma'am,' said he, 'if my oath informs me correctly. May God keep you, I must go.'

He rode off in search of far-famed companies.

Chapter 13

ARNIVE was vexed that Gawan's young man did not tell her where he had been sent to. 'When that fellow returns, whether it be day or night, see to it that he waits for me till I have had a word with him,' she told the Gate-keeper. 'Use all your skill to achieve it!' There was no denying she was angry with that squire. She then went in again to discover more from the Duchess, but the latter took good care not to let Gawan's name pass her lips, since he had asked her not to. Thus she left his name and lineage unsaid. The sound of trumpets and other instruments rang out merrily up in the Palace, and they hung many tapestries as back-rests on the walls. They did not walk there on anything but finely woven carpets. – An impecunious host would have been alarmed! Everywhere round the walls in profusion settees had been placed with downy cushions and the whole bespread with costly quilts.

After the toils he had endured, Gawan was still asleep at midday. His wounds had been bandaged so expertly that if a friend had lain beside him and he had enjoyed her love, it would have soothed him and done him good. He was more disposed to sleep than that night when the Duchess gave him so much ado. He awoke as it was drawing near to evensong. Nevertheless, in his sleep he had fought once more – in the lists of love with the Duchess. Now, so I am told, one of his chamberlains brought in clothes of shimmering brocade weighed down with their gold thread.

'Let us have more of these clothes,' said my lord Gawan, 'all of the same fine quality, and see to it that they are ready for the Duke of Gowerzin and handsome Florant, who has won distinction in many lands.'

Gawan sent a message by a page to his host Plippalinot that he was to send Lischois along to him, and accordingly Lischois was sent up in the care of his lovely daughter. Lady Bene came leading Lischois by the hand from the good will she bore Gawan, and also for the reason that when Gawan had left her in tears on the day he had ridden away from her and his valour had won him fame, he had promised her father a fine gift. And now the Turkoyt too was there, and Gawan could be heard welcoming him in friendly fashion, after which they both sat down beside him and waited for their clothes to be brought. These turned out to be of unsurpassable quality and were brought for all three. There was a master-weaver named Sarant, from whom Seres* took its name, and he was of Triande. In Secundille's country there is a place called Thasme, which is larger than Niniveh or spacious Acraton. Ambitious to earn fame as his reward, Sarant devised a cloth-of-gold called 'saranthasme'† – his work brought great ingenuity to bear. Don't ask if it makes a fine show – it fetches an extravagant price! Those two and Gawan donned these clothes and ascended to the Palace, where there were a throng of knights on one side and fair ladies on the other of whom a good judge would have said that the Duchess of Logroys was most lustrous. The host and his guests came and stood before the dazzling lady whose name was Orgeluse. Gawan freed the two courtly princes, Florant the Turkoyt and handsome Lischois, without conditions for the Duchess of Logroys's sake, for which – innocent of deceit as she was wise in all that goes to make a woman's glory – she thanked him.

Meanwhile Gawan had glimpsed four queens standing beside the Duchess and courteously asked the two princes to stand forward and then bade the three younger ladies bestow the kiss of welcome on them. Now Lady Bene too had accompanied Gawan to the Palace and here she was very well received.

His lordship was disinclined to go on standing. He asked the two to go and sit among the ladies as they chose, and to be requested to do so did not displease them overmuch.

'Which is Itonje?' noble Gawan whispered to Bene. 'She

* China.

† The true etymology is from Byzantine Greek *hexarantismos*, a tissue with six-fold ornamentation.

must let me sit beside her.' The lovely girl pointed her out, since Gawan wished it.

'The one with the red lips, brown hair and bright eyes. If you wish to speak with her in private be discreet,' said decorous Lady Bene, who knew of Itonje's languishings and that the noble King Gramoflanz was paying homage to her heart with the utmost chivalrous devotion.

Gawan sat down beside the maiden – I am telling you as I was told – and embarked on what he had to say with discretion of which he was a master. For her part too young Itonje was possessed of decorous ways fully appropriate to her young life. The question he had taken it upon himself to ask her was whether she was already apt for love.

'My lord, whom should I love?' was the girl's wary answer. 'Since the day I opened my eyes there has been no knight to whom I ever spoke a word, except what you yourself have heard today.'

'Nevertheless,' replied my lord Gawan, 'reports could have reached you by which you would have learnt of high fame won by courage in knightly pursuits, and of who, from his strength of heart, can offer service for love's reward.'

'No word has been said to me of serving for love,' answered the lovely girl, 'only that many courtly knights serve the Duchess of Logroys both for love and for her hire. No few of them have had jousting here close enough for us to watch it. Yet not one came so near as you have come to us. Your victorious battle much enhances this distinction.'

'Against whom are the Duchess's company of so many picked knights campaigning?' he asked the comely girl. 'Who is the man that has lost her favour?'

'Roys Gramoflanz has done so,' she replied, 'the man who wears the very garland of high merit by common accord. This is all I know about it, sir.'

'You shall have better acquaintance of him,' said my lord Gawan, 'since he is hard on the tracks of fame and pursues it zestfully. I have heard from his own lips that, driven by an inward urge, he has come to offer his service, if you would

317

deign to accept it, and is seeking help to console him through your love. That a king should receive love's pain from a king's daughter is as it should be. Madam, if your father was called Lot, you are the one he dotes on and for whom his heart is weeping! And if your name is Itonje, it is you who are the cause of his suffering. If you have a true heart inside you, you must make an end of his sorrows. I will be the go-between. Take this ring, madam. – The handsome fellow has sent it you. I shall manage this in your best interest, take heart and leave it all to me.'

She changed colour so that her whole face was as red as her lips, and then suddenly turned pale. She stretched out her hand in shy confusion to take the ring, and knew it at once ...

'It is now quite clear to me, sir,' she said, 'if I may so speak in your presence, that you have come from the man for whom my heart has so strong an urge. If your manners are not wanting, they will inspire you to secrecy. This gift was sent me once before from the noble King's own hand, the ring is his true token, since he had it from my hand. I am altogether innocent of his sufferings, for I have granted him, in thought, whatever he asked of me, and this he would quickly learn, could I ever pass beyond these walls. I have kissed Orgeluse, who seeks to encompass his death in the way you know. That was a Judas kiss, of which one still hears much today. It was utterly faithless of me when, under compulsion, I kissed Florant the Turkoyt and the Duke of Gowerzin! I shall never be fully reconciled with those who bear unrelenting hatred towards King Gramoflanz! Say nothing of this to my mother and my sister Cundrie,' Itonje then begged Gawan. 'My lord, you asked me to receive Orgeluse's kiss on my lips – though I have not forgiven her – and it has wounded me to the heart. If the King and I are ever to know happiness, the remedy lies in your hands. He loves me above all women for sure, and I intend that he shall have the benefit of it. – He has my favour beyond all other men! May God inspire you with help and counsel so that you leave us happy at last!'

'Tell me how, my lady,' said Gawan. 'He has you out there, you have him here: and yet you are apart. If there is any loyal service I could do for you from which your noble lives could profit, I would undertake it without fail.'

'You shall dispose of the noble King and me,' she answered. 'May your help and God's blessing take charge of our love so that I, wretched woman, can bring his sorrows to an end. Since all his happiness depends on me, and as I am a faithful woman, the desire in my heart must always be to grant him my love.'

Gawan heard from what the young lady said that her thoughts were running on love and that she felt a lively animosity towards the Duchess. She thus cherished both love and hate. Yet on his side he was guilty of a greater fault towards the innocent girl who had told him of her troubles, for he had not mentioned it to her that one mother had borne the two of them, as indeed they both had Lot for father. He offered the girl his assistance, and she thanked him with a secret nod for uttering words of comfort.

But now the time had come to bring up to the Palace into the presence of many ladies sheet upon sheet of table-linen, white as white could be, together with bread. A separation had been decreed whereby knights had a wall to themselves away from the ladies. Lord Gawan saw to the seating. The Turkoyt sat at Gawan's table, Lischois shared a platter with Gawan's mother, the handsome Sangive, the radiant Duchess shared with Queen Arnive, and Gawan asked his two comely sisters to join him, and this they duly did.

Unversed in the culinary art, I could not name half the dishes that were brought in with all ceremony. Fine-looking maidens served the host and all the ladies. Opposite, along their wall, the knights were waited on by men-at-arms in number. Restraint inspired by respect held these young men back from jostling with the young ladies: they had to be seen decorously apart, whether they were bearing viands or wine. The knights and ladies might well call it a feast, for such a thing had never come their way since Clinschor had subdued them with his spells. They had remained unknown to one another despite their living behind one and the same Gate, with the result that they had never so much as exchanged a word. Gawan now made it possible for this company of knights and ladies to

319

meet, and this afforded them much pleasure. Gawan was not
without his own pleasure either, but he had to steal glances at
the dazzling Duchess who held his heart in thrall.

The day now began to stumble so that its brightness was all
but laid low and you could see Night's harbingers – innumer-
able stars – hastening through the clouds to claim quarters for her.
Then swiftly behind Night's banners, Night herself came up.

Many fine chandeliers hung all over the Palace, most elegant
to see. They were soon set with their candles, and quite apart
from this, candles were brought in fantastic numbers to all the
tables. The story goes on to say that the Duchess shed such
brightness that even if no candles had been furnished, there
would have been no night near her! I heard it said of the sweet
woman that her radiance of itself shed daylight!

Unless you intend to malign him you must grant that you
have never seen a host so joyful. – Joy was universal there.
Glances fraught with zestful longing passed to and fro, thick
and fast, between knights and ladies. If any who had shrunk
back from strangeness grew more intimate, I will not take them
to task.

Gluttons apart, and by your good leave, they have had their
fill there. The boards were all removed. My lord Gawan then
asked if there were any good fiddlers at hand. There proved
to be many worthy squires there well versed in string-music.
Yet however great their skill, they had to play old dances –
no new dances were ever heard there like the many that have
come here from Thuringia! Now thank the host: he did not
thwart their enjoyment. Bevies of handsome women passed
before him. Their dance had this decorative pattern – knights
'let in' among ladies! Their aim was to fend off sadness. You
could also see fine knights footing it there with a lady on
either hand. And you could also detect the pleasure of those
knights who had a mind to offer service for love – a request
that was allowable – and who, poor in cares as they were rich
in joy, passed the time with talking with sweet lips, of which
there were no few there.

Gawan, Sangive and Queen Arnive were sitting quietly be-
side the dancing company. The lovely Duchess came and sat

next to Gawan. He took her hand in his, and they talked of one thing and another. Gawan was glad she had joined him. His sadness dwindled, his happiness was in spate, with the result that his sorrows all vanished away. However great the pleasure of the dancers, Gawan's was greater still.

'Give a thought to your comfort, sir,' said Queen Arnive. 'You ought to rest your wounds now. If the Duchess has decided to be mistress of your coverlet and bear you company this very night, she will prove bountiful in aid and remedies.'

'You ask her that,' replied Gawan. 'I am in the hands of you both.'

'I will have him in my care,' said the Duchess. 'Have these people go to bed. I shall tend him better tonight than any lover ever tended him. Let Florant of Itolac and the Duke of Gowerzin be looked after by the knights.'

The dance came to a sudden end. Young ladies with radiant faces were sitting here and there with knights alternately, and if one of these sued for noble love and met with a sweet response, his happiness got even with his sorrows. Their host was heard calling for drink to be served to them, much to the regret of suitors. Yet the host was a suitor as much as his guests, he too was burdened by love, and to him they seemed to be sitting there too long. – Noble love was racking his heart too!

This drink was their dismissal. Squires led the knights away, lighting them with twists of candle-dips. Then my lord Gawan commended his two guests Lischois and Florant to them all, much to their liking. Then without delay the two retired to rest. The Duchess was mindful to wish them good night. And now with elegant inflexions in which they were well versed, the entire company of ladies withdrew to seek repose. Sangive and Itonje left, as did Cundrie.

Bene and Arnive then saw to it that his lordship was comfortable, and the Duchess too took care to be at hand to assist him. These three led him away to his ease. In a chamber, Gawan saw two couches standing on one side. Now I shall not tell you how these were adorned, the tale is approaching other matters.

'Now make this knight whom you have brought here very comfortable,' Arnive told the Duchess. 'If he asks your help, the help you give will do you honour. I will say no more to you than that his wounds have been bandaged so skilfully that he could now bear arms. Nevertheless, you should sympathize with him in his plight: if you can soothe his pain that would do him good. If you can raise his mettle, that will benefit us all. Now go to it with a will.'

After taking leave of her lord, Arnive left, with Bene bearing a light before her.

Gawan barred the door.

If these two know how to steal love now, I am loth to conceal it. I can easily tell you what happened there, except that those who divulge secret matters have always been accused of impropriety, and well-bred people still deplore it, so that one who does so damns himself. Let decorum be the lock that guards Love's rites.

Now imperious Love and the fair Duchess had caused Gawan's happiness to be quite consumed. But for his lover he would have perished. If the philosopher, and all who ever sat them down and fathomed abstruse arts, Kancor and Thebit,* and Trebuchet the Smith (who engraved Frimutel's sword, source of a great marvel), and the physicians with all their skill – if all these had wished him well with concoctions of efficacious herbs, his sharp distress would have ended in bitter death nevertheless, but for a woman's company!

I will make it short. He found the authentic hart's eye† which helped to make him well again so that all that was baneful left him – a herb showing brown against white. A Briton on his mother's side, Gawan fil li roy Lot sought soothing balm for bitter pain with noble aid to good effect till day dawned. Yet the aid he had was of such a kind that it was kept

---

* It has been very plausibly suggested that these two names arise by scribal error from Thebit benchore (T̄ābit ibn Qurra).

† Wild dittany. Harts were believed to cure themselves from arrowfire with the aid of this herb: and Gawan is bruised by bolts, and, it has been suggested, Cupid's darts.

hidden from all that company. Later he saw to the well-being of all the knights and ladies, so that their sadness was all but banished.

Now hear how the squire fared whom Gawan had dispatched towards Bems-on-Korcha in the land of Löver.

King Arthur and his Queen were there, accompanied by a bevy of dazzling ladies and a veritable flood of courtiers. Now listen to what the squire does.

It was early of a morning when he took his errand in hand. The Queen was in chapel reading her psalter on bended knee. The squire knelt before her and offered her a joyful gift. She took the letter from his hand and saw writing on it which she recognized before the youth she saw kneeling there could name his lord.

'A blessing on the hand that wrote you!' said the Queen addressing the letter. 'I have not been without anxiety since the day I last saw the hand that formed this writing.' She wept abundantly and nevertheless was glad. 'You are Gawan's squire?' she asked.

'Yes, Ma'am. He sends you what is his to send: unswerving loyalty, and with it news of small joy, unless you have a mind to make it great. His honour was never at such a wretched pass. My lady, he sends you further news: he would live a life of noble pleasure if he were told that you would console him. You can easily see from the letter more than I can tell you.'

'It is clear to me,' she said, 'for what purpose you have been sent. I shall do him noble service by bringing him a delightful bevy of ladies who, believe me, excel all others of my time. Excepting Parzival's wife, and Orgeluse, I know none of such quality in Christendom. Since Gawan rode away from Arthur, I have been violently assailed by fear and sorrow. Meljanz of Liz told me he had seen him since at Barbigœl. Alas, Plimizœl,' she continued, 'that my eyes ever lighted on you! What sorrow befell me there! I never saw Cunneware de Lalant again, my sweet and noble companion. Many things were said there which breached the code of the Table Round. It is four and a half years and six weeks‡ since noble Parzival rode out from the Plimizœl in search of the Gral. At that same time Gawan, noble man, set out for Ascalun. It was there that Jeschute and Ekuba said farewell to me. Deep regrets for those worthy people have since disturbed my peace of mind.' The Queen confessed to having many sorrows.

'Now do as I say,' she told the squire. 'Leave me and keep out of sight till the sun is well up and everyone – knights, squires and the Great Household – are in and about the court. Then briskly trot up to the courtyard and without bothering who holds your horse, hurry from there to where the noble knights are standing. They will ask you for news. In what you say or do behave as though you had just escaped from a fire so that they will scarce control their impatience to learn what news you bring. What does it matter if you elbow your way through the crowd to the rightful lord, who will not forbear to welcome you? Hand him this letter. From it he will quickly learn your news and your master's wishes. These he will grant by common consent. And I will tell you more. You are to address me publicly where I and other ladies can see and hear you. Try to win us over to the best of your ability, if you wish your master well. And tell me, *where* is Gawan?'

'That will not be divulged,' said the squire. 'I shall not say where my lord is, but, by your leave, he dwells amid joys and pleasures!'

The lad was content with the Queen's instructions. He left her in the way you have heard and returned as he had been told to do.

Punctually at mid-morning the squire rode up to court as publicly as could be. The courtiers judged his clothes to be those of a squire. His horse was gashed by the spur on both flanks. Following the Queen's instructions, he at once leapt down from his horse and was surrounded by a milling crowd. If his mantle, sword and spurs – not to mention his horse – went astray, he cared but little. He hastened to where the noble knights were standing, and they at once asked him for news.

* See p. 432.

People say that it was the time-honoured custom there that no man or woman dined at court before the court was paid its due: news of strange adventures fully worthy of the name!

'I shall tell you nothing,' said the squire. 'I have urgent business. Of your courtesy, do not be offended, but kindly tell me where the King is. I should have liked to speak with him sooner. I am on tenterhooks to discharge my mission. You will no doubt learn the news I shall tell. Then may God move you to help and sympathy!'

The squire's mission pressed on him so hard that he did not care who jostled him till the King saw him and welcomed him. He handed Arthur that same letter, which, as Arthur read it, could not fail to evoke conflicting emotions of happiness and sorrow.

'A blessing on this sweet day,' he cried, 'by whose light I have learned that reliable news of my noble nephew has reached us! If it lie in my power to do manly service, and if loyalty to the ties of blood and companionship avail me, I shall do as Gawan asks me in this message! Tell me,' he went on, 'is Gawan in good spirits?'

'Yes, Sire, by your leave, he has Joy itself for companion,' replied that politic squire. 'But if you abandoned him he would lose his honour. Indeed, who could be happy in such circumstances? Your aid will snatch him up to heights of happiness, your support will chase his cares from his heart and out beyond Sorrow's gate! He sends his devotion to the Queen all this way, and it is his wish that the Company of the Table Round remember his past services and bethink themselves of their loyalty, and refrain from spoiling his happiness and on the contrary advise you to come.'

All those nobles asked the King to comply.

'Take this letter to the Queen, dear friend,' said Arthur. 'Let her read it and say why we should rejoice and of what we should complain. To think that King Gramoflanz can confront my family with such saucy arrogance! He imagines my nephew Gawan to be another Cidegast, his slaying of whom has brought him trouble enough! I shall add to his troubles and teach him better manners!'

The squire went to where he was well received. He gave the Queen the letter which caused many eyes to brim over when her sweet lips had read all that was written in it about the wrong Gawan complained of and his request to them. The squire spared no art in his efforts to win over all those ladies, nor was it in vain.

Gawan's kinsman the mighty Arthur ardently sought his Household's approval for this expedition. 'Nor was courteous Ginover guilty of losing any time in trying to persuade the ladies in favour of the proud sortie!

'Was there ever born so fine a man – did I dare believe it – as Gawan of Norway?' asked Keie testily. '*After* him! *Seize* him! But maybe he's somewhere else? If he dodges like a squirrel you'll soon have lost him!'

'I must hurry back to my lord, Ma'am,' said the squire to the Queen. 'Pursue his interest with all the advantage your station affords.'

'See to this squire's comfort,' she commanded one of her chamberlains. 'Take a look at his horse. If its flanks are much gouged with spurring give him the best to be had on the market. If he has any other needs – of ready money to redeem bond, or of clothes – he is to be supplied. Now give Gawan my humble respects,' the Queen continued. 'I shall excuse your departure to the King – and give your master his compliments.'

And so the King went ahead with his expedition, with the result that the constitution of the Table Round was duly honoured that day. The news they had learnt that noble Gawan was still alive had roused their spirits. The solemn custom of the Table Round was observed there in all harmony. The King sat at the Table together with those who were entitled to sit there for having won fame as the reward of their endeavours. All those Knights of the Table Round derived pleasure from this news.

Now let the squire return whose message has been heard. He set out betimes. The Queen's chamberlain gave ready money, a mount and change of clothes. He rode off happily; for what he had achieved with Arthur meant that Gawan's fears were over. He arrived back after I cannot truly say how many days.

At Schastel marveile, Arnive was delighted, since the Gatekeeper had sent to tell her that the squire had returned in excellent time, after taxing his mount to the full. Arnive went unseen to waylay him where he was being admitted to the Castle. She asked him about his journey and to which place he had ridden out.

'It shall remain unsaid, Ma'am,' answered the squire. 'I dare not tell you. I am bound by oath not to reveal it. My lord would be displeased if I were to break my oath by telling and would think me lacking in discretion. Ask him about it yourself, my lady.'

She tried to corner him with question after question, but this is what the squire replied. 'You are detaining me to no purpose, Ma'am. I shall do as my oath commanded me.'

He went and found his master. Florant the Turkoyt, the Duke of Gowerzin and the Duchess of Logroys were sitting there among a great company of ladies. The squire went up to them. Gawan rose to his feet, took him aside and welcomed him back.

'Tell me, my friend,' he said, 'what message they have sent me from Court, and whether the news be happy or anxious. Did you find the King there?'

'Yes, my lord,' answered the squire. 'I found the King and his Queen, and many other distinguished persons. They send you their compliments and the news that they will come. They received your message so worthily that rich and poor alike were glad, for I told them you were alive and well. I found a prodigious crowd there. Further, the Table Round, thanks to your message, had its Company seated about it. If a knight's fame ever had force, I mean in regard to noble qualities, then your fame is crowned most fairly above others' far and wide!'

The squire went on to tell him how it had happened that he had had speech of the Queen, and the loyal advice she had given him. He also told him about the many knights and ladies whom he would be able to see at Joflanze before the time appointed for his duel. Gawan's cares all vanished, in his heart

327

he knew only happiness: he had abandoned anxiety for joy! He forbade the squire to breathe a word of it. Forgetting all his former cares he came back and sat down and continued happily in his Palace till King Arthur came riding to his aid.

Now hear of both joy and sorrow.

Gawan was happy at all times. One morning it so happened that there were many knights and ladies present in that fine Palace. Gawan chose a place on its own in an alcove overlooking the river, and here he sat with Arnive, who could tell many a strange tale.

'My dear lady,' Gawan said to this queen, 'how I should like to ask you about such matters as have been kept hidden from me, if it did not displease you! It is by your generous help alone that I am living in this style, amid such noble pleasures, since if I ever had a manly heart the Duchess captured it by force, but now I have benefited from your kindness so that my sufferings are assuaged. Had not your help and easement delivered me from bonds and bandages, I should have died of love and wounds! It is thanks to you that I am alive. Now tell me, most felicitous of ladies, about the magic that was and is here, and why subtle Clinschor has devised such cogent spells, since but for you they would have cost me my life.'

No young woman had ever grown old with such glory to her sex as this wise-hearted lady had done. 'My lord,' she replied, 'the enchantments he has here are mere curiosities compared with the mighty spells he has cast in other lands. Whoever puts the blame on us saddles himself with sin, for, sir, I will tell you all about him. He has vented his spleen on many peoples. His country is called Terre de Labur. He is a scion of the stock of one who devised many enchantments – Virgil of Naples. *His* kinsman Clinschor did as follows. His capital city was Capua. The paths he trod in pursuit of honour were so lofty that honour did not elude him. The name of Duke Clinschor was on the lips of men and women till disaster overtook him – in this way. There was a King of Sicily called Ibert, and the name of his wife was Iblis. She was the loveliest person ever weaned. Clinschor became her Servitor till she rewarded him with her love. It was for this that the king put

328

him to shame. If I am to tell you Clinschor's secret it must be by your good leave, since it is improper for me to name the circumstances in which he turned sorcerer. – With a cut he was made a capon.'

Gawan laughed loud and long.

'Clinschor suffered this supreme humiliation,' she continued, 'up in Kalot enbolot,* famed for its strength. The king found Clinschor with his wife, he was asleep in her embrace. If his was a warm bed, he had to leave a deposit for it – he was levelled off between his legs by royal hands, the sovereign deemed it his due. The king trimmed him in his body to such effect that he is unserviceable to any woman today for her sport. Many people have had to suffer as a result.

'I refer not to the land of Persia – it was in a *place* called Persida that magic was first contrived. Clinschor repaired there and procured the means of bringing to pass by enchantment whatever he fancies. Because of the dishonour to his body he no longer bears good will to man or woman, I mean those of worthy disposition, for it gratifies his heart to deny them any happiness he can. There was a King of Rosche Sabins, called Irot, who feared this might happen to him, so he offered to give Clinschor any of his possessions Clinschor might desire, in order to escape molestation. Thus Clinschor received from Irot this eminence famed for its strength, and with it the land around it to a radius of eight miles. Upon this rock, as you plainly see, Clinschor then fashioned this ingenious fabric. Of each and every precious thing there is an incredible abundance here. Should any wish to besiege this fortress there would be provisions up here in great variety sufficient for thirty years. Clinschor has power over all those beings that haunt the aether between earth's boundary and the firmament, the malign and the benign, except those under God's protection.

'My lord, since your great peril was averted without fatal effect, the gift made to Clinschor is now subject to you, since

* Qal°at-al-ballūṭ 'Castle of the Oak', Caltabellotta, near Sciacca. Wolfram can count on knowledge of Sicily and Apulia in his aud¡°nce because the Holy Roman Emperors of his day ruled as kings there with in the first place a powerful Hohenstauffen administration.

never again will he concern himself with the Castle and the lands measured out to it. He has publicly declared – and he is a man of his word – that whoever passed through this Adventure should be free from his molestation, and that the gift should rest with that person. You have here as your subjects many people, men, women and girls – whoever his eyes ever lit on in Christendom. Many infidels too, both men and women, were forced to live with us in this Castle. Now let this company return to the various places where we are anxiously lamented! Exile chills my heart. May He Who numbered the stars guide you in helping us and lead us back to happiness! "Which mother bears progeny that becomes its mother's mother? – From *water* there comes ice, and from this, without fail, there comes water again!" When I reflect that I was borne of happiness, if happiness is ever seen in me again, one progeny will have borne another! As a well-bred man you will bring this about.

'It is a long time since happiness deserted me. Thanks to its sail, a ship makes good headway: but a man who walks on that ship moves even faster. If you understand this little parable your fame will soar. You have it in your power to make us shout for joy and take joy to many lands where fear was felt for us. There was a time when I knew happiness. I was a woman who wore a crown, and my daughter too went crowned in great solemnity before the princes of her realm. We both enjoyed high station. Sir, I never plotted mischief to any man, but knew how to give people their due. Please God, I was seen and acknowledged, as of right, as true Queen of a people, since I never wronged anyone. Now let any fortunate woman who has standards of decent behaviour treat simple people well: she might easily fall into so wretched a state that a common serving-lad could show her an escape from the unhappiness that walled her in. I have watched and waited here a long time, my lord, during which none came, walking or riding, who either knew me or rid me from my cares.'

'If I live, you shall be seen happy again, Ma'am,' said my lord Gawan.

On that same day, Arthur the Briton and son of Arnive

who was lamenting here, was due to arrive with a great company to honour the bonds of kinship.

And now Gawan saw many new banners marching towards him and squadrons of horses covering the field all along the way from Logroys and flaunting many a lance with gay colours. Gawan was glad of their coming. When a man waits for reinforcements any delay makes him secretly afraid that they will be of small use to him. Arthur shattered such doubts in Gawan, for oh! how they saw him coming on! Gawan shrank from being observed lest it be seen that his bright eyes had filled with tears – they could not have served as cisterns, for neither was watertight! The tears which Arthur had brought to view were tears of joy, for Arthur had reared him since childhood. Their mutual loyalty, firm and unfeigned, knew no defection – perfidy had never got through its guard.

Arnive nevertheless noticed that Gawan was in tears. 'You must raise a shout of joy, my lord,' she said, 'this would cheer us all. You must be on your guard against sorrow. Here comes the Duchess's army. This will soon console you.'

Arnive and Gawan saw many pavilions and banners being carried on to the meadow, yet among them only one escutcheon whose markings were recognizable to Arnive. She pronounced the name of Isajes, Utepandragun's Marshal. But it was borne by another Briton, by Maurin of the Handsome Thighs, the Queen's Marshal. Arnive was not to know that both Utepandragun and Isajes were dead, and that Maurin had acquired his father's office, as was right and proper. The Great Household rode over the level meadow towards the landing-place. The Queen's men-at-arms took quarters beside a clear and rapid brook well suited to the ladies. Here you could see numerous fine pavilions set up. At some distance away, many tent-rings were staked out for Arthur and for the knights who had come there. No question, they had left very broad tracks behind them on this sortie!

Gawan sent Bene down with a message to his host Plippalinot that he was to make fast the cogs and ferry-boats so that the army should be prevented from crossing that day.

Lady Bene received her first gift from Gawan's luxurious

Booth from his own hands – Swallow, still famed in England as a rare harp today! Bene went happily away, while Gawan ordered the Outer Gates to be barred. And now, in the hearing of young and old, he voiced a courteous plea.

'Over there on the far side, an army has encamped, so mighty that I have never seen squadrons move in greater strength, either on land or sea. If they intend to attack us here I shall offer them battle with your aid.'

They promised to aid him, one and all. They then asked the Duchess if this army were hers.

'I recognize neither men nor escutcheons, believe me,' she replied. 'Perhaps the man who harmed me once before has invaded my lands and fought below the walls of Logroys. But I fancy he will have found the defenders well able to give an account of themselves: my men would have been a match for them with their redoubts and barbicans. If the irascible King Gramoflanz has been fighting there he will have been seeking satisfaction for his Garland. Or whoever they are, they have had to face upraised lances signalling readiness to joust.'

Her words were absolutely true. Arthur had taken much more harm before he was past Logroys, in the course of which action no few Britons were brought down in regular joust. For their part, Arthur's host paid back what they had got in the same coin, so that both sides had been hard pressed.

And now they of whom it has often been said that they would fight to keep their shirts, came on weary from fighting, tough warriors that they were. Losses had been sustained on both sides. Garel and Gaherjet, King Meljanz de Barbigœl and Jofreit fiz Idœl had been captured and taken into the castle before the bohort was concluded. From Logroys the Britons had taken Duke Friam de Vermendoys and Count Ritschart de Navers, too, who had broken but one lance, for no matter at whom he aimed it, that man came down under its masterful thrust! It was Arthur who had taken this famous stalwart prisoner with his own hand. Thereupon, without thought for the cost, charge had become so interlocked with charge that if lances had been trees a whole forest would have been cleared. Jousts beyond number sent the splinters flying. As far as they were concerned, the Britons gave a good account of themselves opposite the Duchess's army. Arthur's rear-guard had had to counter-attack, for their enemy had harassed them all day long, right up to where the mass of the army lay.

Truly, my lord Gawan ought to have informed the Duchess that an ally of his was in her territory! Then there would have been no fighting. But he did not wish to tell her or anyone before she could see it herself. He acted as it suited him and, with costly pavilions, prepared for his march to meet Arthur the Briton. Nobody went short because he was unknown to Gawan. Gawan's generous hand lavished gifts on them with such a will, you would have thought he was tired of living! He made squires, knights and ladies see and take his gifts on such a liberal scale that all agreed true succour had come to them, and they rejoiced aloud.

The worthy knight now ordered sturdy sumpters to be fetched, handsome palfreys for the ladies, and armour for all the knights. A strong force of men-at-arms encased in steel stood ready there. My lord Gawan then did as follows: he took four noble knights aside, so that one became his Chamberlain, another his Butler and a third his Steward, while the fourth was to remember he was his Marshal. This is what Gawan did, and these four carried out his wishes.

Now let King Arthur quietly lie encamped there. Gawan withheld his greeting all day, though it was far from easy for him to refrain. Early next morning Arthur's host rode off towards Joflanze with ear-splitting sound. He formed his rear-guard so as to beat off an attack, but when they saw that there was to be no fighting, they wheeled and followed on his tracks.

Gawan then drew his Officers aside. He wished to delay no longer and commanded his Marshal to ride to the meadow at Joflanze. 'I want my own camping-ground. You will see the great army encamped there. Matters have reached a point at which I must name their lord for you all to know who he is. He is my uncle Arthur, under whose roof and at whose court I was reared since childhood. Now equip my march to that field with such fine gear that its magnificence will be plain beyond all cavil, nor let it be known here within that Arthur has come for my sake.'

They did what he had commanded them. Plippalinot too went into action. In cogs, ferries, fast galleys and barges, squires and attendants with spirited companies both on horse and on foot, had to cross over with Gawan's Marshal. With him they then wound their way along the Briton's tracks.

Now rest assured that they were also bringing a pavilion which Iblis had sent Clinschor as a love-gift, from which the secret had first become known at large that they loved one another. No expense had been omitted to make that tent, and scissors had never cut a better, but for one that had belonged to Isenhart. This pavilion was set up on its own stretch of grass not far from Arthur, and I am told that many others were pitched around it in a spacious ring, making a magnificent impression.

The report reached Arthur's inner court that Gawan's Marshal had arrived and was setting up camp on the meadow, and that noble Gawan himself would be coming before the day was out. This became the common talk of all the Household.

And now honest, loyal Gawan formed his companies with his men and set out on his march with such pomp that I could tell you marvels of it. Many sumpters were loaded with field-chapels and clothes, while many marched under piles of armour, not to mention splendid shields, with helmets strapped on top. Beside these sumpter animals you could see handsome castilians pacing. Knights and ladies were riding at the rear in a tight press. The whole cavalcade was fully a short league in length.! Gawan did not forget to provide each comely lady with a handsome knight for company, and they were fools if their talk did not run on love. Florant the Turkoyt was chosen as companion to Sangive of Norway, keen Lischois rode beside sweet Cundrie, and Gawan's sister Itonje was asked to ride at his side, while Arnive and the Duchess wished to make a pair for their part.

Matters had turned out thus. Gawan's ring was sited in such a way that it had to be approached through the encampment of Arthur's army. How they all gazed before this company had passed through them! For the sake of honour and courtesy, Gawan asked the first lady to halt at Arthur's ring. His Marshal was then bidden to see to it that a second lady rode up close beside her, and then all the others halted all the way round in the same fashion, the mature and the immature, and beside each the knight who attended her and had undertaken to serve her. Thus Arthur's ring was surrounded by ladies on all sides. Only now was thrice-fortunate Gawan received – and, if you ask me, affectionately!

Arnive, her daughter and the latter's children have dismounted together with Gawan and also the Duchess of Logroys, the Duke of Gowerzin and Florant the Turkoyt. Arthur advanced from his Pavilion towards these illustrious persons and welcomed them in friendly fashion, as did also his Queen, who received Gawan and his companions with a wealth of loyal affection. Many kisses were exchanged between many comely ladies.

'Who are these companions of yours?' Arthur asked his nephew.

'I must see my Lady kiss them, it would be a blunder were she not to, for their lineage entitles them to it.' Queen Ginover kissed Florant the Turkoyt at once, and also the Duke of Gowerzin.

They went back into the Pavilion. It seemed to many that the broad meadow was full of ladies. Arthur did not act the lubber – he sprang lightly on to a castilian, rode all round the ring of comely ladies and the knights attending them and courteously welcomed them with his own lips there and then. It had been Gawan's wish that they should all hold still in the saddle till he should ride away with them. Such was courtly usage in those days.

Arthur dismounted and went inside. He sat down beside his nephew and pressed him with questions as to who the five ladies were. My lord Gawan began with the eldest and addressed the Briton in these words.

'If you ever knew Utepandragun, this is his wife Arnive. You were born of the two. Then this is my mother the Queen

335

of Norway and these two are my sisters – are they not fresh and lovely girls?'

There was a new round of kissing. All who cared to look on saw laughter mingled with tears. It was joy that affected them so: their lips knew well how to convey both weeping and laughing under the impact of great pleasure!

'Nephew, I make so bold as to ask who the lustrous *fifth* lady may be,' Arthur said to Gawan.

'She is the Duchess of Logroys,' replied the courteous Gawan. 'I am here as her liege. I have been told you made an incursion against her. Show me what you had from it, don't be shy. You would make a good widow!'*

'The Duchess has your maternal kinsman Gaherjet as her prisoner, and Garel, who did a knight's work in countless charges. The fearless man was snatched from my side, for one of our charges had penetrated with its full impact right up to their barbican. – *At them now!* – What feats were performed by the noble Meljanz of Liz! He was taken captive up to the castle under a white banner to which a Black Arrow of Sable stained with Heart's Blood had been added, in portrayal of a man's suffering. The company riding beneath it as their battle-sign all shouted 'Lirivoyn!'. The prize they had won so gloriously they took up to the castle. To my sorrow, my nephew Jofreit, too, was captured and led in. Yesterday I had command of the rearguard, that is how this hurt was inflicted on me.'

The King had much to say on his losses.

'I declare you free of any dishonourable act,' said the Duchess tactfully. 'You never had my greeting or favour. You may have done me some harm without my having deserved it. Since you have come and attacked me, may God show you how to make amends. You have ridden out to the aid of a man who, had he fought with me, would have found me defenceless and thrust at me on the open side! If he wants to renew the contest it will be settled without swords!'

---

* Because of Arthur's losses. Or: 'You could be kind to a widow', that is, to Orgeluse, Cidegast's widow.

'How would you consider it if we were to cover this meadow with yet more knights, since we are well able to do so?' Gawan asked Arthur. 'I am sure I can persuade the Duchess to free your men and order her knights along with supplies of new lances.'

'You have my agreement,' said Arthur.

And so the Duchess sent home to summon her worthy men. I do not imagine there can ever have been a more splendid concourse anywhere on earth.

Gawan asked leave to continue on his way to his encampment, and the King granted it. Those who had been seen to arrive with him, now accompanied him to their quarters. With all its chivalric splendour, his camp made a luxurious impression free of all taint of poverty.

No few rode into Gawan's camp who had deeply regretted his long absence. As to Keie, he had now recovered from the joust beside the Plimizœl. He examined Gawan's luxurious turn-out closely.

'With my lord's brother-in-law Lot we stood in no fear of rivalry or separate camp-rings,' said Keie. He was still brooding on the fact that Gawan had not avenged him when his right arm had been broken. 'God's wonders never cease. – Who gave Gawan this gaggle of ladies?' went on Keie, whose mockery of friends was scarcely seemly. A loyal-hearted man rejoices at a friend's advancement; a disloyal man cries out in sorrow when something pleasant befalls his friend and he is there to see it. Gawan was blessed with both honour and fortune: if any man wants more, where are his thoughts leading him? Dastards are full of spite and envy. On the other hand, it gladdens a man of spirit when his friend's honour stands firm and routs dishonour. Gawan, in whom treacherous spite was lacking, was ever-mindful of manly loyalty, so that there was nothing at all wrong with it when he was seen basking in Fortune's favour.

You ask 'How did the man of Norway care for his train of knights and ladies?' Arthur and his retinue were given the opportunity of feasting their eyes on all the wealth of noble Lot's son! But they are entitled to sleep, you know, after supper! I would never begrudge them their rest.

337

Before sunrise next morning an entire force of the Duchess's knights rode up fully armed. Their crests were visible by the light of the moon from where Arthur and his men were encamped. Through these latter the knights now marched to the farther side where Gawan lay with his broad ring. A man who can command such support through the force of his brave right hand must be given high credit for it! Gawan asked his Marshal to show them where they should encamp, and following the latter's instructions, the noble troop from Logroys pitched many rings of fine pavilions on their own. It was mid-morning before they were lodged. But now new cares are approaching.

Illustrious Arthur sent his envoys to the town of Rosche Sabins with this request to King Gramoflanz: 'Since it is unalterable that he will not waive his duel with my nephew, my nephew will grant it him. Ask him to meet us soon, since he is known to be so high and mighty that he will not forgo it. Another would have stopped short of such presumptuousness!'* Arthur's envoys went on their way.

My lord Gawan took Lischois and Florant and asked them quickly to show him Love's soldiers from many lands who had served the Duchess devotedly in the hope of high reward. He rode up to them and received them so well that all acclaimed noble Gawan as a gallant gentleman.

This done, Gawan left them and returned. What followed he did in great secrecy. He went into his wardrobe, cased his body in armour immediately in order to discover whether his wounds had so far healed that the scabs did not fret him. He wished to exercise his limbs, seeing that so many men and women would be witnessing his duel in a place where discerning knights could judge whether his dauntless hand had triumphed that day. He had asked a squire to bring him Gringuljete, and he now gave him the reins, for he wanted some brisk movement so that he and his charger should both be fit for battle.

No sallying-out of his was so little to my liking. My lord

* Or: Another would have taken him to task for it.

Gawan rode away from the army far out over the plain. May Good Fortune watch over him!

Beside the River Sabins he saw a knight motionless in the saddle whom we might well dub a flintstone of manly vigour. A hail-storm to knights, perfidy never got through to his heart. He was so feeble of body that he failed to carry what men call 'Dishonour' at all, not so much as a span nor even half a finger's length! You may well have heard tell of this man before, since the story has now returned to its true stem.

Chapter 14

I F Gawan is going to contend there with the lance I could never be so fearful for his prowess. I ought also to be concerned for the other: but I shall shed my fears, for in battle he was a whole army against one man. His crest had been brought from heathen lands far away overseas. His surcoat and his horse's trappers were even redder than ruby. The warrior was in quest of adventure: his shield was riddled with lance-thrusts. From the tree which Gramoflanz guarded he too had broken a twig for a wreath so gay that Gawan recognized it and was assailed by the fear that the King was waiting for him there. For had Gramoflanz ridden out to attack him, a clash could not have been avoided, even with no ladies to witness it.

Both mounts were from Munsalvæsche, and, urged on by the spur, they raced towards each other into the charge at full tilt. This joust was done not on dusty gravel but on clover green as green and hung with dew. The pain they have to endure distresses me. Their charge was all that could be desired, since both were of a line of jousters. The man who gains the victory here will have won little and lost much – he will always deplore it when understanding comes. For they are joined in loyal affection that remains unscarred, now as in the past.

Now listen to how this joust went – with a mighty onrush, yet in circumstances both must regret. Illustrious kinship and lofty fellowship had met there to fight a bitter battle in all enmity. The happiness of whichever prevails there will be forfeit to sorrow.

Each delivered his thrust to such effect that these kinsmen and companions could not fail to bring each other down, mounts and all. And this is what they set about forthwith – it was as though they were hammering in wedges or pickaxing with swords! As a result of their fighting, the chips from their

340

shields and the green grass were evenly blended there! They had to wait too long for a decision. They had gone to it early, yet no one undertook a settlement. For you see they were alone.

Now would you like to hear more, of how Arthur's messengers had met King Gramoflanz and his army meanwhile? It was on a meadow by the sea. On one side there ran the Sabins, on the other the Poynzaclins – the two rivers flow into the sea here. On its fourth side, the meadow was guarded by the capital city of Rosche Sabins, which enfolded it with walls, moats and many lofty towers. Over a space of a mile by half a mile the retainers had camped on this meadow. Here Arthur's messengers rode past many knights who were complete strangers to them, mounted archers and numerous men-at-arms encased in armour and equipped with lances. Hard upon them yet other great companies were marching up with swinging step under a crowd of banners.

Trumpets rent the air, and you could see the whole army come alive, keen to march to Joflanze without delay. There was jingling of ladies' bridles, for King Gramoflanz's ring was ringed with ladies!

If I can master a tale I will tell you who had come to Gramoflanz's assembly for his sake and lodged upon the greensward. If you have not heard of it before, let me make it known to you. From the water-girt town of Punt his noble maternal uncle King Brandelidelin had brought him six hundred dazzling ladies each of whom could rest her eyes on the sight of her lover armed to do knightly deeds and win renown. Those Punturteis were in good heart on this foray!

If you will take it on trust from me, the handsome Bernout de Riviers was there whose mighty father Narant had left him Ukerlant. He had brought over the sea in cogs a lovely bevy of ladies whose radiant looks were acknowledged beyond all cavil, two hundred of them unmarried girls, two hundred with their husbands. If I have their number right, five hundred illustrious knights well able to do mischief to their adversaries had come with Bernout, son of Count Narant.

In this way, King Gramoflanz intended to avenge the loss of his Garland in single combat and decide which should be

341

judged most glorious before a host of witnesses. The Princes of his realm were there with their knights in great force, together with many ladies. There were some fine-looking people to be seen there.

Arthur's envoys made their way here. Let me tell you in what state they found the King. Gramoflanz was seated on a thick mattress of palmat-silk quilted over with a broad cloth-of-gold. Young ladies, vivacious and lovely, were casing the proud king's feet in jambs of steel beneath a broad canopy of costly, shimmering brocade woven in Ecidemonis and wafted high above him upon a dozen lances. Arthur's messengers having arrived, they now addressed the proudest of the proud in these terms.

'Sire, we have been sent by Arthur, who was noted for having distinguished himself on occasion. And indeed, he does not want for lustre, though you are minded to diminish it. How did you arrive at such a thought as to wish to vent your displeasure on his sister's son? Had noble Gawan done you a greater wrong, he could have counted on each and every member of the Table Round, since all who claim their seat there are his loyal companions.'

'I shall deliver this duel that has been sworn unflinchingly with this same hand,' replied the King, 'and to such effect that before this day is out I shall have chased Gawan either to glory or disgrace! I have heard reliably that Arthur and his Queen have come in force. I bid them welcome. If the malign Duchess has been setting him on against me, Pages, you must prevent it, since it remains unalterable that I shall fight the duel. I have so many knights that I need fear no violence. But whatever it is my lot to suffer from one man, that I will endure. For were I now to refrain from what I have set my mark on, I should be giving up my love-service. God knows, that man has to thank the lady to whose mercy I have surrendered all my life and joy, since hitherto I have always scorned to engage a single enemy. Only because noble Gawan's toils have borne such fruit am I pleased to fight a duel with him. Thus my valour stoops: I have never fought against such puny opposition. I have fought – none denies it, make your own inquiries

342

if you please – with men who conceded fame supreme to this my hand! I have never taken on an adversary one-to-one. Nor should the ladies praise me if I gain the victory today. It warms my heart that the lady for whom this duel is to be fought has been set free, as I am told. One has heard that so many strange lands do far-famed Arthur's bidding that, very likely, *she* has come here with him – the lady I shall serve till death through joy and anguish as she commands! How should I acquit myself better, if it is my good luck that she herself deigns to witness my service?'

Bene was seated beside the King, who had cushioned his arm on her. She had no objection to this duel, having seen his prowess in battle so often that she had no fears on that score. Had she known that Gawan was her lady's brother and that these grim matters concerned her lord, her contentment would have vanished. She had brought the King a ring which the young Princess Itonje had sent him in token of her love, the ring her illustrious brother had brought across the Sabins.

Bene had come by fast galley on the Poynzaclins with news she did not withhold: 'My mistress has set out from Schastel marveile accompanied by many ladies!' She reminded the King how her mistress had told him through her of greater attachment and esteem than any young lady of tender years had ever sent a man, and that he was to keep her sufferings in mind, since to deserve his love meant more to her than anything else she could have. This raised his spirits mightily. Nevertheless, he is wronging Gawan. If this were the cost of having a sister I would rather be without one.

Accoutrements were now brought in of such magnificence that no man constrained by love to strive for ladies' favour, be he Gahmuret or Galoes or King Kyllicrates, could have decked out his person better to please the fair! No finer brocade was ever brought from Ipopotiticon, from spacious Acraton, Kalomidente or Agatyrsjente, than was chosen for his adornment. He kissed the ring which the young Princess Itonje had sent him as a love-token, and so convinced was he of her steadfastness that whenever care weighed him down, her love was as a shield to him.

343

And now this King was fully armed. Twelve young ladies on stout ponies took a hand whose business it was each to hold a pole supporting the costly cloth-of-gold beneath which the King was to ride – this fair company were carrying it to shade the warlike man! On two other young ladies riding beside him, admittedly the best-looking and no weaklings either, the King rested his mighty arms!

With no more delay, Arthur's messengers departed, and on their way back came to where Gawan was fighting. Never had these pages been so sorry. True-hearted as they were, they shouted at the top of their voices to make his peril known.

Things had almost reached the point where Gawan's opponent had won. The latter's strength was so superior that Gawan, noble warrior, would have known defeat, had not those pages recognized and named him so indignantly. The man who had given him battle abstained from any further show of it and flung his sword far from him.

'Accurst and contemptible I!' cried the stranger amid his tears. 'Fortune must have abandoned me for this infamous hand of mine ever to have known this battle – how grossly it has blundered! I accept the blame. Misfortune has come out and parted me from Fortune, and so I display my old blazon* again, as so often in the past! To think that I have been attacking noble Gawan here! So doing, I have vanquished myself and waited for Misfortune, Fortune having fled from me the instant battle was joined.'

Gawan heard and saw his grief. 'Alas, sir, who are you? You speak so kindly towards me. If only these things had been said before while I still had my strength. I should then not have lost my high renown which you have taken from me here. I should like to know your name and where I could find my renown if I should seek it later. As long as it pleased *my* Fortune I always faced up well to one man opposite me.'

'Cousin, I shall make myself known to you, at your service now and always. I am your kinsman† Parzival.'

* His Liege-Lady Misfortune's coat-of-arms.
† Parzival's paternal great-great-great-grandfather Mazadan was Gawan's maternal great-great-grandfather.

'Then it turned out well,' replied Gawan. 'Perverse folly has been straightened out here. Two hearts that are but one have shown their strength in fierce enmity. Your hand has overcome us both. Now regret it for our sakes. If your heart be true, you have subdued yourself.' Having said this, Gawan was able to stand no longer, so weak had he become. He tottered giddily, for his head was buzzing, then fell full length on the grass. One of Arthur's pages darted forward and pillowed his head, and then the handsome boy unlaced his helmet and fanned a breeze across his face with his white peacock-feather cap. These attentions of the page brought new strength to Gawan.

And now companies from both armies were arriving with their forces on either side, each advancing to the positions that had been marked out for them with mighty logs burnished till they shone – Gramoflanz had met the cost since he was the challenger. There were a hundred of these gleaming trees with (so I am told) fifty on either side at a distance of forty courses, each to each, shooting their bright rays. No one was to step between them, for here the battle was to be fought. Gramoflanz and Gawan had given each other their hands on it that their people were to keep out, as though held back by castle-walls or fosses.

As to that battle which had now been arranged, various detachments from both armies had just arrived on the scene hoping to observe who would win. They were curious to learn who was fighting there so manfully and on whom it had fallen to oppose him. Neither army had brought its champion to the duelling-ground, and it struck them as very odd.

It was after this combat had ended on the flowery mead that King Gramoflanz arrived, eager to avenge the loss of his Garland. He heard that a sword-duel had been fought there fiercer than any seen before. And indeed those who had given each other battle had done so for no cause. Gramoflanz rode out from his company towards those battle-weary men deploring their exertions from the bottom of his heart. Yet although he was spent in every limb, Gawan had sprung to his feet, and so both combatants were standing together there.

Now Bene had ridden with the King into the ring in which

345

the rigours of that duel had been endured and there she saw Gawan – him she had chosen to be the crown of her sublimest joy! – with all his strength gone. With a shriek of deepest grief she leapt down from her palfrey, threw her arms around him and clasped him tight.

'A curse on the hand that taught your fair body such pain!' she cried. 'For, truly, your countenance was a mirror of manhood outshining all others!' She seated him on the grass, unable to hold back her tears and then, sweet child, wiped the blood and sweat from his eyes, for his armour he was very hot.

'It grieves me to see you in such discomfort, Gawan,' said King Gramoflanz, 'except that I wish I myself had inflicted it on you. If you will come back to this meadow tomorrow and do battle with me I shall be pleased to await you. At this moment I would rather take on a woman than your feeble person. Without better report of your strength, what glory could I win from you? Now rest this night, you will need it, if you are to answer for King Lot.'

Mighty Parzival was showing no signs of pallor or weariness in his limbs. He had just unlaced his helmet as the noble King set eyes on him.

'Sir,' said Parzival, 'let me stand for my cousin Gawan in any matter in which he has offended you. I am still in good fighting trim. If you intend to vent your anger on him I shall stop you with my sword!'

'Sir,' said the Lord of Rosche Sabins, 'he will render the due to me tomorrow which is owing for my Garland, with the outcome that either its fame will be exalted and made perfect, or he will chase me to where I shall tread the path of shame! I do not doubt that you are a stout fighting-man, but this duel is not for you.'

Bene turned on the King. 'You treacherous cur!' are the words her sweet lips uttered. 'Your heart is in the hand of that same man whom your heart is hating! To whom have you surrendered yourself in Love's name? She has to live by that man's favour! You have pronounced your own defeat – Love has lost her rights in you! For if you ever loved, it was in bad faith!'

After this outburst the King spoke with Bene aside. 'Madam, do not be so angry at my fighting this duel,' he begged her. 'Stay here with your lord. Tell his sister Itonje that I am truly her Servitor and mean to serve her in every way I can.'

When Bene heard it confirmed that her lord was her lady's brother and was pledged to do battle there on the grass, Grief's oars pulled a whole shipload of direst sorrow into her heart, for she was a loyal soul.

'Out with you, you cursed man!' she said. 'Loyalty is a thing you never knew!'

The King rode off with all his company, while Arthur's pages caught the combatants' horses, which were fighting their own duel in sight of all.

And now Gawan, Parzival and Bene rode away to their own great company. Parzival had won such honour with his manly prowess that they were glad at his coming, for when they saw him arrive they all acclaimed him.

I shall tell you more if I can. Experienced men in both armies were talking of this one man, in that they were praising the knightly deeds of him that had won the palm – Parzival, if you agree.* He was so handsome, too, no knight was ever better favoured as men and women declared when Gawan brought him in and kindly saw to it that he was robed – identical clothes of precious stuff were fetched for both! And now it became known everywhere that Parzival had come, of whom they had heard so often that he had won high renown, as many confirmed.

'If you wish to see four ladies of your lineage and other comely women besides, I will gladly accompany you,' said Gawan.

'If there are noble ladies present do not let me be a source of offence to them,' replied the son of Gahmuret. 'All who heard me vilified beside the Plimizœl will detest the sight of me. May God keep their womanly honour in His sight! In my eyes, ladies will always be a source of bliss. I still feel

---

* Wolfram is at pains to placate the pro-Gawan faction in his audience as he leads Parzival back into the limelight.

so deeply disgraced that I am loth to seek their company.'

'There is nothing for it,' replied Gawan, and he led Parzival away to where four queens kissed him. It pained the Duchess to have to kiss the man who had spurned her overtures, when she had offered him both love and lands after he had fought below the walls of Logroys and she had ridden so far in pursuit of him. – Her embarrassment gave her much ado. As to radiant Parzival, he was artlessly wheedled into allowing all his shame to be led captive from his heart, so that, freed from his misgivings, he grew cheerful.

Gawan for good reason forbade Lady Bene on pain of loss of his favour to reveal to Itonje with her sweet lips 'that King Gramoflanz hates me so because of his Garland', or 'that we two will give each other battle tomorrow at the time appointed for the duel. You are not to speak a word of it to my sister and are to repress all signs of weeping!'

'I have good cause to weep and let my sorrow be seen always, since whichever of you two falls, my mistress will mourn for him. She is slain on either side. What else can I do but lament for my lady and myself? How does it help that you are her brother? You are resolved to wage war on her heart!'

By now all the army had marched in, and dinner was ready for Gawan and his companions. Parzival was asked to share a platter with the lively Duchess to whom Gawan had particularly commended him.

'Are you going to recommend a man to me who rails at us women?' she asked. 'How shall I look after such a man? Nevertheless, I shall attend to his needs, since you command it. If he seizes on *that* what do I care?'

'Madam,' replied the son of Gahmuret, 'you do me wrong. I know myself to be so versed as to refrain from mocking the whole sex.'

If it was there, they gave sufficient and served it up with great ceremony. Girls, women and men dined pleasurably there. Itonje did not fail to note from Bene's eyes that she was crying to herself, as a result of which her face, too, took on a woebegone look and her sweet mouth refused to eat.

'What is Bene doing here?' she asked herself. 'Did I not

348

send her to the man who has my heart out there, yet which throws me into such turmoil here? What have I to suffer now? Has the King rejected my love and devotion? His loyal and manly heart will win no more of me than that poor I must die of heartfelt grief for him!'

By the time their meal was over it was past noon. Arthur and his consort the Queen Ginover rode with some knights and a bevy of ladies to where handsome Parzival was seated among the fair, and etiquette prescribed that he had to see himself kissed in welcome by many lovely women. Arthur paid him all due honour and earnestly thanked him for having won high renown noised so far and wide that by rights he must take the palm above all men.

'When I last met you, Sire,' the Waleis told King Arthur, 'my honour was attacked. I was mulcted of so much honour that I was almost bankrupt of it. But now, Sire, if you mean what you say, I have heard that some small honour is attested in me. Difficult though it would be to convince myself, I should nevertheless gladly believe it if those others would believe it, too, from whom I went in disgrace.'

Those who were sitting there declared that he had won such exalted honours throughout many lands that his honour was entire.

And now the Duchess's knights arrived where handsome Parzival was seated at Arthur's side, and the noble King received them punctiliously in his host's pavilion. For spacious though Gawan's pavilion was, Arthur, urbane man, had taken his seat outside in the meadow with the company sitting round him in a ring. Strangers were assembled here together: but to tell you who they all were, Christians and Saracens, by name, in detail, would be a lengthy business. Who were Clinschor's army? Who were the formidable men who sallied forth from Logroys so often, fighting for Orgeluse? Whom had Arthur brought? – If one were charged with naming and proclaiming all their seats and domains, one would be hard put to it to single them out. Yet they were all at one in declaring that Parzival was beyond compare so dazzling in his person that women must dote on him, and that in all that made for distinction, Noblesse had cheated him of nothing.

The son of Gahmuret rose to his feet. 'Let all present quietly sit and help me with a thing whose lack I suffer most keenly. By some strange mystery I was parted from the Table Round. I ask those who were once my Companions, by exerting their companionship, to help me back to it!'

What he had asked, Arthur graciously accorded him. Then, stepping aside into a small group, Parzival voiced a second request, namely that Gawan should make over to him the duel he was to fight next day at the appointed hour.

'I shall be happy to wait for the knight men call Rois Gramoflanz. Early this morning I broke a twig from his tree for a garland so that he should come and attack me, for it was expressly and solely to do battle with him that I entered his country. Cousin, I could scarcely expect to find *you* here – never have I regretted anything so much! I imagined it was the King come to give me battle. Let me take him on as I was intending, Cousin. If his renown is ever to be brought low, it is I who shall inflict such damage on him as will well and truly content him. My rights have been restored to me here, dear Cousin, so that I can live as a comrade towards you. Remember too that we are related, and leave this duel to me. My manly mettle shall not remain hidden!'

'I have many kinsmen and brothers* here with the King of Britain. I shall let none of you fight in my stead. I rely on my good cause that, with luck, I shall gain the victory. God reward you for offering to fight: but I am not yet that far gone.'.

Arthur had heard what was being asked. He put an end to their conversation and went back with them and sat in the ring. Gawan's Butler, who was not without attendants, saw to it that his young gentlemen brought in a store of precious cups of gold encrusted with gems. This outpouring over, the company all went to their quarters.

Night indeed was coming on. Parzival gave thought to examining all his equipment. If any of the leathers had snapped

* The only brother of Gawan named in *Parzival* is Beacurs.

he had them splendidly restored and he asked them to get a new shield, since his had been holed clean through with thrusts and blows. They had to bring him a very stout one, and it was done by men-at-arms who were strangers to him, some French men among others. As to the charger the Templar had ridden against him in a joust*, a squire had applied himself to it so well that it was never better dressed since that day. It was now night and time to sleep, and with all his equipment at his feet this is what Parzival did.

For his part King Gramoflanz was annoyed that another man had fought in defence of his Garland that day; but his people neither dared nor were able to compose the matter. He deeply regretted that he had lost his opportunity. And what did this warrior do? Since he was accustomed to winning glory by the time day was breaking, both he and his mount were armed. You ask if fabulously wealthy ladies bestowed his adornment? It was lavish enough without that – he adorned his person for love of a young woman whose steadfast Servitor he was.

Now Parzival too had stolen out unseen. He freed a stout lance of Angram from its pennant and was fully armed besides. As the warrior rode, alone as he was, towards the burnished tree-trunks where the duel was to be fought, he saw the King waiting there. The tale avers that without saying a word each thrust his lance through the other's shield to such effect that the splinters went whirling high into the air from their grips! They were both adept at jousting and also with other weapons. Over the expanse of that meadow the dew was marred, while their helmets were jangled by keen swords biting deep. They both fought fearlessly. The grass was trampled down and in many places the dew was trodden in. I am sorry for the red flowers and even more for those warriors, who were enduring sharp distress without timidity. To what man they had not wronged could this be unsullied pleasure?

And now Lord Gawan was preparing himself for the hazards of his duel. It was fully mid-morning before it was learned

* Chapter 9.

that bold Parzival was missing. 'Is he out for a reconciliation?' He was not acting as though he were! – He was fighting so manfully with one who was applying himself to battle too. By now it was high morning.

A bishop sang Mass for Gawan. There was a great press of armed men there, and you could see knights and ladies already on horseback in Arthur's ring before the chanting began. King Arthur himself stood on foot where the priests perform the Office. After the benediction, Lord Gawan armed himself. Already before Mass he had been seen wearing his steel jambs on his shapely legs. Ladies began to weep. The whole army marched out to where they heard the sound of sword-play, the crackle of sparks hewn from helmets, and mighty blows being driven home.

It was King Gramoflanz's custom to scorn fighting with one opponent, but it now seemed to him as though he were being attacked by six. Yet it was Parzival alone who was giving him proof of his fighting qualities. He had taught him a lesson in good manners such as is still esteemed today, since never after that time did Gramoflanz arrogate to himself the honour of challenging two men at a time. For, out there, one man is giving him more than he can cope with.

Meanwhile, on both sides, the armies had arrived at their marks on the broad green meadow and were appraising this bitter sport. The bold warriors' horses had come to a standstill, and their noble riders were thus fighting a hard, fierce battle on foot. Time and time again those stalwarts tossed their swords to change the edge.

In this way the King Gramoflanz was receiving harsh payment for his Garland, and this kinsman of his lady-love was suffering small joy from him, so dearly was noble Parzival paying for radiant Itonje, from whom by rights he ought to have benefited. Men who had sallied out many times to win renown, they were now having to pay dear with their strife. The one was fighting to extricate a friend: the other, Love's subject that he was, was doing her bidding.

And now my lord Gawan appeared at the point where the proud bold Waleis had all but won the victory.

Brandelidelin of Punturteis, Bernout de Riviers and Affinamus of Clitiers, these three, rode up to the scene of the encounter bare-headed while Arthur and Gawan rode on to the meadow towards the battle-weary pair from the other side. The five of them agreed to end the fighting. It seemed the right moment to end it also to Gramoflanz, who formally conceded victory to the man they saw opposing him. And others had to say the same.

'My lord King,' said King Lot's son, 'I shall do to you today as you did to me yesterday when you asked me to rest. Now *you* rest today – you need it. Whoever forced this duel on you reduced the strength you can pit against me. I could now face you single-handed though you only take on two at a time! Tomorrow I will dare it alone. May God make the just cause manifest!'

After pledging that he would come to the meadow the next day to do battle with Gawan, the King rode off and joined his followers.

'Nephew,' said Arthur to Parzival, 'though it so happened that you begged leave to fight the duel and to your intense sorrow Gawan refused to let you, you have nevertheless now fought it with the man who was waiting for him, whether we liked it or not. You stole out from among us like a thief, otherwise we should have prevented you from taking part. Now Gawan need not be angry, however much they fête you on your victory.'

'The high distinction my cousin has won does not trouble me,' replied Gawan. 'If I *must* undertake a duel, tomorrow is still too soon for me. If the King would release me from it I should account it very reasonable on his part.'

The army rode in with all its many companies. Comely ladies were to be seen there and no few knights, so caparisoned that no army was ever possessed of such adornments. The tabards of the Knights of the Table Round and the Duchess's train were resplendent with cloth-of-gold from Cynidunte and fabric brought from Pelpiunte. Their horses' trappers too were dazzling bright. In both armies, handsome Parzival was praised so highly that his friends could have been well pleased. In

Gramoflanz's army, indeed, they declared that no knight on whom sun had ever shone had come to them so formidable, and that whatever the feats on either side he alone must have the glory. Even now they did not know the name of this man whom all acclaimed supreme.

Gramoflanz's people advised him to send a message to Arthur asking him to ensure that no other man of his company came out to fight with him, but that Arthur should send him the right one. For it was with Gawan son of King Lot that he wished to do battle. Two well-versed pages, commended for their fine manners, were sent as envoys.

'Now remark minutely whom you would judge fairest of all those lovely women,' said the King. 'You are also to take especial note of the lady at whose side Bene sits – attend closely to how she comports herself. Secretly observe whether she be happy or sad. You will see from her eyes whether she is pining for her lover. Be sure to give my friend Bene this letter and ring – she knows to whom to pass it on. Go about this discreetly and you will have done well.'

Now on the other side it had come about that Itonje had learnt that her brother and the dearest man a girl had ever taken to her heart were engaged to fight one another and were not to be dissuaded from it. Her sufferings then burst through her shyness. Whoever approves her anguish does so without my support, since she has not deserved it.

Itonje's mother and grandmother took her aside into a small pavilion made of silk. Arnive reproached her for the wretched state she was in and rebuked her for misbehaving. And now there was no avoiding it: she freely confessed what she had concealed from them for so long.

'If my brother is going to cut off my heart's dear life,' said she, 'he would have very good reason not to.'

'Tell my son to come to me at once,' said Arnive to a young gentleman-in-waiting, 'and to contrive to come alone.' The squire duly fetched King Arthur. It was Arnive's intention to let him hear for whom lovely Itonje was pining so grievously, in the hope that he might remove the cause.

Meanwhile King Gramoflanz's pages had arrived at Arthur's court and alighted on the meadow. One of them saw Bene sitting outside the small pavilion and beside her a young lady who was saying to Arthur, 'Does the Duchess think it a fine thing that my brother should slay my admirer at her caprice? He should think it a shameful deed. What wrong has the King done him? He should let the King benefit from the fact that I am his sister. If my brother has any perception, he will know our love to be clear and unclouded, so that if he is loyal he will be sorry. If he brings about my death through bitter grief following the King's, let him be arraigned before you!' Such was the sweet girl's complaint to Arthur. 'Remember you are my uncle. By the affection that unites us, settle this dispute!'

'Alas, my dear Niece, that you give proof of such noble love while still so young!' Arthur replied at once, wise in his experience. 'You are bound to rue it, as did your sister Surdamur for love of the Greek Emperor. Sweet, charming girl, I could put this duel by if I knew that his heart and yours are gathered in one. Gramoflanz son of Irot is of so manly a temper that the duel will be fought out unless your love forestalls it. Has he on festive occasions ever set eyes on your dazzling looks, on your sweet red lips?'

'That has never happened,' she answered. 'We love without having seen each other. But in the abundance of his love and in hope of true companionship he has sent me many precious tokens. From me, for my part, he has received what goes with true love and has banished all doubt between us. The King is steadfast in his attachment to me, and his heart is free of guile.'

At this point Lady Bene recognized King Gramoflanz's pages who had come to seek audience with Arthur. 'There should be nobody standing here,' she said. 'With your permission I shall order this crowd to withdraw beyond the guy-ropes. If my lady lets herself be moved to such passionate laments for her darling, it will soon be common talk.'

Lady Bene was sent outside. One of the pages pressed the

355

ring and letter into her hand. They had also clearly heard the torment her mistress was in. They said they had come to seek audience of Arthur, if she would kindly arrange it.

'Go and stand way over there till I tell you to come to me,' she said.

Back inside the tent, sweet young Bene reported that messengers had come from Gramoflanz and were asking for King Arthur. 'I judged it inappropriate to make them aware of this conversation. One might then have asked what grudge I had against my lady to let them see her all in tears as she is.'

'Are they the two pages I saw trotting to the ring in search of me?' asked Arthur. 'They are boys of high lineage. What if they are so well-bred and well-behaved that they are fitted to share in our counsels? One or the other is wide awake enough to have read the signs of my niece's love for his lord.'

'I know nothing of that,' replied Bene. 'Sire, with your gracious leave, the King has sent this ring and letter. One of those pages gave it me when I went outside the tent. Here, my Lady, you take it.'

The letter was kissed over and over again. Pressing it to her breast, Itonje said: 'Sire, read for yourself whether the King sues me for my love.'

Arthur took the letter and found there, from one who knew what it is to love, all that faithful Gramoflanz spoke through his own lips. Arthur could see from the letter that so far as his understanding went he had never in all his days seen love so complete. In it stood words most fitting for love:

I salute her whom it is right I should salute, from whom service earns me salutation. Young lady, it is you I have in mind, since you solace me with hope. Our loves keep company together – this is the root of my abounding joy. Since your heart is constant toward me, your solace outweighs all other. You are the clasp above my steadfastness and banisher of my heart's sorrow. Your love will help me to achieve it that no misdeed of any kind will ever be seen in me. To your goodness I can truly ascribe constancy that does not shift its place – as the Antarctic Pole* stands opposite the North Star and

* The text has: *polus artanticus*. The later *Willehalm*, however, refers to *polus antar(c)ticus*, though some MSS. read *artanticus*.

neither quits its place, our love shall stand in loyalty and never go apart. Now, noble young lady, remember me and all the suffering I have lamented to you. Do not be slow to help me. If any man for hatred of me should wish to part you from me, bear it in mind that Love has power to requite us both. Take care lest you wound woman's honour, and let me be your Servitor. I shall serve you to the best of my ability.

'You are right, dear Niece,' said Arthur. 'The King salutes you in all sincerity. This letter tells me such a tale, I confess I never saw so marvellous an invention on the theme of Love! You must put an end to his anguish, and he must do the same for you. You both leave it to me. I will put a stop to this duel! Spare your tears in the meantime. You were nevertheless taken prisoner! Tell me, how did it come about that you fell in love with one another? You must give him your love as hire, since he is willing to deserve it.'

'The one who engineered it all is here,' said Arthur's niece Itonje. 'Neither of us has ever referred to it. If you wish it she will arrange for me to see the man to whom I have given my heart.'

'Show me her,' said Arthur. 'If I can, I will see to it for his and your sakes that your wishes in this matter are fulfilled so that you find happiness together.'

'It was Bene,' said Itonje. 'There are two of his pages here as well. If you value my life, will you try to discover whether the King, with whom all my happiness rests, desires to see me?'

Discreet as he was courteous, Arthur went out to those pages and, when he saw them, welcomed them. One of them then addressed him.

'Sire,' said the boy, 'King Gramoflanz requests you for the sake of your own honour to fulfil the vow that was made between him and Gawan. And he further requests you, Sire, that no other man come to fight with him. Your army is so vast that were he to overcome them all in turn it would not be right or proper. You should have Gawan take the field, for it was agreed that the duel was to be with him.'

'I will clear us from that charge,' Arthur told the pages. 'My nephew was never more sorry that he did not fight there in person. As to the man who fought your lord, his victory is of his very nature, since he is Gahmuret's son. All who have come here in these three armies from all directions have never heard of a warrior so valiant in battle. All that he does turns to glory! I speak of my kinsman Parzival of the radiant looks, whom you shall see. In view of Gawan's predicament with his oath I shall comply with your sovereign's message.'

Arthur, Bene and these two young gentlemen rode up and down. Arthur drew the pages' attention to the dazzling appearances of many ladies. They also saw numerous crests that rustled high on helmets. It would not harm a mighty man today to behave so companionably. They remained in the saddle, while Arthur pointed out the notables to the pages throughout the army, where they gazed to their hearts' content on the very pick of knights, maidens and ladies, many comely people.

The army was in three parts, with two spaces between, and Arthur now rode with the young people right out on to the meadow away from the army.

'Bene, sweet girl,' he said, 'you heard the woeful tale my niece Itonje told me? – She cannot hold back her tears. My friends here may well believe it when I say that Gramoflanz has all but quenched Itonje's radiant looks. Now assist me, you two, and also you, friend Bene, to have the King ride over here to me today and nevertheless fight the duel tomorrow. I shall bring my nephew Gawan to meet him on the meadow. If the King rides through my army today he will be all the more formidable tomorrow, for Love will give him a shield here such as his adversary will wish to be quit of – by which I mean high mettle inspired by Love that wreaks such havoc in close combat with one's enemy. Let him bring some courtiers. I will mediate between him and the Duchess. Now go about this business discreetly, my dear companions, and you will reap much credit. I must make further complaint to you. What, wretched man, have I done to King Gramoflanz that he treats my family, perhaps deeming it a trifle, to such great love and hatred? Any fellow king of mine has good cause to treat me considerately. If he intends to reward with hatred the brother of the girl he loves, he has only to reflect in order to see that when his heart teaches him such thoughts it has turned traitor to Love.'

'If my lord aims at being thought truly courteous, he should refrain from whatever *you* say is disagreeable, Sire,' said one of the pages to the King. 'You are aware of the old quarrel, in view of which it is better my lord should stay where he is rather than ride over here to you. The Duchess still maintains her feud with him and complains of him to all and sundry.'

'Let him come with only a few,' replied Arthur. 'In the meantime I shall have obtained a truce from the noble Duchess regarding the feud, and I shall give him a fitting escort, for my nephew Beacurs shall receive him at half-way. He shall proceed under my safe-conduct, nor let him think it a dishonour. I shall show him some distinguished people.'

The pages took their leave and went. While Arthur stayed alone in the meadow, Bene and the two pages rode into Rosche Sabins and out on the farther side where the army lay encamped. It was the happiest day in Gramoflanz's life when Bene and the pages addressed him. He felt he had received news which Fortune herself had devised for him.

He said he would be glad to come. Company was chosen. Three Princes of the Realm rode out beside their King. His maternal uncle King Brandelidelin did likewise. Bernout de Riviers and Affinamus of Clitiers each took a companion suited for the way. This made twelve in all. Young gentlemen-in-waiting beyond counting and a host of stout men-at-arms were appointed for the journey. – 'What clothes were those knights wearing?' Brocade refulgent with its load of gold! The King's falconers rode at his side so that he could ply his sport. For his part, Arthur had not neglected to send handsome Beacurs to meet him half-way and escort him. Over the expanse of fields, wherever he saw a way through bog or brook, the King rode in pursuit of game – and even more in keenness for Love. Beacurs received him there, and the encounter was a happy one. With Beacurs, upwards of fifty comely pages had arrived, young dukes and counts who shed the lustre of high race. With them there rode some kings' sons too. There was a great exchange of welcomes and salutations by the pages on both sides, they became acquainted with one another in perfect amity.

Beacurs was of dazzling appearance, and the King lost no time in asking who the handsome knight might be. 'He is Lot's son, Beacurs,' Bene told him.

'Heart,' he mused, 'now find the maiden who resembles this youth riding here so delightfully! She who sent me the hat made in Sinzester, together with her sparrowhawk, is truly his sister! If she shows me further favour I would take her alone above all earthly riches, were the earth double its size! Her love must be sincere. I have come here in the hope that she will be merciful. Until now she has given me such encouragement that I am sure she will do something for me that will raise my spirits.' Her handsome brother took Gramoflanz's hand in his: it too was white and fine.

Now in the army it had come about that Arthur had obtained a truce from the Duchess. She now had ample recompense for the loss of Cidegast, whom she had mourned so intensely, so that her anger was all but overlaid – Gawan's embraces had brought her to life, and her hostility had ebbed away.

Arthur the Briton took courtly ladies fresh and lovely of person, both married and unmarried, into a separate pavilion, a hundred all told. Nothing more delightful could have happened to Itonje, who was also sitting there, than that she was to see the King. Not for one moment did she cease to feel happy, yet one could read from her bright eyes that Love was tormenting her.

Many knights of splendid appearance were seated there, but Parzival outshone them all in looks. Gramoflanz now rode up to the guy-ropes. The fearless King was wearing a tissue woven in Gampfassasche, stiff with gold and shedding its rays far and wide.

Those who had just arrived dismounted. A crowd of Gramoflanz's pages ran ahead of him and pushed their way into the pavilion. The chamberlains cleared a broad path in the direction of the Queen of the Britons. The King's uncle Brandelidelin entered the pavilion before King Gramoflanz and was received by Ginover with a kiss, then the King was welcomed in the same way. The Queen kissed Bernout and Affinamus too.

Arthur then turned to Gramoflanz and said: 'Before you think of sitting down look round and see if you love any of these ladies and kiss her. You may both have leave to do so here.'

A *billet-doux* he had perused out there in the fields told him who his lover was – I refer to his having seen the brother of the girl who had secretly declared her noble love to be his above all the world. Gramoflanz's eyes sought and found the one who loved him, and his happiness soared high enough. Since Arthur had allowed them both to welcome each other with a greeting, he kissed Itonje on the lips.

King Brandelidelin took his seat beside Queen Ginover, and for his part King Gramoflanz sat down next to the girl who had suffused her bright face with tears. As yet this was all she had had from him. Unless he is to punish innocence he must speak to her and offer to serve her to win her love. And she could take it upon herself to thank him for having come. Yet none heard them say a word. They were just content to look at each other. But when I catch proper speech I shall examine what they say and whether it be 'No!' or 'Yes!'

With a 'Now you have had time to say all you want to my wife', Arthur led the fearless warrior Brandelidelin into a lesser pavilion a short way over the field. At Arthur's request, Gramoflanz and his companions remained seated, and little loth were those knights to do so in the dazzling company of the ladies. Their pleasure as they passed the time with them was such as might well content a man who sought it as solace for his troubles.

Drink was now brought before the Queen. If the knights – and not to forget the ladies – drank their fill they had a better colour for it.

Drink was also taken out to Arthur and Brandelidelin, and when the cup-bearer had left, Arthur opened with these words: 'Now suppose, Brother, that they went to work in such a way that your nephew the King were to slay my nephew. If he then wished to bring a love-suit to my young niece, who is now telling him of her troubles over there where we left them sitting together, she would never show him any inclination – were she to behave sensibly – and for his plans would treat him to such hostility as would affront him, if he expected anything of her. Where love is tinged with hatred, happiness is denied entry to the constant heart.'

'Brother,' replied the King of Punturteis to Arthur the Briton, 'these two who are in feud with one another are our maternal nephews: we must prevent this duel. Then there can be no other outcome than that they love each other with all their hearts. Your niece Itonje must first command my nephew to waive the duel for her sake, if he is suing for her love. Thus this duel and all its threat will be well and truly set aside. Help my nephew, too, to regain the Duchess's good will.'

'That I shall do,' said Arthur. 'My nephew Gawan has such authority with her that as a well-bred woman she will leave it to him and me to settle the score. Then you compose the quarrel on your side.'

'I shall,' replied Brandelidelin, whereupon the two went back to the pavilion. There the King of Punturteis resumed his seat beside courtly Ginover. Parzival, no less radiant in looks, was sitting on the further side – eye never lit on a man more handsome. Arthur went from there to his nephew Gawan, who had already been told that King Gramoflanz had come. Then, hard upon that, it was announced in Gawan's presence that Arthur was dismounting in front of his tent, so he ran out on to the green to receive him.

They got the Duchess to agree to a reconciliation, but only on these express terms: that if her beloved Gawan would renounce the duel for her sake, she would grant peace; and further she would be reconciled only if the King would withdraw his accusation against her father-in-law, Lot. This she asked Arthur to convey to him. Arthur, politic man, went away with these conditions. Gramoflanz then had to let his Garland go. And whatever hatred he entertained for Lot of Norway melted away like snow in sunshine for lovely Itonje's sake, untroubled by the faintest resentment. This came about while he was sitting beside her – he agreed to all she asked him!

And now they saw Gawan approaching with a brilliant company. I could not unfold all their names for you or whence they derived their titles.

And now for affection's sake rancour was put aside.

Proud Orgeluse and her noble mercenaries and also Clinschor's squadron – a section of it, not the full complement – were seen arriving. The walls of Arthur's pavilion below the cupola were now removed. Earlier, Arthur had invited the good Arnive, Sangive and Cundrie to the solemn proceedings of this peacemaking. Let any who considers this a trifle deem grand whatever he fancies. Gawan's companion Jofreit led the dazzling Duchess by the hand into the pavilion, where, well-bred and discerning, she waited for the three queens to enter first. Brandelidelin kissed them, and Orgeluse too welcomed him with a kiss. Gramoflanz went towards her to make peace, but also hoping to win her good will. Orgeluse kissed the King with her sweet lips in sign of reconciliation and felt a great urge to weep. She was thinking of the death of Cidegast. Even now her woman's anguish compelled her to mourn for him. Set it down to fidelity if you like.

Gawan and Gramoflanz also set the seal on their reconciliation with a kiss. Arthur gave Itonje away to Gramoflanz in marriage, for which he had performed much service, an event which delighted Bene. Cundrie was given to Lischois, Duke of Gowerzin, whose love for her inflicted many a pang on him – his life had been bare of any happiness till he knew desire for her noble love. Arthur offered King Lot's widow Sangive to the Turkoyt Florant, and indeed that prince gladly took her as a gift well worth cherishing.

Arthur was generous in giving ladies away – he never wearied of bestowing such gifts! But this was all discussed and agreed beforehand.

Now when these matters had been transacted in full, the Duchess announced that Gawan, having served her for her love with high distinction acclaimed by all, was rightful lord of her lands and person, an announcement which saddened her knights-servitor, who in the past had broken many lances aspiring to win her love.

Gawan and his companions, Arnive and the Duchess together with a radiant bevy of ladies, and noble Parzival, Sangive and Cundrie too, all took their leave; but Itonje remained there with Arthur. Now let nobody say where a finer wedding-feast took place. Ginover took charge of Itonje and her lover the noble King, who, spurred on by love for her, had distinguished himself many times with deeds of arms.

Many a man rode to his quarters racked by love for a high-born lady. We can omit to tell what they had for supper, since whoever was partnered in noble love wished day to be night.

Goaded by his pride, King Gramoflanz sent a message to his people at Rosche Sabins to strike camp, where they lay beside the sea, and come with his army before dawn, and that his Marshal was to choose a site amenable to an army. 'See to it that all my arrangements are magnificent, and that each prince has his own ring of tents.' It was meant to make a sumptuous display.

The messenger set out, and now it was night. There were no few unhappy men there who had been brought to that pass by women. For when one's service comes to naught and one finds oneself unrewarded, one speedily succumbs to misery – unless a woman lends a helping hand.

Now as to Parzival, he was thinking of his lovely wife and all her modest charm. Would he address himself to another and offer service for her love and take to unfaithful ways? From such love he refrains. His manly heart and person have been maintained by great fidelity, with the result that no woman was ever possessed of his love other than Condwiramurs, fairest flower that blows.

'How has Love treated me,' he pondered, 'since I first knew Love? After all, I am of Love's lineage. How then have I lost Love? If I am to strive for the Gral, desire for the chaste embraces of her whom I left too long ago must ever harass me. If my eyes are to show me pleasure while my heart speaks to me of sorrow, the two are at odds with one another. No one will ever grow high-spirited from such a situation. May Fortune guide me to what is best for me to do!'

His armour lay nearby. 'Since I lack what the happy ones

command – I mean Love, who cheers the sad thoughts of many with the aid of her delights – since I have been cut off from my part in this, I do not care what happens to me now. God does not wish my happiness. If our love, mine and hers, which compels me to languish for her, were such that severance went with it and doubt and despair preyed on our minds, I could easily arrive at another. But as things are, the love she inspires has taken away from me all other love and hope of happiness. Thus I find no release from my pining. May Fortune give joy to those who desire it, final and lasting! God grant joy to all these companies! As to me, I shall ride out from amid these joys!'

He reached for his armour, which he often managed on his own, and had soon encased himself in it. He is now intent on new hardships. When the joy-forsaking man had all his armour on he saddled his horse with his own hands. He found his shield and lance ready. His riding away so early in the morning was loudly lamented. As he set out, day was breaking.

Chapter 15

MANY people have grown impatient at the Sequel's being locked
away from them. Some I could name failed to fathom it, hard
though they tried. I shall now withhold it no longer, but make
it known to you in plain narrative, since in my mouth I bear
the lock to the story of how gentle, handsome Anfortas was
made well again. This story reveals to us how the Queen of
Belrepeire maintained her chaste and womanly thoughts till
she reached the place of her reward and entered a realm of
high bliss. Parzival shall bring this to pass, if my skill avails
me.

I shall now recount such toils on his part as never before,
compared with which any fighting he had put his hand to was
child's play. If I could waive my obligation to this story I
would not wish to hazard him, I myself should be loth to do
so. But now I shall commend his fortunes – that portion of bliss
which is his – to his own heart, in which daring resided with
modesty. For his heart had no dealings with cowardice. May
this give him firm assurance that he will keep his life!

Since it has fallen to Parzival's lot, a very champion of all
battles will face him on a dauntless expedition. This selfsame
courtly person was an infidel all ignorant of Christianity.

Parzival rode briskly across an open space towards a great
forest – towards that mighty stranger! It is wonderful that I,
a poor knight, can describe to you the magnificence that Infidel
wore as his crest. If I were to tell you about his wealth till you
were sick and tired of it, I should still have to go on describing
it if I meant to say anything at all! All that Arthur disposed of
in Britain and England would not buy the jewels on this
knight's tabard with their pure and noble qualities! It was rare
and costly, believe me – rubies and chalcedonies would not have
fetched that dazzling tabard! Pairs of salamander-worms in
Mount Agremuntin had woven it in the fire. It was overlaid

with precious gems of the true water, both lustrous and opaque. I cannot name their virtues.

The Infidel's desire was for love and the winning of fame, and they were for the most part women who had given him the things with which he adorned himself so sumptuously. Love conducted zest and spirit into his manly heart, as she still does with her suitors today. To crown his high fame he wore on his helmet an Ecidemon: once they have scented it, venomous reptiles have no further lease of life, thanks to the nature of this small creature. In Thopedissimonte, Assigarzionte, Thasme and Araby, there was not to be found such brocade as his mount was wearing for its trappers. The handsome, unchristened man aspired to women's reward: it was for this that he adorned himself so elegantly. His high heart compelled him to strive for noble love.

This same doughty youth had anchored in an inlet where the forest came down to the sea. In keeping with his power and wealth he had twenty-five armies of which none understood another's tongue, while as many separate territories were subject to him, Moors and other Saracens of varied aspect. In his host, drawn from far and wide, there were many strange arms and armaments.

For his part, this lone man had left his army and ridden out into the forest in search of adventure to stretch his limbs. Since these kings assumed the right to seek battle in pursuit of glory on their own, I shall let them ride. Yet Parzival did not ride alone. There went in comradeship himself and Courage, which fights so manfully that ladies would be bound to praise it, unless their frivolity sent them raving.

Here, two who are as gentle as lambs, yet are lions for valour, are going to seek each other's harm. Alas, that broad though the earth is, they did not pass each other by, this pair that fought for no cause! I would be anxious for the man whom I have brought this far, had I not the consoling thought that the power of the Gral must save him. And Love, too, must defend him. He has served both with unswerving devotion.

My skill does not give me the wit to narrate this battle as it happened in all detail.

The eyes of each lit up on seeing the other approaching. The hearts of each rejoiced, yet sorrow lurked there unseen. Each of these unblemished men bore the other's heart within him – theirs was an intimate strangeness!

Now I cannot keep this Infidel from the Christian and prevent them from coming to blows. This ought to sadden all who are known to be good women. For each of these men was exposing his life to fierce attack for his mistress's sake. May Fortune settle it without loss of life!

The Lioness bears her cub stillborn, it is roused to life by its father's roars. These two were scions of crackling lances – picked from prowess in countless jousts! They were indeed no mean jousters, to the cost of the lances they squandered. From a free canter they shortened rein and, beginning their charge, were intent not to miss their marks. No point of their routine was overlooked: they took a firm seat in the saddle, shaped themselves to the joust and gripped their mounts between their spurs. They rode their encounter with this outcome: the collars of both were severed by stout lances which did not bend, so that splinters flew up from the shock. The Infidel was incensed that this man had kept his seat opposite him, since Parzival was the first to have done so of all he had ever engaged with. 'Were they wearing swords of any sort when they spurred towards each other?' Keen ones, and very broad. Their skill and courage were soon displayed there. The Ecidemon creature received no few wounds, giving the helmet beneath it good cause to lament! Their chargers grew hot and weary, for their riders sought advantage by wheeling and wheeling. Thus both leapt down from their mounts, and now their swords rang out in earnest.

The Infidel did much hurt to the Christian. His war-cry was 'Thasme!', and when he shouted 'Thabronit!' he advanced one step. The Christian was formidable in the many swift rushes they made at one another. Their battle had reached a point at which I cannot withhold the comment that I deeply deplore their fighting, in that one and the same life and blood are so unmercifully attacking one another. When all is said, they were sons of one father, bedrock of purest loyalty.

The Infidel had always been open to Love and was thus great-hearted in battle. He aspired to win renown for the sake of Queen Secundille, who had given him the land at Tribalibot. She was his shield in peril. The Infidel was gaining the upper hand: what am I to do with the Christian? Unless he turns his thoughts towards Love, the outcome will inevitably be that this battle will gain him death at this Infidel's hands. – Prevent this, O potent Gral, and radiant Condwiramurs! The man who serves you both stands here in the greatest peril he ever knew!

The Infidel threw his sword high up, a rain of blows forced Parzival to his knees. Whoever wishes to name them 'two' is entitled to say 'Thus did *they* fight.' Yet they were no more than one. Any brother of mine and I make one person, as do a good man and his good wife.

The Infidel did much hurt to the Christian. His shield was of a wood called asbestos, which neither rots nor burns. Rest assured, he was loved by her that gave it. All round the boss, there were inlaid in the metal of its flanges turquoises, chrysoprases, emeralds and rubies, gemstones of many kinds, each with its own water. On the dome of the boss itself there was a stone whose name I shall reveal to you – in the East they call it 'anthrax', but here it is known as 'carbuncle'. Queen Secundille, in whose favour he wished to live, had given him as device the pure beast Ecidemon to be escort of her love: it was her wish that he should display it.

Loyalty in purest essence was fighting there. Great loyalty was at grips with loyalty. Both had yielded up their lives to ordeal by battle for Love's sake. Each had given his hand in pledge. The Christian had placed his full trust in God since leaving Trevrizent, who had counselled him so warmly to ask help of Him Who has power to hearten those in trouble.

There is no gainsaying the Infidel had mighty limbs. When he shouted 'Thabronit!' (where Queen Secundille resided at the foot of the Caucasus Mountain), he gained new courage to assail the man who till now had been spared such an overload of fight – Parzival had been a stranger to defeat, never having suffered it, though many had got it from him.

They swung their arms with expertise, fiery flashes leapt from their helmets and a bitter wind rose from their swords. God save Gahmuret's offspring there! This prayer is meant for both the Christian and the Infidel, whom I have lately named as one. And were they better acquainted they would regard it so themselves. They would not have laid such high stakes: for the price put on their fighting was their happiness, their good fortune and honour, no more. If he cherishes bonds of affection, whichever proves victorious will have lost his joy in this life and found heartfelt grief without end.

Why are you so slow, Parzival, not fixing your thoughts on that chaste and lovely woman – I mean your wife? Have you no wish to live on?

The Infidel was accompanied by two things on which his best strength depended. First, he cherished a love enshrined in his heart with constancy. Second, there were precious stones which with their pure and noble virtues gave him spirit and enhanced his strength. It vexes me that the Christian is growing weary from fighting, from forward rushes and the dealing of strong blows. If Condwiramurs and the Gral are unable to come to your* aid, then, valiant Parzival, you could have one thought to hearten you: that the charming, handsome boys Kardeiz and Loherangrin – whom his wife had conceived from his last embraces – should not be left fatherless so soon! If you ask me, children chastely begotten are a man's supreme blessing.

The Christian was regaining strength. He was thinking – and it was not a moment too soon – of his wife the Queen and of her noble love, which he had won with play of sword on Clamide beneath the walls of Belrepeire, while fire leapt from helmets under blows! 'Thabronit!' and 'Thasme!' were now countered by answering shouts, for Parzival had begun to cry 'Belrepeire!' And now from four or more kingdoms away and just in the nick of time Condwiramurs came to his aid with the power of her love, and I should say chips to the value of some hundred marks went flying from the Infidel's shield.

The stout sword of Gaheviez was shattered by a blow on the

* Text: his.

Infidel's helmet which brought the bold and mighty stranger to his knees. It was no longer pleasing to God that Parzival should wield a weapon robbed from a corpse, as though this were right and proper: for this was the sword he had taken from Ither, knowing no better in his youthful ignorance.

The Infidel, who had never before gone down from a sword-blow, quickly leapt to his feet again. The issue is still undecided. The verdict between them lies in the hand of Him on high. May He avert their dying!

The Infidel was magnanimous. 'It is clear to me, warlike man,' he said, politely shaping his mouth to French of which he had a knowledge, 'that you would go on fighting without your sword. But what honour would I gain from you then? Refrain, valiant warrior, and tell me who you are. I declare that had your sword not snapped you would have won my fame, all that has been accorded me over the years. Now let there be a truce between us till we have rested our limbs and recovered somewhat.'

They sat down on the grass. They were both well-bred as well as brave, while in age they were neither too old nor too young for fighting.

'Now believe me, Knight,' the Infidel went on to the Christian, 'that in all my days I never saw a man more entitled to the fame one wins in battle. Condescend, sir, to tell me your name and lineage, then my voyage to these parts will have prospered.'

'If I am to comply from fear,' replied the son of Herzeloyde, 'and grant this under duress, none need trouble to ask it of me.'

'Then I will name myself first,' replied the Infidel of Thasme, 'and be saddled with the reproach. I am Feirefiz Angevin, with such a plenitude of power that many lands pay tribute to me!'

Hearing these words, Parzival asked the Infidel 'What entitles you to call yourself "Angevin"? Anjou, with all its fortresses, lands and towns, is mine by inheritance. Sir, I pray you, choose another style. If I am to lose my lands and the noble city of Bealzenan, you will have done me violence. If either of us is an Angevin, I claim by true descent I am he! Nevertheless, I have been told for a fact that there is a fearless warrior living in the heathen lands who has won love and fame with chivalric exploits, and is called my brother. Those people have given him the palm. Now, sir,' continued Parzival, 'once I had seen your features I would tell you if you are the one described to me. If you will go with me that far, sir, bare your head. If you will take my word for it, I shall not attack you till it is helmeted again.'

'I have little fear of any harm from you,' replied the Infidel. 'Even if I were wearing no armour at all, you would be overcome, seeing that your sword is shattered. All your skill in war cannot save you from death, unless I am pleased to spare you. Before you started to wrestle I should send my sword ringing through mail and skin.'

The gallant, mighty Infidel evinced a manly bent, for with a 'This sword shall belong to neither of us!' the fearless knight flung it far out into the forest. 'If there's to be any fighting here,' he added, 'even chances must prevail. Now, sir, by the care that formed your breeding, since it seems you have a brother, tell me what he looks like,' said mighty Feirefiz. 'Describe his face to me and what sort of complexion they named to you.'

'It is like a parchment, with writing,' answered Herzeloyde's son, 'black and white, in patches. That is how Ekuba described him to me.'

'I am he,' replied the Infidel.

Neither wasted any time. They at once bared their heads of their helmets and coifs. Parzival found treasure trove, the most precious he had ever lit on. The Infidel was recognized immediately for he was marked like a magpie. Feirefiz and Parzival ended their strife with a kiss. It was more fitting for them to be friends than bitter enemies. Their contest was settled by loyalty and affection.

'Happy I, that I ever set eyes on the son of noble Gahmuret!' cried the Infidel joyfully. 'All my gods are exalted by it. My goddess Juno may well rejoice in the glory of it. It was my mighty god Jupiter who bestowed this bliss on me! Gods and goddesses, I adore your power for ever! May the light of that planet be praised under which I set out on my quest for adventure to you, terrible, charming man! Praised be the breeze and the dew which descended on me this morning! Lucky the women who are destined to see you, gentle unlocker of love! – What felicity will have been theirs!'

'You speak well,' said the man of Kanvoleiz, 'I would speak better, if I could, and with affection. But, alas, I am not so versed that I could exalt your noble reputation with words – God knows, I do not lack the will. Whatever arts my heart and eyes command, they allow of nothing else than that your fame is leader and they the chorus. I know for a fact that I was never harder pressed by any knight.'

'Jupiter neglected nothing in your making, noble knight,' said Feirefiz. 'Do not address me formally any more. – After all, we have one father.' And with brotherly affection he begged him to spare him formal modes and to address him familiarly.

This was not to Parzival's liking. 'Brother,' said he, 'your power and wealth rival the Baruc's, and you are also my senior. If I have any manners, my younger years and poverty should restrain me from taking such a liberty as to use familiar terms with you.'*

The lord of Tribalibot praised his god Jupiter in many ways. He also lauded his goddess Juno highly for arranging the weather so that he and all his army made their landfall from the sea at the point where he and Parzival had met.

They sat down for the second time, with all due courtesy towards each other.

'I shall make over two rich lands to you,' said the Infidel, resuming their conversation, 'which shall serve you in perpetuity – Zazamanc and Azagouc. Your father and mine acquired them when King Isenhart died. Valiant man, he abandoned none who relied on him – except that he left me fatherless! I have not forgiven my father this wrong. His wife who bore me died pining for the love she had lost in him. I should much like to see that man. I have been told there never was a better knight. The purpose of my voyage in such state is to find him.'

* Parzival addresses Feirefiz with the familiar 'thou' only when he has become King of the Gral.

'I have never seen him either,' said Parzival. 'I have been told that he achieved great exploits – I have heard of them in many places – and that he knew both how to extend his fame and exalt his glory in battle. All thought of misconduct fled away from him. He was at the service of the ladies, and if they were sincere they honestly requited it. He practised that for which the Christian faith is still honoured today, namely steadfast loyalty. Helped by a constant heart, he subdued all falsity in his doing. This is what those who knew the man you would like to see were kind enough to tell me. Were he still alive I am sure you would commend him, since commendation is what he strove for. This requiter of ladies was impelled by his service to joust with King Ipomidon below the walls of Baghdad, where in Love's name his noble life was rendered up to death. – In regular joust we lost the man who sired the two of us.'

'Alas for affliction that has no redress!' cried the Infidel. 'Is my father dead? I may well say that I have lost happiness, and yet before my eyes I have proof positive of having found it! For in one and the same hour I have both lost and found it. If I lay hold of truth, both my father and you, and I, too, were but one, though seen as three distinct entities.* No wise man in search of truth counts father and children as related.† On this field you were fighting with yourself. I came riding to do battle with myself and would gladly have slain myself. By fighting on so doggedly you defended my own life from me. Jupiter, record this marvel: thy power succoured us by coming between us and death!'

He laughed (and wept in secret). His infidel eyes began to sprinkle water as though to the glory of the Baptism. (The Baptism teaches steadfast Love, since our New Law is named after Christ, in Whom steadfast Love was witnessed.)

The Infidel spoke, I will tell you what he said. 'Let us not sit here any longer. Ride with me a short way. I shall command the finest army to which Juno ever gave sail-wind to

* When Feirefiz comes to be baptized he will clearly make no bones over the Trinity.

† Traditionally, as against canonical notions, the first degree of relationship was between grandfather and grandchildren, cf. p. 420.

374

quit the sea and encamp on terra firma for you to review them. Truly, and without misleading you with empty boasts, I shall show you a host of illustrious men who do me homage. You must ride there with me.'

'Have you such control over your people that they will wait for you today and for as long as you are away from them?' asked Parzival.

'Unquestionably,' replied the Infidel. 'Were I to absent myself for half a year they would wait for me, high and low, without exception. They would not dare go anywhere. Their ships are so nobly provisioned to lie there in harbour that neither horses nor men need go ashore, except for water from the springs or fresh air over towards the meadows.'

'In return, you shall be shown ladies of radiant beauty,' Parzival told his brother, 'and the delight which they occasion, and also many courtly knights of your own noble lineage. For Arthur the Briton lies encamped here with his illustrious following. I took leave of them only this morning, together with a most charming company – we shall indeed see comely ladies there.'

When the Infidel heard women named – they were his very life – he said 'Take me with you. And also answer this question. Shall we see our kinsmen when we arrive at Arthur's? On the subject of Arthur's style of life I have heard that he is very famous and lives magnificently.'

'We shall see *dazzling* ladies there,' replied Parzival. 'Our ride will not be in vain, for we shall find our own true race, people of whose blood we are born, with some crowned heads among them.'

They both got up. Parzival remembered to retrieve his brother's sword and thrust it back into the noble warrior's sheath. Thus the anger and hostility between them were ended, and they rode away together as friends.

News of them had already been received at Arthur's before they arrived there. That day throughout the whole army there had been sorrow in which all shared that noble Parzival had left them. After due counsel, Arthur resolved that he would not ride out but would wait for Parzival there for a whole week.

Gramoflanz's army had also arrived there. Many broad rings of gaily adorned pavilions were set for him, and there those proud worthies were lodged. The four brides could not have been entertained more pleasurably.

At this juncture a man rode in from Schastel marveile with a report that a battle had been observed in the Pillar up in the watch-tower and that any sword-fight until then 'is nothing compared with this battle!' – such news did he tell Gawan as the latter sat beside Arthur. No few knights began to discuss whom the battle could have been fought by.

'I know who fought it on one side,' King Arthur broke in. 'My kinsman of Kanvoleiz, who left us early this morning!'

At this point the two rode in.

Their helmets and shields had been attacked by swords in a fashion that did honour to warfare. Both carried hands well-versed in tracing the lines of war, for in war, too, art is required. They rode along Arthur's ring. Many eyes followed them where the Infidel rode so unbelievably richly caparisoned!

The field was covered with lodges. They turned past the high pavilion towards Gawan's ring. Did anyone acquaint them with the fact that people were pleased to see them? I imagine this was done. Gawan quickly followed them, for he had seen from Arthur's court that they had ridden towards his own pavilion. There he received them with every mark of pleasure.

The two were still wearing their armour. Courteous Gawan soon had them unarmed. The beast Ecidemon had had his share of the fighting! The surcoat the Infidel was wearing had also suffered badly from blows. It was a saranthasme studded with many precious stones. Below it his tabard was visible – piled, bepictured, snow-white. On it here and there costly gemstones were set. Pairs of salamander-worms had woven it in the fire. The lady who had given him this caparison had hazarded her love, lands and person – I mean Queen Secundille! – while he in turn gladly did her bidding in times of happiness or hardship. It was her heart's desire to bestow her riches on him, for his high fame had achieved her love.

Gawan asked his people to see to it that the fine caparison of surcoat, helmet and shield were not taken away anywhere, or anything broken off it. The tabard alone would have been beyond the means of a lady of slender means, so costly were the stones on all four pieces. But a lofty love can well adorn a knight when the will is coupled with the wherewithal and with fine craftsmanship besides. The proud and wealthy Feirefiz was most assiduous with his homage to win the ladies' favour, thus not one denied him her reward.

Feirefiz's armour was removed. They gazed at this mottled man, and all who liked to talk of marvels had ocular proof of one there – Feirefiz's skin was strangely patterned!

'Make me acquainted with your companion, Cousin,' said Gawan to Parzival. 'He looks so dazzlingly elegant, I never saw anything like it.'

'If I am your kinsman,' Parzival answered his host, 'then so is he. Let Gahmuret assure you of that. This is the King of Zazamanc, where my father so gloriously won Belacane, who bore this knight.'

Gawan duly kissed the Infidel. Mighty Feirefiz was black and white all over his skin, except that about half his mouth showed red.

Luxurious clothes were brought for them from Gawan's wardrobe. And now fair ladies were arriving. The Duchess had Cundrie and Sangive kiss him first, then she and Arnive kissed him. Feirefiz was delighted to see such lovely women, I fancy it was very pleasant for him.

'Cousin,' said Gawan to Parzival, 'your helmet and shield tell me of new hardship you have undergone. You and your brother have both had to bear the brunt of battle. From whom did you get such cruel treatment?'

'You never heard of a harder battle,' answered Parzival. 'My brother forced me to defend myself in desperate circumstances. Self-defence is a charm against death! My stout sword shattered from a blow I dealt this intimate stranger! But he showed little fear – he threw his own sword out of reach. He feared to commit a sin on me, before we traced our relationship. Now I enjoy his good will, which I shall always be glad to deserve of him.'

'I was told of a battle gallantly fought. Up in Schastel

marveile on the Pillar on my watch-tower you can see all that happens within a range of six miles. My uncle Arthur said that one man fighting there at that time must be you, Cousin from Kingrivals. You now bring confirmation, though it was already set down to your account. Believe me when I tell you, we would have waited a whole week for you here while a magnificent festivity was being held. Your fighting together troubles me. Rest under my roof and recover from it. Nevertheless, having fought, you know each other all the better for it. Now be friends where you were enemies.'

Gawan supped all the earlier that evening because his cousin of Thasme, Feirefiz Angevin, and Feirefiz's brother had still not broken their fast. A broad circle of long, thick mattresses was made, and these were covered with quilts of many kinds made of thick palmat-silk. Over this were ample lengths of quilted brocade. It was Clinschor's wealth that was on display there. I also heard that four sumptuous brocades were put up to join and make a square for people to lean against. Below them were soft cushions of down overspread with quilts, with the aforesaid back-cloths fixed above them. This ring embraced an area sufficient to take six pavilions without crowding their guys. But I would be an incompetent narrator were I to let these marvels run on.

My lord Gawan sent a message to Arthur to tell him who had arrived, saying it was the mighty Infidel the heathen Ekuba had praised beside the Plimizœl. Jofreit fiz Idœl told Arthur the news, which greatly pleased him. Jofreit asked the King to sup early and then set a brilliant train in motion with knights and a company of ladies, and to go there with all ceremony and so arrange matters that they could receive proud Gahmuret's son with the honours due to him.

'I shall bring all the distinguished people I have here,' answered the Briton.

'He is so courtly that you will all be delighted to see him,' said Jofreit. 'Indeed, you will see marvels in him. He comes from a region of great wealth – none could raise the price of his armour, there is not one who could afford it. If you were to lay all the lands of Löver, Britain and England, and from Paris

378

along to Wissant, against it, this would fall short of meeting it.'

Jofreit had now returned after informing Arthur what he should do if he wished to receive his kinsman the Infidel. The seating in Gawan's ring was determined according to protocol. The Duchess's following and the companions in a group were seated to Gawan's right. On the other side, Clinschor's band of knights had fallen to with gusto. Opposite Gawan at the far end, seats had been appointed for the ladies, and it was there that Clinschor's ladies were sitting, many beauties among them – Feirefiz and Parzival sat in the very midst of a bevy of dazzlers. Florant the Turkoyt and noble Sangive, the Duke of Gowerzin and his wife Cundrie, were sitting opposite one another. Nor, I fancy, were Gawan and Jofreit unmindful of their old comradeship, for they were sharing a platter. The Duchess with the bright glances was sharing with Queen Arnive, and they both applied themselves with a will to entertaining each other. Gawan's grandmother sat beside him, with Orgeluse on the farther side of her.

Unseemliness was revealed in full flight from that ring – the viands were brought in for the knights and ladies with discernment and propriety.

Mighty Feirefiz observed to his brother Parzival 'Jupiter contrived this expedition of mine to my good fortune, in that his aid has led me here where I see my noble kinsmen. I have every cause to commend the father I have lost, since he came of an illustrious line.'

'You shall see more people whose distinction you cannot fail to acknowledge, many valiant knights ranged around Arthur, their Patron,' said the Waleis. 'Very soon after this meal is over you will see the noble people coming who have been much praised. As to Members of the Table Round now present, only three are sitting here: our host and Jofreit. Some time or other I won the honour of being asked to sit at it and I complied with their request.'

The cloths were removed from the tables at which the ladies and gentlemen were sitting. It was time to do so, they had had their repast. Their host Gawan rose and earnestly begged the Duchess and his grandmother to take Sangive and sweet Cundrie and go to where the mottled Infidel was sitting and entertain him. Feirefiz Angevin saw these ladies approaching and rose to receive them, as did his brother Parzival. The lovely Duchess took Feirefiz by the hand and asked all the knights and ladies who had risen to their feet to be seated again. At this point Arthur rode up with his people to a great sounding of trumpets, tabors, flutes and shawms – Arnive's son was approaching with much crashing and blaring! The Infidel thought this jolly business grand!

In such style did Arthur ride to Gawan's ring in the company of his wife and many handsome knights and ladies. The Infidel could see there were people there whose fresh complexions showed them in the bloom of youth. King Gramoflanz was still a guest of Arthur, and his sweet and faithful mistress Itonje was also riding along that path.

The Company of the Table Round alighted there with its bevy of comely ladies. Ginover gave precedence to Itonje in kissing her cousin the Infidel, then herself approached Feirefiz and received him with a kiss. Arthur and Gramoflanz received this heathen with warm sincerity. They both offered him their humble duty, and other of his kinsmen gave him marks of their good will. Feirefiz Angevin was quick to understand from them that he was among good friends.

Men, married women and many charming girls took their seats. If they felt enterprising and knew how to sue for love, knights could find sweet words from sweet lips, for many fine ladies sitting there allowed such suits without pique. No *good* woman was ever known to upbraid a man who claimed her help: she still has the privilege of saying 'No' – or 'Yes'. If happiness can be said to have a yield, only true love affords such revenue. It was in this style I saw those nobles living: service *and* reward were seated there side by side. The sound of one's mistress's voice is a most helpful sound that can come to her friend's rescue.

Arthur sat down beside Feirefiz. Neither hung back from answering the other's questions, pleasantly, fully and to the point.

'God be praised for giving us this honour of seeing you

here,' said Arthur. 'No man ever came from the infidel lands
to those of the Christian rite whom I would more willingly
serve in any way you wish.'

'All my misfortunes were cut short when the goddess Juno
arranged for the winds to blow my sails to these western king-
doms,' Feirefiz told Arthur. 'You behave most like a man
whose fame is spoken of over a vast region. If you are called
"Arthur", your name is celebrated far and wide.'

'The man who praised me to you and others did himself
honour,' replied Arthur. 'It was his own good breeding that
prompted him more than any desert of mine, it was from
courtesy that he did so. Yes, I am called "Arthur", and I would
gladly learn how you came to this country. If it was some lady
you admire that sent you out in quest of adventure, she must
be very attractive in view of the great distance you have
traversed. If she did not defraud you of your reward it will en-
hance the service of ladies. But if you have been left unre-
warded, the whole sex will have to face the anger of their
Servitors.'

'It is much the reverse,' replied the Infidel. 'Now let me tell
you how I came here. I lead so powerful an army that the
defenders of Troy and those who besieged them would have to
leave me free passage, if both sides were still alive and sought
to bring me to battle. They would not be able to win the
victory but would instead suffer defeat at my and my men's
hands. I have achieved the honour by deeds of arms in many
cruel tests that the Queen Secundille accords me her favour.
Whatever she wishes is my wish too. She has given my life
direction. She commanded me to give open-handedly and so
recruit good knights, I should please do so for her sake. And
this indeed was done. – Many distinguished knights covered by
their shields have been appointed to my following. In return,
her love rewards me. I display an Ecidemon on my shield as
she commanded me. Wherever I was in peril and as soon as
my thoughts were on her, her love has come to my aid, giving
me far more encouragement than my god Jupiter.'

'It is entirely your nature, inherited from your father and
my cousin, Gahmuret, that you should journey into distant

lands in the service of ladies,' said Arthur. 'I will tell you of chivalric service than which greater has never been given for the adorable person of any woman on earth – I mean the Duchess sitting here. Much forest has been cleared in the hope of winning her love! It has been the cause of many a good knight's forfeiting his happiness and of dashing his élan.' Arthur told him all about her war and also about Clinschor's company, who were sitting there on all sides, and the two battles Feirefiz's brother had fought on the broad meadow at Joflanze. – 'And whatever else he has experienced on occasions when he did not spare himself. He is in quest of a lofty goal: he aspires to win the Gral! I desire you both to tell me the lands and peoples you came to know through war.'

'I will name those who are in command of my knights here,' replied the Infidel. 'King Papiris of Trogodjente and Count Behantins of Kalomidente; Duke Farjelastis of Affricke and King Liddamus of Agrippe; King Tridanz of Tinodonte and King Amaspartins of Schipelpjonte; Duke Lippidins of Agremuntin and King Milon of Nomadjentisin; Count Gabarins of Assigarzionte and King Translapins of Rivigitas; Count Filones of Hiberborticon and King Kyllicrates of Centriun; Count Lysander of Ipopotiycon and Duke Tiride of Elixodjon; King Thoaris of Orastegentesin and Duke Alamis of Satarchjonte; King Amincas of Sotofeititon and the Duke of Duscontemedon; King Zoroaster of Arabia and Count Possizonjus of Thiler; Duke Sennes of Narjoclin and Count Edisson of Lanzesardin; Count Fristines of Janfuse and Duke Meiones of Atropfagente; Duke Archeinor of Nourient and Count Astor of Panfatis; the lords of Azagouc and Zazamanc and King Jetakranc of Gampfassache; Count Jurans of Blémunzin and Duke Affinamus of Amantisin. One thing I thought a disgrace. In my country, people claimed that no better knight ever bestrode war-horse than Gahmuret Angevin. It was my wish, and also my way, that I should travel till I found him. So doing, I gained battle-experience. I embarked on the sea in great force at the head of an army drawn from my two lands. My ambition was to do deeds of arms. Whatever lands were good and warlike I nevertheless subdued them, far off into remote regions. Two mighty queens accorded me their love, Olimpia and Clauditte. Secundille, now, is the third. I have done much for love of women. And now only today do I learn that my father Gahmuret is dead. But let my brother, too, tell of his trials.'

'Since I departed from the Gral,' said noble Parzival, 'I have shown much knightly activity in battle, both in tight places and in the open, and have lowered the reputations of divers knights unused to it before. These I will now name for you. King Schirniel of Lirivoyn and his brother Mirabel of Avendroyn; King Serabil of Rozokarz and King Piblesun of Lorneparz; King Senilgorz of Sirnegunz and Lord Strangedorz of Villegarunz; Count Rogedal of Mirnetalle and Lord Laudunal of Pleyedunze; King Onipriz of Itolac and King Zyrolan of Semblidac; Duke Jerneganz of Jeroplis and Count Plineschanz of Zambron; Count Longefiez of Tuteleunz and Duke Marangliez of Privegarz; Duke Strennolas of Pictacon and Count Parfoyas of Lampregun; King Vergulaht of Ascalun and Count Bogudaht of Pranzile; Lord Postefar of Laudundrehte and Duke Leidebron of Redunzehte; Lord Colleval of Leterbe, the Provençal Lord Jovedast of Arles and Count Karfodyas of Tripparun. This happened wherever tourneying was to be had while I was riding in quest of the Gral. Were I asked to name my opponents to the last man it would exceed my knowledge: I must of sheer necessity leave many unmentioned. Yet I believe I have named all whose names were made known to me.'

The Infidel was heartily pleased that his brother's renown stood so high from having won so many great distinctions. He thanked him warmly for it, for he derived honour from it too.

Meanwhile Gawan had given orders for the Infidel's magnificent panoply to be brought into the ring as though without Gawan's knowledge. They all judged it a masterpiece. Knights and ladies fell to examining the tabard, shield and surcoat. The helmet was perfectly proportioned, and they all joined in admiring the rare and noble stones which had been set in it. Let no one ask me of what kinds they were, the heavy and the light: Heraclius or Hercules, and the Greek Alexander could tell you better, and yet another, the wise Pythagoras, who was an astronomer and beyond dispute so sapient that no man since Adam's time could equal him in understanding, *he* could speak from great knowledge of precious stones.

The ladies there were whispering that if Feirefiz had proved false to the woman who had adorned him in it, his reputation would have been sadly tarnished. Because of his exotic complexion, as it seems to me, some were so well disposed towards him that they would gladly have borne with his service. Then the four of them, Gramoflanz, Arthur, Parzival and their host Gawan, withdrew, leaving the mighty Infidel to the attentions of the ladies.

Arthur made preparations for a festivity to be held on the meadow next morning without fail, formally to receive his kinsman Feirefiz. – 'Apply your best thought and energy to enlisting him as a fellow member of the Table Round.'

They promised one and all to do their best, unless Feirefiz himself were against it. In the event, mighty Feirefiz undertook to be their Companion.

After the good-night cup they all went to their rest. It was to the pleasure of many on the morrow when (if I may so express myself)* 'the sweet, bright dawn shone out'.

Arthur son of Utepandragun could be seen actively engaged in making ready a magnificent Table Round of drianthasme.† Now you heard before how they fashioned a Table Round on the meadow beside the Plimizœl. The present one was cut to the same pattern, circular, and with every mark of splendour. They made a ring of seats all round on the dewy greensward, so wide that from there to the Table Round it was fully the length of a jousting charge. This Table Round lay there all alone at the centre not for any use it gave, but for its name. A man of low degree would have good cause for embarrassment had he sat beside those worthies – it would have been a gross misdemeanour to have partaken of their fare.

This ring was measured out in the bright moonlight and arranged to splendid effect. By mid-morning, when people saw

* Wolfram, author of some very fine dawn love-songs, is indulging in self-irony.
† Cf. 'saranthasme', p. 316.

that the ring was ready, its magnificence was such as would have been beyond the means of a petty king. It was Gramoflanz and Gawan who met the main expense of it. Arthur was a stranger in that country, nevertheless he made a handsome contribution.

Night has rarely fallen without the sun's ushering in the day thereafter, as is its wont. And it was precisely this that happened there – the day shone out upon them, sweet, clear and brilliant. Many a knight sleeked his hair, then set a garland on it. You could see the fair skin of many ladies, unfeigned as nature made it, enframing red lips – if Kyot is telling true. Knights and ladies were wearing clothes not cut in just one country. Women's head-dress was worn low over the forehead or high, according to their national customs. This company had been assembled from over a wide area, and their fashions varied accordingly. No lady without a gallant dared take her seat at the Table Round on any pretext. But if a lady had accepted service that aspired to her reward and had engaged herself to bestow it, she rode to the ring of the Table Round. The others had to forgo it and just sat there in their tents.

When Arthur had heard Mass, Gramoflanz was seen arriving together with the Duke of Gowerzin and the latter's companion Florant. Each made his separate plea for membership of the Table Round, and Arthur was quick to grant it. And if any man or woman were to ask you who was the richest and mightiest from any land of all who ever sat at the Table, you could not answer them more accurately than that it was Feirefiz Angevin. So let the matter rest there.

They marched towards the ring in grand style. Some ladies were jostled there and would have gone down had their palfrey not been well girthed. You could see masses of splendid banners arriving on all sides. The bohort was ridden in a wide sweep round the ring of the Table. It was a matter of courtesy that none should ride into the ring – the meadow outside was large enough for them to gallop their horses, mingle charge with charge, and delight the ladies' eyes with feats of horsemanship.

At length they rode to where their seats were and where the elect were to feast. Chamberlains, stewards, butlers had to bring the meal to table with due regard to ceremony. I fancy they gave the company sufficient.

Each lady sitting there beside her gallant was enhanced in reputation. Many had been served with high exploits inspired by hearts desiring them. Feirefiz and Parzival had a delightful choice of ladies for their critical assessment, over there and close to hand. For on tilth or meadow, complexions more fair or redder lips were never seen in such profusion as in that ring, a cause of great pleasure to the Infidel.

Hail to this day of advent! Blessed be the utterance of her sweet speech as it is heard from her lips! They saw a virgin approaching – her clothes fine and costly and well cut in the French fashion! Her hood was of rich samite blacker than genet. On it there gleamed a flock of Turtle-doves finely wrought in Arabian gold in the style of the Gral-insignia. She at once became the focus of all their curious gazes. Now let her hurry to the scene. Her wimple was high and white, and her face was shrouded with many a thick fold and hidden away from sight.

She came riding over the field smoothly, despite her ambling gait. Her bridle, saddle and palfrey were beyond dispute costly. They at once let her ride into the ring. The knowing lady – no fool of a girl she – rode right round the ring. They pointed out to her where Arthur was sitting, and she was quick to salute him. What she said was in French. The object of her coming was to seek pardon for a wrong she had done and ask a hearing. She begged the King and Queen to help her and approve her declaration. Then immediately she turned to where she saw Parzival sitting close at Arthur's side and, losing no time, leapt down from her palfrey on to the grass and with courtesy, of which she had no lack, knelt before Parzival. Through her tears she craved his good will in such sort that he should set aside his anger towards her and pardon her – *sans* kiss of reconciliation. Arthur and Feirefiz warmly seconded her plea.

Parzival nursed great resentment towards her, yet at his friends' request he set it aside, sincerely without malice.

The noble woman whom none can call comely at once leapt to her feet and, bowing, thanked those who had helped her back to favour after great error. She unwound her wimple and flung it into the ring, hood, ribbons and all. Cundrie la surziere was immediately recognized, together with the Gral-device she wore, and they all gazed their fill on the sight. For she still had the same features which so many men and women had seen approach the Plimizœl. You have heard her visage described to you. Her eyes were still as they used to be – yellow as topaz; her teeth long; her mouth bluish like a violet. Except that she hoped for praise, she need not have worn that expensive hat on the meadow beside the Plimizœl, for the sun would have done her no harm – its treacherous rays could never have tanned her skin through her hair !

She stood there ceremoniously and uttered things they deemed of high import.

She began her speech at once in these terms. 'O happy you, son of Gahmuret ! God is about to manifest His Grace in you ! I mean the man whom Herzeloyde bore. I am bound to welcome particoloured Feirefiz for Secundille's sake and for the many high distinctions he has won so gloriously since boyhood days.' Then, addressing Parzival: 'Now be modest and yet rejoice ! O happy man, for your high gains, you coronal of man's felicity ! The Inscription has been read: you are to be Lord of the Gral ! Your wife Condwiramurs and your son Loherangrin have both been assigned there with you. When you left the land of Brobarz she had conceived two sons. For his part, Kardeiz will have enough there in Brobarz. Had you known no other good fortune than that your truthful lips are now to address noble, gentle King Anfortas and with their Question banish his agony and heal him, who could equal you in bliss?'

Seven stars she named in Arabic. They were known to the noble potentate Feirefiz who sat before her all black and white. 'Now take note, Parzival,' she said. 'The loftiest planet Zval and swift Almustri, Almaret and bright Samsi point to good fortune in you. The fifth is called Alligafir and the sixth Alkiter, while the nearest to us is Alkamer.* I do not pronounce it in a

* *Zuḥal* (Saturn), *Al-mushtarī* (Jupiter), *Al-hirrīkh* (Mạrs: *Al-aḥmar* is less likely), *Ash-shams* (Sun), *Az-zuhara* (Venus: not so remote through Hispano–Latin transmission), *Al-ḳātib* (Mercury), *Al-qamar* (Moon).

dream: these planets are the bridle of the firmament, checking its onrush; their contrariness ever ran counter to its momentum. You have now abandoned care. All that the planets embrace within their orbits, whatever they shed their light on, marks the scope of what it is for you to attain and achieve. Your sorrow is doomed to pass away – greed alone can deny you your portion. The Gral and its power forbid false companionship. You raised a brood of cares in tender years: but the happiness which is on its way to you has dashed their expectations. You have won through to peace of soul and outlived cares to have joy of your body.'

Parzival was not put out by her news. Tears – the heart's true foundation – streamed from his eyes, so happy was he. 'Madam,' he said, 'if I have been found worthy in God's eyes of the things you have just named to me, and my sinful self and my wife and any children I have are to share in it, then God has been very kind to me. As to any amends you can make to me, you show your sincerity by asking. Nevertheless, if I had not done amiss you would have spared me your anger on one occasion ... Then, most assuredly, my luck was not yet in. But now you are giving me such high gains that my sorrows are at an end. Your clothes bear out your message. When I was at Munsalvæsche with sorrowful Anfortas, all the shields I saw hanging there bore the same device as your habit – you are covered in Turtle-doves! Now, Madam, tell me when or how I am to set out on my path to happiness, nor let me put it off too long!'

'My dear lord,' she answered, 'one man may go as your companion. Choose him. For guidance look to me. Because of the help you bring, do not delay.'

The news 'Cundrie la surziere is here!' went all round the ring, and also what it portended. Orgeluse wept for joy because Parzival's Question was to make an end of Anfortas's suffering. Ever-bold in pursuit of honour, Arthur courteously addressed Cundrie. 'My lady, ride to your quarters and have yourself taken care of as you yourself would have it.'

'If Arnive is here,' she said, 'I shall content myself with any shelter she gives me now until my lord's departure. If she has been freed from her captivity, let me see her and the other ladies to whom Clinschor has meted out his malice by keeping them prisoner now many a year.' Two knights handed her on to her palfrey, and the worthy maiden rode off to find Arnive.

And it was time, too, for them to have finished their repast. Parzival was sitting beside his brother whom he then asked to be his companion, and Feirefiz proved willing to ride with him to Munsalvæsche. Then at once throughout the ring the company rose to their feet. Feirefiz had a great request to make. He asked King Gramoflanz to give proof of the unflawed love that joined him and Feirefiz's cousin Itonje. 'You and my cousin Gawan must lend a hand and see to it that none of the kings and princes we have here, or barons, not to mention landless knights, leaves this place without looking at my treasures. I should be disgraced if I were to go away without bestowing a single gift! All the strolling entertainers here can look to me for largesse. Arthur, I have a favour to beg of you – not to let the great lords scorn it, but actively to win them over and by your own example guarantee them against loss of dignity. They never met so rich a man! And give me messengers to send to my haven, where the presents are to be disembarked.'

They promised the Infidel that they would not leave the meadow for four days, and he was pleased, so I am told. Arthur gave him experienced messengers to send to the harbour. Feirefiz son of Gahmuret took ink and parchment. His missive was not lacking in marks of authenticity, I fancy no letter ever had more.

The messengers promptly set out while Parzival began a speech as follows. He told them all in French, as Trevrizent had declared when he was with him, that no man could ever win the Gral by force 'except the one who is summoned there by God'. The news spread to every land that it was not to be won by force, with the result that many abandoned the Quest of the Gral and all that went with it, and that is why it is hidden to this day.

Parzival and Feirefiz made the ladies very sorry for themselves. They rode into the four sections of the army and took leave of all the people. They would have regretted it had they not done so. Then they both set out happily, fully armed against attack.

On the third day gifts were brought from the Infidel's army to Joflanze of such splendour as was never conceived of. Any king acquainted with a gift from Feirefiz benefited his land with it forever after. No man, in terms of what was proper to his rank, had ever been shown such rare gifts. All the ladies had costly presents from Triande and Nourient.

I do not know how this army dispersed: but Cundrie and the two rode away.

Chapter 16

ANFORTAS and his people were still suffering an agony of grief. From loyal love they left him in his plight. For he often asked them to let him die and indeed would soon have done so had they not, as often, shown him the potent Gral.

'If you are loyal I know you will be moved by my sorrows,' he told his knights. 'How long am I to continue in this state? If you claim justice for yourselves, you will have to atone before God for wronging me. Since the day I first bore arms I was always willing to do your wishes. I have paid in full for any disgrace that may have befallen me and which may have been seen by any of you. If you have kept your loyalty, release me, by the Order of us who bear Helmet and Shield! For these, as you may often have been kind enough to note, I have resolutely carried to chivalric encounters. I have ranged over hills and valleys, my lance at the ready, and thrust it home in many a joust and used such sword-play as cloyed my enemies, however little it availed me with you. Wretched alien to all happiness that I am, I shall accuse you at the Last Judgment, one man against you all. If you will not let me leave you, your damnation will not be far off. My suffering should arouse your compassion. You have both seen and heard how this disaster overtook me. What good am I now as your lord? It would come as an unwelcome surprise to you if your souls were to perish over me. What new ways have you chosen to follow?'

They would have given him his release but for the consoling hope which Trevrizent had voiced once before, after seeing it written on the Gral. They were now waiting a second time for the man whose happiness had eluded him there, and for that liberating moment when his lips would frame the Question.

The King often kept his eyes shut tight for as many as four days on end. Then they carried him to the Gral whether he liked it or not, and with the malady racking him to the point where he had to open his eyes, he was made to live against his will and not die. This was how they proceeded with him until the day when Parzival and particoloured Feirefiz rode joyfully to Munsalvæsche.

The hour had waited till Mars or Jupiter* had returned angrily in their courses to where they had set out from, with the outcome that Anfortas was abandoned to the pain of his wound, suffering such agony that knights and maidens both heard his frequent cries and saw the doleful glances he gave them with his eyes. His wound was beyond all cure: there was nothing they could do for him. Nevertheless, the story says true help was now on its way to him. They took hold of heart-felt grief.

When sharp and bitter anguish inflicted severe discomfort on Anfortas they sweetened the air for him to kill the stench of his wound. On the carpet before him lay spices and aromatic terebinth, musk, and fragrant herbs. To purify the air there were also theriac and costly ambergris: the odour of these was wholesome. Wherever people trod on the carpet, cardamom, cloves and nutmeg lay crushed beneath their feet for the sake of the fragrance – as these were pounded by their tread the evil stench was abated. Anfortas's fire was a wood of aloes, as I have told you before. His bedposts were of viper's horn. To give relief from the poison, the powder of various spices had been dusted over the counterpane. The cushions on which he reclined were of brocade of Nourient, quilted, not just sewn, and his mattress was of palmat-silk. His bed was further adorned with precious – no other! – stones. The tensed cross-ropes on which the bed beneath him rested were of salamander. On every side it was luxurious, this bed of a man beggared of joy! Let no one try to argue that he ever saw a better. It was elegant and costly from the nature of its gemstones. Hear their names in detail. Carbuncle and moonstone, balax† and gagath-romeus, onyx and chalcedony, coral and bestion,‡ union pearl and optallius, ceraunius and hephæstitis, hieracitis and

* See p. 436.
† Balagius, or a doublet of balas, below.
‡ Probably a doublet of asbestos, below.

heliotrope, pantherus and androdragma, prasius and sagda, hæmatites and dionysias, agate and celidonius, sardonyx and chalcophonus, cornelian and jasper, ætites and iris, gagates and lyncurion, asbestos and tecolithus, galactites and hyacinth, orites and enhydrus, apsyctus and alamandine, chrysolectrum and hyænia, emerald and magnes, sapphire and pyritis. Also, in one place and another, there were turquoise and lipara, chrysolite, ruby, balas and sard, diamond and chrysoprase, malachite and diadochus, peanites and medus, beryl and topaz. Some of these rallied his spirits: the properties of many of the stones there were beneficial medicinally, and they were propitious, too. Those who could handle them expertly discovered many powers hidden away in them. It was with these that they had to sustain Anfortas, their very heart, and source of their abounding sorrow.

But now we shall hear that Anfortas found happiness. Riding from Joflanze into Terre salvæsche, Parzival has come, his cares all gone from him, and with him his brother and a maiden. I was not told what the distance was. And now they would have had fighting on their hands, had not their escort Cundrie saved them from such toil.

They were riding towards an outpost when a whole force of well-mounted Templars in full armour galloped up: but these were well versed enough to see from the escort that joy was coming their way. Seeing all the Turtle-doves gleaming on Cundrie's habit, the commander of the squadron said: 'Our trouble is over! What we have been longing for ever since we were ensnared by sorrow is approaching us under the Sign of the Gral! Rein in! Great happiness is on its way to us!'

At that same moment, Feirefiz Angevin urged on his brother Parzival and spurred to the attack. But Cundrie seized his bridle, and his joust was checked. Then quickly turning to her lord Parzival, 'You will soon be able to recognize their shields and pennons!' the shaggy maiden said. 'They are a Gral company, no others, who have halted there. They are ready to serve and obey you in all things.'

'In that case let the fight be broken off,' said the noble Infidel.

Parzival asked Cundrie to ride along the path towards them.

393

She did so and told them what happiness had come to them, at which all the Templars dismounted on to the grass and, removing their helmets, received Parzival on foot. His greeting was a blessing to them. They also received black-and-white Feirefiz. Then, in tears yet with every sign of joy, they rode up to Munsalvæsche.

The newcomers found a great multitude of people there: fine old knights in number, noble pages, many men-at-arms. The mournful Household had good cause to rejoice at their coming! Feirefiz Angevin and Parzival were well received on the flight of steps leading up to the Palace, into which they then all went.

Here, according to custom, lay a hundred large round carpets, each with a cushion of down on it and a long quilt of samite. If the pair went about it tactfully they could find seats somewhere or other till their armour was taken from them ...

A chamberlain now went up to them bringing them robes of equal splendour. All the knights present sat down, and many precious cups of gold – *not* glass – were set before them. After drinking, Feirefiz and Parzival went to the sorrowful Anfortas.

You have already heard all about his reclining instead of sitting, and how richly his bed was adorned. Anfortas now received the pair joyfully, yet with signs of anguish, too.

'I have suffered torments of expectation, wondering if you were ever going to restore me to happiness. Now, the last time, you left me in such a way that if yours is a kind and helpful nature you will show remorse for it. If you are a man of reputation and honour, ask the knights and maidens here to let me die, and so end my agony. If you are Parzival, keep me from seeing the Gral for seven nights and eight days – then all my sorrows will be over! I dare not prompt you otherwise. Happy you, if people were to say you succoured me! Your companion here is a stranger: I am not content that he should stand in my presence. Why do you not let him go to take his ease?'

Parzival wept. 'Tell me where the Gral is,' he said. 'If the goodness of God triumphs in me, this Company here shall witness it!' Thrice did he genuflect in its direction to the glory of the Trinity, praying that the affliction of this man of sorrows be taken from him. Then, rising to his full height, he added: 'Dear Uncle, what ails you?'

He Who for St Sylvester's sake bade a bull return from death to life and go, and Lazarus stand up, now helped Anfortas to become whole and well again. The lustre which the French call 'fleur' entered his complexion – Parzival's beauty was as nothing beside it, and that of Absalom son of David, and Vergulaht of Ascalun, and of all who were of handsome race, and the good looks conceded to Gahmuret when they saw the delightful sight of him marching into Kanvoleiz – the beauty of none of these was equal to that which Anfortas carried out from his illness. God's power to apply his artistry is undiminished today.

No other Election was made than of the man the Gral Inscription had named to be their lord. Parzival was recognized forthwith as King and Sovereign. If I am any judge of wealth, I imagine no one would find a pair of men as rich as Parzival and Feirefiz in any other place. The Lord and Master and his guest were served assiduously.

I do not know how many leagues Condwiramurs had ridden by then towards Munsalvæsche in happy mood. – She had learnt the truth earlier on, a message had come to her that her sad state of deprivation was over. Duke Kyot and many other worthy men had thereupon conducted her thence into the forest at Terre salvæsche, where Segramors had been felled by a lance-thrust and the snow and blood had so resembled her. There Parzival was to fetch her, an excursion he could well endure!

A Templar reported to him as follows. 'A group of courtly knights have brought the Queen with all ceremony.' Parzival decided to take some of the Gral Company and ride out to Trevrizent's, whose heart rejoiced at the news that Anfortas's fortunes now stood at the point where he was not to die of his lance-wound, and the Question had won him peace.

'God has many mysteries,' Trevrizent told Parzival. 'Whoever sat at His councils or who has fathomed His power? Not all the Host of Angels will ever get to the bottom of it. God is

Man and His Father's Word, God is both Father and Son, His Spirit has power to bring great succour. A greater marvel never occurred, in that, after all, with your defiance you have wrung the concession from God that His everlasting Trinity has given you your wish. I lied as a means of distracting you from the Gral and how things stood concerning it. Let me atone for my error – I now owe you obedience, Nephew and my lord. You heard from me that the banished angels were at the Gral with God's full support till they should be received back into His Grace. But God is constant in such matters:* He never ceases to war against those whom I named to you here as forgiven. Whoever desires to have reward from God must be in feud with those angels. For they are eternally damned and chose their own perdition. But I am very sorry you had such a hard time. It was never the custom that any should battle his way to the Gral: I wished to divert you from it. Yet your affairs have now taken another turn, and your prize is all the loftier! Now guide your thoughts towards humility.'

'I wish to see the woman I have not seen once in five years,' said Parzival to his uncle. 'When we were together she was dear to me, as she indeed still is. – Of course I wish to have your advice as long as we are both alive: you advised me well in the past, when I was in great need. Now I wish to ride and meet my wife who, as I have heard, has reached a place on the Plimizœl on her way to me.'

Parzival asked Trevrizent for leave to go, and the good man commended him to God.

Parzival rode through the night, for the Forest was well-known to his companions. When it dawned, he was approaching a place where many tents had been pitched, a find that pleased him greatly. Many pennants of the land of Brobarz had been planted there, with many shields that had marched behind them. They were the Princes of his own country who were encamped there. Parzival inquired where the Queen herself was quartered, and if she had her own separate ring, and they

* Cf. *Rev.* 3, 15 'I would that thou wert cold or hot, so then because thou art lukewarm ... I will spue thee out of my mouth.'

showed him where she lay surrounded by tents in a sumptuous ring.

Now Duke Kyot of Katelangen had risen early. Parzival and his men were riding up. The ray of dawn was still silver-grey, yet Kyot at once recognized the Gral escutcheon worn by the company, for they were displaying nothing but Turtle-doves. The old man fetched a sigh when he saw it, since his chaste Schoysiane had won him great happiness at Munsalvæsche and then died giving birth to Sigune.

Kyot went up to Parzival and received him and his people kindly. He sent a page to the Queen's Marshal to ask him to provide good lodgment for whatever knights he saw had reined in there. Parzival himself he led by the hand to where the Queen's wardrobe stood, a small tent of buckram. There they unarmed him completely.

Of this the Queen as yet knew nothing. In a tall and spacious pavilion in which numerous fair ladies were lying, here, there, and everywhere, Parzival found Loherangrin and Kardeiz beside her, and – joy perforce overwhelmed him! – Kyot rapped on the coverlet and told the Queen to wake up and laugh for sheer happiness. She opened her eyes and saw her husband. She had nothing on her but her shift, so she swung the coverlet round her and sprang from the bed on to the carpet, radiant Condwiramurs! As to Parzival, he took her into his arms, and I am told they kissed.

'Welcome! Fortune has sent you to me, my heart's joy,' she said. 'Now I ought to scold you, but I cannot. All honour to this day and hour that have brought me this embrace, banishing all my sadness! I have my heart's desire. Care will get nothing from me!'

The boys Kardeiz and Loherangrin, who lay there naked in the bed, now woke up. Parzival, nothing loth, kissed them affectionately. Tactful Kyot then had the boys carried out. He also hinted to those ladies that they should leave the pavilion, and this they did after welcoming their lord back from his long journey. Kyot then courteously commended the Queen's husband to her and led the young ladies away. It was still very early. The chamberlains closed the flaps.

If ever on a past occasion the company of his wits had been snatched away from him by blood and snow (he had in fact seen them on this very meadow!), Condwiramurs now made amends for such torment: she had it there. He had never received Love's aid for Love's distress elsewhere, though many fine women had offered him their love. As far as I know, he disported himself there till towards mid-morning. The men from Brobarz rode up from the whole encampment to gaze at the spectacle of the Templars, who were splendidly arrayed, though their shields were well battered and holed by lance-thrusts delivered at full tilt, as well as gashed by swords. Each was wearing a surcoat either of brocade or samite. They were still wearing their steel jambs, but their other armour had been removed from them.

There can be no more sleeping.

The King and Queen rose, a priest sang Mass. There was much jostling in the ring among the gallant knights who had once fought Clamide. After the benediction all those valiant knights who were Parzival's vassals received him loyally and with honour.

The flaps and side-walls of the pavilion were now removed.

'Which of the two boys is to rule over your country as its Sovereign?' asked the King. 'By rights he shall hold Waleis and Norgals, Kanvoleiz and Kingrivals, Anjou and Bealzenan,' he announced to all those Princes. 'If he attains to manhood, accompany him there. My father's name was Gahmuret, and he left it to me by right of true inheritance. By happy dispensation I have inherited the Gral. Here and now, if I find you to be loyal, receive your fiefs from my son!'

This was done with good will. Many pennants were brought to the fore, and a tiny hand enfeoffed them with broad domains in many regions. Kardeiz was then crowned. Later, he ruled Kanvoleiz and much else that had been Gahmuret's.

Benches were taken and a spacious ring was formed on a meadow beside the Plimizœl, where they were to break bread. After a hasty breakfast, the army made ready for the homeward journey. The tents were all taken down, and they rode back with the young King.

Many young ladies-in-waiting and other members of the Queen's train took leave of her with an open expression of their sorrow. Then his lovely mother and the Templars took Loherangrin and rode away briskly towards Munsalvæsche.

'Once upon a time in this forest,' said Parzival, 'I saw a cell through which ran a swift, clear brook. If you know it, show me the way there.'

His companions told him they knew of one. 'A maiden dwells there, abandoned to lamentation over her lover's tomb. She is a treasure-chest of virtue. Our path takes us very close to her. One never sees her free of sorrow.'

'We shall visit her,' said the King, and for their part they complied.

They rode on straight ahead at a brisk pace and late that same evening found Sigune dead on her knees in prayer. There the Queen saw a harrowing sight. They broke through the wall to Sigune, and Parzival had them raise the stone slab of the tomb for his cousin's sake, revealing Schionatulander, lambent as one embalmed, untouched by decay. Close to his side they now laid her in, who, while she lived, had given him virginal love. They then closed the grave. I am told that Condwiramurs broke out into lamentation for her cousin, her great happiness all gone, since the dead maiden's mother Schoysiane (who was Parzival's maternal aunt) had reared her when she was a child*
– this is why her happiness left her. If the Provençal spoke

* Schoysiane had died giving birth to Sigune, who was taken to Schoysiane's sister Herzeloyde (p. 243). Since Schoysiane had been Bearer of the Gral until she was given in marriage to Kyot of Katelangen, the only time during which she could have reared Condwiramurs was between her change of state and her death. An implication, no more, is that Condwiramurs had lost her mother, whom Wolfram does not name and also otherwise leaves as a complete blank. Wolfram's *Titurel* fragments further complicate the issue. They narrate that the babe Sigune had been given as companion to Condwiramurs, who at first was a suckling like her, but that later Sigune came to Herzeloyde. Rather than imagine a whole shuttle-service of sucklings and Kindergarten, it is safer to assume that Wolfram nods. This note, supported by a scholarly apparatus that would have prompted Homeric laughter in the poet who denied that his *Parzival* was a 'book', is for the comfort of readers with retentive memories.

true, King Kardeiz's tutor Duke Kyot knew nothing of his daughter's death: this story goes straight and truthfully, not curved like a bow. They did what their journey required and rode by night towards Munsalvæsche, where Feirefiz had whiled away the hours pleasantly as he waited for them. They lit candles in such numbers you would have thought the whole forest was on fire. A Templar of Patrigalt in full armour was escorting the Queen. The courtyard was vast. On it many separate companies were drawn up. These all welcomed the Queen, their lord and his son. Then Loherangrin was taken to his uncle Feirefiz. Seeing him all black and white, the boy did not want to kiss him. Noble children are still said to be a prey to fears. The Infidel laughed at this. When the Queen had dismounted, those on the courtyard dispersed, enriched by the happiness her coming had brought. And now she was led to where there was a noble bevy of comely ladies. Beside them on the steps, Feirefiz and Anfortas stood most attentively. Repanse de Schoye, Garschiloye of Greenland and Florie of Lunel were bright of eye and fair of skin, with the added glory of maidenhood. Also standing there, lithe as a wand, was the maiden Ampflise, Jernis of Ryl's daughter, who lacked neither beauty nor virtue. I am told that Clarischanze of Tenabroc was standing there, a sweet girl, her fair complexion quite perfect and with a waist drawn in like an ant's.

Feirefiz stepped towards his lady the Queen, who asked him to kiss her, and she kissed Anfortas too, and expressed her joy at his deliverance. Feirefiz led her by the hand to where she saw their lord's aunt Repanse de Schoye standing, with much kissing to be gone through. Moreover Condwiramur's mouth was red enough already, yet it now had to endure a veritable ordeal of kisses, so that I am much put out that I cannot take on this labour for her, for she was already weary when she arrived among them. Young ladies now led their mistress away.

The knights remained in the Palace which was amply furnished with candles that burned with a brilliant light. And now solemn preparation was made for the Gral.

The Gral was not carried in at all times as a mere spectacle for the Household, but only for particular festivities. That evening, time past, when they were desolated over the Bloody Lance, the Gral had been brought in because they needed help and imagined consolation was at hand – only Parzival had soon left them to their sorrows. But now it will be carried in to them in jubilation, since their sorrows are now utterly vanquished.

When the Queen had removed her travelling clothes and donned her head-dress, she came in a style altogether queenly. Feirefiz received her at a door. Now when all is said, it is beyond dispute that no one ever heard or spoke at any time of a woman more lovely. Moreover, she wore on her person a cloth-of-gold woven by a skilful hand according to that weave devised by Sarant in Thasme so ingeniously. Shedding her radiance about her, she was escorted in by Feirefiz Angevin. Three great fires redolent of wood of aloes had been made along the middle of the Palace. There were forty carpets and more seats than on a certain occasion when Parzival had also seen the Gral brought out. One seat was magnificent beyond all others. On it, Feirefiz and Anfortas were to sit beside the lord of that Castle. Those who wished to give service when the Gral was to appear, behaved with discretion and understanding.

You heard enough before as to how they carried the Gral into the presence of Anfortas. They are now seen to do likewise before noble Gahmuret's son and Tampenteire's daughter. The maidens do not keep us waiting – for here they come in due order everywhere, to the number of five and twenty.

The appearance of the first-comers, with their hair falling in locks, struck the Infidel as comely; but those who came hard behind them he judged even lovelier, the gowns of all most costly. The faces of all those maidens were without exception sweet, charming, winsome. Following them all came fair Repanse de Schoye, a maiden most rare. By her alone, no other, I am told, did the Gral let itself be carried. Great purity dwelt in her heart. The flesh without was a blossoming of all brightness.

If I were to tell you how they began to serve them, how many chamberlains offered water for their hands, what tables they brought in ... beyond what I mentioned to you before ... how vulgarity fled that Palace, all the trolleys they wheeled in laden with precious cups of gold and how the knights' seating was arranged ... the tale would grow too lengthy. Thus for brevity's sake I shall move fast.

With ceremony they received from the Gral meats both wild and tame: for this man mead, for another wine, each according to his custom; mulberry wine, tinctured, clary. Fil li roy Gahmuret found Belrepeire in different case when he first came to know it.

The Infidel inquired how the empty cups of gold became full at the Table – a marvel he delighted to watch!

'My lord,' replied handsome Anfortas who had been given to him as table-companion, 'do you not see the Gral straight in front of you?'

'I see nothing but an achmardi,' replied the particoloured Infidel. 'My young lady carried it in to us, the one standing there before us, wearing a crown. The sight of her pierces my heart. I imagined myself so strong that no woman, wed or unwed, could rob me of my happiness. If I was ever the recipient of a noble love, it has become odious to me. Bad manners usurp the good in me when I confide my troubles to you – I have done nothing to deserve it of you. What is the use of all my wealth? And all the fighting I did for ladies' sakes? And any gifts I may have bestowed? Am I to go on living in such torment? O mighty god Jupiter, why didst thou have to send me here to endure such hardships?'

The power of Love and his low spirits made him blench where he was white. Radiant Condwiramurs now all but found a rival in the fair maiden of the dazzling skin, in whose love-snare the noble stranger Feirefiz was now held fast. His former attachment was suddenly all over, and he wished to forget it. What did Secundille's love avail her now, or her land of Tribalibot? A maiden was inflicting such pangs on him that this son of Gahmuret of Zazamanc thought little of the love of Clauditte, Olimpia, Secundille and other women elsewhere, far and wide, who had rewarded him for his service and fostered his reputation.

From the pallor of Feirefiz's white patches, handsome Anfortas saw that his companion was in torment and that his spirit had abandoned him.

'I am very sorry, sir,' he said, 'if my sister is the cause of your suffering pangs such as no man endured for her before. No knight has ridden out to serve her, thus none has ever had reward of her. She has been at my side in great sorrow, and her looks have suffered somewhat for her having had so little pleasure. Your brother is her maternal nephew, he can perhaps help you in this affair.'

'If as you say the girl wearing a crown over her unadorned hair is your sister, then advise me how to win her love,' replied Feirefiz Angevin. 'All the longing in my heart is for her. If only all the fame I have ever won with the lance had been for her sake, and she were then to grant her reward! The tournament knows five lance-strokes, and I have delivered them all! The first is straight ahead in massed charge; the second known to me is to the right obliquely; the third awaits the others' charge, selecting one's adversary; then I have ridden the good thrust at full tilt in regular joust, one to one; and I have not neglected the thrust in pursuit. Of all the days since the shield became my shelter, this is my day of deepest affliction. At the foot of Agremuntin I thrust at a knight all of fire – but for my surcoat of salamander and my other covering, my shield of asbestos-wood, I should have been burned to a cinder in that joust! In whichever places I earned fame at risk of life and limb, ah, if only your adorable sister had been *she* that had sent me there! I would still be her emissary for war! I shall always resent it in my god Jupiter if he does not avert this great sorrow of mine.'

The father of these two was Frimutel. Seen beside his sister, Anfortas had the same features and complexion. The Infidel's gaze rested on her and repeatedly came back to Anfortas. And for all the viands that were being carried to and fro, not a morsel passed his lips, though he sat like one who was feasting.

'My lord,' said Anfortas to Parzival, 'I believe your brother has not yet seen the Gral.' And Feirefiz himself told his host that he did not see it, which struck all the knights there as mysterious. The aged, bedridden Titurel, too, came to hear of it.

'He is a heathen man,' he said, 'and should not aspire without benefit of Baptism to have his eyes share with the others' in contemplating the Gral. A fence has been raised before it.' – This message he sent to the Palace.

His lordship and Anfortas told Feirefiz to note the people's sole source of nourishment and they explained that all infidels were debarred from seeing it. They urged him to receive the Baptism and with it buy everlasting gain.

'If I were baptized for your sakes, would Baptism help me to win love?' asked the infidel son of Gahmuret. 'Until now, all that I have endured in love or war has been as nothing. Whether it be a short time or a long since shield first covered me, I have never been more distressed than now. Good manners require me to conceal my love, but my heart has no power to keep it secret.'

'Whom have you in mind?' asked Parzival.

'Whom else but that dazzling young lady, the sister of my companion here? If you will help me win her I will give her wealth and sway over broad territories.'

'If you will allow yourself to be given Baptism,' said his host, 'you will be in a position to seek her love, dear man. – I can now address you familiarly, since our possessions are just about equal, on my side thanks to the Gral.'

'Help me, Brother, to win your aunt's friendship,' answered Feirefiz Angevin. 'If one gets Baptism by fighting, send me there at once and let me deserve her reward. I have always liked the music of splinters flying in jousts and swords ringing on helmets.'

His host laughed much at this, and Anfortas even more.

'If this is your way of receiving Christianity,' said Parzival, 'I will bring her under your governance by due process of Baptism! You will have to break with your god Jupiter and give up Secundille. Tomorrow morning I will give you such advice as will be apt to your purpose.'

Before the time of his ailment, Anfortas had won a far-flung reputation with knightly exploits in Love's cause. His heart was naturally inclined towards kindness and generosity and indeed he had won many plaudits. Thus there were sitting there in the presence of the Gral three of the best knights who ever followed the Shield: for they did not flinch from danger.

If you agree, they have eaten their fill. Tables and linen were decorously removed from them all. In keeping with service rendered, all the young ladies bowed. When Feirefiz Angevin saw them turn away from him his sadness was intensified. She who held his heart in her noose carried the Gral away, Parzival having given leave to go.

As to how the Mistress of the Household herself withdrew, or how they went about providing comfortable bedding for the man who, because of Love, nevertheless lay uncomfortably, or how the retinue of Templars gave the guests their ease after hardship endured – all this would make a long tale of it. I will tell you about next morning.

When the light of dawn shone out, Parzival and the good Anfortas, intent on a solution, agreed to invite Love's victim, the lord of Zazamanc, into the Temple and the presence of the Gral. At the same time Parzival summoned the wise Templars. Thus companies of men-at-arms and knights were standing there when the Infidel entered. The font was a ruby, the round, stepped pedestal on which it stood was of jasper. – It was Titurel who had installed it so magnificently.

'If you want my aunt,' Parzival told his brother, 'you must forswear all your gods for her sake and be always ready to fight the Adversary of God on high, and faithfully observe God's Commandments.'

'Whatever will assure me of winning that maiden shall be done and seen to be done, fully and faithfully,' answered the Infidel.

The font was tilted a little towards the Gral and it immediately filled with water, neither too hot nor too cold. An aged priest with silvery hair was standing there who had plunged into it many a babe from heathendom.

'You must believe in the One and Only God on High,' he said, 'and snatch your soul from the Devil. God's Trinity gives its yield universally, and in even measure. God is Man and His

405

Father's Word. Since He is Father and Son, Who are held in equal honour together with His Spirit, with the furtherance of all Three this water will fend off heathenry from you. With the power of the Trinity He from Whom Adam took his likeness entered the water for His baptism. Trees have their sap from water. Water fecundates all things made that are called "creature". We see by means of water. Water gives many souls a splendour not to be outshone by the Angels.'

'If it will soothe my anguish, I shall believe all you tell me,' said Feirefiz to the priest. 'If her love rewards me, I shall gladly fulfil God's Commandments. Brother, if your aunt has God, I believe in Him and her – never was I in such need! All my gods are forsworn. I have broken with Secundille too, whatever honour she had by honouring me. In the name of your aunt's God, baptize me!'

They then treated him according to the Christian rite and pronounced the baptismal blessing over him. As soon as the Infidel had been baptized and the baptismal robing was over, they supplied him with the young lady, that is, they gave him Frimutel's daughter, an event for which he had waited with cruel impatience. As to seeing the Gral, until the holy water covered him he had been blind: but afterwards the Gral was unveiled to his vision.

After this christening, Writing was seen on the Gral to the effect that any Templar whom God should bestow on a distant people for their lord must forbid them to ask his name or lineage, but must help them gain their rights. When such a question is put to him the people there cannot keep him any longer. Because gentle Anfortas had remained in bitter agony so long and the Question was withheld from him for such a time, the members of the Gral Company are now forever averse to questioning, they do not wish to be asked about themselves.

The Christian Feirefiz begged and entreated his brother-in-law to sail away with him and freely share his riches at court; but Anfortas politely dissuaded him from this endeavour.

'I do not wish my urge to serve God to come to nothing. The Gral Crown is of equal worth. Through arrogance I lost it.

But now I have chosen humility. Possessions and love of women are far from my thoughts. You are taking a noble woman away with you who will serve you chastely as good women do. As to me, I shall not deny my Order: I shall ride many a joust, fighting in the service of the Gral. Never again shall I fight for love of woman. There was one who brought bitter pain to my heart ... But I have left all hatred of women behind me. They inspire men with a sublime zest, however little I profited from them.'

Feirefiz again urged Anfortas to come away with him in his sister's honour, but Anfortas held his ground and declined. Feirefiz Angevin then wanted Loherangrin to sail away with him; but the boy's mother turned it down. King Parzival too added a word.

'My son is destined for the Gral, and if God permits him to attain discretion must serve it with a willing heart.'

Feirefiz enjoyed and disported himself there for eleven days and departed on the twelfth. When the mighty man asked leave to escort his wife to his army, Parzival's affection moved him to sadness – The idea of Feirefiz's riding away filled him with regret. He arrived at the decision with his familiars to send a great company of knights beyond the Forest with Feirefiz. Anfortas, gentle, valiant knight, rode out with him as escort of honour. Many maidens there could not restrain their tears.

From here they had to make fresh tracks towards Carcobra. Gentle Anfortas sent a message there to the Burgrave to remind him that if he had at any time received rich gifs from Anfortas he was now to honour his vassalage with éclat and guide his brother-in-law – 'and *his* wife, my sister, through the Forest of Læprisin to the broad and lonely haven.' And now it was time to take leave, for the Templars were not to go farther. Cundrie had been chosen to deliver this message. The Templars took their leave of the mighty, courtly man, and off he rode.

The Burgrave did not fail to perform what Cundrie asked – mighty Feirefiz was received there in grand chivalric style. There was no question of his being bored there, since no time was lost in guiding him further on his way with a guard of honour. I do not know how many domains he rode through till he came to the broad meadow at Joflanze.

They came upon some people, and Feirefiz immediately asked where the army had gone. Every man had returned to his country in accordance with his marching orders. Arthur had gone to Schamilot. The man from Tribalibot was free to ride at once to his army. The latter lay in the haven, desponding at their lord's absence. But now his return brought fresh spirit to many a good knight. The Burgrave of Carcobra and his men were sent home with splendid gifts. Cundrie found important news awaiting them: messengers had followed the army to say death had claimed Secundille.

Only now could Repanse de Schoye be glad of her journey. Later in India she bore a son named 'John'. They called him 'Prester John', and, ever since, they call their kings by no other name. Feirefiz had letters sent throughout the land of India describing the Christian life, which had not prospered so much till then. (Here we call it 'India': there it is 'Tribalibot'.) Feirefiz asked Cundrie to tell his brother in Munsalvæsche how he had fared since their leave-taking, and that Secundille had died.

Anfortas was glad that his sister was undisputed mistress over so many territories.

The authentic story has now reached you concerning Frimutel's five children – how they acted in good part and how two of them died. The first was Schoysiane, who in God's eyes was perfect in her loyalty. The second was Herzeloyde, who thrust falsity from her. To win eternal gain, Trevrizent had dedicated his sword and chivalric life to God's sweet love. The heart of handsome, noble Anfortas harboured courage and chastity together: as his Order enjoined on him, he rode many jousts fighting not for ladies but the Gral.

Loherangrin grew to be a strong and valiant man in whom fear was never seen. When he was of an age to have mastered the arts of chivalry he distinguished himself in the service of the Gral.

Do you want to hear more? Some time after these events

there was a lady ruled her lands, perfect in her integrity. Possessions and high lineage were hers by inheritance. It was her nature always to act with unfeigned modesty. Human cravings found no expression in her. There was no lack of illustrious men who sued for her hand, some of them crowned heads, no few princes of her own rank. Yet so meek was she that she gave no thought to it. Many counts of her country made it a bone of contention with her – they demanded to know why she was so slow to take a husband fit to be her lord. But for all their angry remonstrations, she had entrusted herself entirely to God. Though she had given no offence, many vented their animosity on her. Thus she called an assembly of her barons.

Many envoys from distant lands made their way to her, but she abjured all men other than the one assigned to her by God – that man's love she was pleased to cherish.

This lady was Princess* in Brabant. A husband was sent from Munsalvæsche. Destined for her by God, he was brought by the Swan† and taken ashore at Antwerp. He proved to be all she could wish for. He was a man of breeding and was inevitably accounted outstanding for looks and courage in all the kingdoms to which knowledge of him came. A courtly, perspicacious, tactful man. One who gave sincerely and generously without wincing, as a person he was without fault.

The lady of the land received him graciously. Now hear what he had to say. It was heard by rich and poor, who were standing here, there and everywhere.

'My lady Duchess,' he said. 'If I am to be lord of this land, I have left as much behind me. Now hear what I wish to beg of you. *Never ask who I am!* – Then I can stay with you. But if I am chosen for your questioning you will have lost my love. If you cannot take this warning, then may God remind me of He knows what.' She gave a woman's pledge – which thanks to her affection later proved infirm – that if God left her her

* As Mistress of Brabant, historically a Duchy as here, this lady was a Fürstin ('Princess of the Holy Roman Empire').

† After his barefaced preparations, Wolfram here assimilates the Lohengrin legend to that of his Gral, see pp. 418ff.

reason she would do her husband's bidding and never go against what he had asked.

That night he knew her love. He then became Prince in Brabant. The wedding celebrations went magnificently. Many lords received at his hands the fiefs to which they had title. That same man became a good judge. And he often practised chivalry and irresistibly claimed the palm.

Together they got lovely children. There are many people in Brabant today who are well informed about this pair – her receiving him, his departure – they know that her question banished him and how long he had been there. And indeed he was very loth to go. But his friend the Swan brought back a small and handy skiff. Of his precious heirlooms he left a sword, horn and ring. Then Loherangrin went away. If we are going to do right by this story he was Parzival's son. He travelled over paths and water back to the keeping of the Gral.*

Why did the good woman lose her noble, charming lover? When he came to her from the sea he warned her against asking questions. Erec ought to say a word here – he knew how to administer a rebuke.†

If Master Chrestien of Troyes has done wrong by this story, Kyot, who sent us the authentic tale, has good cause to be angry.‡ The Provençal narrates definitively how the son of Herzeloyde achieved the Gral as had been ordained for him after Anfortas had forfeited it. The authentic tale with the conclusion to the romance has been sent to the German lands for us from Provence.

I, Wolfram of Eschenbach, intend to speak no more of it than what the Master uttered over there.

I have named Parzival's sons and his high lineage correctly, and have brought him to the goal which a happy dispensation intended for him, despite his setbacks.

When a man's life ends in such a way that God is not robbed

* The original is equally ambiguous, see p. 419.

† In *Erec*, the hero roughly rebukes his wife for speaking after he has forbidden her to do so, deliberately overlooking the fact that she does so to save his life.

‡ See pp. 428ff.

of his soul because of the body's sinning and who nevertheless succeeds in keeping his fellows' good will and respect, this is useful toil.

If I have any well-wishers among good women of discernment I shall be valued the more for my having told this tale to its end.* And if it was done to please one in particular, she must own I said some agreeable things.

---

* Wolfram thus seems finally to shed the disguise of 'Kyot' and claims for himself the credit for having completed the story of the Gral.

AN INTRODUCTION TO
A SECOND READING

WOLFRAM embarked on *Parzival* at a time when Hartmann
von Aue (*c.* 1170–1215) had established his reputation as the
leading German narrative poet with his courtly religious master-
pieces *Gregorjus* and *Der arme Heinrich*, with his early adap-
tation of Chrétien de Troyes's Arthurian romance of *Erec*, and
then, perhaps overlapping in time somewhat with *Parzival*,
his classic version of Chrétien's *Yvain*, also in the Arthurian
vein. In coming out with a third adaptation from Chrétien's
Arthurian *œuvre*, Wolfram was well aware that jealous com-
parisons would be made with Hartmann's work, so, knight
first and poet after, as he himself says, he threw down his
gauntlet and challenged Hartmann by name to see to it as
doyen of German Arthurians that young Parzival be well
received at Arthur's court – else Hartmann's heroine Enite and
her mother Karsnafite would be dragged through the mill!*
It is in the same spirit of vigorous rivalry that Wolfram fabri-
cates a jousting victory for his Orilus, a mere duke, over
Hartmann's hero King Erec on the latter's home ground.†
Wolfram's bid to outdo Hartmann, however, goes much further
and deeper. We have already seen his disclaimer that *Parzival*
was a book in the scholarly Hartmannian sense. It was Wolf-
ram's ambition to deliver a narrative whose content would
thoroughly transcend what passed for Christian chivalry at that
time as presented in an authoritative idealized form by Chré-
tien, though also subtly mocked by Chrétien himself in a
Cervantean manner.‡ Whereas there are strong hints towards
the end of Hartmann's *Erec* and *Iwein* that their heroes have
gone beyond the Arthurian ideal, Wolfram's *Parzival*, develop-

* See p. 83.
† See p. 78.
‡ It cannot have been given to many writers both to launch a new
literary vogue and to point to the seeds of its decline.

ing the leads of Chrétien's unfinished *Perceval* in grandiose fashion, takes its hero explicitly and definitively to the loftier sphere of the Gral. The markedly greater freedom which Wolfram allows himself within the established canons of adaptation into German was due not only to the situation of his completing an unfinished mystery story, but also, and more importantly, to his own artistic temperament, the unusual boldness and exuberance of which had already found expression in his love-poetry. Yet Wolfram found as early as his fifth chapter – the third in chronological order of composition – that he had reckoned without his traditionalist audience, among whom a knowledge of the fashionable French was widespread, so that half-way through his poem he decided to mask his creative activity behind a pseudo-source – 'Kyot the Provençal'. As self-elected spokesman for 'literary' poets, Gottfried von Strassburg, without naming him, takes Wolfram severely to task for his bold attempt to usurp the laurel wreath, and sets it firmly on Hartmann's head.*

In leading his hero towards the Gral community, Wolfram does not reject or even devalue average 'Arthurian' society in favour of an esoteric or mystical ideal. Contrary to what some have alleged, *Parzival* is devoid of mysticism in the strict sense, except for elements of the strange yet moving blend of amorous and religious feeling of the maiden Sigune for her slain suitor Schionatulander. As the creator, on Chrétien's matrix, of the lay hermit Trevrizent, who confesses his nephew Parzival as knight to knight without humiliating him, Wolfram was not one to condemn the chivalric activities in which he shared with such gusto. He brings out the zest and colour of the chivalric life with great force, knowledge, charm and splendour through his handling of Parzival's father Gahmuret in two episodes of his own creation (Chapters 1 and 2); of the knightly exploits and progression in love of Gawan in six brilliant episodes based on Chrétien (Chapters 7, 8, 10–13); and of a number of minor

---

* See my translation of Gottfried's *Tristan*, Penguin Classics (1960 etc.), p. 105.

characters for the most part lovingly portrayed. As will be seen, Parzival's virtually exclusive outward activity, the activity which wins him the Gral when at last he pursues it in the right spirit, is that of knightly combat. The chivalric orders had from the outset enshrined lofty Christian principles in their statutes, which, however, were often more neglected than observed. It was Wolfram's aim through a sympathetic discussion of knighthood as reflected in the early life of Parzival to raise this *latent potential* in the general chivalric order. In order to do so Wolfram had to shield the knighthood from the wounding arrogance of the ascetic clergy, who took the uncharitable view that as men of blood knights were damned. Apart from his positive teaching, mainly through the mouth of Trevrizent, Wolfram furthered his aim by the simple device of having no other clergy in his story than those required for the formalities of baptism, marriage and celebration of the Mass, leaving confession and discussion of such burning questions as homicide, rebellion against God and religious despair to his laymen. Comparison with the corresponding passage in his source guarantees Wolfram's intentions here, for in the *Perceval* the hermit has a chapel, a priest and a deacon, all absent from Wolfram's adaptation.

Although destined to the Gral from on high, Parzival also had to achieve it by effort. Wolfram, or at least his mouthpiece Trevrizent, represents this achievement as unique for all time, though Anfortas is there to remind us that even if one is born and elected to the Gral one can lose it. Despite this suggestion of uniqueness, however, the message conveyed by the poet is the antithesis of discouragement to all knights. The writing on the Gral in its function of news-flash from Heaven designated Parzival as Elect: but since the Creation so are we all – elect to fill the choir forsaken by the fallen angels. Leaving his First Paradise, Parzival inevitably failed at his first attempt to enter the Second from a state of mind engendered by inexperience and ignorance: but so do we all, always excepting the enviable few blessed with the *sancta simplicitas*. In conquering his pride which reached desperate proportions towards God, Parzival perfects himself for his pre-ordained place in the Second

Paradise, symbolized by the Gral Domain. Beneath the bewildering wealth of narrative detail in *Parzival* there is the clear outline, even graph, of the eternal Christian story, which went out of high literary fashion so long ago. According to what may be called 'the trampoline effect' of Christian doctrine regarding the regeneration of Man, the deeper one falls the higher one may rise. With his rejection of God, as though the bond between Maker and Creature were a feudal relationship, Parzival falls far lower than his purely chivalric counterpart, Gawan, and of course rises far higher, indeed to the summit of lay Christendom in the whole world, the Kingship of the Gral. It is the powerful paradox of this story that its hero, who is unique, presents a pattern for all knights in all audiences. And, we may be sure, it was a paradox which cost them nothing at all to surmount, either emotionally or intellectually. For if a pot-hunting crack-jouster could win the Gral, Wolfram was suggesting to them, why not they too? Their Grals were waiting.

Wolfram excludes the clergy, as he also excludes the peasantry, purely for the purpose in hand. Apart from his demand for tactful confession for the knighthood, he has no intention of criticizing, let alone challenging the institutions of the Church. It is significant that immediately before confessing Parzival out in the wilds where there is no cleric to discharge this office, Trevrizent enjoins reverence for the priesthood in an extended passage in the clearest possible terms.* Before, during and after Wolfram's time there is historical evidence of a deep desire in lay circles to be more closely associated with clerical institutions in piety somewhat short of the taking of monastic vows. Various solutions were found to meet this longing, both for men and women. Sigune's life in the forest as an *inclusa* is a case in point. Wolfram's solution, that of a Gral community, is of course purely poetic and symbolic, yet the *way* which he points out to his imagined Gral was one of great immediacy to his courtly listeners.

Because Chrétien drew a causal connection between Perceval's

* See p. 255.

sins of riding out in search of Arthur and leaving his mother to die of grief, and his failure at the Gral Castle, there has been discussion as to whether Parzival's failure was not of the same nature. In the course of his long exchange with Parzival in the German poem, Trevrizent, it is true, specifies three past sins on the part of the hero: the slaying of his kinsman Ither, whose blood-red armour despoiled from the corpse he is still wearing; his failure to show the sympathy he felt by asking Anfortas what ailed him; and his heartless abandonment of his mother. These shortcomings are named in that order, and there is no attempt by Trevrizent to establish causal connections. In fact, Trevrizent's estimate of their nature is hinted at in his charitable allusion to the Failure at a time when he is still unaware that he is conversing with the guilty party: he says that the man was 'tump', that is, 'young and inexperienced'. Further light is thrown on how Wolfram would wish us to view the matter by his observation that in taking her son into the wilds to keep him from the chivalric life, Herzeloyde was 'cheating him of his royal style of life', an excess of motherly solicitude over which the virile Wolfram shakes his head. The boy's nature was bound to assert itself at the first contact with knighthood. And so it proved. Similarly, when Parzival slew Ither it was under the provocation of a very hard blow and against vastly superior armament – and a jolly good javelin-shot it was through the one chink in Ither's armour! Young Parzival's sins, then, including his Failure at Munsalvæsche, were not of a nature to overtax either his confessor's or God's powers of forgiveness. What *did* place Parzival's soul in eternal jeopardy was his general state of mind. Trevrizent has some deep words on family feeling and on homicide, but it is to Parzival's state of mind that he addresses himself chiefly. And with what marvellous gentle tact! For whereas Parzival's first tutor showed a fine forbearance in adjusting the green young man's weaponry with an 'Allow me!', the second has a raw and rebellious soul to guide and save.

For Wolfram it was the way to Kingship of the Gral community that mattered, not tenure of the office or the life there. Apart from the two moments of high festive ritual coinciding with Parzival's first and second visits, the concerns of Munsalvæsche are dealt with sketchily, leaving many blanks to be filled in. I have suggested above that one of the symbolic aspects of the Gral milieu was that of the Second Paradise. On the other hand it is no Utopia, no blue-print for a recombination of human proclivities that will miraculously convert anti-social into social leanings to make a stable harmony. Without some powerful moral influence emanating from the Gral which Wolfram fails to mention, Gral Society even in his bare description would not last a week. It would be an amusing literary exercise for an able pen to portray the inevitable disintegration, and Wolfram himself could have done the job as well as any. As it stands in his text, the function of Gral Society, beside its symbolic connotations, is to inculcate an image of self-discipline in young men and women in joint service to God – coupled with and despite high living. The Templars' duty of defending the mysterious boundaries of the Gral Realm against often formidable intruders was of course congenial in part: but it meant fights to the death if need be, perhaps tournaments and dancing, but no flirtations. The food and conditions on the other hand were good, as were the horses, despite their lack of oats – there were no peasants at Munsalvæsche to raise them – or was there a Gral Manger? There was always the chance of sudden preferment to a distant throne and a full normal life as a sovereign whilst discharging the higher function of spreading the faith. Gral maidens, too, would find fulfilment in the same way. That we are to see the Templars as men of flesh and blood requiring self-control with regard to the exquisite girls produced on festive occasions is shown by the fateful lapse of no other than the Gral King with a lady beyond the walls.

Unbelievably, it was possible to fall from this Paradise, even for one who was born within and for it, like Anfortas, though excusably, since it was his First. Yet this had to be. Like the Question, it belonged to the mechanics of the story, since without the Gral King's fall, how could an outsider (albeit of the same Family), a pattern for us others, battle his way through to the Kingship of the Gral? We are left to believe that in the whole history of the Gral Family there was and was to be this one exception. But one was enough. It gave Parzival, the exemplar of a full-blooded Christian knight, his chance to come in from the world after mastering his religious problem.

A brief examination of how Wolfram contrives this vital exception, for which he owes nothing to Chrétien beyond the bare narrative datum, will illuminate his barefaced style of fabulation, whereby he relies on the sense of humour of the quick-witted to twig what he is up to and leaves the others – including, alas, many scholars – to be duped. First, Parzival's mother Herzeloyde, sister to the reigning King of the Gral, has to be got outside Munsalvæsche. This is done according to the rule that Gral *maidens* are sent out *openly* to marry. Second, Herzeloyde's husband Castis dies before the marriage is consummated: one would hope that Gahmuret, the father of a future Gral King, would marry a virgin, even if he himself were already married and the sort of man whose 'tilting would have been more on the mark' than Parzival's on finding an unprotected beauty asleep in her pavilion.* Third, Herzeloyde's first husband left her two kingdoms, Waleis and Norgals. Don't cudgel your brains wondering what sort of law of inheritance they had in Waleis and Norgals: focus on the name of the man – 'Castis'. A man whose name is so near to Latin *'castus'* 'chaste' is not likely to breed, indeed the likeliest diagnosis of the unnamed cause of his death was his fear of doing so. Gahmuret was otherwise, and so we have a son out in the world who combines in his heredity the virility of his father's line with the spirituality of his mother's, though we note in the men of the Gral Family that they too were no mean fighting-men, such being Wolfram's bias.

Another sign of how little it was to Wolfram's purpose to present a viable Gral régime is seen in his reckless incorporation of the Lohengrin legend, or rather the legend of the Knight with the Swan,† into his Gral narrative. Whereas the legend of Prester John, the Christian Priest-King spreading the faith somewhere in Asia or Africa, was highly compatible with

---

* See p. 80.

† Wolfram takes Loherangrin's name from the hero of the unconnected story *Garin le Loherain*.

Parzival through the hero's oriental half-brother Feirefiz, what came to be known in Germany as the Lohengrin legend was not. In wiring this legend on to *Parzival*, Wolfram's first move as far back as Chapter 9 (unless he tinkered it in later) was to have another rule at Munsalvæsche that *men* are sent out *in secret* to rule lordless lands. His second move, in Chapter 16, is' to have the Gral receive a signal 'to the effect that any Templar whom God should bestow on a foreign people for their lord must forbid them to ask his name or lineage but must help them to gain their rights. When such a question is put to him, the people there cannot keep him any longer.' This veto was of course a vital element of the already existent story of The Knight with the Swan, and Wolfram has generalized it to cover the case in hand. He further pegs it down by stating that because Anfortas had suffered for so long owing to the Question having been withheld 'the members of the Gral Company are now forever averse to questioning, they do not wish to be asked about themselves'! Furthermore, contrary to one's legitimate expectation that a future or regnant Gral King, if released from Munsalvæsche, would be employed by Heaven to confer marked religious benefits on his new people, all that Wolfram can do for the Christian Brabanters is to make Lohengrin – his Loherangrin – a just judge. When Loherangrin leaves the Gral Community on this mission we are left guessing who would rule at Munsalvæsche and whether Condwiramurs had borne other sons. Another subject on which Wolfram leaves us uninformed as he rapidly tapers off his great romance is the relationship between Loherangrin's high-minded Duchess and the comically named Duke Lambekin of Brabant, who accepted King Kaylet of Castile's cast-off mistress Alize as wife and whom Kaylet unhorsed at Kanvoleiz only two generations back in Chapter 2. The historical Duke Henry I of Brabant at the time when Wolfram was composing *Parzival*, however, was of a power and calibre to be chosen leader by the German Princes on Crusade in 1197. What motive can Wolfram have had first to belittle then to elevate the House of Brabant in his story? Did these changes of mood reflect the ever-changing political alliances of Wolfram's poetry-loving, yet macchiavellian patron

Hermann? Recourse to standard history-books gives no clear answer to this question, but it does show that Wolfram seized an opportunity here too, since for the greater part of the time during which *Parzival* was in the making, Henry of Brabant had no son. In 1198, when she was seven years old, Henry's daughter Maria was betrothed to Otto of Poitou, rival claimant with Philip of Swabia to the Imperial Crown. In 1204, however, Pope Innocent III felt forced to intervene in support of his protégé Otto to forbid the proposed marriage of Philip's nephew, the future Emperor Frederick II, with this same Maria. In this year, too, the sonless Henry received authority from Emperor Philip *to name a daughter as heiress in Brabant*. At last, in 1207, a son was born to Henry, but Philip's concession will not have been easily revoked.* A date of AD 1207 for Wolfram's decision to incorporate his Loherangrin plot in *Parzival* accords well with what is known of the latter's general chronology.†

There was an Unseen Hand on Parzival's bridle, yet he also had human helpers in his stubborn efforts to win the Gral. Parzival is helped at vital points in his quest by his own clan in the narrower and wider sense, notably by his maternal cousin Sigune (whose name in Upper German pronunciation is an anagram of 'cusine') and by his maternal uncle Trevrizent. We have to unthink such modern institutions as the police force and insurance, and the medical and welfare services to be able to begin to conceive what kinship meant to people living under feudal conditions at the beginning of the thirteenth century. Earlier, in the Germanic languages, there had been one word for 'father-and-son(s)', echoes of which occur in *Parzival* in passages where the bond between father and son is not considered to be a degree of relationship, the first degree being that between grandfather and grandsons.‡ The feeling for kinship

* In 1214, Otto, now Emperor, in order to seal a *rapprochement* with Brabant, married the 22-year-old Maria. Henry's throw was a bad one, since Otto's fortunes were soon to be shattered at the Battle of Bouvines. The last we see of Maria does not surprise us: it is within the strong walls of Cologne, piling up huge debts for Otto at hazard.

† See p. 8, and pp. 423 and 435.

‡ See p. 157.

is very strong in *Parzival*, see for example the emphasis on the
'identity' of the hero and Feirefiz even though they are only
half-brothers.* This rises to a veritable mystique in Wolfram's
Willehalm. Sigune names Parzival at their first meeting, certifies
his integrity of heart and guides him away from the formidable
Orilus, slayer of the dead suitor in her lap. At their second
meeting, Sigune upbraids Parzival for his failure at Munsal-
væsche, retracts her earlier assessment of his integrity and for-
mally outclans him, so that soon, after being publicly disgraced
by Cundrie and renouncing Arthurian society and then God,
he will consider himself all on his own. At their third meeting,
matured by suffering like Parzival, Sigune charitably readmits
him to the clan, and shows him the way which, under Provi-
dence, leads to Trevrizent. It is after Trevrizent's teaching and
confession of the already near-penitent Parzival that outward
signs of Parzival's return to Grace are manifested. Parzival is
twice saved from repeating his sin of slaying a kinsman, first
his rather distant cousin Gawan and then Feirefiz. Wolfram
relates the latter event specifically to the slaying of Ither and to
Providence. The sword snatched from Ither's corpse shatters on
Feirefiz's helmet: 'It was no longer pleasing to God that Par-
zival should wield a weapon robbed from a corpse ...' These
two crucial duels are Wolfram's work, since *Perceval* breaks off
before them. Despite the pleasant delays over Itonje's love-
intrigue† they show what a firm grip Wolfram has taken on the
story. The importance of blood-relationship and of the action of
the Gral Clan, however, does not rest with the already some-
what old-fashioned Germanic feeling for the kindred, for this
profound poet in the last resort traces the descent of the entire
human race, Christian and heathen alike, back to Father Adam,
so that the whole world is kin. In his magnificent introductory
prayer in *Willehalm*, Wolfram finds a sublime extension for
Adam's Family in these terms: 'I am Thy child and Thy kind
expressly, wretched though I be and Thou so mighty. Thy
humanity gives me kinship. The Paternoster names me un-

* See p. 374.
† See pp. 316ff.

equivocally the child of Thy Godhead. And the Baptism gives me an assurance which has redeemed me from despair. I believe and know that I am Thy namesake. Wisdom beyond all knowledge, if Thou art Christ then I am Christian.' It does not surprise us that the Wolfram who is disturbed in *Parzival* at the Devil's being permitted to make such mock of so civilized a people as the Saracens,* in *Willehalm* voices the passionate plea through Lady Giburc that the Infidel should not be slaughtered like cattle if the Christians win a defensive war. For, like all mankind, the Saracens are God's own handiwork.

It would have been astonishing if with his insatiable universal curiosity Wolfram had not been fascinated by the Muslim world. As with most of his contemporaries, however, the factual knowledge he was able to acquire of it is pathetic. This need not surprise us, since to the discredit of the then more highly civilized people, the Muslims too showed a lamentable inability to penetrate the curtain dividing them from the Franks, though it is to their eternal credit that they were far more tolerant than Western Christians where religion was concerned, once fighting was over: their tolerance was written into law and a graduated tax-system. Since Christ is an honoured prophet in Islam, it is not conceivable that Muslim poets would attribute Zeus or Wodan to the Christians as gods, yet the very curious Wolfram can do no better than have his Feirefiz pray to Jupiter and Juno, and by the time he is writing *Willehalm* he can throw in Tervigant (our Termagant), Kahun and – an offence he would have avoided, had he recognized it – Mahumet. This multiplicity of Muslim 'gods', taken over from the French *chansons de geste*, is no doubt a *tu quoque* reflecting Christian sensitivity in religious polemical exchanges on the subject of the Trinity. In *Parzival*, really all that Wolfram knows about the Muslims is that they had darker faces, produced marvellous textiles, had easier access to gold and precious stones, were more advanced in medicine and astronomy, used mounted archery and employed Parthian tactics: Wolfram's 'wheeling and retreating' (*wenken unde vliehen*) is the *karr wa farr* still to be observed

* See p. 232.

by Col. Lawrence during his desert campaigns. Wolfram's Baruc* of Baghdad is an inverted Pope of Rome fused with an anti-Emperor, and when Wolfram asserts 'They get their papal law from Baghdad, and, so far as it is free from crooks and crannies, deem it straight!'† he is mocking not only dubious decretals from the Lateran but also his own ignorance of the East. Wolfram shows no knowledge of the degradation of women in harems or under the veil, nor of the freedom of Andalusian ladies beyond the imaginings of the much-chaperoned noblewomen of Christian Europe. Moreover, to his Saracenic 'knights' he attributes the same code of love as to his Christians: service for reward.

Parzival was begun about the turn of the twelfth and thirteenth centuries. Only a few years before, Temujin was proclaimed paramount chief of the Mangkhol. Except perhaps for revisions, *Parzival* was completed before 1210. By this time Temujin had been confirmed in his sacred title of 'Jinggis-khan'. By 1221 Jinggis had shattered the Shadom of Khwārizm in what is now Western Persia, and by 1223 his Mongols were in the Eastern Caucasus and in Southern Russia. Tremors of these not too distant events are discernible in *Willehalm*, in which Wolfram depicts the seething of heathen oriental peoples greatly outnumbering the Christians who, so it was believed, formed but Twelve of the Seventy-two Tongues. How could this be? In the fullness of time, but before the coming of Antichrist, the Gospel *must* reach the ends of the earth. Wolfram had two dreams of the incorporation of the heathen into the Christian world: in *Parzival* through the Gral mission of Parzival and his progeny, whereby Templars and Gral maidens were sent to distant thrones,‡ with, as the outstanding examples, the converted Feirefiz and his Gral-bearer wife Repanse de Schoye, parents of Prester John; and in the *Willehalm*-torso, by extrapolation from itself as much as from its French source,* through

* Wolfram took this pseudo-title from Hebrew *bāruḳ* 'blessed'.
† See p. 20.
‡ Wolfram could not add 'in heathen lands' since this would have frustrated his incorporation of the Lohengrin legend, see pp. 419ff.
* *La Bataille d'Aliscans.*

the marriage of Emperor Louis's daughter Alize with Renne-
wart, the lost son of the mighty Saracenic 'Emperor' Terramer.
Armed aggression is remote from the thoughts of our soldierly
poet, and by the time of the Fourth Crusade in 1204, to which
Wolfram refers obliquely, the crusading ideal was thoroughly
discredited in the eyes of thoughtful laymen. Indeed, the fias-
cos of the Second Crusade and of the Battle of Hattin in 1187,
for which the clergy had promised victory, were one of the
major contributory causes of the emergence, first in France and
then in Germany, of a more independent secular literature *by*
knights *for* knights, of which Chrétien's *Perceval* and Wolf-
ram's *Parzival* are ornaments.

'Oriental' elements are lacking in Wolfram's source. Their
prominence in *Parzival* can be safely ascribed to the known
exotic tastes of Wolfram's great patron, the Landgrave Hermann
of Thuringia, which Wolfram evidently shared with him, a
true marriage of minds. Given the chronological order of
composition of Chapters 3-6; 1-2; 7-16, it is easy to see how
Wolfram dangles his newly conceived Feirefiz before his
audience towards the end of Chapter 6 to lead in to the begetting
of him in Chapter 1 in the land of the Moors, his own free
composition and first offering to Hermann.

Like some other masterpieces of literature, *Parzival* affords
an example of the piling of Pelion on Ossa, of the work of one
genius reared upon that of another, the *Perceval* of the great
Chrétien de Troyes. Chrétien was the creator of Arthurian
romance for the courts and with some support from his immedi-
ate predecessors and from his contemporary, Thomas of Britain,*
can be regarded as the father of European narrative. Comparison
of *Parzival* with the unfinished *Perceval* affords the rare oppor-
tunity of looking over the shoulder of genius at work, as Wolf-
ram goes about the task of recreating and completing the story.
Comparison of Chaucer's *Troilus* with the *Philostrato*, once
attributed to Boccaccio, provides a similar opportunity in our
own medieval literary history. A thorough study of the case in

---

* See The Penguin Classics (*Tristan*), already cited, in which I have
translated the surviving fragments of Thomas's *Tristran*.

hand would run to several volumes. My aim here is to draw attention to the bare fact that readers of French can share in this pleasure to an acceptable degree by comparing my translation with L. Foulet's modern French rendering of the *Perceval*.* At the present time, when negligible and even expendable authors claim absolute originality and independence for their productions it is salutary to dwell on the fact that poets of the order of Wolfram and Chaucer saw nothing amiss in adapting existing works to their purposes. Helped by the traditionalist outlook of their audiences, though not infrequently also at odds with it, such poets correctly assessed the role of tradition in the art of communication and would have consigned aspirants to absolute originality to Bedlam, which is where they in fact are.

Chrétien's unfinished *Perceval*, with its rather sudden changes of attention from Perceval to Gauvain (Wolfram's Gawan), has often struck critics as formless. Some of Chrétien's and Wolfram's contemporaries, obviously lacking in empathy and in insight into basic plot-structure, thought that Gauvain, not *Perceval*, should win the Graal. Reading between the lines of *Parzival* one senses that Wolfram had to deal with a pro-Gawan faction in his audience. He knew that the royal boy who was isolated from chivalric contacts by his mother *must* reveal his inborn nature in the face of all obstacles. Wolfram may also have thought that the sequence of Chrétien's episodes, here given the numeration of Wolfram's,† could be arranged thus, with the thirteenth episode barely begun:

* *Chrétien de Troyes. Perceval le Gallois ou le conte du Graal.* Cent Romans Français, Paris, 1947.

† Normally called 'books', they are called 'chapters' here.

Wolfram's completed pattern is in any event thus:

		16		
		15		
	12	13	14	
7	8	9	10	11
	4	5	6	
		3		
		2		
		1		

In other words, perhaps following the general pattern of Thomas's *Tristran* with its opening episode on its hero's parents, Wolfram has added Chapters 1 and 2, which are devoted to Gahmuret, who begets Feirefiz to carry the Infidel strand of the story (1), and Parzival, exemplar of deeper Christian chivalry (2); has completed Chapter 13, at whose end he knots the Gawan- and Parzival-actions by bringing the two heroes on to a collision course incognito – a device already familiar from Chrétien's *Yvain* and Hartmann's *Iwein*; in Chapter 14 Wolfram narrates the actual duel and merciful recognition of the combatants; in Chapter 15 he similarly knots together the Feirefiz- and Parzival-actions, with a second duel incognito explicitly ended by divine intervention after Parzival's first taste of defeat in battle; finally, in Chapter 16 Parzival enters at last into his own as King of the Gral, taking Feirefiz with him to inevitable conversion and then return to the East to beget Prester John on the maiden who had carried the Gral. Over and above this, Wolfram greatly expands what Chrétien gave him for Chapter 9 to make it his central doctrinal chapter on salvation and the Gral.

At the beginning of Chapter 13, where the *Perceval* breaks off, Wolfram is of course not an entirely free man, since he has to observe the narrative logic of what has gone before, derived from Chrétien's major incidents. Yet it is significant that as soon as his source dries up, Wolfram embarks on a festivity and spins out the new marvels of Clinschor. As a result, he only just manages to knot the Parzival- and Gawan-actions at the very end of Chapter 13 to preserve the vital Parzival-sequence – the vertical central column in the cruciform pattern above: 3 (young Parzival), 5 (First Visit to the Gral), 9 (Parzival with Trevrizent), 13 (as just discussed), 15 (Parzival and Feirefiz), 16 (Parzival Gral King). 9, which deals with the turning-point in Parzival's life and the nature of the Gral, is at the absolute centre of the pattern.

For a century and a half, though in diminishing numbers, there have been critics who have denied at least part of these innovations to Wolfram, and for little other discoverable reason than that as from half-way through his *Parzival*, Wolfram claims to be following one 'Kyot the Provençal', sender of the 'true version'. Ideally and for the most part in practice, scholarship is conducted according to the convention that all other scholars are of the highest possible intelligence and perspicacity. Thus if any wish to take Wolfram's statements on Kyot at their face value they are free to do so, even if these statements are utterly lacking in external support and even if they ironize, not to say mock themselves. I myself respect this convention for its optimism and courtesy, and because most scholars out of touch with reality are innocuous and self-supporting. Nevertheless, it is my hope that one day a far more learned, formidable, and above all blunt scholar than I will arise to bury the 'Kyot controversy' for ever. Let it suffice to say here that although a writer Guiot de Provins is known, none of his writings deals with any aspect of the Gral story, nor is one attributed to him by inference; that Guiot de Provins was no Provençal but of course a North Frenchman from a town between Troyes and Paris (though very probably Wolfram used his name); that appeal to pseudo-sources to authenticate one's own fabulations in a traditionalist age was far from unknown; that there is no single romance of the Graal in French or in any other language which narrates a number of Wolfram's innovations in sequence; that Wolfram drags in Kyot towards the end of Chapter 8 in order to validate a very minor figure because he is going to splash Kyot big in Chapter 9 (just as he had used his 'trailer' technique in Chapter 6 in order to focus expectation on Feirefiz, who was to be engendered in his next Chapter, 1).*

In Chapter 9, when Wolfram is about to reveal the nature of the Gral through Trevrizent, he refers to wranglings with his listeners over the Gral 'earlier on', that is when Chapter 5 was being recited: but now he is ready for them. For if from their knowledge of French or by hearsay his audience had resented the discrepancies between his version in Chapter 5 and the corresponding episode of *Perceval*, then 'Kyot's' version would confute and rout them. The cock-and-bull concomitants of Wolfram's full-scale counter-attack with 'Kyot' in Chapter 9 would charm the quick-witted with its reckless humour and fob off the dull.

A very fair reviewer of the whole field of Wolfram studies named in the Bibliography below, recently cited as surviving obstacles to interpreting 'Kyot' as a narrative device: i) Wolfram's surprising reverence for the House of Anjou (Gahmuret, Parzival and Feirefiz are 'Anschevin'); ii) Wolfram's allusions to – more accurate would be 'analogy with' – the Knights Templar, who were hostile towards the Germans; iii) Wolfram's astonishing knowledge of French literature; and iv) the many points of agreement with French Graal tradition after Chrétien.

Concerning the last item, this same critic admits that these points of contact occur not in a single coherent narrative but widely scattered in different monuments. With regard to the Knights Templar, Wolfram can have disliked their politics whilst admiring their statutes and their task of guarding nothing less than the Holy Sepulchre; similarly Wolfram must have been greatly impressed by the brilliance and far-flung connections of the House of Anjou – by its inheritance of 'Arthurian' panache from the Normans on whom Geoffrey of Monmouth had bestowed it in his *Historia regum Britanniae*; by its link through Eleanor with the prestigious territories of South-West France and through her also with the cult of courtly love; by the military exploits in the East of her son Richard Cœur-de-Lion, who discussed the possibility of marrying his sister to the great

* See p. 164 and footnote.

428

Kurd Saladin and who in any case provided Wolfram with traits for his Gahmuret; and curiously by the fact that the House of Anjou had lands in Styria, with one of whose districts Wolfram associates Trevrizent and from which he took the place-name 'Gandin' as a name for Gahmuret's father (p. 253). This only leaves Wolfram's allegedly astonishing knowledge of French literature to be accounted for. But so much of Wolfram's knowledge is astonishing, whether it be of falconry, organized warfare, precious stones, the planets, or general lore. His mind was so avid of colourful information, and on the other hand French literature was so much the rage and accessible at the German courts where acquaintance with French was far from rare, that it would be at least mildly surprising if this poet – twice the recreator of narratives in Old French – had not laid by a great store of it in memory. Like chivalric activity, poetry was his own game.

It seems, then, that there are no cogent reasons why the fairest and most tolerant of critics should not regard Wolfram's 'Kyot' as an entertaining fiction and a narrative device.

The question of Wolfram's literacy was discussed above.* Those who think he could read will not mind him reading French. Close comparison of *Parzival* with *Perceval*, however, strongly suggests that unlike Gottfried's command of French, Wolfram's was far from perfect. One typical misunderstanding of his seems to have been of a word for a 'carving-dish' – of silver – which he interpreted as 'carving-knife' in the plural. But what matter? To a man of Wolfram's temperament and imagination such minor irritations to narrative logic produced pearls. With two silver knives on his hands, Wolfram invents a function for them. They are made to remove the ice-like 'glass' deposited on the Lance from Anfortas's wound, a deposit nothing else would master. Of silver though they were, they would have cut through steel! To assess the full effect of this sally on the knights of Wolfram's audience one has only to recall that in battle their lives depended on nuances in the temper of steel.

* See p. 10.

As a narrator, Chrétien composed vivid and memorable scenes involving few persons and strung them together in almost dreamlike succession. Two things which contributed to this effect were the clarity and intensity of the foreground against an elusive and often mysterious background. In his re-creation of what Chrétien gave him, Wolfram on the other hand constructed a very highly organized background. Whereas Chrétien was sparing with names in *Perceval* in the manner of the folktales from which he ultimately derived his romances, Wolfram revels in names and allots to their owners precise places in geography (whether real or fanciful), feudal rank, and membership of great ramifying families within the three or four generations of the living. In this aspect of his style Wolfram is much nearer to epic than romance, and indeed in *Willehalm*, which re-creates a French feudal epic, he comes as near to classic epic as the rather unepical courtly measure and his resolve not to shock the ladies will let him.

The fullness and complexity of background in *Parzival*, with all their explicitness and cross-coupling, make for a realistic style, often echoed in his choice of images, which do not halt at the smithy or the woodman's clearing. Yet Wolfram's realism is a unique graphic style in which 'reality' is evoked by poetic means. For example, when Ither reverses his lance and brings it down on Parzival, the lad's blood 'sprayed through his pores in a cloud'. Or 'he rode over rough country where few plantains were to be seen', where the experienced eye detaches the fact that when traffic has worn away all the herbage the tough plantain remains. Or when Parzival came to Belrepeire he saw the torrent below its walls flying 'like bolts well feathered and trimmed when the tensed crossbow hurls them with throbbing string'.

This same poetic realism also governs the heroes' movements through time and space. Study of the errancies of Parzival and Gawan through places real or unreal, but regularly named, has shown that Wolfram had a coherent map of them in his head which the reader could reconstruct for himself, and that he uses locality and scenery symbolically. The reader's attention is particularly drawn to the environs of the suggestively named Munsalvæsche – 'Mount Savage' or 'Wild Mountain' – which guards the Gral and whose situation Wolfram hides. The best hint Wolfram drops on the whereabouts of Munsalvæsche is that Parzival rode thither from Belrepeire in a day – though a bird would have been hard put to it to cover the distance! Parzival's steed is thus momentarily Wolfram's Pegasus. Belrepeire, in turn, had been reached from Graharz through high mountains. And Graharz had been reached from Nantes in one day, yet such was Parzival's ignorance on this his first ride on a war-horse that he forced a two days' march from it. Finally, Nantes had been reached in three days dry-shod via the Forest of Brizlan (Broceliande) from 'Soltane' presumably somewhere in Herzeloyde's land of Waleis (Wales?), as though lands of the Celtic fringe were linking up in folk memory. Munsalvæsche, then, and its whole region of Terre salvæsche somewhere beyond the river Plimizœl and 'Young Forest' as viewed from Britain, is mysteriously hidden, as is only fitting for a goal which only the Elect can reach. As such, it again appears as a sort of earthly Paradise, hidden like that of the Alexander story near the sources of the four rivers Pishon, Gihon, Tigris and Euphrates. It is significant for *Parzival* that Alexander in medieval legend penetrated to the walls of Paradise, was there given a Stone and told to go away and practise humility by a donnish old saint, on which theme the Stone permanently enshrined a lecture. For, placed in one pan of a scales, it could be raised up by no weight of gold in the other however great, whereas a feather lifted it at once. Wolfram describes the impregnability of the Gral Castle in terms very similar to those used of Paradise in the early German *Alexander*, which Wolfram knew. Alexander's need to cast out pride and seek God's mercy through humility is also parallel to Parzival's. The spiritually controlled weight of the Stone and the rejuvenating powers ascribed to the Stone in some versions, must have contributed to Wolfram's notion of his Gral, also a stone, while a phrase used of Alexander's Stone in one Latin version, *lapis exilis* 'small or slight stone' at least affected some manuscript

431

readings of *Parzival*, if not Wolfram's original text itself, since a synonym for the Gral in Chapter 9 adopted by Lachmann and by all editors since is *lapsit exillis*.

This is far from exhausting the symbolic geographical overtones of Munsalvæsche, not to mention the scenery of Gawan's quest. Those of chronology are scarcely less suggestive.

Until recently the two cumulative time-references in *Parzival* had been thought abrupt. In Chapter 9, Parzival and Trevrizent recall the former's first visit to the hermit's cell (in Chapter 5) rather in the time-skipping manner of Virginia Woolf through an object – Taurian's lance, which Parzival had purloined in Trevrizent's absence. Taking his first date from there, Trevrizent tells his nephew that it was four and a half years and three days past, and he confirms it from his psalter. In Chapter 13, Queen Ginover is found by Gawan's messenger kneeling in chapel with her psalter. She tells him that Parzival had left the Plimizœl four and a half years and six weeks before, and she too knows this without consulting her psalter. Recent acute scrutiny of these passages and their implications[*] has shown that there is nothing abrupt or esoteric about Trevrizent's or Ginover's reckonings. Just as we have forgotten what life was like without piped water, electric lighting and sanitation, so most of us have 'forgotten' the liturgical calendar. We know from the text that Trevrizent gave his computation on Good Friday. The Queen gave hers forty days later, which, following the liturgical calendar, brings us to the Vigil of the Ascension – and that is why she is on her knees. But the liturgical calendar is determined by an Easter which can move as much as five weeks. Thus the link between the liturgical and secular calendars was not immediately apparent. A possibility of coordinating the two calendars was seen in the exceptional circumstance of Easter falling on the same day five years apart in 1203 and 1208, years that fall comfortably between 1200 and 1210, the time-span arrived at by independent critical means for the composition of *Parzival*, whereby the same caveat with regard to the absolute dating of the poem must be issued as for the incor-

[*] See 'A List of Works in English for Further Reading', p. 448.

poration of the Lohengrin legend*: Wolfram seems to have revised *Parzival* at a later date, if not at a series of dates. Working back from the highly symbolic Good Friday in Chapter 9, when the seeds of Parzival's regeneration were sown, to his Visit in Chapter 5, it was found that he reached Munsalvæsche at Michaelmas, the Feast of St Michael, who in his role as Vanquisher of Satan-as-Dragon by force of arms, enshrined much of the chivalric ideal. At Michaelmas, the passage in which Michael casts down the Proud Rebel was prescribed reading in church, *Rev.* 12, 7–12, together with *Matth.* 18, 1–10, which deals explicitly with pride and innocence. Applying this to Parzival in Chapter 5, we see that his condition is highly ambiguous. With the trappings of a knight, like St Michael, and as ready to fight the Dragon of Pride, Parzival in fact has that Dragon within himself, and it is from within himself that he must cast it down. In the nightmare in Chapter 2 before she gave birth to Parzival, Herzeloyde had dreamt of him as a fierce Dragon, as a great ruler to be, as a Prince of this World; and now here he is at Munsalvæsche in armour the colour of blood, armour despoiled from a kinsman, having lost the child's innocence discoursed of in *Matth.* 18. It is no accident of Wolfram's use of imagery after this that Parzival's first positive deed on leaving Munsalvæsche behind him is to mend the marriage he had broken, by literally knocking Dragons off the arrogant Orilus (Chrétien's li Orgueilleus = 'the Proud'): 'The Dragon on Orilus's helmet took a wound, and wound was added to wound ...' That Parzival also knocked the Dragon *out* of Orilus is shown by the latter's humble attitude when receiving his wife back to favour. Nevertheless, Parzival's own pride is still so fierce that after his public humiliation by Cundrie in Chapter 6 for 'failing' at the Gral Castle, he – did he but know it – casts himself down to the depths by withdrawing his allegiance from God.

A light reader might consider the foregoing to be a very loose piece of writing, since the subject under discussion was Time, not Heraldry or Parzival's state of mind. But it is typical of Wolfram's art, as of few others', that so much is linked with

* See p. 419.

so much else. The previous paragraph was the direct outcome of pursuing Wolfram's internal chronology in terms of symbolic time. The perspicacious young American scholar to whom we owe the interlocking of the two calendars even claims that Parzival's question to his uncle as to how long ago it was since he was last there, initiates a process whereby Parzival was to be brought into harmony with the liturgical calendar and the divine plan of salvation.

Another order of time in *Parzival*, astrological time, has now to be considered, a sort of time which is naturally in keeping with the liturgical through the Creator. Because Wolfram does not use technical language when speaking of the movements of the planets and perhaps also owing to a lack of unanimity of the manuscripts in one instance, his symbolic intentions are clearer than the purely astronomical ones. The former, however, are the more important.

In Chapter 9, when looking back to the time of Parzival's first visit to Munsalvæsche, Trevrizent tells his nephew that Saturn, the highest (that is, most distant) planet was at such a point in its course that because of the intense cold of its influence it caused Anfortas greater agony in his wound than ever before. For the first time there was blood on the Lance, the original wounder of Anfortas, after it had been inserted homeopathically to still the pain. Wolfram's intention was thus clearly to present the expectancy of the Gral Company that Parzival would deliver Anfortas with almost unendurable intensity. It is, however, an exaggeration to call Parzival's Failure at this juncture 'a deviation from the Cosmic Plan', which is a rather heretical notion; for God will have foreseen Parzival's spiritual unfitness, which is corrected within five years.

Saturn was widely regarded as baleful. In his *Astrolabe*, written for his son Lowis studying in Oxford, Chaucer writes that astrologers call it a fortunate ascendant 'whan that no wykkid planete, as Saturne or Mars, or elles the Tail of the Dragoun,* is in the hous of the ascendent ...' In *Parzival*, Wolfram tells us that other 'high' planets affect Anfortas's wound too, as does the moon with its changes. Which those

* See p. 246, second footnote.

434

other high planets may be is perhaps filled in, however strangely or teasingly, in Chapter 16 at the time leading up to Parzival's appearance as deliverer, and again to emphasize Anfortas's agony. 'The hour had waited till Mars or Jupiter had returned angrily in their courses to where they had set out from ...'

The word which Wolfram uses for a precise point of departure or return, when he uses one at all, means 'mark', and scholars have been much exercised to discover what he had in mind.

One set of starting-points can be rejected out of hand, namely the primordial ones. At the beginning of the *Divine Comedy*, Dante refers to these initial positions, to the sun 'mounting with the stars which were with it when God first set them in motion'. The reference here is to the First Spring of the Year. But, as was seen, the time of year which Wolfram had in mind was the onset of Autumn. The following suggestions have also been put forward. i) After their apparent retrograde motion occasioned by the rotation of the earth round the sun, the planets return to their points of departure, the point of intersection of the epicycles of the Ptolemaic system, after which their apparent motion accelerates. ii) The point referred to is the point of transit into a planet's 'house' or 'mansion', a position of great astrological potency. iii) The point intended by Wolfram is the point of 'opposition' to the sun, and so that, when the sun sets and a planet rises, that planet is very potent. In this case, Wolfram's 'mark' might best be rendered as 'station'. The propounder of this interpretation, quoted at length above on the subject of the liturgical calendar, notes further that if Wolfram had had the actual conditions of 1203 in mind, Saturn would have been fast approaching opposition to the sun at Michaelmas, and that in 1208 Mars and Jupiter were within 4° of longitude of one another prior to conjunction, though whether this was of benign or malign import in any system is not stated.

In Chaucer's and surely all other systems, Mars exerted a malign influence. But Jupiter? And what of Cundrie's statement towards the end of Chapter 15, implying that at least Saturn, Jupiter, Mars and the Sun (in their Latino-Arabic names), if not all Seven, portend good fortune for Parzival and therefore better fortune for Anfortas, though not immediately for his wound? Add to this the baffling offhandedness of the preferred manuscript of *Parzival*, the one followed by all editors: 'till Mars *or* Jupiter ...', followed by plural number in both the verb and the possessive adjective, though some minor manuscripts read 'Mars *and* Jupiter ...'

Was Wolfram just muddled in his syntax, or unfair? There are strong reasons for believing that Wolfram was pulled up by a theologian after the recital of Chapter 9 for an unguarded statement that the Neutral Angels could have been saved, since Trevrizent retracts in Chapter 15.* Unless a historian of science and a student of medieval German literature in happy conjunction can interpret this constellation of facts satisfactorily, the possibility cannot be ruled out that in a similar way Wolfram was pulled up by an astronomer-astrologer (perhaps by the one who supplied the Arabic names of the planets) for mismanagement of these heavenly bodies, and so was forced to tinker with his text again. Wolfram's is one of the boldest and firmest voices in narrative poetry, and he was never bolder or firmer than when bouncing his listeners – one has only to think of Kyot. But unless it is a joke, simply the laughing off of an error, 'Mars *or* Jupiter ...' is stylistically most uncharacteristic and weak. With an eye to the conditions in 1208, Wolfram's original text may well have read 'Mars *and* Jupiter ...'† in keeping with the plural verb and possessive adjective; but after he was pulled up Wolfram emended 'and' to 'or' to avoid being pinned down. In this event, as on other known occasions, he will have sacrificed those copies of his work in progress that were out and away beyond his control. In other words, it is suggested here that Wolfram's astrological scheme broke down, so that what we have, though highly suggestive item by item, is opportunistic, not schematic. This would be a sad thing, since Wolfram's seriousness over Saturn and the Wound is unmistakable. Saturn, however, takes just under thirty years to complete its revolution round the sun, and so was not at

* See pp. 232, 240 and 396.
† In other circumstances 'Mars *and* Jupiter ...' would have the appearance of a *lectio facilior* as against 'Mars *or* Jupiter ...'

Wolfram's disposal in Chapter 16. If this planet was potent in Chapter 5 for any of the reasons i)–iii) above, Wolfram knew that its powers must have waned five years later, though if it had begun in its house it might still linger there. Thus Saturn was out, leaving, of the 'higher' planets, Mars and Jupiter, and that is why they are named *at all* in Chapter 16. If they were not acceptable in a bunch, then they would have to be accepted as alternatives – let the astrologers work it out for themselves!

In conclusion, the following brief remarks may also serve the reader as clues through the engaging labyrinth of *Parzival*.

According to Wolfram, the fundamental two-way bond of rights and obligations between God and Man, lord and vassal, man and wife, parents and children, kinsman and kinsman, Knight-servitor and Lady, was *triuwe* – 'steadfast love'. God Himself showed this feudal bonding-sentiment supremely by *condescending*, as Lord of the Universe, to take on a human shape and give His life on the Cross.

Another aspect of the two-way bond, this time nearer to economic activity, was the reciprocity of service and reward: service here on earth, reward in Heaven; service out on campaigns, bounty back at court; service for a lady out on the tourneying field, her favour if possible in bed – though opportunities had to be snatched to cheat surveillance. Only in his third involvement does Gawan achieve a correct and viable relationship with a member of the opposite sex; for his make-believe affair with Obilot was service without reward, his lightning wooing of Antikonie without service almost brought reward, but with Orgeluse arduous service was at last richly rewarded by her person in marriage. The dialectical progression is obvious. Parzival's difficulty of adjustment was with God, and here, too, one detects at least a triad: religious instruction at rising levels of insight, from his mother, from Gurnemanz, and from Trevrizent. It is further significant for Wolfram's sense of structure that Parzival, too, goes through three stages in his relations with the other sex, though in other terms than Gawan's: with Jeschute (ignorance-innocence); with Liaze (calf-love); with Condwiramurs (marriage and fulfilment). That

437

Wolfram fully intended this last progression is proved by the fact that he invented Liaze for the middle term, since a Liaze-figure is lacking in the *Perceval*.

The attentive reader will have noticed how Wolfram tends to harp on ladies who accept the service of knights but fail to reward them, and also on how well he praises the fair. The key to this is to be found in his Apology. Because of an unrestrained expression of anger over treatment meted out to him by one lady he lost the favour of all the others. There can be no doubt that the offence he gave was contained in a song, no longer extant, of 'lost service', in which he must have upbraided the lady for bilking him of his due. One only has to recall how in Chapter 12 of *Parzival*, Wolfram affects to lose his temper with the exacting Orgeluse – Gawan should have given her a green-gown there and then, as has happened to many a fine lady since. So much for Wolfram's manly pride: concurrently this superb soldierly tactician uses the marvellous gallery of femi-nine characters he creates to work his way back to the ladies' favour.

In the original, Wolfram's Templars are *templeis*. Since he gives us a Gral Temple, it seemed legitimate to render *templeis* as 'Templar': yet it would be wrong to read into this term, by association, any more than is told of these knights in *Parzival*.

A. T. HATTO

438

A GLOSSARY OF PERSONAL NAMES

The names included here are those of the active characters of Wolfram's story, together with those of their relations, dead or alive. Omitted are such names as those in catalogues (for example, those on pp. 382 and 383), and names belonging to the sphere of general medieval knowledge, such as Absalom, Alexander, Aristotle, Astiroth, etc.

ADDANZ Son of Lazaliez; grandson of Mazadan, Parzival's great-grandfather in the male line.

AFFINAMUS OF CLITIERS A companion of Gramoflanz.

ALIZE Sister of King Hardiz of Gascony; wife to Duke Lambekin of Brabant.

AMPFLISE (1) Queen, then Queen-Widow, of France, and Gahmuret's 'Lady' in the formalized 'Lady-Knight-servitor' relationship.

AMPFLISE (2) Daughter of Jernis of Ryl; Gral maiden.

ANFORTAS Parzival's maternal uncle; Gral King until succeeded by Parzival.

ANNORE Queen of Averre; loved by Galoes of Anjou.

ANTANOR 'THE SILENT' A knight at Arthur's court.

ANTIKONIE Sister to King Vergulaht of Ascalun.

ARNIVE Widow of King Utepandragun of Britain; mother of Arthur.

ARTHUR King of Britain; son of Utepandragun; grandson of Brickus; great-grandson of Mazadan; husband of Ginover, who bore him Ilunot; brother of Sangive; maternal uncle of Gawan.

ASTOR Duke of Lanverunz.

BEACURS A brother of Gawan.

BEAFLURS A fairy; wife to Pansamurs and mother of Liahturtel-tart.

BELACANE Queen of Zazamanc, first and abandoned wife of Gahmuret, and mother of Feirefiz.

BENE Daughter of Plippalinot.

BERNOUT DE RIVIERS Count of Ukerlant, inheriting from his father Narant.

BRANDELIDELIN   King of Punturteis; maternal uncle of Gramo-flanz.

BRICKUS   Son of Mazadan; grandfather of Arthur and progenitor of Arthur's line. (Brickus is doubtless a corruption of Britus, via Bricus.*)

CASTIS   King of Waleis and Norgals; partner in unconsummated first marriage of Herzeloyde.

CIDEGAST   Duke of Logroys; first husband of Orgeluse; slain by Gramoflanz.

CLAMIDE   King of Iserterre.

CLARISCHANZE OF TENABROC   Gral Maiden.

CLAUDITTE (1)   Daughter of the Burgrave Scherules; playmate of Obilot.

CLAUDITTE (2)   A queen loved by Feirefiz.

CLIAS 'THE GREEK'   A knight at Arthur's court.

CLINSCHOR   Duke of Terre de Labur; maternal nephew of Virgil of Naples; the lover of Iblis; a castrated sorceror.

CONDWIRAMURS   Wife to Parzival; daughter of King Tampenteire, from whom she inherited the land of Brobarz as Queen in her own right; cousin of Sigune; maternal niece of Gurnemanz.

CUNDRIE 'LA SURZIERE'   Sister of Malcreatiure; messenger of the Gral.

CUNDRIE   Daughter of King Lot of Norway and Sangive, and thus sister to Gawan and maternal niece of Arthur; later, wife to Lischois.

CUNNEWARE   A titular Duchess of Lalant (=Lalander); sister to Orilus and Lähelin.

DODINES   A knight at Arthur's court; brother of Taurian.

EHKUNAT   A count; brother of Gurzgri's wife Mahaute.

EKUBA   An infidel Queen of Janfuse.

ENITE   Wife to Erec.

EREC   Son of King Lac; a hero of his own Arthurian romance.

FEIREFIZ   Parzival's infidel half-brother; son of Gahmuret and his first wife Belacane; later baptized and married to Repanse de Schoye, on whom he begets Prester John.

FLEGETANIS   An infidel astronomer and man of science.

FLORANT OF ITOLAC, 'THE TURKOYT' (an exotic name of in-

* This seems sufficient reason to make Brickus ancestor of the British and Arthurian line, leaving Lazaliez as ancestor of the Angevins. The text does not allocate Brickus and Lazaliez thus specifically.

determinate meaning) A companion of Lischois in the service of Orgeluse.

FLORIE OF KANADIC Loved by Arthur's son Ilinot.

FLORIE DE LUNEL A Gral maiden.

FLURDAMURS A paternal aunt of Parzival; wife to Kingrisin, and mother of Vergulaht and Antikonie.

FRIAM Duke of Vermendoys.

FRIMUTEL Parzival's grandfather in the female line and a Gral King; unlike his father Titurel no longer living.

GÁBENIS A prince of Punturteis (Brandelidelin's kingdom).

GAHERJET A maternal cousin of Gawan and knight of Arthur's suite.

GAHMURET Parzival's father by Herzeloyde, Feirefiz's by Belacane; younger son of Gandin, King of Anjou; brother of Gandin's successor Galoes whom he succeeds; knight-servitor of Ampflise.

GALOES Parzival's paternal uncle; elder brother of Gahmuret and successor to King Gandin of Anjou; knight-servitor of Annore.

GALOGANDRES Duke of Gippones

GANDILUZ Son of Gurzgri, Gurnemanz's son, and Mahaute.

GANDIN King of Anjou; Parzival's grandfather in the male line; son of Addanz; father of Galoes, Gahmuret and Flurdamurs; husband of Schoette.

GAREL A knight in Arthur's suite.

GARSCHILOYE OF GREENLAND A Gral maiden.

GASCHIER 'THE NORMAN' A maternal nephew of Kaylet.

GAWAN The hero of the subsidiary and complementary action of *Parzival*; son of King Lot of Norway and Sangive; maternal nephew of King Arthur; brother of Beacurs, Surdamur, Cundrie and Itonje; marries Orgeluse; distant relation to Parzival through their common ancestor Mazadan, a maternal great-great-grandfather of Gawan's. Otherwise and elsewhere the paragon of Arthurian knighthood.

GINOVER As Arthur's wife, Queen of Britain; mother of Ilinot. No pedigree, though related to King Segramors.

GRAMOFLANZ King of an unnamed land whose great fortress and royal residence is Rosche Sabins; son of Irot; maternal nephew of Brandelidelin; slayer of Cidegast; marries Itonje.

GRIGORZ King of Ipotente.

GRINGULJETE 'WITH THE RED EARS' A Gral war-horse which passes to Lähelin, from him to Orilus, from him to Gawan, to Urjans, to Lischois, and back to Gawan.

GURNEMANZ Prince of Graharz; Parzival's first tutor; father of Schenteflurs, Lascoyt, Gurzgri and Liaze; grandfather of Schionatulander; brother-in-law of Tampenteire; maternal uncle of Condwiramurs.

GURZGRI Son of Gurnemanz; brother of Schenteflurs, Lascoyt and Liaze; husband of Mahaute; father of Gandiluz.

GUVERJORZ King Clamide's castilian war-horse.

HARDIZ King of Gascony; brother of Alize.

HERLINDE A lady in some way dear to Vridebrant.

HERNANT A king slain by Vridebrant on account of Herlinde.

HERZELOYDE Parzival's mother by Gahmuret; granddaughter of Titurel, daughter of Frimutel; sister of Anfortas, Trevrizent, Schoysiane and Repanse de Schoye; partnered in unconsummated marriage with Castis, from whom she inherited Waleis and Norgals, as Queen.

HIUTEGER A Scottish duke under Vridebrant.

IBERT King of Sicily; husband of Iblis; castrator of his cuckolder Clinschor.

IDER SON OF NOYT A knight; slayer of Lascoyt; a formidable opponent at beauty competitions militant; known also from *Erec*.

IDŒL Father of Jofreit.

ILINOT Son of Arthur and Ginover; knight-servitor of Kanadic, and dead in her service.

IMANE DE BEAFONTANE A young lady abducted by Meljahkanz.

INGLIART 'WITH THE SHORT EARS' Gawan's war-horse, lost unwittingly to Parzival at Bearosche.

IPOMIDON OF BABYLON King of Niniveh; slayer of Gahmuret; brother of Pompeius.

IROT King; father of Gramoflanz; brother-in-law of Brandelidelin.

ISAJES Utepandragun's Marshal.

ISENHART King of Azagouc; son of Tankanis; knight-servitor of Belacane and slain in her service by Prothizilas; maternal cousin of Vridebrant.

ITHER OF GAHEVIEZ King of Cucumerlant; Utepandragun's maternal nephew; husband or lover of Lammire; related to Parzival by blood only through his grandfather (Parzival's great-great-great-grandfather) Mazadan, though Gahmuret claims him as 'maternal kinsman'; 'the Red Knight' until Parzival assumed that title by slaying him.

ITONJE Gawan's youngest sister, wooed unseen and won by Gramoflanz.

IWAN   Count of Nonel, father of a Gral maiden.

IWAN   A knight in Arthur's suite.

IWANET   A young kinsman of Ginover and squire at Arthur's court.

JERNIS   Count of Ryl; father of the Gral maiden Ampflise.

JESCHUTE OF KARNANT   Sister of King Erec; wife of Duke Orilus.

JOFREIT   Son of Idœl; maternal kinsman of Arthur; companion of Gawan.

JOHN, PRESTER   Son of Feirefiz and Repanse de Schoye, Christian priest-king in India.

KARDEFABLET   Duke of Jamor; brother-in-law of Lyppaut.

KARDEIZ (1)   Son of King Tampenteire of Brobarz; brother of Condwiramurs; lost his life for love in unknown circumstances.

KARDEIZ (2)   Son of Parzival and Condwiramurs; twin brother of Loherangrin, inheritor of Parzival's secular thrones of Brobarz, Anjou, Waleis and Norgals.

KARNAHKARNANZ LEH CUNS ULTERLEC   Count, overlord and rescuer from Meljahkanz of the abducted Imane; the first knight ever seen by Parzival.

KAYLET OF HOSKURAST   King of Spain and of Castile; maternal cousin of Gahmuret; husband of Titurel's daughter Rischoyde; maternal uncle of Killirjacac; paternal kinsman of Schiltunc.

KEIE   Lord High Steward and Seneschal at Arthur's court.

KILLIRJACAC   A count of Champagne, Kaylet's maternal nephew.

KINGRIMURSEL   Landgrave and Burgrave of Schanpfanzun (thus his landgraviate rests on inherited title and not on territory), paternal nephew of Kingrisin; cousin of Vergulaht.

KINGRISIN   King of Ascalun; father of Vergulaht by Flurdamurs, Gahmuret's sister; paternal uncle of Kingrimursel.

KYLLICRATES   King of Centriun, in Feirefiz's suite.

KYOT   Duke of Katelangen (Catalonia had Counts of Barcelona); brother of Tampenteire and Manpfilyot; father of Sigune by Schoysiane; paternal uncle of Condwiramurs.

KYOT LASCHANTIURE, ALIAS 'THE PROVENÇAL'   Wolfram's alleged source (see pp. 428ff).

LAC   King of Karnant; father of Erec.

LAHEDUMAN   Count of Muntane; in Poydiconjunz's army.

LÄHELIN   King; brother of Orilus and Cunneware de Lalant; conqueror of Herzeloyde's lands of Waleis and Norgals.

LAHFILIROST   Burgrave of Patelamunt in Zazamanc.

LAMBEKIN Duke of Brabant and Hainault (see p. 419); brother-in-law of Hardiz.

LAMMIRE A paternal aunt of Parzival, appointed to rule within Styria by her father Gandin of Anjou (see p. 429); wife or mistress of Ither.

LANZIDANT A count of Greenland; page to Queen Ampflise.

LASCOYT Count; son of Gurnemanz.

LAZALIEZ Parzival's great-great-grandfather and son of Mazadan.

LIADARZ Son of Count Schiolarz; page to Queen Ampflise.

LIAHTURTELTART Son of the fairies Pansamurs and Beaflurs; page to Queen Ampflise.

LIAZ A count of Cornwall; son of Tinas; page to Gawan.

LIAZE Daughter of Gurnemanz; cousin, through the latter's sister, of Condwiramurs.

LIDDAMUS Duke; vassal of Vergulaht, and seemingly also a sovereign lord.

LISAVANDER Burgrave of Beauvais; vassal of Meljanz.

LISCHOIS GWELLJUS Duke of Gowerzin; in the service of Orgeluse; later marries Gawan's sister Cundrie; companion of Florant.

LOHERANGRIN Son of Parzival and Condwiramurs; twin brother of Kardeiz; for a time Duke of Brabant by marriage, as Swan Knight.

LOT King of Norway; father of Gawan, Beacurs, Surdamur, Cundrie and Itonje by Sangive.

LYBBEALS OF PRIENLASCORS Gral knight, slain by Lähelin, first owner of Gringuljete.

LYPPAUT Duke, lord of Bearosche; vassal of Meljanz; father of Obie and Obilot; brother of Marangliez; brother-in-law of Kardefablet.

MABONAGRIN Cousin of Clamide and former Lord of Schoydelacurt; slayer of Gurzgri.

MAHAUTE Sister of Ehkunat; wife of Gurzgri; mother of Gandiluz (and, according to *Titurel*, also of Schionatulander).

MALCREATIURE A dwarf; brother of Cundrie la surziere; the gift of Secundille to Anfortas, who gave him to Orgeluse as page.

MANPFILYOT Brother of Kyot of Katelangen; paternal uncle of Condwiramurs.

MARANGLIEZ Duke of Brevigariez; brother of Lyppaut.

MAURIN 'OF THE HANDSOME THIGHS' Ginover's Marshal.

MAZADAN A fairy, ancestor of the House of Anjou and of Arthur's line; Parzival's great-great-great-grandfather; husband of the fairy

Terdelaschoye by whom he had Lazaliez (Angevin line) and Brickus (Arthurian line).

MELJAHKANZ Son of King Poydiconjunz; abductor of Imane.

MELJANZ King of Liz; maternal nephew of Poydiconjunz; suitor then husband of Obie.

MIRABEL King of Avendroyn; brother of Schirniel.

MORHOLT OF IRELAND Imported cyclically from the *Tristan*, where he is brother to the elder Isold, Queen of Ireland.

NARANT Count of Ukerlant; father of Bernout de Riviers; fell at Belrepeire.

NOYT Father of Ider.

OBIE Elder daughter of Lyppaut; sister of Obilot; mis-wooed and, thanks to Obilot and Gawan, won by Meljanz.

OBILOT A child, younger daughter of Lyppaut; sister of Obie; 'Lady' of Gawan in make-believe Lady-Knight-servitor relationship.

OLIMPIA An eastern queen loved by Feirefiz.

ORGELUSE Dowager-Duchess through marriage to her first husband Cidegast; loved by Anfortas; wooed and won by Gawan.

ORILUS Duke of Lalander (= Lalant), brother of Lähelin and Cunneware; husband of Jeschute; slayer of Schionatulander and Galoes; a 'Burgundian'.

PANSAMURS A fairy, husband of Beacurs, father of Liahturteltart.

PARZIVAL The hero of the main action of *Parzival*, scion of i) the Gral Family and ii) the House of Anjou, i) through his mother Herzeloyde, ii) through his father Gahmuret; King of the Gral and baptizer of his half-brother the infidel potentate Feirefiz (father of Prester John); husband of Condwiramurs, and, by her, father of Loherangrin (Gral) and Kardeiz II (Secular).

PLIHOPLIHERI A knight slain by Orilus.

PLIPPALINOT Knight-ferryman near Schastel marveile; father of Bene.

POMPEIUS King of Niniveh; brother of Ipomidon.

POYDICONJUNZ King of Gors; father of Meljahkanz; brother-in-law of Schaut; maternal uncle of Meljanz.

POYTWIN OF PRIENLASCORS A knight.

PROTHIZILAS A duke; vassal of Belacane.

RAZALIC A prince in Azagouc.

REPANSE DE SCHOYE Daughter of Frimutel and Gral-bearer; sister of Anfortas, Trevrizent, Schoysiane and Herzeloyde; later wife to Feirefiz and mother of Prester John.

Rischoyde Sister of Frimutel; wife to Kaylet.

Ritschart Count of Navers.

Riwalin King of Lohneis (imported cyclically from a version of *Tristan*, in which he is Tristan's father).

Sangive Daughter of Utepandragun and Arnive; sister of Arthur; with first husband Lot, to whom she bore Gawan and his brother and sisters; with second husband Florant.

Schaffilor King of Arragon.

Schaut King of Liz; brother-in-law of Poydiconjunz; father of Meljanz.

Schenteflurs Son of Gurnemanz; brother of Lascoyt, Gurzgri and Liaze; cousin of Condwiramurs, as whose ally he was slain by Clamide and Kingrun.

Scherules Burgrave of Bearosche under Lyppaut and his Marshal, father of Clauditte (1).

Schiltunc Father-in-law of Vridebrant; paternal kinsman of Kaylet.

Schiolarz Count of Poitou; father of Liadarz.

Schionatulander A prince; knight-servitor of Sigune, in whose service he was slain by Orilus before their love was consummated; according to *Titurel* son of Gurzgri and Mahaute, with the rank of Dauphin of Graswaldan, and page to Gahmuret.

Schirniel King of Lirivoyn; brother of Mirabel.

Schoette Gandin's Queen in Anjou; mother of Galoes and Gahmuret.

Schoysiane Daughter of Frimutel; sister of Anfortas, Trevrizent, Herzeloyde, Repanse de Schoye; wife of Kyot of Katelangen; died giving birth to Sigune.

Secundille Queen of Tribalibot (India); a mistress of Feirefiz.

Segramors A King in Arthur's suite, related through his mother to Ginover.

Sigune Daughter of Kyot of Katelangen and Schoysiane; Parzival's cousin; 'Lady' of Schionatulander who as her knight-servitor was slain by Orilus; to reverence her beloved suitor she became an *inclusa*. Wolfram created the *Titurel* fragments in which to elaborate the tragic love-story, see p. 11.

Surdamur Daughter of Lot and Sangive; sister of Gawan and Itonje; wife of the Greek Emperor Alexander (see p. 296 and footnote).

Tampanis Chief squire to Gahmuret.

TAMPENTEIRE King of Brobarz; brother of Kyot of Katalangen and Manpfilyot; brother-in-law of Gurnemanz through his nameless wife, father of Condwiramurs and Kardeiz I.

TANKANIS Father of Isenhart.

TAURIAN 'THE WILD' Brother of Dodines.

TERDELASCHOYE A fairy, if not 'of', then closely associated with Mount Feimurgan; wife of Mazadan and ancestress of the House of Anjou and of the Arthurian line. (For reasons best known to himself, Wolfram has reversed the elements of the name of the widely known Feimurgan/Famorgan <*Fata morgana* of Terr de la Joie.)

TINAS Father of Liaz.

TITUREL First King of the Gral in the known line; father, still sustained by the Gral, of Frimutel, who was slain in chivalry, and of Rischoyde; grandfather of Anfortas; great-grandfather of Parzival.

TREBUCHET A famous and ingenious smith.

TREVRIZENT Son of Frimutel; brother of Anfortas, to do penance for whom he renounced chivalry and became a hermit; maternal uncle and second and crucial tutor to Parzival; maternal uncle of the *inclusa* Sigune.

TURKENTALS A prince of Waleis or Norgals.

URJANS A prince of Punturteis; a ravisher.

UTEPANDRAGUN King of Britain, grandson of Mazadan; son of Brickus; husband of Arnive and father of Arthur and Sangive.

VERGULAHT King of Ascalun; son of Kingrisin and Flurdamurs; brother of Antikonie; cousin of Kingrimursel; cousin of Parzival.

VIRGIL 'OF NAPLES' Maternal uncle of Clinschor. (The poet Publius Vergilius Maro was believed in the Middle Ages to have foretold the birth of Christ, to have mastered magic arts and to have made a fool of himself in amorous escapade, though not to the point of losing his manhood like his nephew Clinschor. Virgil is thought to have studied Greek in Naples, wrote most of his *Georgics* there and was buried not far away.)

VRIDEBRANT King of Scots; son-in-law of Schiltunc.

A LIST OF WORKS IN ENGLISH
FOR FURTHER READING

Blamires, D., *Characterization and Individuality in Wolfram's 'Parzival'*, Cambridge, 1966.

Gibbs, M. E., *Wiplîchez wîbes reht*. A study of the women characters in the works of Wolfram von Eschenbach. Duquesne Studies, Philological Series, 15, 1972.

Green, D. H., and Johnson, L. P., *Approaches to Wolfram von Eschenbach*. Five essays. Mikro-kosmos, Band 5, Bern-Frankfurt am Main-Las Vegas, 1978.

Groos, A., 'Time reference and the Liturgical Calendar in Wolfram von Eschenbach's *Parzival*', *Deutsche Viertel jahrsschrift für Literaturwissenschaft und Geistesgeschichte*, Jg. 49, 1975, pp. 43–65.

Richey, M. F., *Essays on mediæval German poetry*, Oxford, 1943. Revised 1969. (Wolfram's love-lyrics in part translated.)

Richey, M. F., *Gahmuret Anschevin*. A contribution to the study of Wolfram von Eschenbach. Oxford, 1923.

Richey, M. F., *Schionatulander and Sigune*. An episode from the story of Parzival and the Gral, as related by Wolfram von Eschenbach. London, 1927. Revised edition 1960.

Richey, M. F., *Studies of Wolfram von Eschenbach*, London, 1957.

Sacker, H., *An introduction to Wolfram's 'Parzival'*, Cambridge, 1963.

Springer, O., *Wolfram's 'Parzival'*, in *Arthurian Literature in the Middle Ages*, a collaborative history edited by R. S. Loomis, Oxford, 1959.

Weigand, H. J., *Wolfram's 'Parzival'*. Five essays with an introduction, edited by Ursula Hoffmann. New York–London, 1969.

Excellent articles on themes or aspects of *Parzival* have been published in English by British, Commonwealth and American scholars in various learned periodicals. They can be found for the years 1945–69 in the standard modern bibliographie raisonnée: Bumke, J., *Die Wolfram von Eschenbach Forschung seit 1945*, Munich, 1970.